The Good People

Other books by Patrick Harpur:

The Savoy Truffle
A Complete Guide to the Soul
The Philosophers' Secret Fire: A History of the Imagination
Daimonic Reality: A Field Guide to the Otherworld
Mercurius; or, the Marriage of Heaven and Earth
The Rapture
The Serpent's Circle

To Anya

First Published by Strange Attractor Press 2017, in a hardback edition of 100 copies and an unlimted paperback edition.

Original cover art by Leon Sadler.
The engraving at the end of the book is Emblem 36 of Michael Maier's *Atalanta Fugiens* (1617).

A CIP catalogue record for this book is available from the British Library.

ISBN 978-1-907222-40-5

Strange Attractor Press
BM SAP, London, WC1N 3XX, UK
www.strangeattractor.co.uk

Printed and bound in Estonia.
Distributed by The MIT Press, Cambridge, Massachusetts. And London, England.

THE GOOD PEOPLE

PATRICK
HARPUR

Author's Note

The Good People is a modern fairy tale set in west London in the early summer of 1989, just before the collapse of the Berlin wall and of South Africa's apartheid; a time of global flux when signs and portents appeared. Amongst these was a rash of strange objects appearing in the sky and a resurgence in the belief that humans were being abducted by aliens from another world.

While the book is fiction, its unusual or supernatural events are based on fact – but understated because, as is well known, fact is too unbelievable for fiction.

"It was in a mist the Tuatha de Danaan, the people of the gods of Dana... came through the air and the high air to Ireland."

Lady Gregory; *Gods and Fighting Men*

"And if any gaze on our rushing band,
We come between him and the deed of his hand,
We come between him and the hope of his heart."

W.B. Yeats: *The Hosting of the Sidhe*

ONE

The early days of June had been hot and that day promised to be no exception. The newly risen sun mounted a sky of unstained blue, illuminating the London borough of Acton like reason itself.

Bernadette O'Rourke, a widow of sixty-eight, was the first to arrive at the derelict shopping precinct. As she set up her fruit and vegetable stall, she considered the bacon, eggs, fried bread and tea which she would buy at the Golden Plaice the moment it opened at six o'clock. Although it was already warm, Mrs O'Rourke was well muffled against any possible inclemency: she wore thick brown boots, grubby green trousers, a purple cardigan under a ragged quilted jacket and a headscarf decorated with faded orange flowers. A movement in the corner of her eye caused her to glance up at the white clock tower which was high enough to be visible from anywhere in Acton.

"God save us all!" she exclaimed. "Whatever next." She took a long hard look at the thing near the tower but, while able to believe her eyes, was neither able nor willing to form an opinion of it. She crossed herself and returned to the arranging of her produce. Then, as a precautionary afterthought, she took off her jacket, turned it inside out, and put it on again.

Maeve Allingham, aged fifty-seven, was wearing only a light dressing-gown over her thin nightdress when she stepped out through the French windows into her garden. Dew soaked through her sheepskin slippers; a faint mist lay like steam over her lawn. The low sun, wedged between two rows of terraced houses, was just heating up from red to gold.

Later, Maeve would remember the unusual silence, without the swish of cars on the High Street or the annoying bleep from the pedestrian crossing; without even birdsong. Now, she was only conscious of the slope of still air between her and the fiery disc of the sun. 'It looks like a gold coin,' she thought, and the simile recalled the vision of William Blake who had not seen the sun thus, but as an innumerable company of the heavenly host singing 'Holy, Holy, Holy is the Lord God Almighty.' She was inclined to believe that Blake, like all Romantic poets, was telling what Nanny used to call 'a story'.

She turned her back on the sun and absent-mindedly dead-headed a few early roses. She looked up at the white clock tower. The drab building on which it was erected – formerly the town hall and now assembly rooms – was screened from view by trees and houses, so that the tower looked singular and exotic. The low parapet above the clock suggested a minaret, as did the red-tiled roof above. Maeve could easily imagine herself in Fez or Istanbul, awaiting the muezzin's first stirring wail of the day. The hands on the clock face pointed at twenty to six. Her husband was an early riser, but even his routine, and her supporting act, did not begin for another fifty minutes. 'Nearly an hour's grace,' she thought, feeling suddenly as free of care as Persephone picking wild flowers in the sunlit meadow.

At that moment she heard or sensed an anomalous sound: a low rumble, but whether from above like a distant jet, or from below like Hades' brazen car boring towards the surface, she couldn't tell. In the patch of clear sky beside the tower, an untoward sight met her eyes – so untoward that she could not altogether believe them at first. She watched whatever it was for what seemed like a long time. Then, without warning, it moved. Maeve instantly became very frightened indeed.

Thirty-year-old Heather Wright had been dreaming that she was asleep in her bedroom when, all of a sudden, it was brilliantly lit up from an unknown source outside her window. She awoke at that moment, wholly alert. Her curtains were drawn, but she was filled with the certainty that, were she to open them, some tremendous spectacle would greet her.

She was disappointed to find that the light which shone through the broad window was nothing out of the ordinary. She was about to go back to bed when she glanced up at the clock tower in order to ascertain how early it was. What she saw was definitely not ordinary. Even as she watched – her legs suddenly weak, her jaw slack – it flashed: once, twice. A current of something like lightning passed through her and diffused itself like a presence throughout the room. Later, she would think of the experience as akin to having a magical lens inserted behind her eyes, at the very root of her perception; a sliver of crystal which conferred powers of insight into the phenomenal world. Now, it seemed that without moving her eyes she took in all her surroundings: the clothes on the floor, the furniture, the shrubs outside, the street, London – the whole world, in fact. In a single glance she was privileged to see the precious invisible thread by which all creation was bound together. Then, even as she watched, the source of her illumination disappeared in the twinkling of an eye.

Heather stood, frozen in the moment, at the window. Everything seemed to have returned to normal. Or had it? There was definitely a residue of the experience, as if the crystalline lens had melted into her head like rice paper. Her brain throbbed with subdued excitement. It felt as though she had been activated. She wanted desperately to tell someone what had happened, to capture the moment before its after-image altogether faded.

Quickly she pulled on a coat over her pyjamas and dashed out into the deserted street. She hoped to catch a glimpse of the wonderful object but there was no sign of it. She ran in her bare feet as far as the former shopping precinct where an elderly woman was arranging fruit on a stall. For some reason she wore her quilted jacket inside out.

"Did you...?" began Heather breathlessly. "Did you see...?"

"That?" said the woman, pointing towards the clock tower. "Ah God, wasn't it a sight for sore eyes?"

Alistair, the Reverend Allingham, stood dumbfounded in the kitchen, unable to believe his eyes. A series of little thrills ran through his body. The hand which held the letter trembled. His eyes refused to follow the order of the sentences but darted backwards and forwards over the words, as if to devour them in one ocular gulp. He scrutinised the signature, wondering if it could really be genuine, if it might not be a cruel hoax. Half-running to his study, he fished out another of the Dean's letters and compared the handwriting. The scribbled signatures tallied. It was too good to be true. For one blinding moment, not only was his decision to take on an inner city parish vindicated, but his whole life, for God's sake, was justified.

He returned slowly to the kitchen, unconsciously clasping the letter to his heart.

Maeve was standing by the electric kettle which was coming to the boil. She did not return her husband's greeting but continued to stare dumbly at some petals in the palm of her hand. Yes, she remembered that she had been dead-heading the roses. But the curious thing was, that her next memory had her standing at the end of the garden facing the house when, by rights, she should have been standing next to the roses with her back to the house. She had wandered back indoors, puzzling over this discrepancy. Had she dropped off for a moment? It didn't seem likely. What's more, she felt funny. Her joints ached as if she had been passed through a wringer. It was peculiar since she had felt so well only a few minutes before. 'Either I'm getting the 'flu,' she thought, 'or I'm getting old.' She dropped the petals into the waste bin and rubbed her eyes which were stinging in a nasty way. Pollen, she supposed. The count was unseasonably high. But it was not just her body that felt funny. Her mind had gone all... all spongy on her. She couldn't concentrate it. She felt dazed in a way she had not felt, God forbid, since that unhappy event of her childhood in Five-Acre field. On the whole, she reckoned, this early rising had not been such a great idea; perhaps she would have a cup of tea and go back to bed.

However, making tea was easier said than done. The routine was no longer automatic. She manipulated the teapot as if wearing those long mechanical gloves used to handle radioactive substances. She had to work her fingers deliberately, clumsily, as if they were steel claws. She was aware, but remotely, of Alistair's excitement as he sat at the table, jiggling his legs like a little boy.

"Well?" he said. "Aren't you going to ask me what my news is?" He waved his letter.

"Where did that come from? The post doesn't come till six-thirty."

"Wake up, dear," said Alistair with a touch of impatience. "It's quarter to seven now."

"Your watch is wrong."

"No, it's not. Look at the cooker clock." Maeve looked. The clock on what she still called the stove said a quarter to seven. She rubbed her eyes which itched as if dust had been thrown into them. "Are you feeling all right, Maeve? That's a nasty rash on your face and neck." Maeve touched the area with her fingertips. Sure enough, the skin on her neck, extending up over her jaw and onto the side of her head, was lumpy and inflamed as though it had been exposed to some toxic blast. But this was a small thing compared to the cold premonitory shock she felt at the news that the time was a quarter to seven.

"This letter…" Alistair began portentously.

"It can't be quarter to seven," Maeve interrupted. "I'll prove it to you." She walked briskly into the drawing-room, out through the French windows and looked up at the clock tower. The world tilted under her feet. Her hands flew to her mouth. "Oh God."

The hands on the clock pointed to just after a quarter to seven. But that was impossible – it couldn't be later than six. It couldn't be more than a quarter of an hour ago that the clock had said twenty to six. She had clearly seen it while dead-heading the roses, a moment before returning to the house and switching on the kettle. There had been nothing to delay her, except...

She saw it again, suddenly, in her mind's eye – the way it hung there and then, in a flash, moved very close to her, no further than the end of the garden. Surely it was a different shape now from the one it had been high up? Or was there more than one of them? She was breathing too quickly. 'Be sensible, Maeve,' she heard Nanny's voice telling her. 'Keep calm.' She must have dropped off or, good Lord, blacked out, for there was no doubt about it: somehow she had mislaid about fifty minutes of her life.

She blinked her irritated eyes and stroked the raw patch on her face. It took a supreme effort of will to get a grip on herself, but it was necessary because Alistair was liable to panic if he saw her so thrown. She breathed deeply and went back to the kitchen.

"You were right," she said. "I must be still half-asleep." She was in control again now but she couldn't rid herself of this sensation of remoteness, of plate-glass having been inserted between her and the world. She watched her hand lift a teacup to her mouth. Was she dreaming? She surreptitiously pinched herself on the leg. She was awake all right, but not in the usual sense of the word.

"Listen, will you?" Alistair was saying. His legs were jiggling again. "It looks like we're going to have a visitor. An important one." He paused and, when Maeve failed to press him, added: "Mwawa, actually."

"I already knew that," Maeve replied with an effort. "He's coming for 'Christ in Action'. It was in the papers."

"No, no. I don't mean England. I mean here. He's coming here, to this house." Alistair could still hardly believe the letter. Bishop Mwawa in his house! It meant that he couldn't fail to figure prominently at the Conference, of which the Bishop was to be the centrepiece. There'd be a couple of cardinals, three or four South American priests, of course – the Conference was nothing if not ecumenical – but no-one of Mwawa's stature. He was not only an Anglican bishop but black and African as well. He had been in the front-line struggle for years, arrested more than once and, rumour had it, tortured. He lived in the real world. His presence at the forthcoming 'Christ in Action' Conference – his imprimatur, as it were – raised it to global importance. And it was probable – practically certain – that Bishop Mwawa would within a few short weeks be standing in this very room!

Maeve focused on her husband with difficulty, partly because of her eye disorder and partly because he himself seemed blurred. His face had aged since coming to Acton. It was covered in tiny creases like a paper bag which has been screwed up and opened out again. It was a kindly face, but the strong bones and nose tended to emphasise the weakness of the chin. A vacant smile became fixed on his lips when the face was in repose, as though he were afraid of being caught looking severe. His eyes, too, had a blurred look beneath the pale lashes and brows. Instead of turning grey his sandy hair had simply thinned and faded into a nondescript colour. Poor old Alistair. She had no intention of damping down his joy, but the dubious, almost sensual intensity with which he contemplated the imminence of the Bishop made her speak sharply: "Why? Why is he coming here?"

"It goes against the grain for him to stay at the palace or a posh hotel. He wants to show solidarity with the poor, to stay somewhere humble, in the inner city."

"I'm never quite sure where that is. Do we qualify as inner city?"

"Of course we do. Not literally perhaps, but this is exactly the kind of neglected multiracial area that – anyway this isn't the point..." Alistair was nettled. Why was Maeve being so pedantic? It was unlike her not to throw herself into his triumphs. God knew they were few enough.

Maeve, however, was feeling too dazed and detached to suppress an heretical thought: she didn't like the look of Bishop Mwawa. Admittedly she had only seen him on TV, moving through a crowd of supporters in a township, discreetly clenching his fist in salute, calling for the release of his old comrade, Nelson Mandela. Close-ups showed deep-set, intelligent, cunning eyes. The purple shirt and ostentatious silver cross irrationally increased her suspicion that he was prey to vanity. She wondered, too, about Mrs Mannheim, his personal assistant and renegade white woman, who was never more than three paces behind his elbow. While the bishop was all smiles, Mrs Mannheim's face never cracked.

"But why not Brixton?" she insisted. "That's the obvious place for him to stay. Or even Shepherd's Bush. Much handier for the BBC."

"As a matter of fact, Brixton was mooted," Alistair admitted, liking Maeve's tone less and less, "but the Black leaders expressed reserve about welcoming him. You know how touchy they can be. Besides, their profile's a bit on the high side. Shepherd's Bush is out of the question. No-one suitable to play host. It was my articles in *Theology Now* which made them think of me." Alistair's articles had attracted attention less for their content as for striking the right note. He had the knack of sounding as though he were the first person to notice – and condemn – pernicious regimes. He avoided inflammatory political terms – fascist, racist – and wrote instead of struggle, tragedy, atrocity. He was speaking somewhat in that vein now.

"...don't you see, Maeve? At last the establishment will see that our own struggle, here, in Acton, is essentially the same as Bishop Mwawa's. He's showing solidarity – showing that oppression is not some abstraction, remote from our lives, but all around us. He cares deeply about the victims of our own beastly class-ridden English injustice..."

Maeve was unable to concentrate. She knew he was right, of course. His fervour, his dedication, were virtues she admired. It was just that she had heard the same words so often. She shouldn't be thinking it, but Alistair's jargon seemed suddenly automatic, his rhetoric worn out, like that of a man who protests love too often and too much. "Goodness! Look at the time," she interrupted during a pause in the flow. "And I'm not even dressed yet." She kissed his hot indignant cheek. "I'm very pleased about the Bishop, dear. It'll put you on the map at last, and not before time."

Climbing slowly up the stairs, she instantly forgot all about Bishop Mwawa. 'I've lost fifty minutes,' she thought. 'What's *happening* to me?'

Alistair wandered out into the garden. Although mollified by Maeve's parting words, he still felt a bit let down. He sometimes thought that, lately, his wife had not been, well, quite as supportive as she might be. He suppressed the thought at once. Maeve was magnificent, a rock. It was a gross betrayal, base ingratitude to suggest otherwise. He'd be lost, lost without her. She had a naturally acerbic edge to her, that was all. It was probably an Irish thing. He admired it. It kept him on his mettle.

He strolled down the narrow lawn, peering vaguely at the flowerbeds which Maeve despaired of keeping in order, and allowed his imagination free rein. He saw himself meeting Mwawa's flight from Jo'burg or, perhaps, Harare where he retreated when things got too hot in the south. They greeted each other like two old comrades, like two freedom fighters, amidst the fireworks of the press's flash bulbs. The vicarage would become, for the duration of the Conference, the focus of church activity.

A shadow fell across his fantasy: was his house too… spacious, too well-appointed? He was not comfortable in a large four-storied house (albeit terraced) when all the other houses in the street were split into flats and frequently overcrowded. But then again, perhaps it was as well that the vicarage was not too small. The Bishop had suffered enough hardship. It was thrilling to think of the conversations they might have long into the night; of the way he would be at the Bishop's side during the hours of the Conference. If anything vindicated all Alistair's tribulations and recompensed him for his dwindling congregation or for the blank stares of the local youth, it was this visit.

Alistair's happier train of thought was broken by something that caught his eye on the lawn: a large oval shape had been etched into the grass. It appeared too regular to be a 'fairy ring' of subterranean fungi; it looked more like a scorch mark, as if a giant iron had been laid on the grass and left too long. It ruined what smoothness he had laboured with mower and weed-killer to obtain. He made a mental note to ask someone what could be sprayed on the oval to arrest the spread of this latest pestilence.

TWO

About three hours after her revelation, Heather was enough in her right mind to think about getting properly dressed. She threw on a few loose garments of cotton and silk which she fastened with bits of fabric at the wrist, neck and waist – a style of dressing which Julian called 'athletic chic'. She added bracelets, dangly earrings and plain flat shoes to diminish her height. She wasn't actually all that tall; she only thought of herself as such because her ballet teacher had told her she was too tall ever to become a successful dancer. With the self-knowledge acquired during Jane's therapy, she wondered if perhaps her teacher was not merely being tactful, avoiding the issue of her talent. At any rate, while she was reconciled to failure in her chosen career, she still bore marks of her ballet days. Her long dark hair was severely scraped back, either hanging in a pony tail or pinned up in two plaited loops like a Russian peasant; her hand gestures were expressive, graceful and, to untheatrical eyes, affected. She walked in that distinctive springy way – feet turned out at the end of muscular legs, as if she were forever on the verge of leaping into the air. Recently, she had given up the rather zealous use of make-up preferred by Julian in favour of the spare natural look characteristic of Jane. What she lost in one sort of dramatic effect, she gained in another: her face under its tight frame of hair had a Pre-Raphaelite ethereality, with its pale skin, delicate nose and small curly mouth. Her eyes, as might be expected, were large, dark and wide apart – what Julian in one mood called soulful and, in another, dog-like.

Heather walked around her basement flat, touching things, savouring them. The lethargy of the past weeks had been dispelled. She felt aerated, fizzing with energy. The daily struggle against pointlessness which had plagued her in the aftermath of her affair – four years, seven months and nine days was a long time – was over. Her life would now never be the same again – could now, for the first time, begin. Nothing else mattered except the imperative to re-enter, recapture the brilliant world of pure meaning she had perceived beneath the contingent surface of this one. Nor was it the impossible dream which all the big orthodoxies led you to believe (all those grand words like salvation, redemption, samadhi, nirvana). No, it was just a question of opening your eyes to *reality*, pure and simple, which was always there, right in front of you, waiting to be stepped into as naturally as being born.

Her rooms still glowed in the aftermath of her illumination and, judging by this light, it was easy to see which piece of furniture was out of place. It was important to conform your surroundings as closely as possible to the marvellous hidden order of things. She lost no time therefore in earmarking those possessions which would obviously no longer do. She gathered up a lampshade here, a coffee table there, a rug, a kitchen chair, the bathroom curtains – and dumped them outside in the street. There, with luck, they would be claimed – re-cycled – just as she had recovered from the gutter a lacquered screen and a perfectly good clothes' horse.

While she laboured, she continued to wonder whom (if she couldn't tell the whole world) she could *tell* about the morning's event. The Irish vegetable woman didn't count. It was even doubtful whether she had, as she claimed, seen it too; for how could anyone see it and remain so calm, almost indifferent? The old bat was probably a few bricks short of a load. She couldn't even wear her jacket the right way round. Heather's first instinct, inevitably, had been to tell Julian. But that was just habit and out of the question. Time was, she might have given some friend a buzz; but, running through the list of names in her head, she realised how many people she had lost contact with during the Julian period. Besides, her friends were mostly too busy or too married. Even before Julian she had grown sick of forever talking to their answering machines or their Portuguese nannies.

The less cluttered the flat became, the more Heather was pleased. She threw out another chair, with a wonky leg, and then – why not? – a whole sofa she'd never much liked. She felt lighter by the minute. The decks, she felt, were being cleared for action. As an afterthought she bunged out a full bookcase as well. Wherever the future led her she wouldn't be needing all those heavy improving books, that was for sure. She dusted off her hands and made a cup of herbal tea which she carried out into the small walled garden. She sat on the overgrown patch of lawn and allowed herself the luxury of recalling *the thing*. Just remembering it made her insides start up like a power plant and begin to hum. The obvious person to tell – the memory seemed to put this into her head – was Jane. As soon as this came to her she couldn't *wait* to tell her. Jane had made it clear that certain days, such as this one, were sacrosanct (she needed time away from her clients to 're-energise her personal space'); but she couldn't possibly resent Heather's intrusion when the news was so crucial, so positive, so good. Without finishing her tea, Heather sprang indoors, pirouetted along the passage and out of the front door.

It would have been quickest to take the Tube to Ealing Common – Jane's semi-detached was not far from the station – but Heather viewed the Underground with revulsion. It wasn't so much the susceptibility to fire and IRA bombs, airlessness and criminal elements, as her own claustrophobia which, on the increase since her teenage years, had for some reason grown acute since Julian had left her for his wife. Besides, buses were cheaper, and she needed to watch every penny since going on the dole. To accept unemployment benefit was to accept a measure of guilt. She was not a deserving case. She could easily find work, on the creative side of things, as she had done in the past – in an art gallery, at a fashion designer's, with a video company. But now she needed time to herself – for herself, as Jane put it. The vacuum created by Julian's defection provided the ideal opportunity to get herself together, sort out the career which had so far eluded her and generally take charge of a life which, left to its own devices, had failed to deliver the goods.

As she approached the bus stop in the High Street, a pile of rubbish in the doorway of an empty shop moved. A red-faced old lady, all but buried in bags and litter, sang out:

"La-di-da. Di-da, di-da." Heather instinctively rummaged in her bag and held out a pound coin to the unfortunate woman. "Pooh," she remarked, taking it. "Pooh-pooh-pooh." Heather smiled at her.

Waiting at the bus stop she looked around her with interest, hoping to recapture some tiny fraction of the vision which had earlier been vouchsafed to her. Every few paces there was a patch of festive colour courtesy of the litter which adorned the street like the residue of a carnival. Passers-by wore bright summer clothes. They etched sharp purple shadows into the pavement. The shop fronts were unprepossessing but, if you lifted your eyes, the façades of the second storeys presented a wholly different picture of the street – a variety of brickwork and tiled roofs and architectural styles to delight the eye. They reminded Heather of an impulsive trip she had taken to Morocco two years ago, a respite from the anxiety attaching to her affair with Julian. Her first choice had been India, with its promise of superabundant teeming life and, above all, its holy men who, encountered as if by chance in narrow gullies or remote mountain passes, said the one thing that made sense of your life. However, it came to her in the travel agency that India was too well-trodden by exactly the same kind of earnest truth-seeker as herself. All the great gurus had surely scurried away like yetis into mountain caves by now, leaving their second division colleagues to be besieged in gigantic ashrams by intense Americans and humourless Swedes. She had changed her mind on the spot.

Being driven in a jalopy across the fringe of the Sahara towards Marrakesh, she saw the only thing which remotely compared to that morning's experience: just as she had raised her eyes above street-level a moment before, so she had been invited to do the same by her unshaven taciturn driver.

"Atlas," he had said, pointing a finger. Sure enough, on the horizon there was a jagged line of brown mountains, not exactly what the word 'Atlas' conjured up, but monumentally impressive nevertheless. Above them hung a stratum of cloud. "Atlas," the driver repeated, stabbing his finger at the windscreen. "Yes," said Heather. "I see."

But she had not seen. All at once, lifting her eyes higher, to the sky above the cloud-topped mountains, she saw that what she had assumed was further cloud was, in fact, a vast range of white peaks so high above the dun foothills as to be incomprehensible to her sight. "Oh... I *see...*" But she had never seen anything like them. The astronomical tonnage of the soaring snow-bound crags, holding up the sky, imparted by some weird inversion a sensation of weightlessness, as if without moving she had been wafted on to the roof of the world. And it seemed momentarily as though her hunger for some overarching meaning had been appeased.

As she boarded the number 51, Heather looked up above the roofs at the white clock tower standing like a sentinel over Acton. The sky around it was as blue and innocent as the day was long. Perhaps whatever had been there in the early hours was still there, invisibly. The thought set Heather's innards churning and her brain throbbing in time to the deep bass note of the bus.

Maeve was arrested at her front gate by the sight of an electric blue piece of plastic trapped in the low broken picket fence which divided her property from next door's. Irritatingly, it could not be plucked out without trampling over the small rectangular flowerbed which did duty as a front garden (not that this was really an obstacle since the bed had failed to evince any of the flowers she had planted months ago, and was now given over to weeds and a few bare stalks). No, the trouble was, the blue plastic evoked an emotion out of all proportion to its mere presence; an emotion beyond irritation and bordering on despair. The epitome of litter, it spoke of a heartless chaos which threatened her orderly existence.

Never one to flinch from truth, Maeve stared up and down Marlborough Gardens, the grandiose name of her run-down street. With the perspective granted her by the level blue eye of plastic, she could no longer see what Alistair had initially described as an authentic and colourful community; she could no longer feign joy in being, finally, at 'grass roots level'. She was afraid of her sordid surroundings – the stacks of rubbish on the pavement which children in cheap nylon track suits set fire to; the bad spelling of graffiti on garden walls; the cacophony of pop music mingling with the shouts of the rowing family at number twenty-three; and above all, the litter – tin cans, wrappers and packets which, together with the semi-permanent piles of household junk, betrayed the contempt of the inhabitants for their surroundings. Amidst all this squalor, what was one small piece of plastic? Maeve couldn't be bothered to pick it up. She turned away and walked with dragging steps down Marlborough Gardens towards the High Street.

She could not shake off the feeling of unreality which had been with her since early morning. Her body ached as if her limbs had been wrenched and all her organs rearranged. Her eyes still itched; the rash on her neck and face showed no sign of abating. Her head throbbed. She wondered whether she should visit the doctor again. He had not been especially helpful the last time, being at a loss to explain her recent increase in weight except by the mysterious formula 'fluid retention', a condition for which she'd been given tablets. They made her pee a lot, but they weren't helping. The tall, slim woman of a few months ago had become fleshy and round-shouldered; the slender waist, thick; the shapely legs, cylindrical; the feet inclined to swell in the flat sensible shoes. Her face had not changed. It was still pretty – an appropriate word in the light of its clear girlish complexion – but few noticed this because it was not made up and, in repose, appeared prim, not to say severe. This impression (not unlike Nanny Bryce's) doubtless derived from her school-teaching days, and was augmented by her habit of keeping her greying hair permanently pinned up and of wearing austere, unfashionable but 'good' clothes. Closer inspection, however, revealed flaws in this severity: the hair constantly strayed from its pins and floated in wisps around her face, while the clothes rebelled against uniformity with missing buttons, small frayings and the odd tear. The more she aged, the more Maeve resembled her parents – mildly eccentric and down-at-heel members of a minor Anglo-Irish aristocracy.

Maeve also wondered whether her discomfort might not have something to do with the morning's event – that sudden menacing *thing*, the disorienting loss of time – but she couldn't assemble any concrete thoughts in connection with it; nor could she face the effort of trying. It was easier to follow the promptings of duty and habit, and therefore to go shopping as she always did on that day. Side-stepping a pile of dog's muck, she entered Khan's newsagent's on the corner.

Mr Khan was standing behind his counter as if he hadn't moved since Maeve had last been in. He stood very straight, with a faraway look in his eyes, as if he were a sea captain and his shop, the bridge of a ship. His face was strong, slightly hawkish and rather handsome – similar (as she'd pointed out to Alistair) to Imran Khan, the Pakistani cricket captain, whom her husband so admired. Fittingly, a radio was on and tuned to the test match. Maeve had not paid attention to Alistair's analysis of the previous day's play and so she didn't even know which teams were involved. England, presumably; but who were they playing?

"Good morning, Mr Khan," she said. The shopkeeper inclined his head. While Alistair found Mr Khan's taciturnity disconcerting, Maeve found it restful. She liked the way he brought his eyes into focus on his customers, with the merest hint of amusement. "Just popped in to see if my husband's magazine has arrived." Mr Khan raised a finger, turned and disappeared through the strips of multi-coloured plastic curtaining which screened his back room.

Maeve examined the newspapers on the counter. The disreputable tabloids were displayed less prominently than the heavyweights. She scanned them quickly for any evidence of IRA bombings – she always felt a sense of guilt at its outrages even though she had long ago disavowed her Irish nationality – but, luckily, there were none. Indeed there'd been a lull since the awful deaths in Hyde Park a few years ago and, more recently, at the Grand Hotel in Brighton where the prime minister had narrowly avoided injury. But the populace was still jumpy, still vigilant for suspicious packages left in department stores and Tube trains. Instead, the papers were full of Gorbachev and his policy of perestroika. What was he up to? Was it all some diabolical plot to lure the West into a false sense of security? It seemed too good to be true. And yet, looking at Gorbachev's photograph, Maeve saw warmth in his smile and a human expression very different from the closed obdurate faces of previous Soviet leaders. She hardly dared believe it, but perhaps it was true – perhaps Gorby was bringing the Cold War to an end.

Mr Khan returned, holding *Theology Now* slightly at arm's length. The low murmur of the cricket commentator was accompanied by a sudden muted roar. Clearly a wicket had fallen. Mr Khan permitted himself a suspicion of a smile, which Maeve returned uncertainly. Perhaps Pakistan was playing. Or did Mr Khan support England? She didn't like to ask. She paid for the magazine, and left.

Acton was a well-defined place for London. The High Street ceased at a definite point to both east and west where it changed into a no-man's-road between Shepherd's Bush and Ealing respectively. However, compared to fashionable Chiswick, a mile or so to the south, it was a bit of a backwater. Property prices had begun to rise late, and then largely owing to the promise of a glittering new shopping mall, similar to well-heeled Ealing's, which was to be built on the site of the derelict precinct, now filled with a tide of market stalls.

Meanwhile, the shops were as uncertain as the shopping. Every time Maeve went out, it seemed, one had closed and another opened. Dress shops did not last more than a few months; the lone health food shop, weeks. Maeve enjoyed the market most, even though there was nothing amongst the junk to buy except, once a week, fish from the back of a lorry and vegetables from her – and everyone's – friend, Mrs O'Rourke. But she liked listening to the vendors hawking their wares in an exotic array of accents from cockney to Gujarati. Mrs O'Rourke's was pure Galway.

There were more Irish in Acton than Asians, Poles or even West Indians. Not Northern Irish, of course – they were another race – but Irish from counties as far apart as Wexford and Kerry, Sligo and Cork. It distressed her that, whenever a bomb went off, the shadow of suspicion fell over her parish. It was nonsense, of course – although most were probably Republicans, they were no more Provos than she was. Yet it also worried Maeve that there were pockets of the Irish community – those that frequented that dreadful pub, The Castle – which were not above suspicion. Far from it, as everybody knew.

More generally, it distressed her that the Irish apparently made little effort to better themselves – for instance, to fight their way out of the tower blocks and into their own flats, as the government was encouraging. In the hierarchy of Acton's ethnic groups, the Irish were bottom of the heap. They were impossible. They were the more disturbing to Maeve because their accents evoked a childhood she hoped to have put behind her. A snatch of brogue overheard outside the charity shop could make the ground shudder like a bog and plunge her on the instant back into Ireland. She could almost swear that she could smell the soft rain, the smoke from turf fires or the warm coconut aroma of yellow furze. Such memories, heart-shaking in their immediacy, were never separate from their presiding genius. His name was Patsy Collins.

As Alistair was making his way down the High Street towards the first parish visit of the day, a curious and frightening thing happened to him. Sidestepping a group of boys jostling four-abreast on the pavement, he was forced into the foyer of a shoe shop where he came face to face with a disturbingly familiar old man. Alistair took in his appearance at a glance: he was tall, even spindly, with a self-effacing stoop; his face was finely wrinkled and ascetic-looking; the distinguished nose and faint smile might have suggested an absent-minded professor, were it not for the incongruity of his dress – a bomber jacket, jeans that flapped loosely round his thin calves, and a pair of grubby trainers. This uniform, already dated among the youthful, looked sinister on a man of his years. He made as if to pass Alistair by, but, seeing the expression of distaste on the vicar's face, matched it with one of his own, and stopped. Alistair looked more closely at the alien yet familiar features. They composed themselves into a face known to him intimately. His own face, in fact.

Inadvertently reflected in a full-length looking-glass built into the shop front, Alistair had glimpsed himself as another might see him, before he had time to put on the face which greeted him every morning in the shaving mirror. It had been a disconcerting sight. He smiled at his stupidity and walked on. But he wasn't able to dismiss so easily the fright his reflection had given him. It was not caused by his oddly disheartening appearance so much as by the recollection, evoked by his own image, of an occurrence in his earlier life.

It had taken place in 1949, during his second year at university. By and large this had been a happy period for Alistair. Freed from the harshness of public school and the loneliness of home, he had thrown himself into the life of an undergraduate. He made friends, discovered girls, got drunk, read voraciously. He understood the peculiar blessing of being at university. It was a time of grace, between adolescence and the duties of full manhood, in which nothing was expected of him except that he should study and explore all possibilities for their own sake, before necessity fixed him in a more or less rigid pattern of life. In this spirit he was drawn towards a small but enthusiastic circle of occultists.

Its members were more or less serious and, for the most part, benign. They eschewed the blacker arts and discussed natural magic, the Kabbalah, Hermetic and Neoplatonic philosophy, angelology and so on, while engaging in sporadic psychical research. They gave dinners in honour of such visiting luminaries as Dr Falkenburg, the commentator on Cornelius Agrippa, and Professor Hayadi, whose work on the numerology and magical proportions of the Temple of Jerusalem still languished in obscurity. They took tea with leading mediums who gave impromptu sittings, or with aged former initiates of the Golden Dawn who could be relied on for indiscreet anecdotes about Aleister Crowley and W.B. Yeats. Once, delightfully, they entertained to cocktails a Mrs van der Houf, an incarnation of the Comte de St Germain – one of Madame Blavatsky's seven Masters of Wisdom – who sharply enjoined them never to eat members of the bean family.

All this was a heady and often amusing brew for a young man like Alistair, whose religious propensities led him naturally to an exploration of the supernatural. He wanted stronger meat than the dull Anglican liturgy; he desired personal experience – *gnosis* – of the transcendent. He practised yogic techniques and meditation, experimented with his diet (more than once smoked hashish), and learnt a little Hebrew in order to read the *Sepher Yetzirah*. Thus he needed no second invitation to participate in the raising of Manu-Cacu, the Merciful Daemon of the Eleventh Sphere. He didn't exactly believe in the objective existence of such entities – any more, for instance, than he believed in an evil separate from the corrupt will of men. He was, after all, a Christian. But he vaguely thought that the ritual might produce some stimulating subjective effects. Mostly, like the others, he just wanted to scare himself a little.

In the event, the ceremony was a damp squib. Everything was arranged according to the letter of Crowley's instructions – the disposition of circles, pentagrams, symbols and daggers – and yet the mighty invocations produced nothing more than a sudden draught and a sinister flickering of candles which Alistair privately attributed to the opening of a nearby door. He went to bed that night full of port, stilton and firm resolutions not to waste his time with hocus-pocus.

At six minutes past three, according to his bedside clock, he awoke with a start. Thinking he had left a light on, he tried to get out of bed. He found that he couldn't move. Nevertheless he could see that the illusion of having left a light on was created by a sickly viscous yellow, more substance than illumination, which pervaded the room from an invisible source. He felt at once that something was terribly wrong, but he couldn't put his finger on it. He struggled in vain to move his paralysed limbs. His room, high up on the corner of his college, was charmingly angular. Slowly the source of his disquiet was borne in upon him: the angles of the room were wrong. They had become subtly deformed, a fraction more acute or obtuse, so that he had the impression of waking in a parallel universe where everything in the normal world was replicated, but distorted. The creeping horror he experienced was out of all proportion to the circumstances. It seemed to him that things were not merely out of kilter but positively evil. The walls were crawling, alive, and, like the non-light, felt rather than seen to have a disgusting texture. If he had considered evil at all, he had thought of it as morally, even physically threatening; he had never reckoned on this disgust.

The atmosphere in the room deteriorated further. In the corner of his eye he saw someone or something sitting at his desk, with its back to the bed. It was at once alien and familiar, very like the reflection in the looking-glass outside the shoe shop. Even as he caught sight of it, it in turn seemed to sense his presence. It began to revolve its head. Alistair had a premonition that the figure would also be a replica – of himself subtly, hideously altered. It occurred to him that if he looked into this Doppelganger's face, he would lose his mind.

The next thing he remembered was good clean sunlight breaking through the crack in the curtains. The room was restored to its old self. The chair at the desk was empty. The event had been nothing but a nightmare. Hadn't it? On the other hand, it had been unlike any dream he had ever had before or since. He wondered if he was going a bit mad, toyed with the idea of seeing a trick cyclist. When nothing further occurred, he dropped the idea with relief. He was left with the possibility that the vision, as he thought of it, had been real – a notion supported by its clarity and solidity. It was surely more than coincidental, too, that it had happened on a night when he had been party to a magical conjuration. He remained perplexed and fearful. For weeks he had to steel himself to go to sleep.

Alistair abandoned occultism and began to reflect intensely on spiritual matters in general and Christianity in particular. The Anglican Communion now looked more like a sanctuary than a dull routine. The decision to take holy orders crept up on him unawares. Only now did he begin to consider how large a part fear had played in his ordination. The truths of science and reason had broken down in his room on that night, and he needed some other counterbalance to evil. He found it in the powerful apotropaic magic of Christ. He came to believe that, if anything, his nightmarish vision had been providential – that God had used it to bring about his repentance. At any rate, Alistair changed his degree course from philosophy to divinity and, within three years of leaving university, found himself a slightly bewildered curate in the heart of a Derbyshire parish. In the light of his unequivocal Christianity, coupled with marriage to an eminently sensible schoolteacher, he was able to banish that dark stain on his memory. In time, he even learnt to smile indulgently at his adolescent fear, as he might smile at a child's fear of a bogey man.

All children have places which are sacred to them. But Maeve was conscious from her earliest years of a larger sacred landscape which was not personal – a network of hallowed spots which, belonging to the wilderness beyond, encroached on the walls of Eden, as her father's demesne was named. To each of these places tradition ascribed a mystery or significance which Patsy Collins, who worked for her father, would relate. Although only in his late twenties, he seemed to have accumulated a store of knowledge beyond his years.

As he drove her to town in the trap or phaeton, he would point out a haunted crossroads, a copse you shouldn't pass during a new moon, a blackthorn it was perilous to shelter under. Such landmarks were sometimes more obvious – a bush, for example, whose branches were alive with a flutter of rags and ribbons, attached by wayfarers who had said a rosary there; the Altar Rock where Masses had been said by priests outlawed by the British; or holy wells guarded by gaudy statues of Our Lady, around which were strewn votive objects. The spirits of tree and stone and water were older than the saints and revered long before a church militant had wisely commandeered them.

Sometimes Patsy would pull up at a particular place and, letting the reins drop, roll a cigarette and mention some tale of ghosts or miraculous healings. Through his eyes Maeve saw a landscape in which every natural object had glamour. Centuries' worth of stories – the history of Ireland, in fact – overlaid the land in layers, like stones in a dry-stone wall. The very air was thick with possibilities so that it would be unexceptional to meet, without even knowing it, a saint in the boreen or the devil on Divil's Hill.

Most thrilling, though, were the raths or 'fairy forts' – circular banks and ditches of impenetrable antiquity which farmers were tempted to dig up for the treasure they were said to hold. Few dared to do so for fear of incurring the wrath of the *Sídhe*. One exception, according to Patsy, was a man called O'Rahilly who had boasted one night in the pub that no superstition would prevent him from breaking into the rath on his land. And hadn't a very old man whom nobody knew stood up then and, with a queer look, strongly advised against such a scheme, unless of course O'Rahilly wished to leave his children fatherless? O'Rahilly had gone ahead all the same. He found no treasure; but the really strange thing – here Patsy gave Maeve a meaning look – was that your man *was alive and well* to this day.

Sídhe was a word Patsy uttered but rarely, and then in a lowered voice. It was pronounced 'shee', like a whisper. The *Sídhe* were the ancient inhabitants of Ireland, driven underground by later invasions. Patsy was descended from them. He had seen these ancestors more than once, riding into the raths which were merely entrances to that otherworld where the *Sídhe* danced and hunted, feasted and fought; where it was summer when it was winter with us, and vice versa. They were terrible ones for shape-shifting, appearing now larger than life, now smaller. They could assume the appearance of whatever took their fancy. A pig in a field might not be what it seemed; even an insect or a cloud of dust might not be *right*. They could help a man with his work or deal him a stroke, leaving him dead or paralysed. They could steal young men to help them in their games or young mothers to suckle their new-born; and while these were *away*, a body in their likeness, or the likeness of a body, was left lying in their beds. Some said they took the dead, who had been seen dancing among them. Their music was too beautiful to be endured. Many people, including Patsy, often called them – more in hope than expectation – the Good People.

In the beginning, the taint of eerie ambiguity which attached to Patsy as an intermediary between her and the *Sídhe*, excited more than it disquieted Maeve. It was simply part of what it meant to be Irish. She accepted the interpenetration of natural and supernatural just as she took the fairy forts for granted, as untamed outposts among the broken fields. There was even a fairy place within the precincts of Eden: a large oval tumulus lying along the edge of a copse, overgrown with brambles. The locals called it Maeve's Grave. Patsy explained that her namesake, the Queen of the *Sídhe* herself, was buried there – a contradiction, since the Good People were well-known to be immortal.

Maeve was fascinated by the uncanny mound. How glorious it would be to see the steep side of Maeve's Grave swing open on silent hinges and pour forth a fairy troop in all their fantastic array! She pictured the tall riders caparisoned in green and gold; she could almost hear the clatter of their red-eared horses' hooves and the terrible gaiety of inhuman laughter. At the same time, how she feared seeing them – dreaded meeting those famous eyes, preternaturally lustrous, silver-flashing, cold.

Once, at noon on a heavy August day, when the land lay suspended and breathless in the heat, Maeve steeled herself to clear a space in the brambles and, lying with her ear pressed to the mossy mound, fancied she could hear the beautiful intolerable bleat of uilleann pipes, and the muffled thud of dancing feet. She ran then from that unearthly sound, pursued by the thud of her own heart, as if her life depended on it.

THREE

The number 51 squeaked and jerked its way along the congested High Street, straining to break through the traffic into the open road towards Ealing Common. Heather sat at the front of the upper deck where, as a child, she had pretended to be the driver. On the pavement below, a group of black boys took it in turns to dance around a ghetto-blaster, as around a camp-fire, outside the Youth Centre. Farther on, some scruffy men, already drunk, were lounging or swaying outside the Co-op. A heavy, defeated-looking woman with dishevelled greying hair was giving one of them, younger than the rest, some money. Looking up, he caught Heather's eye and triumphantly brandished his fist at her. She waved back. On the other side of the road, she could see a throng of people weaving in and out between the stalls of the market, participating – like the undulating youths, the swaying drunks – in a ritual dance of which only she seemed conscious.

From behind, a random man on the street resembled Julian. As little as a day ago, when she still saw him everywhere, her heart would have hammered against her ribs. But now, knowing what she did, she didn't even bother to turn and check his face. She had been freed from all that. Never again would she wait for his 'phone call or his ring at the doorbell with that perpetual ache of anticipation which his presence never quite dispelled. In the same way, while his love-making had always been satisfactory, it never quite assuaged her hunger for it, almost as if her real longing was for something else. Heather had never faked an orgasm; but, as the affair wore on, she began to suspect that, in a deeper sense, all her orgasms had been fakes.

"I hate you, I hate you," she had bawled at the empty chair in which Jane had invited her to imagine Julian. But, in truth, it wasn't possible to hate Julian, whose self-laceration had been greater than anything Heather could have inflicted. His adultery amazed him; his monologues of remorse grew into hyperbolic epics that left Heather helpless with laughter.

"Anger and pain," Jane observed, "are at the root. You're angry and hurting but you don't allow yourself to acknowledge it. You're programmed from infancy, like all women, to suppress it." She proceeded to draw unpleasant diagrams of this anger festering at the roots of Heather's psyche. But there was a positive side, too: green insistent shoots were germinating in the darkness, pushing up against the crust of pain which had to be dissolved by blissful tears, like rain after drought.

Heather admitted that she'd been pretty miffed by Julian's treatment of her, but 'miffed' was not at all what Jane had in mind. She was after something more primal. Accordingly she set Heather to pummelling a pair of cushions that represented her father. Heather recollected some childhood injustice or other and managed some embarrassed smacks on the heads of the cushions. She promptly felt guilty, and then felt guilty about feeling guilty. But in time, under Jane's firm but caring direction, she learnt to stage a tantrum or two in order, as it were, to prime the pump for tears. "Go on," urged Jane, "cry it all out." But her eyes obstinately remained dry. Perhaps Dad was the wrong target after all. He was a dear old thing, gone down five years since into the earth he'd spent a lifetime as an archaeologist digging up. Mum had been cremated a year later, leaving Heather more or less alone in the world, but with enough money to buy her flat outright. Neither of them had given her as much attention as she wanted – they were too wrapped up in each other – but it was difficult to believe that she was repressing a tidal wave of wrath and pain on that account. She understood and liked them (the same was true of Julian). According to Jane, she was too understanding. She had been conditioned to 'understand' – to value everyone above herself and to make no fuss. Whatever the truth of this, Heather knew that something at least was wrong with her because she was unhappy in matters of the heart and, in every other department, unfulfilled – until now. If only she had known beforehand – before all the therapy, meditation, diets, aerobics and improving books – that you didn't always have to be fighting off depression; that you could be unblocked and enlightened in the twinkling of an eye. Paradise was only a heartbeat away, a hidden order within the fallen world where you could take your ease like the original lovers, walking with God in the cool of the day.

When she reached the quiet tree-lined crescent in which Jane lived, Heather slowed her pace. A shadow of doubt occluded her high spirits: what would Jane make of the visitation? What if she saw it simply as another symptom? How could she be persuaded that further therapy was superfluous? Heather paused to stroke a marmalade cat sunning itself on a wall. She pictured Jane's taut face, with its compassionate expression. Her long-suffering hazel eyes matched her hair, cut short as befitted her strength, but prettily fluffed in a way that bespoke femininity. She would nod wisely as Heather spoke; her concern would be communicated in an affected hesitancy of speech. "Don't worry too much about the meaning of your experience, right?" she would say. "Tell me what it means to you. Tell me how you feel about it. OK?"

But was this approach appropriate? The evidence of her own eyes earlier that day suggested that there were things outside the merely psychological, the only human. As she reached Jane's front gate, Heather hesitated to open it. Instead, she closed her eyes and summoned up the Cube.

When she had first looked up at the clock tower, she had had the impression, either through some optical illusion or in fact, that it was shaped like a disc which instantly sprang up into a square. It was as if that particular stretch of sky was solid, and the malleable Cube had landed on it with such force as to flatten itself before springing back into its proper form. It hung or hovered there, in mid-air – a two-dimensional square of glimmering metal like an opaque window onto a world behind the sky. Although it was impersonal, it was not neutral. It was somehow focussed on her like the pupilless eye of a Greek statue. Only then did it tilt slightly to reveal two more sides, a third dimension which suggested a cube rather than a square. At the same time it emitted (or did it merely catch the sun's rays?) its piercing flashes of light, both natural and intelligent, like Jehovah in the burning bush.

For a moment Heather was ravished all over again by that blinding instant of truth. She felt herself re-activated, her body resonating in time to the high-energy hum in her brain. Just as she opened her eyes, she noticed a flaw in one of the Cube's facets. Not a flaw, she decided, but a sizeable depression – a faint concave circle like a porthole in the silvery wall which, on reflection, was as much fluid as solid, more quicksilver than steel.

She snapped her eyes open with the shock: there was someone tall and imposing standing behind the semi-transparent depression.

Heather's chief fear was that she would somehow allow her experience to fade away, be forgotten. She urgently needed to make contact with others who had had the same experience, who were perhaps more advanced on the path to understanding the mystery of the Cube. In her heart of hearts she knew it would be unforgivable if she did not bend all her energies towards achieving permanently the state of perfection promised by the Cube's lightning-strike. There'd be no rest for her in all eternity unless she entered into communion with the One and All.

Jane's house had a blind and shuttered look. There was nothing for her there. Courtesy required her to inform Jane that her therapy was no longer needed – and that was all. Even if she were able to express a fraction of what she had undergone and planned to undergo, she would never be able to make Jane understand. As she approached the house by its front path, she was struck by the *rudeness* of the front door. It was sticking its tongue out at her. Closer to, she saw that the illusion was created by the local newspaper protruding from the letter-box. She rang the doorbell and, while waiting for Jane to answer, idly plucked the newspaper out and glanced at the back page. There, in front of her disbelieving eyes, in the small ads section, was a ruled box. It contained nothing except five words and a telephone number. The words might have been written especially for her. But of course, they were written for her. They were charged with awful significance, like a secret code only she could interpret. Without waiting a moment longer she bounded back down the path to the gate. Then she broke into a run. The words in the advertisement read:

ARE YOU WATCHING THE SKIES?

Heat wavered above the road. Patches of tar turned soft. The air was congested with dust and fumes. Breathless and already fagged out by her shopping expedition, Maeve leaned against the Public Library's wall. In the High Street there was nowhere to sit; it was designed to keep people upright and moving. A quiet cup of tea was nowhere to be had except at the Golden Plaice which really, Maeve felt, should have been another take-away, had its Chinese proprietors not been reluctant to waste the space.

Outside the next door's Youth Centre, four black boys were standing around a vast ghetto-blaster placed in the middle of the pavement. One of them was improvising a complicated undulating dance to the blaring music. In spite of her natural revulsion from the sound, Maeve drew nearer to watch the fascinating dance which switched rapidly between slow stylised movements and jerky, witty ones. Her concentration was broken when one of the three spectators flicked an empty cigarette packet on to the ground. Maeve spoke reflexively, sharply:

"Pick it up!" The youth stared at her incredulously. He glanced at his neighbour, a huge Rastafarian to judge by his dreadlocks and the legend, emblazoned across the back of his T-shirt, *Weed of Wisdom*. The Rasta swung around to face Maeve.

Her legs turned spongy: it appeared for a second that the young giant had no eyes – or, rather, that his eyes were long, convex and completely dark. They stretched around his face to the hairline, like the eyes of an insect.

Maeve staggered slightly and, dropping her shopping basket, instinctively stretched out an arm and leaned against the wall of his chest. The man was taken aback; but, recovering himself, he supported Maeve with an arm around her shoulders.

"Hey, lady, take it easy," he said gently. Then, turning to his friend: "You heard the lady. *Pick up the packet*, man." The boy did as he was told.

"Sorry, sorry," said Maeve, recovering. "I was just... thrown by your..." She gestured vaguely at his face.

"Me dreadlocks give you the willies?"

"No... no. Your sunglasses."

"They isn't no ragamuffin shades, lady" – he sounded hurt – "they is primo quality". All the same he obligingly removed them and looked down on Maeve with interest.

"I'm sure they are," she said, withdrawing from the Rasta's embrace. "It's not that. It's more that I saw something... I mean, I saw..." Realising that she was unequal to the task of explaining, she smiled helplessly and began to edge away.

"What's so scary 'bout a pair of shades?"

"Oh... nothing. Just I being idiotic!" The Rasta laughed.

"You kill I, lady."

"Sorry to have bothered you. Please go on with your dancing – it's really awfully good."

'What,' Maeve wondered as she limped away, '*was* so scary about the sunglasses?' Nothing, nothing. Except that... except that, for the teeniest moment, when the young man turned towards her, why had she seen a pair of long tilted eyes, almond-shaped and – worst of all – completely black? And why had they seemed *familiar*? It was obviously a day for seeing things – she suddenly remembered the extraordinary thing by the clock tower. How had she forgotten it? It was as if it had slipped her mind deliberately, leaving her all bemused so that instead of getting on with things, she had been wandering about reflecting on the dismal condition of the world or dreaming of Ireland. She was becoming impossible. But why was there no disturbance in the streets after that outrage in the sky? Had she been the only one to see it? Surely, *surely* not. Obviously, it had to be explained. 'Finish the shopping quickly,' she commanded herself, 'and then *report* that wretched thing.'

She glanced nervously up at the clock tower. The sky was empty except for a sun muddied by the turbid atmosphere. Even William Blake would not be able to discern a heavenly host singing 'Holy, Holy, Holy' in that blotched yellow spot. If it penetrated the filthy air at all, it was hostile, aiming its carcinogenic death-rays through holes ripped in the ozone. It was in league with the foul air and acid rain to do everybody in. In Acton death came in secret, hidden inside the very commodities on which life itself depended. Was her own fluid-retaining body simply clogged in sympathy with the rivers and seas where fish breathed in toxic waste and birds were grounded by oil spills and poor turtles were throttled by passing plastic bags? She toiled up the High Street, trying to drag her mind away from these unwonted apocalyptic thoughts and back to the business of the day.

On the forecourt of the Co-op Maeve had to run the usual gauntlet of men in all stages of intoxication, from the moist and affectionate to the angry and bitter. Most were Irish; many had come from, or were on the way to, the Castle where by all accounts any class of behaviour was tolerated. Maeve handed over some change to a bashful lad still sober enough to ask for it and pushed her way into the shop.

She looked gloomily at her shopping list. All she had written on it was: food. Not helpful. She set off with her trolley. Nothing on the shelves inspired her. Food was as boring as the lumpy body that needed it. It was even, like air and sunlight, a menace. Lately she had begun to think that she could taste the pesticides and preservatives. Meat was spoilt by the flavour of adrenalin from the fear of the slaughtered beasts. And then there was all the bother of checking to make sure nothing came from South Africa, lest she break the embargo that Alistair insisted on. He was quite right to, of course; but what a palaver.

All too soon the tills were ahead of her and still she had bought nothing. She turned back, irritably scratching the rash on her neck, and recklessly set about the shelves. A tin of corned beef, a packet of frozen peas, spaghetti, half a pound of rubbery Cheddar, six 'farm-fresh' eggs (yes, but what *sort* of farm?), a sliced white loaf, a tin of sweet corn and another of cocoa – these items, precious little to relish among them, had just dropped into the trolley when an electrifying voice sounded behind her:

"La-di-da," it said loudly. "La-di-bloody-da."

Maeve's heart sank even lower. Half-turning, she glimpsed a scarlet-faced old woman in the aisle behind her, squatting in a nest of plastic bags. Whether the chant of la-di-da was aimed at her, Maeve couldn't be sure – the bag lady might be talking to herself. But as soon as Maeve moved smartly on, the woman gathered up her nest and shuffled after her.

"Would *Modom* care for some *pommes de terre*? No. Modom bloody wouldn't. Pooh-pooh. Would Modom like a little wine? Ha-ha. A Medoc? Ha-ha. A Chablis? Ha-ha. A Bergerac? Got a lovely big nose, that one. Ha-ha-ha. Pooh-pooh-pooh."

Blood rushed into Maeve's face. She lowered her head and pressed on as fast as she could without actually running. It was a thing she absolutely dreaded – being accosted by mad people. They belonged to another world, nothing could be done with them. They were impossible. Especially this one who, despite the caricature of a posh accent, was obviously educated and therefore all the more sinister. What had brought a middle-class French-speaking woman to this pass? It didn't bear thinking about.

The bag lady was gaining on her, singing snatches of *Carmen* as far as Maeve could make out. Any moment now there'd be, oh God, a *scene*. Scenes were the one thing she dreaded. Other shoppers, she noticed, were making themselves scarce. They seemed to be shooting her glances less of sympathy than of accusation.

"La-di-da-di-da... Pooh-pooh-pooh!" The litany went on, not a yard from her back. With blazing face Maeve paid the check-out girl, who looked at her as if she had brought this on herself. Then, afraid of being physically collared, she broke into a run towards the door.

Alistair's last mission of the day was to have tea with Mrs Silcock, who had missed church on two Sundays owing to arthritic legs that could only be shuffled along with the aid of a walking frame. He rang the front doorbell and pushed open the door which, courageously, Mrs Silcock didn't lock because of the pain and effort needed to answer it.

"Coo-ee! I'm in the kitchen!" she called. Alistair walked along the dingy passage to the kitchen. "Only I've made a coffee cake, vicar. I told my friend, Mrs Jenkins, 'I've made the vicar a coffee cake,' I says. 'I hope he likes it.' I bought a cherry cake as well. In case you didn't fancy mine."

"I'm sure I shall, Mrs Silcock. Indeed yes."

"You go through to the front room, vicar. Put your feet up. I'll bring the tea through in a minute. Coffee cake was my Harold's favourite. It was all he could eat at the end. 'Everything else goes right through me,' he used to say."

"Can I help you at all?"

"No, vicar. I can manage. You go through."

"Really, a mug of tea in the kitchen would be absolutely fine. I don't want you to go to any trouble. I'll just sit here, shall I, and we'll have a mug of tea together. Far more friendly." He squeezed himself behind the narrow formica table.

"Well..." Mrs. Silcock looked doubtful. "I don't know as I've got a mug."

"Oh well. Anything then. We won't stand on ceremony, eh?"

"Just as you like." Inexplicably she began to shuffle out of the kitchen, leaning heavily on her walking-frame. Alistair half-rose to assist her but there was nothing, short of carrying her, that he could do. "You watch the kettle for me, vicar," Mrs Silcock called breathlessly over her shoulder.

"Certainly, certainly." Alistair looked at his watch. Then he looked around the kitchen. It was poky and, in the heat of the day, stuffy.

He couldn't help comparing it unfavourably to the spacious kitchen of his privileged childhood where, on winter days, he was allowed to sit with a book in a warm corner, while servants bustled around him. The only child of elderly parents, he had been brought up in a world unchanged since Edwardian times; and, despite his free-thinking university days, he doubted whether he would ever have entered modernity had he not met Maeve during his first curacy. They had been like siblings at first and she, the elder sister. She had knocked much bookishness out of him and some sense in. She had teased him out of his earnestness, taught him social graces, taken him in hand. They never quarrelled except when he teased her about her charming Irish accent which was now, unfortunately, all but lost.

He could hear Mrs Silcock labouring along the passage. He jumped up and took the tray she was balancing on her walking-frame before she dropped it. It struck him as eccentric that she should keep all these things – cups, plates, sugar, milk, cutlery, doilies – in her front room, where they were hardly handy.

"You've let the kettle boil dry, vicar. I don't know. You men," reproved Mrs Silcock, her face blotchy with the strain of movement.

"Have I? Sorry, sorry." He never knew what to *say* to Mrs Silcock, nor, half the time, what to make of the things she said. So many of his flock were like her. Maeve seemed to understand them – at least she always knew what to say. Perhaps it was a knack one was born with.

"As I say," said Mrs Silcock (had she said?), "I've had the Blocks Men in. Couple of Micks. You can hardly understand a word they say." Alistair frowned at what he took to be a reference to two Irishmen.

"Blocks Men?"

"For the drains, vicar."

"You've had problems with your drains?"

"Problems? They're a shocker, the drains. The Micks was saying, all the drains in London is shot to pieces – haven't been touched since Queen Victoria did them. It was all right when there was one house, one family, but now it's all flats. The drains weren't built to take that many people... Bit of cake, vicar? The coffee I made myself – or the other?"

"Oh, er, either. Really." Alistair was not paying full attention to Mrs Silcock. She was happy to ramble on, provided you grunted agreement occasionally. He was thinking instead how disappointing

Acton was, in so many respects; how shocking it was that injustice and racial prejudice were so widespread, even among the victims of such vices, the very people on whose behalf he was fighting.

"You say, vicar."

"Oh. Right. That one, please."

"The cherry."

"Fine, fine."

"Suit yourself, vicar."

His appointment to Acton, after much petitioning of the bishop, had been the culmination of a change which had overtaken him during the last decade. He had come to feel – in his fifties, with death no longer so remote – that his cosy Gloucestershire living was only an extension of his sheltered childhood. His thoughts began to turn to a more real world. He grew uncomfortable in his own church which, by virtue of its traditional rural calm, seemed to give tacit support to the structures of oppression. The very beauty of his wisteria-covered vicarage made him fret. He was haunted by a recurring dream in which thousands of people, huge-eyed like famine victims, extended pleading arms towards him. Tortured by the need to do something, he rose high in a society which smuggled bibles into regimes where they were proscribed. He could almost envy the Russian Christians for whom prayer was a political act and every rite of worship spiced with danger.

"...we're floating on an ocean of sewage right now, the Blocks Men said," Mrs Silcock was saying. "A couple of years' time, I'll be up to my neck in other people's muck. What a shocker. I hope I go before that happens. I mean, you don't mind so much if it's your own."

"No," agreed Alistair vaguely. "I suppose not." With the move to his inner city parish came the thrilling intuition that he was approaching the heart of things. At last his religion could put on muscle. He knew, of course, that Christianity was a creed of weakness: Jesus had neither reformed Jewish legalism nor led a revolution against Roman imperialism – He had submitted to the Cross. But Alistair was too humble ever to contemplate imitation of this sacrifice; and, besides, what was appropriate to an age of martyrs was no longer valid now, when the teachings of Jesus were best placed in the service of human rights. He was fond of quoting to Maeve an epigram of Dag Hammarskjöld's: 'In our era, the road to holiness necessarily passes through the world of action.' That his road had so far only passed through the hands of Mrs Silcock and her ilk was something of a disappointment – something he trusted that Bishop Mwawa's visit would remedy. He tried now to give his whole attention to Mrs Silcock, in order to discern how he might be of service to her.

"... it'll cost millions to fix the sewers. Millions. Nobody's going to pay for what they don't see. We'll all have to move up a floor. Of course my trouble is" – she lowered her voice and raised her eyes – "I've got these darkies upstairs. Don't get me wrong. I like a curry myself, only I don't fancy it coming down the walls. That's my trouble, you see, vicar: their carzey's right over my bedroom. I can hear everything, if you take my meaning. All the pipes go down inside my walls. When I think of all that curry coming down and bunging up the drains, well, it puts you off. Ready for a slice of my coffee now?"

"Thank you, no. I really have to be going." He felt slighted somehow, rather as he had felt when the Patriarch of Moscow rejected his smuggled bibles because they didn't correspond to those sanctioned by the Russian Orthodox Church.

"Suit yourself," said Mrs Silcock.

Maeve was quite shaken by her run-in with the mad bag lady in the Co-op. She never touched strong drink – a sherry before Sunday lunch was her limit – but she could have done with one now. She settled for a cup of tea at the Golden Plaice, sitting at the window table where she could watch life in the sunlight passing her by. It was utterly unlike her to feel so depressed. Not depressed exactly, more... dislocated. In this mood, the last thirty years seemed to have been written in water. There'd been Alistair to look after; fêtes and jumble sales; flower-arranging, coffee mornings, the little confidences of parishioners and so on. But did it, as Anne had taken to saying, amount to more than a hill of beans? She had at least brought Anne up reasonably well. Except that, in truth, Anne had brought herself up. A complaisant child with no taint of Irishness, she had spontaneously adapted Nanny Bryce's precepts, relayed by Maeve, as her own. Preferring a cordon bleu course to university, she signed on as cook to a man who delivered yachts to the West Indies. She married the man, Gary, who now owned a marina in

Florida. Her figure was unaltered in spite of producing two children, Carly and Gary Jnr. In photographs she looked tanned, pretty and youthful as only Americans can. Her face was unlined, ingenuous; its expression refused to be anything except – ghastly word – positive. Maeve barely recognised her.

She had visited Anne four – no, five – years ago, and it had exhausted her. She never got used to the heat. Her grandchildren seemed preoccupied with interests more appropriate to teenagers, and with the gratification of desires that were, well, trivial. However, she was careful not to be a bore and harp on the past, and they let her watch *Miami Vice* with them. They each had TV sets in their bedrooms to avoid squabbling over which channel to watch. Maeve was secretly appalled at their ignorance of quite basic things such as the Second World War and the Bible. But when it came to clothes, records, comics, videos and sex, they were precocious.

Anne rarely cooked any longer. She taught her mother to telephone for pizzas or to say 'Five burgers, four fries to go'. Her town had no centre; her house was planted on parched earth behind a strip of buildings which was continuous with the next town. The strip ran parallel to a golden beach where they spent much of the long days. A disproportionate number of leathery old people lay like reptiles on the sand, waiting for the sun to mummify them. Some glistened with oil, others wore metallic sun-reflecting beaks. The children either needled each other or sat vacantly under headphones, occasionally rousing themselves to play a half-hearted game of Frisbee or to sit on stools at the beach bar, eating ice-cream. The sky throbbed, white hot, overhead; the sea was a blue mirror, frilled in the foreground with lacy wavelets.

It was here, dozing under an umbrella, her Trollope unread beside her, that Maeve was first overwhelmed by the homesickness which now afflicted her again as she sat in the Golden Plaice, watching the heat beat up off the High Street. Strangely, it had not been then (as it was not now) a homesickness for England, but for the lush greenness of Ireland. Moreover, and more strangely still, the Ireland of which she day-dreamed was not the countryside around Eden but the legendary one hundred and twenty-six acres of mountain and rough pasture overlooking the Atlantic, which belonged to Patsy.

In fact, the land in question had passed to his older brother. But, somehow, Patsy never mentioned it without a proprietorial air, and he mentioned it a good deal: the way bands of weather did be rolling in off the sea – visible isobars of low-flying cloud, sheets of rain and sudden rods of sunlight; the way the place never looked the same twice, with the cloud-shadows scudding over the green slopes crisscrossed by white dry-stone walls; the way dark streams frothed like Guinness over stony beds, and turf smoke hung in a blue haze over the farmhouse on still summer evenings.

No, the land Collinses had farmed since time began didn't belong to Patsy. Rather, as he said with a fierceness in his voice, but without bitterness, accepting a second son's lot: '*I belong to that land.*' Indeed, despite the many disputes over land ownership, there was a point beyond which the Irish didn't own the land but were claimed by it, just as a nation may own its history but is always possessed by its myths. In Ireland the land pre-empted the separation of history and myth by remaining the background to both. The battles of the former were fought alongside the battles of the latter on fields uncultivated by time. Every landmark had a name of mythological origin. On Collins land, or just below it, men and *Sídhe* had always intermarried and lent each other warriors. Despite – or because of – the fact that Maeve had Eden and, in particular, Maeve's Grave to belong to, she dreamed of and yearned for Patsy's acreage, land she had never laid eyes on.

'*I belong to that land,*' Patsy had insisted – and the land had agreed. It killed that poor slow-witted bachelor brother of his by breaking his leg in a hard winter. He was found on the mountain, dead of exposure, with his hands and feet stuck in the carcass of a sheep for warmth. It looked as though Patsy, the clever one, educated by the Jesuits, had been right to rebel against his parents' wishes and to refuse to enter the Church. "I'd as soon work the land of an Englishman," he confided to the tiny Maeve, "as become a priest, with nothing better to do than frighten old biddies and ride around free on the buses all day." Not that his disrespect for the priesthood prevented him from attending Mass nor, every fourth Garland Sunday or so, 'leppin' up Croagh Patrick in me bare feet.'

Maeve read of Patsy's inheritance and departure from Eden in a sorrowful letter of her father's sent to the English boarding-school. She thought little of it for, by this time, she had learnt to regard Patsy with an exasperation the equal of Nanny Bryce's. For example, she and Nanny would be out walking when Patsy would stick his head round the stable door and shout coarsely:

"One hundred and twenty-six acres, Miss Bryce! What d'you think of that?"

"What does he mean, Nanny?"

"Really, that man is becoming impossible," Nanny would reply, not allowing the evenness of her expression to falter. However, a faint insight retained from her early years made Maeve think that she might after all have some idea of what Patsy meant.

"It was a cube," said Maeve. It was hard to pin down exactly what she had seen. She thought of it as a cube – *the* cube – which hovered in the sky a little above and to the left of the clock tower. But, trying to picture it again, she thought that for the space of a heartbeat (or had she merely imagined this?) it had been the shape of a teardrop, expressed from the true blue eye of the cloudless sky. Or again, it was as if a hairline crack in the fabric of the universe had allowed the thing to drop through, like oil into water, so that it contracted at once into its cubic form. "Definitely shaped like a cube." She was aware of how improbable, not to say hopelessly non-aerodynamic, her description sounded.

"And what was it made of, madam?" the policeman asked impassively.

"I don't know. It was silvery. Dullish silver. Some kind of metal perhaps? It was more like quicksilver than anything else." It didn't sound convincing. All the same, the policeman dutifully wrote down her words. "It just stayed there."

"How long for, madam?"

"I can't be sure. Half a minute perhaps. Then it moved."

"In which direction?"

"Towards me. North-west."

"It passed right over you then?"

Maeve shook her head. She felt foolish and, worse, afraid. She couldn't focus her mind on what had happened next without being gripped by something very near to panic. "Well, how big was it, madam?" The policeman was being extremely patient with her. Maeve shook her head again. She felt weak and even – good God – a little tearful. She took hold of herself.

"It wasn't all that large."

"Big as a house? An aeroplane?"

"No. Smaller." But even as she spoke, she vividly recalled how the cube had been quite small at one moment, as it hung above the tower, but then, at the next, it had suddenly been as big as a pantechnicon, very near to her and *round*. She couldn't look at that. She rubbed her eyes as if to erase the sight. "About twenty-five feet," she managed to add.

"Twenty-five feet wide?"

"All round. I told you, it was cubic." She wasn't ready to admit to this new circular or oval shape which had been large enough to block out everything else from view, just as if it had jumped silently yet at inconceivable speed from the tower to right in front of her eyes. Not that she had seen it jump. It had simply been there one second and here the next. She didn't feel able to describe this to the policeman. It would sound ridiculous.

"What then, madam?"

"I can't remember. I didn't see it go, but it must have. Next thing, it just wasn't there any more."

"I see." The policeman wrote. Maeve had intended to tell him everything, calmly. But now she was trembling. She wanted only to be alone, outside the police station, taking deep breaths. She had meant to say how, absurdly, she had 'lost' nearly an hour, but now she felt it would only weaken an already weak story. She felt, too, an obscure shame, like the victim of an assault who can't remember the smallest detail of the assailant's appearance.

"I suppose you think I'm quite mad."

"No, madam." The policeman smiled for the first time. "In this job you learn to spot a loony at a hundred paces."

Maeve hauled her basket home. She was angry at her inept performance. The policeman had said he could do nothing, advised her not to worry. At least he had not suggested that it was all a trick of the light or something. He'd taken it seriously. All the same, she felt like an idiot. Pausing at her gate she noticed that the offensive rag of blue plastic was still lodged (how could it not be?) in the teeth of the fence, like some malign nonbiodegradable agent of decay. Its evil eye, epitome of all litter and waste, willed that the world be brought to ruin. 'I could at least pick that up,' thought Maeve. But her back ached and her swollen legs were painful and she couldn't bear the thought of picking up her heavy basket again once she had put it down. 'I'll do it later. Definitely.'

FOUR

At seven-thirty precisely, Heather arrived at an opulent house in Chiswick, near enough to the river to smell the stringent tang of reeds. She had planned to take the Tube – it was only one stop, for God's sake – but, faced with the awful yawning mouth of the station, had opted at the last minute to walk the whole way, breaking now and then into a run so as not to be late. She checked the address for the fifth time against the piece of paper on which it was written. Her secret, formerly dormant nervous system which had waited all these years to be activated by the Cube was lighting her up from the inside as if, like a Geiger counter, it could sense the proximity of some revelatory treasure.

She had called the telephone number in the local paper. The voice of the man who answered was guarded.

"Well, are you?" he had asked abruptly.

"Am I...?"

"Watching the skies."

"Yes. That is, I saw something. Hovering. It changed shape. Into a Cube. It... it flashed."

"Are you making this up?"

"Of *course* not. Who are you, anyway?" A silence.

"We have to be careful. A lot of nutters ring this number."

"I'm not a nutter. I thought you might know what's going on."

"I do know."

Heather caught her breath. Some certainty in the man's voice made her believe him. They had arranged to meet in a pub.

She pushed the gate open and walked up the narrow overgrown path. The house showed no signs of life. She glanced nervously at her directions: it was the right address. Or had Murdo McQuillan – as the man was called – misled her? Was it a trick? A hoax?

She remembered her first impression of him, fastidiously sipping a tomato juice and holding up, as arranged, a copy of the local paper. She felt she would have recognised him without it by the way he discreetly stood out from the other customers, mostly big-bellied men who jingled keys in their pockets and stared at her legs. Murdo was thin and intense. Black eyebrows which met above his bony nose and fierce dark eyes gave him a frowning look. His jaw muscles worked as if he were constantly clenching his teeth in anger or pain. His clothes – jeans, shirt, jacket – were all black.

They had chatted; or, rather, Murdo had answered monosyllabically the nervous questions that Heather put to him, all the while examining her face as if for signs of that nuttiness he had suspected on the 'phone. He was – had been – a painter. His life had changed completely when – his face broke into a rare smile – he had met Katy.

"You fell in love?" Heather assumed. Murdo looked puzzled. "Perhaps," he said. "But, you see, the point is" – he glanced around him, lowered his voice – "Katy's a *contactee*."

Heather pressed the door bell. She heard no ring from inside. In the silence of the small untended front garden, the rhythmic trill of her nerves was very loud. A startled brown bird beat off through the bushes. The bass accompaniment of her heart missed a pulse. If Murdo was the genuine article, as Heather fervently believed he was, she would in a few short minutes be meeting Katy; and, if conditions were favourable (Murdo had stressed this), someone more important still.

"You, too, are a contactee," Murdo had said. His words hung between them.

"Am I?"

"There's no mistaking contact."

"No. I suppose not."

"They spoke to you?"

"Who?"

"The Guardians, of course."

Heather was overcome by the matter-of-factness with which he spoke of these mysteries.

"Is that what they're called?"

"We call them that, for convenience."

"They didn't speak exactly," she said. "There was this *flash*, and suddenly everything was clear to me... a great burst of energy, light, understanding. Like a sun going off inside me." She had spoken some more in this vein, growing more excited, desperate for this wise man to understand her and to explain her experience.

"Keep calm," advised Murdo. "What happened to you is only the beginning. The Guardians have it all in hand. Come to this address..." He gave her the piece of paper, adding the date and time. He rose to leave. "I'll tell the Lord Arkon you've made contact. He'll be expecting you."

"The *Lord....*?" But Murdo only put his finger to his lips. "By the way, drink no alcohol. It lowers your energy level." With that he was gone, leaving Heather, her vetting complete, staring guiltily into her glass of lager.

The front door opened on to a young man in his twenties with a smooth, pink complexion and fair wavy hair. He was wearing a worn tweed suit and old, highly polished brogues.

"Come in," he said uncertainly, adding with some embarrassment, "Er, welcome." They faced each other, smiling politely, in a hall with a dark uncarpeted floor and several heavily-antlered stags' heads on the wall.

"I'm Heather Wright. Murdo gave me this –"

"Yes. Of course. Sorry." He stuck out his hand. "Jeremy."

"Hello, Jeremy."

"Hello." Since the young man seemed unsure as to which way he should move, Heather asked:

"Is this your house?"

"As a matter of fact, it is," he apologised. "At least, it was. It's sort of, well, ours now. As it were."

"I see," said Heather, not seeing.

"You're new, aren't you? Yes. Murdo doesn't always have time to keep me abreast of, well, things. In fact he's a bit wrapped up now... always is before meetings. The thing to do," he brightened at his sudden idea, "is to introduce you to Katy. She'll show you the ropes." He led the way to a panelled door and threw it open to reveal a large high room, more like a ballroom than a drawing-room. Rows of chairs had been set out facing, at the far end, a modest platform behind which there was another door. On the platform stood a bare wooden table and two chairs, one of them high-backed and throne-like. About forty people stood around the room in groups.

She tried to assess the nature of the gathering. It had no distinguishing features, either of age, gender, class, dress or general appearance. If these people were the Guardians, they wouldn't stand out in a crowd. One or two of the women were somewhat exotically clothed perhaps, with a suggestion of rough-hewn jewellery and ethnic skirts; and, amongst the men, there was a higher proportion of beards than you might normally expect (a grey-haired man with sunken cheeks wore sandals without socks) – but that was it. In every other respect the gathering might have been designed by an advertiser to represent, in terms of percentages, the British public.

She covertly scanned their faces for signs of special knowledge as Jeremy led her across the room. A sombrely-dressed Indian caught her eye and gravely inclined his head. Otherwise, no one paid any attention to her. Bland normality prevailed, although a detectable air of suppressed excitement suggested that this might be a deliberate mask. Jeremy stopped in front of a poised young woman of about twenty-four with a glamorous mass of auburn hair and feline green eyes, watchful beneath drooping eyelids. Her black waisted jacket and pencil skirt suggested to the intimidated Heather that she was a high-powered business person.

"This is Katy," he announced, a bit out of breath, like one throwing open a treasure chest. "You're looking awfully nice, Katy," he added in a rush. The young woman raised an eyebrow but did not dispute the compliment.

"Hadn't you better see if Murdo needs anything, Jeremy?" she said.

"I suppose I had. Let me introduce..." Heather's name, if he had remembered it, was lost in a murmur as he backed away, his eyes fixed on Katy's face.

"So," she said, "You're the latest contactee."

"I'm not sure," Heather replied nervously. "That is, yes. I s'pose I am. Are you... a *Guardian*?" Katy gave a snort of laughter.

"Oh dear, no," she said, not unkindly, "I'm just a contactee, like you. About half the people here are, to some degree or other. The others are simply believers. Like Murdo, for example."

"What happened to you, Katy?"

"The usual. It was three years ago. I was walking home from a party with two friends. We saw one of the Guardians' crafts. An enormous disc about two hundred feet up, spoked like a Ferris wheel and blazing with different coloured lights. It had a deep effect on me. I nearly went mad trying to convince people of what I'd seen. The other two wouldn't discuss it – it takes people that way sometimes. They can't face reality. They'd rather not accept the implications and change their lives. Luckily I met Murdo and he believed me at once. In some ways he was more seized with the whole thing than I was."

Heather was amazed at this self-possessed girl who could speak so casually of her world-transforming encounter.

"Mine didn't look at all like that," she began excitedly. Katy raised a hand.

"Don't tell me now. You'll have a chance later." Heather was immediately subdued. She must have inadvertently broken one of the rules.

"Sorry," she said, feeling foolish. Katy only smiled. She seemed to understand exactly what Heather was going through. Yet Heather could not imagine a time when she would be able to accept her experience as lightly, recount it as calmly, as Katy who was now watching the door behind the platform, her mind on other things.

"There were only half a dozen Children of the Sky when Murdo and I joined," Katy continued, indicating the gathering with a sweep of her hand. "Now the numbers are growing every week, thanks to him. He practically runs the whole show. Everyone – even the contactees – respect his understanding and knowledge. He's read all the books. Even Pete Kershaw listens to him." She pointed to a tall heavily-built man with a pockmarked face who was holding forth to an admiring group. "Pete's our only abductee. Makes most contacts look like pretty small beer. He was a policeman. They took him from his police car just outside Chelmsford at three in the morning. Of course he remembered nothing beyond the initial contact until he went into regression hypnosis. Murdo's idea, naturally. Pete spoke with three of the Guardians for some time, it turned out. Came up with some astonishing details. I dare say Murdo'll let you hear the tapes when he thinks you're ready." Katy was silent for a moment. "It's frightening to think," she said, shaking her head, "how many abductees there are walking around without being aware of the fact. Don't worry," she added, noticing Heather's stricken expression, "Murdo's sure you're not one. You don't have the signs – memory loss, missing time, fresh scars, headaches, dissociation, that sort of thing."

Katy was prevented from expanding on this worrying subject by Murdo whose appearance on the platform from the door at the back induced a respectful hush. He was dressed as before except that his jacket was now a more elaborate affair in black leather. He gazed benignly down on the gathering as each person hurriedly took a seat.

"Our leader is not quite ready yet," he announced in a low resonant voice, "although it is felt that conditions are favourable for Lord Arkon to manifest himself." He quietened the buzz of anticipation by raising both hands. "In the meantime I'm sure we'd all wish to thank Lord Klonakilty – " he gestured dramatically towards the back of the room. Heather's heart gave a jump. One of the Guardians was here, in the very same room as herself! " – who has kindly made this beautiful house available to us." Everyone clapped until Jeremy was prevailed upon to stand up.

"He's a *Guardian*?" Heather whispered to Katy.

"A peer of the realm."

Although the confusion was resolved, a certain lustre nevertheless clung to the bashful young Lord as he spoke:

"No, really. One only does what one can. I mean, it's I who should thank you. If I hadn't been guided to Katy – and Murdo, of course – well, I'd still be a complete mess... and so on." He sat down abruptly. There was another ripple of applause.

"Drugs," whispered Katy. "Coke, fortunately, not smack. Murdo and I helped him get off it. But it was the Lord Arkon, of course, who provided him, like all of us, with a new life."

Heather was still absorbing this information when, to her mortification, she heard her name being spoken.

"...please welcome our latest recruit, Heather Wright," Murdo was saying, "whom I will now call upon to give her witness."

"Stand up," hissed Katy. "Don't worry. Just tell everyone what happened."

Heather was so nervous under the stare of so many eyes that she could not order her thoughts. Her mouth, bone dry, made an embarrassing clicking sound as she began to speak. Anxious to be absolutely accurate she started her story too far back. Her audience fidgeted as she struggled to supply some brief background information about herself. She hurried on to the morning in question. She told them first of all about her dream. Approving looks were exchanged, giving her confidence. She described the Cube minutely. There was total stillness, except for the tiny scratch of Pete Kershaw's pen as he (perhaps from long habit owing to his former profession) took notes in a neat black book. When she came to describe the sudden flashes, the effect, the vision, Heather faltered. How could she begin to do it justice, that superhuman intelligence and beauty irradiating all things? As if flying to her assistance, the Cube leapt in front of her mind's eye, hanging there calmly in all its meaning. She struggled to give an account of it until her words faded into a helpless gesture at the inexpressible marvel of it all. She sat down to understanding applause.

Questions were tactfully asked. Had anyone else seen the object? Heather told of how she had dashed from the house and found no-one about except the old woman who sold vegetables. She, too, had seen the Cube. There were murmurs of approval. Had she seen the occupants of the craft? Heather was about to shake her head when, suddenly, the Cube moved nearer in memory as though her mind's eye had acquired binoculars. The tall figure was again visible behind the porthole-like depressions in the smooth surface. Its elegant domed head might have inclined majestically towards her, in acknowledgement or approbation. Hesitantly she passed this on to her interlocutors. They were satisfied.

The emotional temperature of the room had crept up by several degrees. Heather returned the encouraging, friendly smiles which were aimed at her from all sides; Katy patted her arm. Her ordeal over, she basked in the contagious warmth.

"Thank you for sharing your experience with us, Heather," said Murdo. "Your witness strikes many chords in the hearts of us all. But now, it is time..." He walked deliberately across to the door behind him. A thrill passed through the audience. Heather could sense that even the relaxed Katy had grown tense, more alert. The lights were dimmed, Murdo held the door open. A taut silence stretched like piano wire across the room. An extraordinary personage swayed through the doorway and took its place on the throne.

Again Maeve scanned her dressing-table. Again there was no sign of the little pot which held her foundation cream. Although she rarely used it, she always knew where it was. She never moved it, she'd seen it only yesterday.

"Get a move on, dear," said Alistair humping himself into his best suit jacket. "You know what the Dean's like." The Dean set great store by punctuality, especially on an occasion as important as his summer 'do'.

"I've only the face to put on. Won't be a minute." She scrabbled among the items on the dressing-table. Was she going blind? The pot had to be there. The reflection she glimpsed in the mirror showed an ageing woman, red in the face, whose newly pinned hair was already escaping in wisps. She grew even more hot and bothered. It wouldn't take much for her to look like that mad bag lady. She took a firm grip on herself and began to touch everything on the surface of the table, naming each object under her breath so as to be absolutely sure of not missing the pot of cream. Things, after all, did not simply dematerialise.

This was exactly the sort of pickle mother used to get herself into. Her possessions were always going missing. 'Pixilation' she called it. Mary the cook, who had another name for them, was the only one who accepted – indeed, praised – the cunning intervention of pixies in everyday life. Maeve smiled to herself, remembering her mother's vague discomfiture and her father's irritation.

Like Alistair – it formed a tacit bond between them from the start – Maeve was an only child, born late to surprised parents. They called England home but in fact father had spent only his school years there and mother, only occasional visits. Father had, naturally, fought for the King in the Great War; but, when a bayonet closed down one of his lungs, he was not sorry to return to County Mayo and to Eden, a modest house by Anglo-Irish standards – Victorian rather than Georgian – where he had been born and which, by then, he had inherited.

He had met mother out hunting in Wexford and was drawn to her sensitive hands and good seat. She gave up riding altogether soon after the wedding – something referred to thereafter as 'mother's accident' had caused her nerve to fail. She never quite adapted to damper, more primitive Mayo after the comfort and splendour of her family home in Wexford. So, while her husband lived and breathed horses, she turned the pages of months-old English magazines or, with a drink at her elbow, watched the thin rain meander like tears down the high windows which overlooked Eden's green pastures.

She never drank anything Irish and never anything but spirits. Scotch, gin and brandy were her main tipples. Only these, she claimed, were proof against the damp. She was superstitious about drink, as if it could homeopathically alleviate the chronic moistness which afflicted both her and Mayo. She never conceded that her drinking was anything other than medicinal, picking up a glass as if surprised to find it there, and swallowing the contents with distaste, as though it were an unpleasant duty. She never became drunk, only more and more beatific, *distraite*. Her reading spectacles went missing two or three times a week. "Come along. The game's over," she would say to the invisible pixies. "Give them back. *Please*." And, in time, the spectacles would turn up, in an unexpected place, but one where she might just plausibly have left them.

Maeve learnt not to rely on her mother. She counted on Mary for meals and, for the rest, on Patsy. Father she hardly saw. It was by the merest chance that mother noticed during a lucid interval that her daughter was 'running wild'; it was nothing short of marvellous that she roused herself to action by securing Nanny Bryce. Once that formidable woman had arrived, mother was content to sink back into the shadows. If called upon to settle household disputes, she would refer the injured party – Mary or Maeve – to Miss Bryce. The words 'Nanny knows best' shortly acquired the force of an axiom.

If mother was all moistness and melancholy, father was fire and choler, full of ambitious schemes destined to fail. He would be obsessed for a month or two with some plan to drain a bog or raise a new breed of cattle; but since his first love was always horses, he soon ran out of steam. He cursed the Irish for their fecklessness but was himself a worse offender – in many ways he was more Irish than the Irish. He was shy with people, and irritable – calm and patient only with Patsy, and with the horses he bred with passion but could hardly bear to part with. When the need for money became pressing he tended to sell another chunk of land.

Both her parents were unfailingly kind – Maeve remembered them with detached affection – but they were shadowy figures, less than three-dimensional compared to Patsy and Nanny, the real flesh and blood in her life and the pair who really brought her up.

Mother was the first to die, in her fifties, during Maeve's second year at boarding-school. In the end, as if her life had been one long premonition, it was a damp-induced chill leading to pneumonia which carried her off, in spite of all her counter-measures. In

Maeve's last term father suffered a stroke. She was recalled from England. He died in the stables (where Patsy had set up a day-bed) only a week after the sale of the last piece of Eden, which the bank manager, admirably unsuited to his job, had not the heart to tell him was no longer his. Maeve returned to England and began her training as a teacher.

"What are you *playing* at, dear?" Alistair's voice jolted her out of her reverie. He was only narky, she told herself, because he was nervous. The Dean's functions always made him nervous. "We'll be late, for goodness' sake."

"I can't find my little pot." She had named every object on the table. The pot was not among them. This tiny lacuna in the continuity of the world gave her anguish. It called up other cracks in reality, such as the nightmare in Five-Acre field a lifetime ago. Such as the missing fifty minutes only this morning. She didn't wish to think about such aberrations of space and time. Besides, there was bound to be an obvious explanation for both of them. It was too obvious to spot, that was all.

But if a pot could disappear so capriciously from a dressing-table, what certainty about anything was left? She began to laugh.

"I'm pixilated!"

To Alistair's alarm her laughter acquired a nasty edge to it. Tears rolled down her cheeks. Incredibly, she was crying.

"Maeve! Dearest, what is it? How can you let a mere pot *upset* you like this?"

"It's not the pot, it's not the *pot*. It's everything. The bloody awful filthy clogged-up world. It's cracking up... coming to an end in front of our eyes... and we do nothing."

"What on earth's brought this on?"

"I don't know. Yes, I do. Ever since I saw that bloody *thing* this morning, everything's been... bloody."

"Thing? What *thing*?"

"You'd laugh. You'd think I was a mad old... bag lady."

"I wouldn't. I *won't*. Tell me."

Maeve spared him nothing. She described the cube, its movements, her fright, the missing time. She began to cry again. Alistair paced the room in silence. Then he said:

"Are you coming to the Dean's?"

"No." She heard the bedroom door shut behind him, the sound

of his footsteps on the stairs, the front door opening and closing. She noticed something hard under her hand, where it rested on the dressing-table. It was her little pot of cream.

Maeve dabbed calamine lotion on her inflamed neck, bathed her sore eyes in Optrex and went to bed early. It was high time she stopped this blubbing nonsense and thought clearly about the cube. She had rather hoped that Alistair might have helped. It was hurtful the way he had simply walked out but, then again, who could blame him? She must have sounded demented. The trouble was, it required a frightful effort to bring any rationality to bear on the cube. It was as if... exactly as if *it didn't want to be thought about.* She pushed this absurd notion out of her mind and, taking up pencil and notepad, forced herself to make a list of all the objects, natural or otherwise, that it might have been: planet, star, cloud, bird, patch of light, optical reflection (?), balloon, airship, helicopter, aeroplane. It was a futile exercise because she was already certain that it was none of these things. She considered each of them as honestly as she could, and then crossed them off.

It was possible, of course, that she had witnessed some freakish atmospheric phenomenon. Something like ball lightning, whatever that was, or, better still, a mirage. Yet it was not just its metallic and cubic nature which militated against this line of thought but its – for want of a better word – intelligence. She couldn't rid herself of the impression that it was watching her, homing in on her. She wrote: 'experimental aircraft'? 'secret weapon'? The words she deliberately avoided, of course, were 'extraterrestrial craft' or 'UFO' which, as far as she was concerned, were synonymous with 'flying saucer.' There'd be plenty of time for absurdities once she had exhausted the previous options. It was doubtful whether the authorities would experiment with a new craft over Acton. It was equally unlikely that a hostile power could penetrate British air defences with a cube. (Five years ago you might have accused the Russians of trying, but not any longer.) Nevertheless, what she must do would be to make enquiries first thing tomorrow morning. If she could establish that the cube had been detected by radar or launched by the RAF – or simply witnessed by someone else – then at least she could rule it out as the thing she feared most: the product of her own mind.

Alistair watched the meter in the taxi ticking up more money than he could easily afford. There would have been no need for a taxi if Maeve hadn't made him late. And how was he to explain her absence? 'My wife can't make it because she's upset about seeing a...' A what? He felt a return of the panic which had caused him to leave the house without a word. Listening to Maeve tell her story had been like listening to someone who seems perfectly normal but who suddenly reveals herself, by some gross fiction, as insane.

But Maeve wasn't, *couldn't* be insane. She had clearly misidentified some commonplace object in the sky. At the very worst she had been prey to a momentary delusion. Alistair did not altogether succeed in reassuring himself. He was even a bit resentful towards Maeve's story – if anyone in the family was fey, it was he. She was the bastion of common sense who could always be counted on to bring him down to earth. Damn it, it was this quality which had attracted him to her in the first instance. And now here she was – actually *bursting into tears*. He hadn't seen her cry since she lost that brooch her old nanny had given her. Was it possible, oh God, that she was having some sort of nervous breakdown? If so, was this thing, this so-called 'cube', a cause or an effect? Alistair wanted, for Maeve's sake, to think about it. But not only did panic preclude thought, but he also possessed no framework in which to think about it. It was outside his experience, outside thought altogether. The only notion that ran like a frightened rat through his mind was: if Maeve were to crack up, it would be the end of the world.

In addition, as the taxi pulled up outside the Dean's residence, Alistair couldn't altogether suppress the ignoble thought that his wife's distress had come at a bad time. The 'Christ in Action' Conference was not far away now. The Powers That Be had hinted that, if he acquitted himself satisfactorily, there would probably be a Canon's chair in it, certainly more prestigious committee work. God knew what peaks he might yet aspire to; the sky was the limit. Everything hinged on Bishop Mwawa's visit. Maeve would have to pull herself together before that.

FIVE

The creature who loomed palely across the dimly-lit platform was, as near as Heather could tell, a middle-aged woman. She was, without being fat, big-boned, fleshy, formidable. Broad white forearms, held like a wrestler away from her flanks, poked out of the billowing sleeves of her purple tent-like robe and ended in thick bangled wrists and powerful, heavily-ringed hands. A silver medallion inscribed with an arcane device depended from the neck which drove up like a white pillar into the base of the monumental head. The prematurely grey hair was tinted with the merest suggestion of pink and stiffly sculpted like candy floss. The white unlined expanse of face possessed a macabre beauty under its theatrical make-up, including dark lipstick and purple eye-shadow. The fierce little eyes, black and shiny like currants pressed into dough, measured the audience as a seasoned actress might assess the fullness of the 'house'.

"Good evening," she said in an unexpectedly high, sing-song voice. "I hope everyone is sitting comfortably."

There were affirmative murmurs, one or two suppressed nervous laughs. Realizing that she had forgotten to breathe, Heather exhaled and glanced sideways at Katy who was frowning slightly as she watched Murdo fuss around the woman, fixing a cushion at her back and fetching a glass of water from the back room. The woman took a few sips and, placing the glass carefully on the table at her elbow, closed her eyes.

A long silence ensued, broken only by the woman's abnormally deep breathing. At last she heaved and shuddered with a profound sigh. Her legs moved apart and her feet lifted, one at a time, before planting themselves more solidly on the platform. Her whole body grew taut as if its envelope of flesh were filling out with sudden muscle. While the eyes remained closed, the head jutted forward and swivelled ponderously from side to side as though taking in its surroundings. Heather wasn't sure if she was imagining it – but was it a trick of the half-light or had the woman's face changed, the eyes becoming deeper set, the nose more aquiline, the mouth more austere? She was further discomfited by a deep grunt which sounded in the woman's vicinity. The grunt expanded into a growl such as a record makes when played at low speed until, finally, recognisable words emerged:

"Children. I, the Lord Arkon, bring you greetings from the Guardians." Although the voice had some connection with the woman's, it was far deeper and more resonant, as if it had lingered in the cavernous body, gathering force. At the same time, Heather had the unreasonable impression that, like bad dubbing, it was not quite synchronised with the speaker's lips.

"The Time of Grief approaches. The natural disasters which even now beset your planet are as nothing compared to what will be. The people of Earth weaken. Every day the air they breathe, the water they drink, the food they eat becomes more unclean, lowering resistance, increasing weakness. There will be no strength left to combat the final catastrophe, when unknown bacteria and viruses will bring a new Black Death to Earth. No medicine will avail. Those who survive will starve; those who escape starvation will be swept up in a wave of cataclysms. The seas will rise up first. Droughts will follow floods and fire. Hurricanes and earthquakes will smooth flat forest and city alike. Friends, there is great sorrow among us, the Guardians, who have watched over your planet since the beginning of time..."

This apocalyptic discourse – deeply stirring to Heather – was now interrupted as Lord Arkon clumsily attempted, through the medium of the woman's body, to remove the white high-heeled ankle-length boots which protruded from the bottom of the voluminous robe. When his purblind, somewhat robotic, hand movements proved inadequate to the task, Murdo solicitously stepped in and deftly whisked the boots from the feet.

"I am not used to the instrument's apparel," explained Lord Arkon. "On my planet our limbs are not confined by such as these." His head swung mournfully in the direction of the discarded footwear. He tested the floor with his stockinged feet and grunted with satisfaction. This activity seemed to have broken his train of thought. Murdo cleared his throat respectfully.

"May we ask questions, Lord Arkon?"

"Yes, as long as time allows. The instrument is tiring. It is a burden for her nervous system to play host to a Being such as I, who inhabits a far higher sphere. Also I sense that the energy flow grows erratic and troubled. The channel will not remain open much longer."

An elderly lady with a severe fringe and a posh accent spoke up at once in a firm voice:

"Would you mind, Lord Arkon, telling us something about your own home?"

"The Guardians' planet lies in the constellation you call the Pleiades," he replied, "which contains thousands of star-systems. It is hard for me to describe because it is beyond your imagination. Everything there is created by thought and sustained by will. However, we have cities much like yours, although immeasurably more beautiful, with many gardens and parks where flowers grow in a profusion of hues beyond your meagre spectrum, where the trees are laden with a thousand fruits unknown to you, and the pavements are inlaid with a myriad precious jewels. All life on our planet co-habits in peace, harmony and joy. Having achieved perfection of existence aeons ago, we Guardians seek only to aid the evolution of other life-forms in the Universe."

"Can't you use your technology, and that, to save us?" a teenaged girl asked tremulously. "Can't you land a ship at the White House and Red Square? Can't you do somethink?"

Heather found the girl's desperation very moving. Lord Arkon answered her gently and with sadness:

"We have already done as much as Eternal Law permits to help you. For example, we have averted nuclear war by influencing, unknown to them, your world leaders. We can influence but we cannot directly intervene. Besides, would the politicians listen to us? No. They would no more listen to us than they listened to the great Guardian who called himself Jesus. Yet, just as he revealed his true nature only to ordinary humble people, so our ships, which constantly appear in the sky over all parts of your world, are ignored or derided by the great and worldly ones and are understood only by those who have eyes to see. It is these, our Sky Children, who are the chosen ones. Nor will we abandon them in their hour of need!"

The audience stirred at these words. Heather had the impression that the previous statements were more or less familiar to the Children of the Sky; but, now, a new note had been struck. It was

Pete Kershaw's turn to speak, as the only person perhaps who had sufficient authority to act as the group's spokesman:

"Is it too much to hope, Lord Arkon, that we might be saved from the coming destruction?"

"No, my child. It is not too much. Your faith will be rewarded. You, and those like you, will be saved when the Earth is brought to ruin. We shall come in a mighty fleet of ships and raise you up to another world. Soon, my children, soon you will –" Here he paused and shifted his instrument's body uneasily. "I cannot stay any longer. But never fear – I will return to tell you more of our common destiny..." The head slumped against the chest which heaved with painful breaths. Clearly the Lord Arkon was withdrawing from the medium.

She opened her eyes and, yawning, looked around her. The lights were undimmed. Murdo busied himself with giving her water to drink and restoring the boots to her feet. She stood up, teetering on the high heels.

"We all want to thank you, Hermione," said Murdo, taking her arm and steadying her stately progress down the shallow steps to ground level. "We know what it costs you." There was a chorus of agreement.

"Yes, it went rather well today," replied Hermione. "The energy was high, so I didn't need the deep trance. I was aware of nearly all that the Lord Arkon said – one or two things are a bit misty still, but I shall remember them, of course. He always recalls them to me. He and I are very close. Kindred souls – although he is, naturally, vastly more exalted than I will ever be. All the same, contact with him, though exhausting, is also exhilarating. One can sometimes glimpse what it's like to inhabit his world –" she sighed wistfully – "it's a purifying... almost a divine experience." As she spoke she turned her great pale head from one person to another, fixing them with her shiny black eyes and gesturing economically, as royalty might. Suddenly the penetrating little eyes lighted on Heather. "You must be the new Sky Child. Don't be alarmed, dear. The Lord Arkon has been in touch with me about you."

"About me?" Heather was overwhelmed. Hermione grasped both her hands and looked intently into her eyes.

"Of course. No one escapes his notice. He intimated that you are a sensitive, like me. You feel it, don't you, dear?"

"I... I don't know."

"You will in time. You will develop your gift. You will be of great help to us. I see it in you." The words might have been meant literally since her eyes bored into Heather like twin X-rays. Close to, she exuded a powerful sweet musk like a condensation of her overbearing presence. Heather felt humble and small, as well as a bit faint. She would have liked to have removed her hands from the firm grip. Hermione smiled, showing two rows of little pointed teeth, and let her hands drop.

"We will gather again in eight days' time," she announced at large, "when the stars indicate that the Guardians will once more be able to clear a channel. Meanwhile, the advanced meditation group will meet here every evening and I shall be available to all of you for individual counselling." She lowered her voice: "We do not know how long we have left..."

Nodding solemnly, the group began to disperse. Each took their leave of Hermione, receiving in turn a confidential word or touch. Murdo stood beside and a little behind her, ready to move people on if they were inclined to linger. Katy slipped her arm through his.

"Come along, Murdo," said Hermione sharply. "We have a great deal to go through this evening before we can rest!" Together they turned towards the door behind the platform like a judge and her clerk going off to confer in the robing room. Jeremy, Lord Klonakilty, was hovering beside Katy.

"Actually," he said to her, "I was thinking of nipping over to the pub for a drink. Non-alcoholic, of course. Would you...?" But Katy appeared not to hear him. She was watching the door to the inner sanctum as it shut. Heather hoped Jeremy might extend the invitation to herself, but he didn't.

Although it was past one o'clock in the morning Heather, an early riser who was normally in bed by eleven, could not even contemplate sleep. She was charged with an extraordinary energy which gushed out of her like blood from a haemophiliac, except that the more she expended the greater the flow seemed to be. She sat, an open wound, in the middle of her sitting-room floor and attempted to meditate. Hermione had stressed the importance of clearing the mind in order to receive the healing influence of the Guardians, whose telepathic powers constantly swept the Earth's surface like great beams of invisible light. Night favoured their reception more than day when the atmosphere was muddied by human traffic.

Heather had forgotten how quiet London nights were in the backwaters of Acton. Darkness pressed in on the uncurtained windows, relieved only by the sudden stark pillar, in the distance, of the floodlit clock tower. The silence highlighted the fizz of energy inside her head until it became so loud as to be unbearable. Concentrate as she might she could not extinguish it. She shifted her buttocks from side to side, unable to compose or even to contain herself. She was overflowing, expanding into the space of her flat which more than ever seemed cluttered and confining, not unlike an Underground station.

The evening's meeting of the Sky Children had been nothing short of momentous. The whole notion of the Guardians, their mission, the imminent end of the world, the probability of rescue, was more than she could absorb. The world had been peeled away to reveal a fantastic reality beneath – so fantastic, in fact, that Heather felt a stab of uncertainty which it seemed ungrateful, even heretical, to acknowledge. Lord Arkon's message had been apocalyptic but that in itself did not disqualify it. On the contrary, what other communication could do justice to her own extreme experience? No, what bothered Heather about the message – she scarcely dared to admit it – was its banality. Any tramp with a sandwich board could have said as much.

Heather shook herself violently from head to toe, trying to rid herself of such scandalous doubt. After all, if the world were ending, how many ways of saying it were there? The adumbration of the Last Days as related by Jesus himself, when he warned against the adoption of false prophets and predicted natural disasters, was not so different from the placards of nutters at Hyde Park Corner. It was a question of authority, perhaps – *who* was prophesying, not *what* was said.

Another doubt pushed up like a black pebble amidst the cataract of her thoughts: was it possible that Arkon was something to do with Hermione, like another aspect of her personality? Heather thrust such scepticism aside. She was, she felt certain, being tested, tempted. She had only to remember one thing: *she had seen the Cube with her own eyes*. It – or its occupant – had communicated a vision of unearthly beauty. She was attuned to receiving signs. Hadn't she been led *immediately* to the newspaper in which Murdo had advertised? It had been no coincidence. Hermione had looked into her eyes and seen that she was a 'sensitive' – a potential vessel for the sublime insights that the Guardians conferred. How could she question the woman's integrity when she had selflessly and successfully emptied herself, as Heather was bound to do, in order to accommodate the harbinger of higher truth? Heather calmed herself with the memory of Lord Arkon: there was no question of his authenticity. He might have used Hermione's body but there was no doubt that his personality was utterly distinct from hers. He and the other Guardians were in all probability watching her now, smiling wisely at her frailty, from vast ships moored in the dark freezing outer reaches of the solar system.

For a long moment her mind was at peace. She relished the stillness. Her eyelids grew heavy at last. Then, away in the distance, she heard the rhythmic dissonant clash of swords on shields as the army of her returning thoughts marched towards her.

After an altercation with the director of Heathrow airport, Maeve was put through to air traffic control.

"My name's Maeve Allingham. I saw something early yesterday morning, at about twenty to six, over Acton. In the air," she added foolishly.

"Yes?"

"I was wondering if you knew of any... any aircraft in that area, at that time – anything that might explain what I saw. I'm perfectly serious." She was flustered now. How was she going to explain? She should have planned more carefully what she would say.

"There's no flight path directly over Acton," the man said brusquely. "What sort of aircraft did you see and how high was it flying?"

"Well, it wasn't an aircraft exactly. I mean, it wasn't an aeroplane. It was an odd sort of thing. Metallic, shaped like a cube. And it wasn't flying. It was hovering or floating – it didn't move anyway. Not at first. It was about a hundred and twenty feet up." She braced herself for the man's laughter or sarcasm. Now that she had blurted it out, it sounded ludicrous. It had been a mistake to 'phone. However, there was only silence at the other end of the line. "Hello? Are you still there?"

"Yes. Hang on. I'll check." She could hear a muffled confabulation. There was a long wait. Then: "I'm sorry. I can't help you. We wouldn't pick up anything on our screens at that height, especially in a built-up area. You probably mistook it for something. A planet maybe, or a kid's balloon – they can look odd sometimes. Light can play tricks."

"Yes. There's probably a simple explanation. Sorry to have bothered you." She rang off. The man had sounded truthful. On the other hand, if there were some kind of irregular flight in the vicinity – a secret aircraft, say – then he might have been briefed to fob off anyone enquiring.

She decided, before her nerve failed, to tackle the Ministry of Defence. She rang the number and was shuffled from one department to another until she came to rest in the office of an air vice-marshal. She described her sighting again, more forcefully this time, to a senior aide. She had nothing to lose, after all. The aide was not a patient man. He had dealt with calls like Maeve's before. People were always seeing things. He was able to deny categorically the existence of any secret or experimental aircraft (but then he would, wouldn't he? thought Maeve).

Maeve became stubborn. His tone got her back up. She knew what she had seen; she wanted an explanation. If none were forthcoming, she could only assume that foreign aircraft came and went as they pleased without let, hindrance or even detection. Such breaches of national security, she suggested, would be of interest to the press. She was not serious about this (she could imagine only too well what the newspapers would make of her story) but it was enough to shake the complacency of the senior aide.

"I can assure you, madam, that British airspace is not under threat from foreign powers. Nevertheless, since you insist, I'll look into your story. If necessary I'll send a chap round to put it on record." He took down her address. She thanked him. They rang off with mutual suspicion.

"I hope I didn't wake you last night," said Alistair politely, lifting his cup of tea to his mouth.

"No." In fact, Maeve had still been awake when her husband came home, stumbling in the darkness of the bedroom; but she had pretended otherwise. "Was it a good do?" She was equally polite as she carefully buttered her toast.

"Oh, you know. The usual faces." Actually it had been more of a success than any previous gathering at the Dean's. Alistair was quite the centre of attention now that Bishop Mwawa was known to be about to stay with him. The Dean's wife had made a point of introducing him to several churchmen hitherto inaccessible by virtue of their eminence. She flatteringly mentioned his articles in *Theology Now*. The Dean had praised his parish work. "One of our front-line troops," he had remarked humorously.

Maeve was in no mood to press her husband, in the normal way, for news and gossip. There was a constraint between them which, almost without precedent, distressed Alistair more than his wife, who seemed sealed off in her own thoughts.

"I've been thinking about... what you were saying last night," he began. This was not strictly true since he was unable to think about Maeve's tale in any constructive way. His immediate concern was to re-establish their old rapport. "There's probably some quite ordinary explanation."

"There's no need to talk about it. It's probably just me. I'll get over it." In fact Maeve longed to talk about it. But she detected in Alistair's voice the brisk note he reserved for those slightly loopy parishioners whom they used to laugh about together. She dreaded looking up and seeing on his face that expression of professional concern.

"But if you're upset, Maeve dear," he went on earnestly, "it upsets me. We ought to talk it through. I'm inclined to believe, you know, that your odd, er, 'sighting' was a dream – a highly unusual dream, of course. What we call a lucid dream."

Maeve stiffened at his use of the pronoun. 'We' indeed. With her own interest in depth psychology, she might be supposed to know rather more about dreams, lucid or otherwise, than Alistair. Yet here he was, tapping the tips of his fingers together like some Herr Professor.

"On the other hand," he went on, "we ought to consider whether it might not have been a projection of the unconscious mind, possibly even a hallucination – a mild one, of course, and only momentary –"

"Please," Maeve interrupted, closing her eyes. If he talked any more in this 'psychological' way she wouldn't be able to bear it. Who really knew what dreams, projections, hallucinations were anyway? Who dared dismiss that multitude of images, terrifying and beautiful like her cube, with meaningless 'explanations' and feeble psychologisms? She could almost wish that Alistair would be, well, more *religious* about her experience; that he would mention the work of the devil or something. At least he would sound as if he took it seriously. "Please," she repeated. "Don't say any more."

The remainder of breakfast was passed in silence. Alistair glanced anxiously at his wife from time to time. Normally he was reluctant to pay too much attention to what he thought of as the mental sphere. In the face of genuine physical suffering, its quirks seemed no more than self-indulgence. However, in Maeve's case, that was out of the question. As he left the table to go about his business, he patted her hand reassuringly. She barely noticed.

As soon as Maeve was left alone with the washing-up, she returned automatically to her reverie about the past which, in her present condition of mental and emotional dislocation, seemed more real than the present. She had ceased to worry whether this dwelling on her childhood was unhealthy or not, and simply gave free rein to her memory. In her current distress and bewilderment the image of Patsy in particular seemed like an embodiment of sanity, an old friend returning to help her. His face came back to her all the more vividly for having been pushed out of her mind these forty years. It was not a typically Irish face: the prominent nose and coppery sheen on the cheekbones suggested more of an aristocratic Red Indian (Native American, she corrected herself) if you overlooked the blue eyes. His body was wiry, the legs slightly bent, the back straight. He was not a great man for the washing or shaving but he always looked spruce on Sundays, in his dark suit and with his black hair brilliantined.

Patsy had been her father's only permanent employee. Hired to look after the horses, he turned his hand to most things – fencing and ditching, turf-cutting, milking. He was invaluable when it came to breaking horses because he knew how to horse-whisper, a secret he had won at cards from a tinker at Ballinasloe horse fair. He worked at his own pace, steady rather than hard, on which Nanny Bryce – herself a martyr to the Protestant work ethic – had occasion to remark:

"If that man stopped drinking he might discover the meaning of an honest day's work."

Maeve couldn't understand what she meant. Of course Patsy drank, but it wasn't *drinking*. It wasn't getting fighting drunk like the men in Slattery's bar; it wasn't getting furtively stewed like mother. He drank as he worked – steadily throughout the day. Not heavily, but 'a nip now and then for the joy that's in it.' The nips were solemn moments after which he would raise his eyes to the land and gaze at it as if for the first time. Sometimes he would focus them on the blue mountains and beyond, and murmur:

"One hundred and twenty-six acres. Think of that, pet."

A month or two after Nanny's arrival, the ritual changed slightly. Patsy broke the customary silence before the nip with a casual remark, something like a toast. "Isn't education a wonderful thing?" he'd say enigmatically; or, more specifically, "Miss Bryce now. I'd say she was a fine sweep of a woman." Maeve could not deny the truth of these observations but she was ashamed for Nanny who had classed him as 'a drinker'.

Meanwhile, days with Patsy were sudden and unpredictable as the weather. And, just as there was no such thing as bad weather – rain was God's way of giving a man a chance to have a smoke – so there were no bad days. Patsy always had time for her and always saw potential adventures in his tasks. Helping him fetch water from the well became a contest to see who could make the other spill the most; grooming a horse prompted epic tales of pile-ups at Grand National fences whose names Maeve had to know by heart; mending a fence was an ordeal by demons of wood and wire for, in Patsy's hands, inanimate objects would become 'lively'; riding the haycocks home to the barn at twilight he taught her to whistle tricky slip jigs. On special days which could not be known beforehand Patsy would abruptly yield to her pleas to be shown his two false teeth. Every day he re-made the world before her very eyes. Nothing was so obvious that it wasn't made mysterious; nothing so obscure that it couldn't be made plain.

Between dusk, when Patsy went home to his bothy, and dawn when he reappeared, his life belonged to himself. Maeve used to lie awake trying to imagine it. She knew he went poaching or to the pub, but she could no more picture him in this life than she could picture him behind the portals of the Catholic church on Sundays. Patsy's other life – his Irish life – was a source of fascination and dread. A sweet dread at first, like the anticipation of seeing his false teeth. But as Nanny began to take over the days, edging Patsy into the outer darkness of Irishness, her fascination grew fearful, the dread unalloyed

SIX

It had been a good idea of Maeve's to foregather at St Luke's and thence to move in a body to the chapel, rather than arrive in twos and threes. Apart from providing cover for those who might otherwise have been too shy to attend, it also gave them a chance to demonstrate unity – to turn up, as Alistair imagined it, in a joyful throng, ready to worship, no matter how different the form of that worship might be. However, the party which straggled over the short distance between his church and the chapel was by no means as substantial as Alistair had expected. It put a damper on the great ground-breaking ecumenical adventure. It had cost him a lot to organise this exchange with the Pentecostals and now, he felt, his parishioners had let him down.

It had been bad enough that only two dozen or so, most of them old or frail, had seen fit to show their faces at the earlier service for the visitors. In spite of this it had gone rather well. His sermon, though he said it himself, had been enthusiastically received, perhaps because the visitors felt the iniquities of South Africa more deeply than his own congregation. He had exhorted the latter to make a better fist of it for the 'return match' – apparently to no effect. They might have shown a bit more Christian spirit. Apart from being an affront to the Pentecostals, whose sense of the ecumenical had been exemplary, their failure to turn out in force showed a distinct lack of support for him personally. Even the ones who now trailed behind him looked apprehensive and glum. His efforts to jolly them along had met with taciturnity. Maeve wasn't helping either. Normally, this was exactly the sort of occasion when her communication skills were invaluable; but, for some reason, she wasn't displaying them. Instead of being the centre, as she usually was, around which his parishioners naturally gravitated, she seemed despondent and detached as she ambled along at the back of the group next to the hobbling Mrs Silcock, who, with her arthritic legs, was the only person to have made a visible effort to attend.

By the time he reached the Pentecostal hut (sandwiched between a building society and the DIY centre, built of wood and roofed with corrugated iron, it couldn't in all conscience be called anything more), Alistair was perspiring freely. It wasn't just the weather which, building up more heat every day, refused to break; it was also the knowledge of how much was at stake – what tangible contribution towards peace and unity could he point out to Bishop Mwawa other than this ecumenical venture?

The Pentecostal delegation was waiting, in three tiers, on the chapel steps. Their black faces, shining above white collars or below smart hats, reminded Alistair disagreeably of Victorian mission photographs in which newly converted natives in European clothes posed stiffly in front of rude jungle churches.

"Welcome, my friends, welcome. A lovely day, praise the Lord, for your historic visit, hah," declaimed the Reverend Caleb Duval, stepping forward with outstretched arms. (At least, Alistair assumed he was a Reverend. He might be a pastor, elder, deacon, prophet, apostle – Alistair reproved himself for his ignorance.) Caleb's fluorescently white teeth shone from a round face that had been buffed to a high sheen, like a grand piano. His heavy-rimmed spectacles drew his eyes out of their sockets as if in advance greeting. When Alistair had first approached him about an exchange of services – as a preliminary to further co-operation – there was no problem, nothing was a problem to Caleb. All was joy. "Be careful I don't convert your flock, Mr Allingham, hah!" he had joked.

"Yes, here we are," said Alistair heartily, shaking Caleb's hand with both of his. "Ready for the fray!"

"The fray?"

"I mean, we're looking forward to meeting your... sharing with you..." He turned to Maeve for help. She was chatting amiably to the woman they had got on so well with at St Luke's. Rosebud? Tulip? No, Hyacinth. That was her name.

"Well, amen to that, Mr Allingham." Caleb nodded to the ranks of his congregation. With military precision they moved forward in a smiling body and swept Alistair's little band into the chapel.

The small building seemed to be already full. The girls were so sweet in their white dresses, the boys so brave in their neatly pressed suits. Alistair's heart went out to them, driven as they were into the arms of God by a society which had at best neglected them, at worst trodden them down, certainly sold them short. The Anglicans were absorbed surprisingly easily into the crowd. Alistair felt an absurd flutter of fear as he was separated from Maeve and pressed into the second row of chairs. Mrs Silcock threw him a panic-stricken look as she was gently frogmarched into position across the aisle by two enormous youths whose hair was carved in geometrical shapes. He stood a head taller than his neighbours, an old man with a wispy grey beard who gravely introduced himself as Matthew, and his teenaged grand-daughter, Valerie, who giggled and thrust a hymn book into his hand. He held it in front of him awkwardly because his elbows were forced into his sides. He didn't recognise anyone from the St Luke's visit except the woman Hyacinth who stood in front of him, slightly to the right. The children next to her might have been hers – she had three, according to Maeve – but there was no husband: he had left her some years ago.

It was a novelty for Alistair to face the altar, a plain cloth-covered table with a wooden cross on it. To the left was a compact electric organ and an all-female choir, twenty strong, who rocked the rafters of the hut with the first hymn. Alistair was unprepared for the sheer volume of sound after the thin drone which died out in the echoing heights of his own church. The quality of voice, too, was strange to him: an intense yet effortless outpouring of song as if every member of the congregation possessed immense but finely controlled lungs. To his ears many of the women appeared to be singing a shade too high, with a stridency verging at times on dissonance. He was almost relieved when the hymn finished and a short Bible reading took place. But there was no easing of the tension generated by the singing in the cramped chapel. Rather, the loud and rhetorical reading by an elder sustained and elaborated the rhythm of the service so that, when the next hymn – at once raucous and mellifluous – broke out, Alistair felt a sudden surge of blood in his veins.

Heat was steadily building. Condensation blurred the small high windows. Alistair had no choice but to abandon himself to the sweat which gathered under his collar and ran down his back. The smell of perfume and after-shave was subverted by a more natural, more powerful musk, like a deep bass note. Alistair breathed deeply and sang out. Beside him, Matthew nodded and smiled and moved his shoulders to and fro in time to the music. Valerie decorated his tenor with a trill of spontaneous grace notes. The hymn was simple and touching; it implored and praised the mercy and love of Jesus. Shafts of tropical light slanted across the exotic upturned faces. As if his bones were thawing after a long frost, Alistair felt his body growing more supple, beginning to sway. He fancied that he might almost be in Soweto, packed into some trembling shanty church, joining his voice to the righteous cries of the powerless and the outcast. He thought with distaste of his own threadbare flock, shivering well apart in the draughty church, impacted within their tight white skins. They were not his people; these were his people. Emotion like a frozen serpent came to life inside him, rising up and painfully constricting his chest and throat. If only this fellow-feeling – yes, praise God, this love of neighbour – could overflow on to the streets, then all differences would be obliterated on the instant.

He gazed at his dry, white, liver-spotted hand where it held the hymn book only an inch away from Valerie's. Hers was soft and chocolate-coloured, with exquisite pink nails and pale palms he wanted to clasp. The hands were so utterly different and yet, for all that, they were only hands, only an inch away, only human.

Caleb launched into his sermon. Alistair was too agitated to grasp the sense of it; instead, he allowed the quavering ecstatic sentences to speak directly to his heart. Like so many small injections Caleb's voice – by turns angry, imploring, cajoling, crooning – sent a series of seismic shocks through his audience, who participated with sharp cries. "Amen!" "Hallelujah!" "Praise the Lord!" The preacher in turn took up these exclamations, elaborated on them and tossed them back to his flock who threw up their hands to catch the invisible word of God. Alistair found that he could scarcely forbear to shout something himself.

While the sermon rained down on him – "Jesus, oh Jesus, enfold us with your love, hah" – Alistair's eyes were continually drawn to Hyacinth. She wore a white dress with blue polka dots and a chic little toque. Her wiry hair was straight except for a fascinating cluster of tiny black curls at the base of her skull. Her dark mesmerising neck was unexpectedly slender on her broad muscular shoulders. She wasn't fat or even plump, but somehow solid. As the sermon ended and she drew herself up to resume singing, there was no suggestion of heaviness. She above all looked cool except for the tantalising dew-drops on her top lip, seen in profile against the light.

The singing rose to a crescendo. Hymn books were abandoned. Everyone was clapping in time to the music. Each clap was in perfect unison like a crack of static in the mounting humidity. Alistair joined in enthusiastically. He was forced to sway from side to side by the swaying of the others in his row. He stared openly at the easy economy of Hyacinth's hip movements as she too allowed the rhythm of the hymn to enter her body. Beside him Valerie had ceased to sing, had begun to bump heedlessly against his side. Her body gave several small jerks. The hymn died away amidst exclamations of praise. Hyacinth turned around just as Alistair had been willing her to. He beamed at her eagerly, expecting to be answered by her broad smile; but her expression was intent, her head cocked and listening, her eyes unfocussed. Valerie let out a moan. Her hands rose up level with her head as though drawn by some magnetic force. An electrical ripple ran through the charged crowd. Alistair's stomach turned over: the poor girl was ill. Hyacinth had foreseen it. She was deftly scooping her chair out of the way and entering Alistair's row. She placed her hand lightly on Valerie's shoulder as the girl, her eyes closed, began to speak in a low breathless voice. In spite of the heat, Alistair shivered. He realised that Valerie was speaking in tongues. The words were unlike any language he had ever heard. In a clear voice, Hyacinth interpreted the utterances of the Holy Spirit. "...the Last Days... Armageddon... the Second Coming..." The message acquired peculiar force from the combined lips of Valerie and Hyacinth. He cast his eyes around wildly, looking for Maeve. She was blocked from view by a wall of black faces. "He will come again... come in judgement... trailing clouds of glory." The familiar words failed to ward off his panic. Something uncanny was loose in the chapel. There was no control except, paradoxically, in the tall figure of Hyacinth herself. She was calm in the midst of her own prophetic speech.

A disturbance on the other side of the aisle nearly caused Alistair to groan aloud and lunge for the door. Mrs Silcock was being lifted to her feet by her huge protectors. Caleb was beckoning her with outstretched arms. "Love," he was saying, "come and take Jesus into your heart. The Holy Spirit is with us. Do not be afraid. He brings gifts of healing..." He was actually laying his hands now on Mrs Silcock's legs. "Pray," he was shouting, "pray that this woman may be made whole by the power of the Lord!" "Amen!" came the response. Mrs Silcock gave a little scream of pain or delight. Caleb was working her legs to and fro. Alistair felt sick and faint. She was flexing her joints, taking tentative steps. He seemed to be seeing her through the wrong end of a telescope. Far away, she bent her knees and executed a few nimble little hops. The chapel was filled with shouts of praise. Alistair's own legs dissolved. With the sound of a low-flying jet, blackness swept over him.

Maeve kept an anxious eye on the back of Alistair's head which poked up above the crowd. It seemed inclined to roll a little. 'Oh dear,' she thought. She had tried to warn her husband about the fervour they were likely to encounter. She had even wondered aloud, in a musing sort of way, whether it would be as straightforward as he wished to throw together two groups of people separated not simply by cultural, but by theological and historical differences as well. He had lowered his head in that listening attitude which indicated that he wasn't taking in a word she said.

Maeve had dragged herself out of bed that morning with an enormous effort. She wanted peace to reflect, rather than to be plunged into a mass of noisy fundamentalist Christians. She had for some time dreaded the embarrassment which such people inevitably caused. In the event, things were not turning out too traumatically. It was good that the Anglicans had been dispersed; it prevented them from huddling in a timid block where they would only inhibit each other. Maeve was quite happy to sing and clap surrounded by friendly Pentecostals, as long as things didn't go too far – as long as there was no compulsory embracing or anything. Besides, she didn't feel that any of it had much to do with her. The worrying sense of dissociation, which had plagued her ever since that fateful morning, had not disappeared along with the itch in her eyes and rash on her face and neck; but, by rendering everything pointless, it had at least proved an ally in the battle against embarrassment. She would have welcomed some of this indifference when the Pentecostals came to St Luke's.

On that occasion her heart had bled for Alistair. He was up half the previous night, honing his especially relevant sermon. But, on the day, his congregation had been thin on the ground. They looked shabby next to the smartly-dressed Pentecostals. The organ squealed, the visitors sang faster than the home team and the honed sermon didn't rouse the guests. Perhaps, in the light of Caleb's recent outpouring, there had been too much emphasis on South Africa and Peace at the expense of the redeeming Christ. The Pentecostal children began to fidget, looking up at the stained glass windows as if hoping to discern there the lineaments of the Holy Spirit. Maeve had closed her eyes and prayed that he would hurry up and finish before the visitors began to slip away. When she stole a glance at him she saw at once that her fears for him were unfounded: his eyes, fixed on some distant Utopia, noticed nothing untoward in the church.

Fortunately, things went more smoothly in the crypt where coffee was served. If the two camps didn't mingle freely they at least showed goodwill towards each other, thanks mainly to the efforts of Hyacinth Lee. Her expansive chattiness and infectious laugh broke through the mutual reserve; only in her large presence did the Holy Spirit remotely look like putting in an appearance.

Maeve would have liked Hyacinth beside her now. They had taken to each other. But Hyacinth was up in the front row with two of her children (Hugh and Kitty to judge by their ages) while she was trapped among strangers, who were too close for comfort, like rush hour on the Tube.

The initial enthusiasm was getting out of hand. The people in her row didn't care how much they jostled in their eagerness to praise the Lord. Maeve craned her neck to see how Alistair was doing; its muscles tensed when she saw his ungainly frame reeling slightly. Her face reddened at the sight of him clapping out of time. There was an intoxicated look about the set of his head. She hoped he wasn't going to make a fool of himself, hoped he wouldn't bawl 'Hallelujah!' or anything. He wouldn't do it properly, it wouldn't sound right in his pedantic voice; it would be excruciating.

The girl next to Alistair gave a little jerk. Maeve knew immediately what was going to happen. 'Please,' she prayed, 'not next to Alistair, please.' The girl quivered slightly. Maeve half-expected the chapel to be filled, as the Bible described, with the sound of a mighty rushing wind; she glanced at the ceiling, afraid that cloven tongues like as of fire were already winging their way down. With relief she saw Hyacinth stepping in and, laying her hand on the girl's shoulder, begin to interpret her odd pronouncements. It struck Maeve that, no matter how inspired the message was, it barely strayed from quite ordinary Christian injunctions. The Holy Spirit rarely deviated, it seemed, from his (or her) set text. Time was running out, according to Hyacinth's translation of the girl's prophecy. Catastrophes would occur; the world would end. No news there, thought Maeve, who felt not only hot and sticky but depressed. To cap it all, a transfigured Mrs Silcock was jigging in front of the altar, pointing with both hands at her healed knees. Alistair, on the other hand, was not bearing up all that well. He dropped his head and then, like a slow motion film of a dynamited steeple, crumpled and fell.

As Maeve pushed her way towards him, she saw Hyacinth clear a space around his body and bend over him with the serene, interested expression of a botanist examining a new species of plant.

Standing at his front door, in the act of ringing the bell, was a girl. Perhaps he should say 'woman'. There was something about her – her straight posture or scraped-back hair – which gave Alistair pause. She turned at his approach and, tilting her chin up, smiled hesitantly.

"Mr Allingham? I wonder if I could have a word with you?"

"What about?" he asked, more sharply than he intended. He had recovered from his faint but he still had a lot on his mind. He felt that he had been very far away, as if coming round from a general anaesthetic. "I mean, is it something that can wait? I'm rather busy. Is it some personal matter or...?" He had been helped outside, into the air, and offered a lift home; but, burning with shame, he had preferred to walk, leaving Maeve to salvage what she could from the Pentecostal fiasco. What he wanted now, more than anything, was solitude.

"Personal?" the girl seemed doubtful. "I suppose it is. But if you're busy..." She made as if to retreat.

"No, no. Come in, come in." Duty forbade him to send her away, no matter how much he wished to be left on his own, to grapple with the shattering experience which had overtaken him while surfacing from the faint.

The girl, who introduced herself as Heather Wright, sat opposite to him in his study. She looked well-groomed, composed, except for the working of her fingers in her lap, as if some inner agitation were leaking out of her extremities.

"I'm not sure why I've come here," she began. "It's just that something can happen and you're not sure what to make of it... not sure who to ask. I mean, if your eyes are suddenly opened as though you'd been asleep all your life, well, that's sort of religious, isn't it? And can you always tell if it's Christian or not? A strange experience might be Christian without your knowing it..."

There was more in this vein, but Alistair found it difficult to concentrate. The girl was barely coherent and, for some reason, hedging – or was it something in the nature of her experience which made it seem so? It occurred to him that she might be struggling to describe something very like that which had happened to him in the chapel. He leant forward abruptly in his armchair.

"What? What 'strange experience'?" The girl flinched at his sudden directness and looked at him with her large tragic eyes.

"It's not easy to say. I mean, in a way it's still going on... getting weirder. You'd probably laugh –"

"No, no. On the contrary..." But his protestation was too quick for she continued to knot her fingers in silence before breathing deeply and beginning on another tack.

"It says in the Bible, doesn't it, that our Saviour will come again. That he'll descend from heaven and we'll be 'caught up into the clouds, to meet the Lord in the air.' Do you think this will happen soon? Is it already beginning?"

Alistair felt deeply tired. The girl reminded him of the overwrought Valerie. He'd had enough apocalypses for one day. The face of Hyacinth rose up unbidden before him. He couldn't think about that yet; he had to answer the girl.

"The prophecies concerning the Second Coming," he forced himself to say, "are not, I suggest, to be taken literally. The first Christians believed that Christ's return was imminent but, as time wore on and he naturally failed to arrive, they had to revise their ideas and put his Coming at ever more remote dates in the future. I further suggest, my dear, that the notion of a Second Coming, together with the descent of the New Jerusalem – as John describes in the Book of Revelation – should be interpreted as the creation of a just society on Earth." He gave a little deprecating laugh. "We needn't necessarily adopt the metaphors of comparatively primitive, first-century Christians whose way of looking at the world was very different from ours."

Heather did not look altogether impressed or convinced. Alistair was suddenly impatient. Why was he indulging this middle-class girl, who obviously had plenty of leisure to cultivate unnecessary neuroses; who allowed her undisciplined mind to run wild in mystical fancies, when she could be doing something useful in the real world? Heather opened her mouth to protest something – his impatience was not lost on her – when the door opened and Maeve's head appeared.

"Oh, I'm sorry. I thought you were alone, Alistair. Are you all right?"

"Yes, yes. Thank you. Perfectly well."

"Good. Well, I didn't mean to interrupt –"

"I was just going," said Heather quietly, rising from her chair.

"Don't go on my account. Please." Maeve smiled at her.

"I've taken up enough of Mr Allingham's time." She didn't return the smile, but gazed anxiously into Maeve's face.

From the kitchen Maeve could hear Alistair showing the visitor out. "Do please feel you can come again," he was saying. "My door is always open," he added with less than strict accuracy. Maeve heard the front door shut and Alistair returning to his study. 'That girl was frightened,' she thought. 'I do hope Alistair was patient.' However, from the look on the girl's white appealing face, she guessed that there had not been that communication on which Alistair so often laid stress.

For his part, Alistair forgot the girl as soon as she was out of sight. He debated with himself whether to tell Maeve about the consequences (if that was the right word) of his fainting fit. Normally he would not have thought twice about it – he was used to telling her everything, thoughtlessly, even childishly. But he found that he simply couldn't tell her about this, not because it had been so personal and, yes, so moving, but because it had also been so silly. For a second he longed to hear her good sense and the easy laugh without which he could never keep matters in perspective; but another part of him couldn't bear to see so precious a thing dismissed in this way.

For what he had seen in that eternity between opening his eyes on the floor of the chapel and re-assembling his usual mundane perception, was Hyacinth's face. This was not in itself remarkable since she was bending over him, her brown eyes not six inches from his. No, the disturbing thing was that he had been ravished by the face as if by a vision of the Black Madonna. He could still see it now, if he closed his eyes: the disembodied face floating above him, set like a jewel in an azure sky and surrounded – here was the silliest bit – by curly pink and gold clouds straight out of some rococo painting. Her hair, like a dark halo, was outlined in golden light; her brow and upper lip were sprinkled with silvery droplets of dew. Unprepared for such an epiphany, Alistair had all but fainted again. In fact he merely closed his eyes on a sight it seemed blasphemous to dwell on, and suffered himself to be lifted, helped to the door, where the summer breeze dispersed the last wisps of those ridiculous, poignant rococo clouds.

SEVEN

As on the first occasion, Jeremy answered the door of the Children of the Sky's headquarters.

"Oh," he said. "Hello." He gazed anxiously over Heather's shoulder as if he had been expecting to find someone else on the doorstep. "You didn't see Katy on your way over, by any chance?"

"I'm afraid not."

There were more people present than before, but whether new recruits or members who had been absent on the previous occasion, Heather couldn't tell. Not wanting to appear pushy she took a seat five rows back and hoped that someone would notice her.

The time between meetings had passed swiftly. Heather had made lists of things to be accomplished – everyday things such as paying bills, doing laundry, buying new washers for her dripping tap – but, when it came down to it, few of these activities seemed worth the candle. Too often the fading light in her back garden alerted her to the fact that another day had been spent watching the inchoate images slide like a waterfall through her mind. She wanted someone to talk to. She fought shy of private 'counselling' with Hermione and hadn't the courage to broach Murdo. Someone like Katy, who understood, with whom she could share the marvel of it all, would have been ideal. But she had neither her 'phone number nor the nerve to call that stern young woman.

Without any great expectations, she had tried the Rev Allingham. Her visit was more in the spirit of an official report than anything else, although she had hoped for the chance to unburden herself. But the vicar's mind had obviously been on other things and, besides, he seemed a bit of a dry stick, a bit wary of religious experience that was not intellectual; a bit of a ninny, in fact. His wife looked more promising, with a smile that was kind and, more important, genuinely curious. But that, too, might have been a professional trick. Anyway, it was probably for the best that there was no opportunity for discussing the Cube. It was not a thing you wanted diminished by rationalisations or clever language.

Jane had 'phoned, asking why she had missed two sessions of therapy. Heather found that she didn't want to tell Jane anything, only announcing that she was perfectly all right; in fact, never better. She found herself laughing at Jane's tender yet sceptical tones, at the exasperating slowness of her voice. Jane had rung off with, amazingly, a touch of huffiness.

The only cloud on Heather's horizon was the Cube. It bulked large in her mind even when it wasn't convenient; it gunned her inner engines too much, presided ominously over the welter of thoughts which backed up inside her head, crowding her out. It was too shiny, too perfect, and laden with a meaning too heavy to comprehend. She longed for a good night's sleep, a respite from all this consciousness; but her dreams ran on where her thoughts left off, like a delirium. Only today she had failed to leave a note for the milkman, having dreamed that she had already done so.

Heather felt honoured when, the last to arrive, Katy slipped into the chair beside her. She was dressed casually this time, in jeans; her mass of hair was unkempt. Her face looked much younger without its subtle make-up. Her eyes were hidden by dark glasses.

"I'm really pleased you came," Heather began. "I wanted to 'phone you. It's awful not knowing anyone who'd believe me or take me seriously. And it's all so tremendous, isn't it? Almost too big to take in..."

"Is it?" said Katy.

"Of course. I mean, don't you just feel like shouting it all out in the street? All those people walking about as if nothing had happened, as if they were safe."

"My UFO didn't do much for me, when I think about it. It was just there. I sometimes wonder if it's worth all the hoo-ha."

Heather was scandalised into silence by these despondent remarks, especially by the acronym 'UFO' which had never crossed her mind in the context of her own encounter. Weren't UFOs rather silly – 'flying saucers' that credulous people or hallucinating hippies claimed to 'see'?

Katy took out a handkerchief and, removing her dark glasses, dabbed gingerly at her left eye which was purple and swollen.

"What happened to your eye?"

"It's traditional, I think, to say that I walked into a door or something. I'd rather call it the result of a domestic upset. Murdo and I don't always agree about Hermione. His enthusiasm can carry him away. Talk of the devil..."

Hermione was making her entrance from the inner sanctum to her platform. If it were possible, the great moon-face was, whether by art or nature, whiter than before; the purple eyelids, heavier. She was holding Murdo's arm proprietorially and leaning against him as if the weight of the world were suddenly too much to bear. Murdo, on the other hand, seemed to have grown in stature. He walked very upright, his dark eyes challenging the audience beneath the joined frowning eyebrows. Beneath the leather jacket he wore a shiny black shirt shot through with a pattern in silver thread. His leather trousers were tight enough to turn his walk into more of a strut. The only sound in the room was the clack of his boots on the wooden platform. He eased Hermione into her massive chair and addressed the audience:

"Children of the Sky, unfortunately the Lord Arkon cannot be with us tonight. Despite Hermione's valiant efforts, she was unable to open a channel through the inharmonious conditions for any length of time. However, she has been in personal contact with Lord Arkon, who even managed to manifest himself to me, in a three-dimensional thought-form transmitted from the mother ship. I can report that he was almost too dazzling to look upon – a face like the sun, a gown studded with stars, eyes as blue as lapis lazuli and deep as the sea... words can't describe him..." His voice wavered; he closed his eyes in ecstasy or pain, swaying lightly where he stood. Heather found it impossible to believe that this enlightened figure, so favoured by the Guardians, could have perpetuated anything so vulgar as a black eye. She unconsciously shifted a few inches away from Katy.

The glorious Lord Arkon had brought disturbing news. The world-catastrophe looked like happening sooner than predicted. The Guardians' sophisticated instruments had detected dangerous seismic movements which, unknown to Earth scientists, were building up in the depths of certain geological faults. The Sky Children were to hold themselves in readiness for the Rapture – that vast operation of snatching up into the heavens all those who had kept faith with the Guardians.

The general tenor of the gathering, subdued to start with, became fearful. A girl with stringy brown hair and a pinched face stood up.

"My family don't believe," she said tremulously. "They'll be left behind. They'll all die..."

Hermione stirred out of her torpor. "It's going to be hard on all of us. The birth of every new age is always painful. But our planet won't entirely perish. Who knows, we might be able to return to it soon and begin again. Think of that! All the mistakes of the past will have been swept away and we'll be able to form at last that true community of pure souls who, under the guidance of the Guardians, will live in peace, harmony, love and justice. Don't dwell on the time of coming cataclysm. Compared to the whole history of Earth, it will last less than the wink of an eye. Dwell instead on the rebirth of Nature, on the great privilege we have been given and on our future happiness."

A military-looking man – thin moustache, straight back, shiny brown shoes – raised his hand. "Everyone knows," he said, "that I came here in the first instance because of Miss Stringham's encounter with a Guardian ship" – he gestured to a nervy woman beside him – "and I'm eternally grateful. But I ask myself: if she can bring in someone who has not been personally contacted, mightn't I do the same? Where is the line drawn?"

"The Guardians know what they're doing, Donald. Or perhaps you think you know better?"

"It's not that, Murdo. You know it's not. Haven't I given up my job, my savings, everything for you... for the Guardians? It's just that I worry. I can't help it. My daughter's only five and a half. I can't leave her –" Strong emotion caused him to break off. The audience was silent, each visibly thinking of someone he or she, too, could not leave behind.

"There will be suffering," replied Murdo flatly. "It can't be helped. We must trust the Guardians."

"I do, I do," said Donald, tears running in parallel lines down his cheeks. "But I can't help wondering – forgive me – if all of us here will be saved. Will there be room? We don't know how many people all over the world may be waiting in groups just like ours. There may be thousands. Will I be allowed to give up my place to my daughter?"

A disconcerted murmur broke out in the audience. Heather waited eagerly for Murdo to set things straight, but he only picked uneasily at the collar of his jacket. Instead, Hermione raised her bulk wearily out of her chair. The hubbub immediately died down.

"We will all be saved," she announced quietly. "Yes, Donald's daughter as well." Her voice was severe, final.

"How can you be sure?" asked Pete Kershaw the abductee. There was a small collective intake of breath. No one expected the group's star member to strike a challenging note. Hermione and Murdo exchanged fleeting glances.

"Shall I tell them, Murdo?"

"Lord Arkon advised against it," he replied. "It's too soon, he said. They won't understand."

"They have trusted us. Now it is our turn to trust them. How gladly I do so." Hermione turned the full spotlight of her face on to her disciples. "There should be no mistrust between us, no barriers... In answer to your question, Peter, I can tell you I'm sure because I am myself one of the Guardians." She cast her eyes down demurely as this revelation swept through the assembled company. The shadowed lids made her face seem, for a second, eyeless. Even Pete Kershaw, a man steeled by years in the Force and immune to abduction into spaceships, looked nonplussed.

"I was as surprised as you," Hermione went on, "and I don't pretend that I possess or will ever possess anything remotely like the Guardians' power and wisdom. Nonetheless, as Arkon explained to me, certain people on Earth have the capacity for Guardian consciousness. My psychic abilities are part of this. All the Guardians, you see, are linked together in one great collective mind. We, too, share in that mind without being aware of it. In these last days many people are discovering their potential for realizing the great mind, just as I am. Although only a part of it, we can also embody the whole of it – the whole vast reservoir of the Guardians' knowledge accumulated over millions of years..."

At this point Murdo interrupted Hermione's flow. Ignoring the fixed stare of her little currant eyes, he took up her thread with the air of a scholar:

"The Guardians are the gods of old, known to every ancient culture from Egypt to China, from Greece to South America. They mated with humans, passing on their genetic material, and taught arts and technology. All mythologies contain accounts of this. For example, in the Bible – Genesis, chapter six – we are told how 'the Nephilim were in the earth in those days, and also after that, when the sons of God came in unto the daughters of men, and they bore children to them'. The Nephilim and the sons of God were, of course, Guardians who came down to Earth in chariots of fire like the ones which the prophet Elijah was later taken up in, just as we shall be – " He broke off as Hermione slumped back in her seat and passed a languid hand across her eyes.

"I may not be able to spend as much time with you from now on," she said weakly. "There's so much for me to learn, so much meditation to perform, if I am to realise the enormous energies which have already begun to stir within. But don't be concerned: keep faith with me, and together we shall ascend ever closer to the source of our well-being." She closed her eyes briefly as if in prayer, and then signalled for Murdo to help her come among the audience.

The Children of the Sky were almost shy of her now that she had acquired her unexpected status. They parted respectfully as she passed, addressing a kindly word to those within her field of vision. Heather was overawed. Everything was happening so quickly. There was so much to take in – nothing less than a wholly new interpretation of evolution, history, theology. Yet she felt that it was right somehow, for only a revelation as grand as this could do justice to her own vision. The early Christians must have been just as dumbfounded: they too were only a few, only ordinary, but bequeathed a profound and holy legacy; and, like them, you had to guard against cowardly quibbling and nit-picking. You had to make the leap of faith in order to embrace the new dispensation.

Although she was hanging well back in the press of disciples, Heather was singled out by Hermione's drilling little eyes, as if the latter already possessed the praeternatural intuition of a Guardian. Heather instinctively bobbed in a sort of half-curtsy, and felt stupid. Hermione spoke into Murdo's ear and, as soon as she had retired to her robing room, he made his way across to where Heather was standing with Katy and Jeremy.

"Hermione would like a private word, Heather," he said abruptly.

"Me?"

"You."

"Are we going now, Murdo?" asked Katy. "I don't feel all that –"

"We've a lot to get through yet," he interrupted briskly. "Jeremy will run you home, won't you, Jeremy?"

"Yes." Jeremy kept his eyes on the black eye. His cheeks were bright pink.

Murdo conducted Heather to the door behind the platform and tapped lightly on it. Not waiting for a summons, he went in. Heather timidly followed.

Maeve withdrew to the privacy of what was called her 'sewing room' (although no sewing took place there) and opened the first of the two books she had taken out of the library. Too ashamed to ask for assistance, she had finally located them among miscellaneous volumes of folklore and curiosities. They were on an unregarded bottom shelf, like outcasts from the world of respectable literature – not unlike herself, she felt, who was lost to respectability by the very act of reading them. Her heart gave a little skip as she noticed that the book had been frequently taken out before. So there were others like her, other closet crackpots. Alert to any sound of Alistair who was working in his study, she began to dip into the pages like a small boy peeking at pornography.

The book was a collection of essays. There were photographs of the authors. Despite the suspicious preponderance of beards, many of them had reassuring letters after their names. Maeve took a sheet of paper she had brought with her and dutifully wrote down some notes:

In a nationwide poll in the USA (1987), more than 50% of the sample believed that Unidentified Flying Objects (UFOs) were extraterrestrial spacecraft manned by people like ourselves. 1 out of 11 adult Americans claimed to have seen one (= 15 million sightings in the US alone). Witnesses not confined to any particular type or group. UFOs reported worldwide. Most seen at night, as coloured lights. They hover or move abruptly at lightning speeds.

At once Maeve was reminded of the 'fairy lights', commonplace around Eden in her childhood. She herself had seen them one night, flying in a straight path from Maeve's Grave to a distant rath. Even father had seen them. No-one ever thought to question them. Maeve turned to a section about the size and shape of UFOs:

Mostly saucer or disc-shaped. Also conical, bell-shaped, triangular, cigar-like. Can be smooth, domed, irregular or winged. Can be without lights. Can be tiny or colossal or anything in between.

It struck Maeve that, if the things were piloted by extraterrestrials, either there were dozens of different species or there was one species with as many different models of spacecraft as earthlings had cars. The belief that UFOs came from other planets was mainly founded on their unmistakably intelligent behaviour. Since the lights followed people on foot or in cars, 'buzzed' aeroplanes or responded to lights flashed at them, it was natural to assume that they were craft with lights on. And when they could be clearly seen, they moved with purpose – swooping down on people, who incurred burns or dizziness; causing car engines to cut out; convincing witnesses that they were under surveillance. On the other hand, since for every witness who suffered physical effects, whose car stalled, whose cat bristled and spat, there were more who showed no effects, it was just as likely – more so, perhaps – that UFOs were all in the mind. Indeed, for every UFO which appeared to several witnesses, there were far more that appeared to uncorroborated individuals. Photographs – if they weren't faked – were rare. Above all, no UFO encounter was identical to any other. They were simply impossible. In all fairness, Maeve had to admit – it was deeply worrying – that the cube was something to do with her alone. (But it had been so *real*. If someone else had been there, wouldn't they – surely – have seen it too?)

Her note-taking was interrupted by Alistair, shouting up the stairs. She quickly thrust the books out of sight and hurried down to the hall. Her husband was holding the telephone receiver away from him as if it might go off.

"Some fellow from Heathrow," he said shortly. His face told her that he guessed what the call was about; it told her that the whole business had gone far enough. He shut his study door a shade too loudly behind him.

Alistair's irritation, however, was not occasioned by Maeve's 'phone call which he had barely registered. It was caused by a 'phone call from the Dean not ten minutes before with some ostensibly good news. Momentous news, actually, which was the talk of Church House. The Archbishop himself had made it known that he was inordinately pleased. So Alistair's irritation was all the more surprising. Since he couldn't immediately trace its cause, he was glad to be able to shelve the matter while he answered the letter he had received that morning:

Dear Mr Allingham,

I understand that you have responded favourably to an approach from your superiors concerning the proposed visit of Bishop Mwawa to London for the duration of the 'Christ in Action' Conference. His Grace is familiar with one or two of your published papers and he has asked me to say how delighted he is to have the opportunity of meeting you and of staying in a part of the capital which is subject to neglect and deprivation. He feels strongly that the struggle for freedom, peace and unity amongst his own people should not be allowed to become insular, but should be broadened to embrace oppressed people everywhere, of whatever creed or colour.

I shall communicate with you again shortly to iron out the details of the Bishop's visit. Meanwhile he joins with me in wishing you every success in your valuable work.

Yours sincerely,
Barbara Mannheim (Mrs)

The letter was tangible proof of the visit, whose reality he had begun to doubt. With a steady hand he wrote of his sense of privilege and honour that Bishop Mwawa should have elected to stay in his humble home. He looked forward to it with keen anticipation. Would the Bishop's wife, he asked, be accompanying him? He hoped so. (He also wrote a memo to Maeve about acquiring new curtains for the best spare-room.) He was sure that Acton would offer many insights, if the demands of the Conference permitted, into the lamentable conditions of ethnic minorities in a typical Western European inner city environment.

Once he had finished he no longer had any excuse for putting off consideration of the Dean's momentous news: Mother Felicitas had announced her intention of attending the Conference. As the Dean said, this was better than getting the Pope. For, in the eyes of millions, Catholics and non-Catholics alike, Mother Felicitas was – more than any Church leader – the embodiment of sanctity. Why then did Alistair find the news disturbing?

Partly, he supposed in a fit of honesty, it was because she might steal Bishop Mwawa's thunder. Alistair's fierce loyalty to the Bishop made him indignant: it was distinctly unfair of this Felicitas to choose this moment to emerge from her seclusion. She was a Catholic, a nun, who had barely left her convent outside Santiago for years and years; she played no visible part in the battle against social injustice. Even while – it was true – exerting a beneficial influence on the Chilean poor and inspiring other similarly down-trodden peoples, she had never even spoken out against it. In fact, she rarely spoke at all. The last time that Alistair could remember was twelve or so years ago, when she accepted the Nobel Peace Prize. The moving ceremony had been on television. He remembered her quiet firm voice. She had mentioned Christ more than once and, it seemed to him, with complete success. It was a tricky name to pronounce at the best of times, let alone on TV, without sounding defiant or pious, hearty or ironical. She gave the impression that she was referring to an old, highly-respected friend and mentor to whom, it went without saying, the prize really belonged.

Try as he might, Alistair couldn't remember what the elderly woman, whom the world's press dubbed a 'saint', looked like. There were no photographs, except the famous one on the cover of *Time* magazine, where, with her back to the camera she could only be seen, as it were, reflected in the radiant faces of the people around her – people who had been bereaved by an earthquake and who now obviously derived comfort from her presence. On television she had been unmemorable in appearance: frail-looking perhaps, nondescript, with poor teeth.

From Alistair's point of view, the most amazing (and the most galling) thing about Mother Felicitas was her effectiveness. Her empire of hospitals had spread right across South America and now had branches on other continents. He couldn't see how it was done. While she had been active, ages ago, in establishing the first of these hospitals in the slums of Santiago, she had in recent years withdrawn behind the walls of her convent. There were rumours that she came out briefly from time to time in order to visit some government or other and to put the squeeze on them for another hospital; but mostly they seemed to spring up of their own accord, wherever they were most needed, with only the barest intervention on her part. The administration was performed by the nuns of her

Order while they and a host of affiliated lay workers staffed the wards on a day-to-day basis. Asked once why she had withdrawn to such an extent from the running of her hospitals, Mother Felicitas had been quoted as saying: 'Necessity. The world's suffering is such that more prayer is the only practical solution.' Alistair was frankly baffled by this.

And now this living myth, this religious symbol, was proposing to attend the Conference. Attention would inevitably – perhaps disastrously – be diverted away from the Issues and on to her. If she pledged support for Bishop Mwawa and others like him, her presence might be of real benefit. But there was no guarantee that she would; no guarantee that she would speak at all. Alistair didn't feel at all sanguine about this new and, frankly, rather disturbing development. He would ask Maeve's opinion as soon as she stopped talking to the man at Heathrow. What was she talking to an airport for? The answer came to him as soon as he had asked the question, and he didn't like it one bit. Surely Maeve wasn't still pursuing that bloody thing of hers when such great matters were at hand, was she?

"Who's speaking?" asked Maeve down the telephone.

"My name's Bob Adams, Mrs Allingham. Air traffic control." He paused as if he had come to the end of his message.

"Yes?"

"Well, um." There was another short silence. "Look, I just wanted to say that I heard about your spotting something, er, unusual the other day. I was here when the boss got your call."

"I see."

"It's true, as he said, that nothing exceptional showed on our screens at the time you mentioned."

"I don't doubt it." After another pause, she added: "Why are you 'phoning me then?"

"I don't really know. I felt I had to... ought to. You see, nothing appeared on our screens that day, but on the day before we tracked an unidentified aircraft across a large part of the south of England. It went at a phenomenal speed. Caused quite a stir. A 747 pilot made visual contact with it for about a minute. All he could make out was a row of lights. That's all."

"What was done about this?"

"Nothing. These things have happened before. There's no policy for dealing with them. Some of us think they're due to faulty equipment – besides which all sorts of things can show up on radar. Others don't know what to think. Me, for instance."

"Don't you report them? To the Ministry of Defence, for example?"

"We have done in the past. Mostly the MOD prefers not to know. They must have a number of similar reports, but what can they do?"

"I 'phoned the MOD myself. A man said he'd look into my story. He said he'd send someone round to see me. You'd be doing me a favour if you repeated what you've just told me to him."

"Well, I don't know. I'm not saying I believe in UFOs. I don't know what I'm saying. I just wanted to tell you that funny things do crop up. I can't help you more than that."

"Nevertheless I'd be very grateful if you would just tell the MOD man. You don't have to commit yourself to anything. You certainly don't have to endorse anything I've said." Before he could protest further, Maeve gave the 'phone number of the air vice-marshal's aide to whom she had originally spoken.

"Well, all right. I'll do it," said Bob Adams, "but don't drag me into anything. Be more than my job's worth if the papers get hold of it. It doesn't do for air traffic controllers to 'see things' on duty."

"I won't say a word, Mr Adams. I won't bother you again. Thank you for being so thoughtful as to call me."

Maeve wandered into the kitchen and put the kettle on. Bob Adams's news had been interesting, but not more than that. She didn't regard it as any kind of proof of the objective existence of UFOs. What was the difference, really, between some blips on a radar screen and some blips in front of the eyes of a tired pilot? What had her own sighting been except a kind of blip which flipped from here to there? A hiccup in the visual cortex would produce as much.

Alistair appeared in the doorway. She could sense any disquiet of his at a hundred paces. "What's up?" she asked.

"Nothing, really. I've just heard that Mother Felicitas is coming to the Conference."

"That's good, isn't it? It'll do wonders for the publicity."

"But will it be the right sort of publicity?"

“Is there a wrong sort? Besides, she might add a touch of holiness to the proceedings.”

“Do be serious, dear. You see, one can’t help having reservations. She never talks, except to ask for money. I’ve never even heard her condemn the Chilean regime.”

“Her presence at the Conference implies criticism of it.”

“I suppose so. But might she not detract attention from the real issues?”

Maeve was silent. She was no longer certain what the real issues were; no longer certain of anything much. She remembered seeing Mother Felicitas on television years ago, at the Nobel Prize ceremony. The thin, prematurely aged figure walked up an aisle, flanked by rich and powerful diplomats, politicians, industrialists, scientists. While the nun delivered her short speech of acceptance, the camera zoomed in on the faces of these men. Tears of pure distilled sentimentality welled up in many of their eyes. It had made her feel queasy. The cameras showed some of them being introduced to Felicitas. They bent over her solicitously, clasping her hand familiarly in both of theirs, as if she were an absolutely splendid little old lady who had done some heroic social work. They didn’t seem to notice the amused glint of blue steel in the nun’s eye, at wallet level, as she murmured something else about money.

Like Alistair, Maeve recalled little of the nun’s appearance, partly because the quality of the TV picture had been poor and partly because the nun’s gaunt face had been shadowed by the old-fashioned wimple she wore. The interviewer congratulated her on the Peace Prize and, more generally, on doing so much good. Mother Felicitas remarked tersely that it was not possible for humans to do good. Doing good was Christ’s prerogative. Fortunately He used humans to do His will. It was easy and pleasant to look after the sick and dying because He was present in every individual. Maeve was struck by the way she mentioned Christ, without special emphasis, as if He were a husband whose affairs she was seeing to while He was away on other business.

The interviewer was eager that she should say a few words about social conditions in the Third World. Instead, Mother Felicitas told an irrelevant story about the woman after whom she had been allowed to name herself. The first Felicitas had been a Carthaginian slave who had converted to Christianity and been martyred by the Romans. While waiting in prison for her execution, she had given birth. Screaming in the agony of labour, she was mocked by her jailers: how, they asked, if she screamed during childbirth, did she expect to endure being torn apart by wild animals? She had replied: "Now *I* suffer what *I* suffer; then Another will be in me who will suffer for me, as I shall suffer for Him."

EIGHT

The dark panelling and the bookshelves – now lined with ornaments and knick-knacks – suggested that the small room had once been Jeremy's study. Since being given over to Hermione, it had acquired the air of an actress's dressing-room or boudoir. A chaise-longue covered in yellow silk, on which Hermione reclined, imparted a period feel – the 1890s, perhaps, or the 1920s. The heavy curtains drawn across the high window, the sweet lingering smell of incense, and the dim pink light evoked the séance room. An electric kettle standing next to the tea tray on a side table struck a sour modern note.

Hermione beckoned Heather over to the chaise-longue and took hold of both her hands as she had done on their first meeting. Heather could feel the cold metal of the many rings pressing into her flesh. In order to reach, she had been obliged to bend at an awkward angle. It was easier – and perhaps what Hermione had intended – to kneel beside the chaise-longue and gaze up into the medium's compelling little eyes. The way her tent-like robe was arranged in careful folds along her reclining body and the great head bent in sorrowful weariness, brought to mind a macabre painting of a grieving Virgin Mary.

"You're not afraid of me, are you, dear?" Heather shook her head and compressed her lips into an approximate smile. "That's good. We shouldn't have anything to fear between us. I want us to be good friends. Isn't that right, Murdo?"

The young man was lounging against a black wooden bookcase, eating from a packet of biscuits. His leather joints creaked as he shifted position to stare with embarrassing frankness at the kneeling Heather.

"Is she up to it?" he remarked with his mouth full.

"Of course she's up to it. Aren't you, dear?"

"I don't quite know what you mean."

"Such a charming voice. I think she's been on the stage, Murdo, I really do."

"I haven't. Not really. I used to dance a bit."

"Dance. Of course. I see it all now. No wonder you're a sensitive. You never told me she was a dancer, Murdo. Our gifts bring responsibilities, don't they, dear? But such rewards, too. You had a rare experience. Ah yes, that was something Murdo didn't forget to tell me, the naughty boy. It's not given to many to encounter the Guardians in such a way. They choose those who are open to higher consciousness, you know."

"Have you seen their ships as well?" Heather blurted out.

"Many times," Hermione replied softly. "But you must already be aware that that's only the beginning. Am I right?"

"Well, I suppose its effect on me was more dramatic than the Cube itself – although I can't imagine one without the other."

"It's not difficult to see their skyships, as I like to think of them. Anyone may see them unless their minds are altogether closed. The skyships are powered by thought alone. That's why they are so elusive, so extraordinarily manoeuvrable compared to our clumsy aircraft. Something of the thought which propels them can be passed on to a sensitive observer, one who is in tune with Guardian consciousness. That's why, my dear, your response was so much deeper than that of observers who merely *look* at the skyships but *see* nothing."

This explanation, at once elegant and far-reaching in its implications, struck Heather with great force. Hermione released her hands and patted her arm.

"I see you understand matters quickly, dear. Just as we thought. It's why I wanted to speak with you. You see, Arkon has privately expressed fears for our planet which I daren't share with the other Children. It's urgent that we form a council of chosen ones to help recruit and prepare people for the last days. There's the business, too, of raising funds..." This last consideration gave her pause. "You're not well off, are you, dear? Social security, Murdo tells me. Never mind. Council members will be exempt from donations."

"Me? On the council?" Heather could scarcely credit it.

"Why not? You have already shown that you have enormous potential. You may even be a Guardian yourself. You'll be invaluable to us in recruiting new members, especially the kind of men who might feel threatened by someone like Murdo."

"But surely there are others... worthier than I. I don't know anything yet. What about Pete Kershaw or... or Katy?"

"Not everyone is as suitable as they appear," confided Hermione. "The Kershaws of this world may seem to hold a privileged position because of the very extremeness of their experience. But this isn't necessarily the case, is it Murdo?"

"Peter was abducted into a skyship because he is too narrow to be awakened in any other way except by main force," said Murdo abruptly. "Even then he learnt very little. His memories of the Guardians are vague. I would say trivial. They couldn't penetrate the barriers by which Peter wilfully sealed himself off from enlightenment."

"Surely Katy –"

Murdo cut her short:

"Katy hasn't proved altogether satisfactory," he said coldly. "It's no concern of yours, but since we will be working closely together, I hope, I can tell you that Arkon has let it be known through Hermione that the relationship between Katy and me has served its purpose. Our destinies are not intertwined." Heather glanced at Hermione for a clue as to how she should react to this information. The Guardian shrugged and let out a high-pitched giggle.

"Murdo took the news very well," she said. "But then he is a highly developed soul." She allowed her shiny eyes to rest fondly on him for a moment. Heather's legs were painful from prolonged kneeling. She stood up.

"Hermione. I don't know what to say. It's a tremendous honour, really, to be considered for the council. But it worries me, being one of... well, the chosen ones."

"You'll come to accept it, dear. Have a little faith in the Guardians. That's all. It's not asking too much is it, that you should trust us a little?" Hermione showed both rows of sharp little teeth.

"It's not that. You see, what I saw when the Cube – the skyship – contacted me was an amazing oneness of everything. Everything separate and itself but at the same time connected to everything else. I can't explain, but I feel it goes for people too. I do think we should be contacting... recruiting others – but only to spread the word and so on. We should be opening out, not forming groups within groups and keeping secrets... and so on." Her face was overheating; her head felt like bursting. She wished she could say what she meant.

Hermione gazed at her with kindliness mingled with a touch of sadness, of pity perhaps, around the mouth. She sighed, drawing on some deep wells of patience within herself.

"Two words, dear: human nature. Your idealism does you credit. I see myself in you. But you do not know human nature, does she, Murdo?"

"I'd say not," said Murdo, biting into another biscuit.

"If only the world were ready for our message... but it is not. The great truths have always been accessible to only the few. The great religions always begin with a few. Humans cannot bear too much truth all at once. They must be prepared for it. Don't you think we would rather be ignorant of the terrible knowledge we carry? Do you imagine poor Murdo here enjoys the responsibility? He is almost crushed by the burden. He only asks for a little help. We are the vessels who will bear the future of mankind beyond the stars and – who knows? – back again." With this short lyrical burst she suddenly seemed out of sorts. "I can't unfold the whole plan in five minutes. This is no time to be self-centred, dear. I know that you will soon realise how much you have to learn. I know you won't let us down. I feel it. Murdo will see to it."

"I'll see to it," promised Murdo.

"I'm so tired," said Hermione. Her eyelids closed like blinds being lowered over windows in a wide blank building.

"Sorry," said Heather. But Hermione had withdrawn to another mental sphere so that Heather was obliged to obey Murdo's signal to follow him from the room.

Maeve woke suddenly in the middle of the night with her head full of a terrible dream. It seemed as though she had only just dropped off, for she had not been sleeping at all soundly of late and, when she did, the fitful oblivion was troubled by anxiety dreams – nothing as bad as this one, but bad enough. They were the more remarkable because, until now, had she been asked to relate her dreams, she would have replied, absurdly, as people do: 'I never dream.' With a feeling of sick dread, she began to recollect the one which had just woken her.

She was in a stately mansion, very like Eden but larger. She had been living there comfortably for many years but without realizing, as she did now, that the house was populated by a huge work-force of servants who were forbidden to appear except to perform duties necessary for the running of the place. Gradually it occurred to her that the servants inhabited whole floors she had never visited. Creatures of basement and attic, they moved about below and above her, ascending and descending a labyrinth of hidden staircases which interlocked with the manifest stairways of the house. As soon as she realised that the house had a life separate from hers, she grew afraid of the legion of servants on whom her leisured existence depended; afraid that, were the building suddenly, in the night, to turn inside out, her portion of it would disappear.

She became obsessed with the idea that she must get to know this shadowy area of her own house, and its inhabitants. She summoned the Housekeeper who was dressed far more gorgeously than she was, in an embroidered crinoline, and whose hair was pinned up and beautifully kept, like Nanny Bryce's. When Maeve told her what she was about to do, the Housekeeper laughed: anyone who explored the servants' region never found their way out again. Nor would she be able to understand the servants' routines, purposes and even their language – and so she would lose her authority which her ignorance of them alone kept intact.

Nevertheless, in fear and trembling, Maeve opened a small door in her vast drawing-room and entered the servants' quarters. There was a host of people there; not just chambermaids and housemaids bearing clean sheets, hot water, coal scuttles and so on, but people she knew to be poor relations. She opened door after door, walked up and down narrow staircases, but she could never pin down a single person long enough to ask the question she couldn't even frame. At last she came to the door of the butler who presided over the whole army of servants. He was sitting in front of a fire in dirty underwear, and he was drunk. His condition was all the more distressing because he looked like Patsy, yet horribly changed. She wanted to dismiss him but she was too frightened. He seemed to intuit her wish. He put his face close to hers and said that she couldn't sack him because she was not his employer – she was not even the mistress of the house. He would take her to meet the true masters.

The next part of the dream was confused. She remembered following the 'butler' down some stairs and then some stone steps. It grew darker, filling her with deeper foreboding. The 'butler' stopped in front of an ancient wooden door with rusty iron hinges which had clearly not been opened for aeons. He unlocked it with a large key and pushed it open.

At this point the atmosphere of the dream changed. The unexpected, dazzling light which greeted her from the circular room created in Maeve the strong impression that she had woken up. The lit room had none of the dream-like quality of the preceding episodes; the door was like an opening on to reality.

Maeve could feel her heart beating fiercely as she waited for her eyes to grow accustomed to the sudden light, which shone from an unknown source. She soon discerned, at the far side of the room, a number of what looked like people. As they moved towards her, with the light behind them, she saw that they were quite small – no more than four feet or so high. The masters of the house were children! But something about the way they moved, with jerky limbs, was terrifying. She tried to run, but found she couldn't break free of the paralysis which, she knew, the children had induced. As they came nearer, she began to make out something not right about them – some deformity about their eyes. With a supreme effort she managed to force her eyelids shut against the sight and, at the same moment, woke up in her own bed, appalled.

She lay there rigidly, feeling the darkness seethe around her, listening to Alistair's quiet breathing. She cudgelled her brains in an effort to make sense of the dream. More and more it seemed that the lit room was a memory rather than a fantasy image. But was it the memory of a previous dream or of some event in her childhood or – please God not – of some more recent event? The sensation of horror kept her aching eyes stretched open until dawn filtered through the bedroom curtains, and she fell into a black sleep.

Heather wondered whether she ought to eat. She had had nothing since a stale croissant mid-morning. It was now getting on for two o'clock the following morning. She had walked home from Chiswick, wrestling all the way with that strange mixture of dread and exultation which Hermione, Murdo and the Sky Children evoked. The combination was not conducive to thought, yet it was imperative that she do exactly that – think of a way of squaring her personal vision with the creed of the Sky Children.

She opened the fridge. There was nothing inside except a carton of sour milk, some shrivelled carrots, a jar of mayonnaise and a fragment of hard cheese. It didn't matter; she wasn't hungry anyway. She was fed by the energy her own mind manufactured out of thin air. Its flow had abated in the interim between the two meetings, but now it was back in spate. The fridge was old and heavy with rounded edges. It looked more organic than mechanical. It looked animate. Heather told herself she wasn't afraid of it.

She had meditated and prayed all week that her mind would be put at rest. She had hoped that this last session with the Sky Children would dispel her uneasiness vis-à-vis the Guardians, for whom she had prepared a number of questions. But Lord Arkon hadn't put in an appearance; and, when it came down to it, she hadn't liked to trouble Hermione.

She extracted an ice cube from the freezer compartment and put it in her mouth. The icy water melted pleasurably down her throat. She was startled by a sound that broke the bubble of silence which, at that hour, enveloped the flat: the fridge, its door left open, had woken up and resumed its duties. Its motor hummed; the door trembled under her hand. If she didn't know better, she might have sworn it was speaking to her. With a sense of pistons thudding within, her own engine picked up speed. It began to generate a fraction more energy than she was comfortable with. She closed the fridge door and patted it. Its blank white face purred at her. She sucked hard on the ice, as if to cool down her thudding insides. She listened to their hubbub. Unless she was mistaken, something in the shape of an idea was being manufactured. As it worked upwards through ducts and tubes, it grew more defined, its angles more precise, until it pushed with crystalline clarity into her head: *the world wasn't going to end.*

More precisely, there wasn't going to be any actual catastrophe. No, instead, the *materialistic view* of the world would end. No ecological or other disaster, but a change of heart would occur. The common perception of the Earth would perish and be replaced by true spiritual insight. This was what her vision had foreshadowed – the melting away of appearance to reveal the reality beneath. The Children of the Sky had completely misinterpreted the spaceships and their occupants. They were merely portents, symbols of approaching transformation. There would be no snatching up of the faithful into extraterrestrial craft – that was like taking Noah's Ark as gospel. Rather, reading the poetic code aright, the task was to rise above this base sensory world to a more spiritual plane.

Heather's whole infrastructure shuddered with excitement. Breathing hard, she gulped down a pint of water. 'Don't panic,' she told herself. 'Think.' But she didn't have to think; she had only to listen to the whisper of a million pre-existing thoughts which fell out of the sky, through her roof, her ceiling, her brain. Each thought was a charged particle of meaning which dropped too fast for its drift to be caught. With a violent effort she was able to concentrate the cascade of thoughts into the shape of her Cube. It hung in front of her, faintly rippling. She was calmer at once. The stately enigmatic figure moved past a porthole. Of course. *He* would save her.

Heather sighed deeply with relief. She lay down on the floor. She had only to think about, to contemplate *him* and she felt centred again. The shadowy personage, both austere and compassionate, transcended everything – Hermione, Murdo, the putative Guardians, herself. He would arrange it all. She would be guided somehow to others, wiser than she, who would help her in the quest. For now, she had merely to empty herself and await orders; and, in the end, the Saviour would raise her up to his own high condition. Heather fell asleep with the beauty of that thought beating all around her, like colossal wings.

NINE

Although the sky was overcast, bringing relief from the direct blast of the sun, there was no significant drop in temperature. The atmosphere was muggy, with reports of thunderstorms heading in from the west. In short, it was far from ideal weather for Maeve to be hauling heavy shopping bags around Acton, especially when she was worn out and haunted by images so vivid and frightening that she could no long swear as to what was a dream and what wasn't. However, she could not put off the shopping she had already delayed for too long. There were essential items to be got, such as loo paper and Alistair's razor blades, for which she now entered the chemist's.

She caught the owner – a corpulent Indian woman in a fuchsia sari – in the act of scolding her young assistant, a slender girl of no more than seventeen. Her head was bowed and her white cheeks showed twin spots of red under the stream of petulance She hurried to re-stock a shelf of deodorants from a large cardboard box. The owner quietened down when she saw Maeve.

"These foreign girls," she explained, "they have to be told everything." Striving to keep her mind on the simple task in hand, Maeve stared vacantly at the shelves. The young assistant approached her.

"Can I help you, madam?" Maeve couldn't remember when she had last been called 'madam' in a shop; it was usually 'love' or 'dear', or nothing at all. She smiled gratefully at the girl.

"No, thank you, I'm just thinking."

"Of course you are. Only she likes me to ask." She nodded in the direction of her employer. Maeve felt sorry for the girl and, wishing to be kind, asked:

"What part of Ireland are you from?"

"County Clare." Her cheeks reddened again, but with pleasure.

"I was born in Mayo myself."

"Were you? I was there a couple of times. I was in Westport to climb Croagh Patrick. It was great gas." She seemed about to elaborate on her pilgrimage up the holy mountain, but, glancing at the Indian woman, returned to her task.

As soon as she had focused her mind long enough to gather together the things she needed, Maeve presented them to the girl who was now manning the till.

"That'll be three pounds, twenty-seven pee, please." Maeve rummaged in her purse.

"Oh dear," she said. "I haven't brought enough money. So stupid of me. I'll put something back."

"How much have you?" Maeve counted out her coins.

"Three twenty-one."

"Ah, give us that."

"I couldn't possibly."

"Sure, you could. We'll not kill ourselves for a few pence."

"No," said Maeve firmly. "I'll put something back." She replaced a packet of aspirin on its shelf. No wonder the owner was impatient – the girl had no idea about conducting business in the proper way. 'We'll not kill ourselves...' indeed. Just the sort of thing Patsy might have said. The girl really was priceless.

But, outside the shop, Maeve suffered a pang of remorse. She felt she had let the girl down in some obscure way; she felt somehow in the wrong when, on the contrary, she had been right. As she continued up the High Street, some unconscious association brought to mind that historical landmark: Nanny Bryce's arrival at Eden.

She hadn't been allowed, she remembered, to accompany Patsy in the trap to bring Nanny from the station because her mother had dressed her up in new, stiff, uncomfortable clothes, and there was to be no risk of dirt or dishevelment. She was flattered all the same that mother was bothering to take such unprecedented care over her appearance.

"You've been running wild for too long, dear," she said, brushing Maeve's hair in a desultory way. "Your father, as you know, is not a rich man. But he has been good enough to bring Nanny all the way over from England, at great expense, to turn you into an educated young woman. So do try not to be naughty, to knuckle down to work and do exactly as Nanny says."

"Is she a Christian Brother?" asked Maeve anxiously, recalling the floggings that Patsy had endured at the hands of those hard taskmasters.

"Of course not, darling. She's Protestant, like us." Maeve was resigned to being Protestant but she had always hoped that this might change in the future so that she could go to Mass with Patsy, by all accounts a mysterious and exciting business compared to the tedium of Matins in their parish church.

With her anxiety about the teaching methods of Miss Bryce allayed, Maeve looked forward to her arrival. She would be somebody new. She imagined Nanny's delight at being driven for the first time by Patsy. It was a long way to the station and back, and there were a number of remarkable places to see. Patsy would be sure to tell her all about them.

She shook hands with Miss Bryce in the hall. She couldn't speak at first because there was so much to take in. Nanny was old, of course – in her twenties – but not as old as Maeve had imagined she would be. She was tall and stood very erect. Her waist was wonderfully narrow, like a lady in a magazine – an impression reinforced by her smart clothes and the make-up which adorned her handsome face. But most dumbfounding of all was the mass of golden hair, pinned up and sculpted around her hat, and the marvellous lustrous eyes which, together, made her the very image of a fairy princess. Maeve could see that even her mother was a little awed by Miss Bryce.

"Did you have a pleasant journey?" asked Maeve politely when prompted to speak. "Did Patsy show you everything?" Nanny's face assumed the determinedly cheerful expression which would become so familiar to Maeve whenever it was a case of encountering the Irish.

"Oh yes," she replied, amusement twinkling in the fine eyes. "Mr Collins told me all sorts of stories." Maeve was taken aback by the clipped English accent; it made her uneasy, as did the subtle emphasis, suggesting ambiguity, on 'stories'.

"Aren't they great?" she said, a touch defiantly.

"Priceless," said Miss Bryce.

It was a word Maeve was to turn over in her mind. The way Nanny said it was new. It opened up previous assumptions, like a scalpel.

"Your usuals, Mr Allingham?" asked Mr Khan, turning down his radio and extracting two newspapers from the display in front of him. Alistair did not hear him immediately. He was thinking: 'It's now ten past eleven. I won't think about her until noon.' But he knew that he would, in fact, think about her long before the promised hour. He couldn't help it – she drifted unbidden into his mind all the time. Paradoxically, her face escaped him most when he exerted, as it were, the muscles of memory; but, left to itself, it re-presented Hyacinth suddenly, spontaneously, causing his body to blaze like tinder.

"What? Ah yes. Thank you, Mr Khan." He took the two newspapers and fished in his pocket for change.

"One hundred and twenty-seven for six," said Mr Khan, with what constituted for him an unusual chattiness.

"I beg your pardon?"

The shopkeeper motioned with his head towards the radio.

"Ah," said Alistair. "The test match." He listened politely for a moment, craning his neck towards the muted commentary. "We're taking a beating, it seems." It didn't displease him that Pakistan were bowling England out for a derisory score. His thoughts returned to Hyacinth. It was her tactile rather than visual presence which maddened him – the dark, butter-smooth pelt oozing dew drops. It was so vivid he could almost stroke it. But the confection of azure sky and pink-gold clouds in which she was set presented a disquieting contrast: their sweetness and innocence was redolent of a gaily-painted Virgin at a wayside shrine. Desperately he told himself that the picture of Hyacinth had been a side-effect of his faint, but he didn't believe it. It was too real for that – as real as if he'd been granted a glimpse into her essential nature and seen there something extraordinary; something, well, *holy*.

"We are indeed," said Mr Khan.

"On the contrary, it's England who –" Alistair stopped himself. Mr Khan did not allay his confusion, but merely moved the corner of his mouth in the suggestion of a smile.

Outside, Alistair paused to take stock. He wanted to tell Maeve about Hyacinth. He wanted her cool common sense to douse the flames of what was becoming an obsession. But could Maeve be relied on? She was behaving funnily, going through a silent phase – pray God it was only a phase – which he had no wish to exacerbate. And then again, even if she were her old self, and he were to tell her, well, she wouldn't laugh – God forbid – but she might smile that nanny-ish smile of hers, and raise her eyebrows and that would be enough; perhaps too much.

Heather sat at her bedroom window, sipping a cup of hot water which, if not exactly pleasurable, was free of toxins and a necessary part of the pure life she was now required to lead. Although it was a little below ground level, the window still afforded her a passable view of the street – a view preferable to the one from the back garden where it was impossible to avoid seeing the clock tower, with all its too-disquieting associations. Days had passed. Three or four, probably; she wasn't sure. They seemed inordinately long in one way; in another, they had elapsed in a flash. A thousand times she had started up to initiate some action, but each time she stopped herself – firstly because no specific course of action sprang to mind and secondly (more importantly) because she was mindful of awaiting orders. Often the Cube would come to her rescue: shining at the back of her mind, its divine occupant would slide his thought into hers. 'Patience,' he seemed to say; and Heather was again, for the moment, content.

Her attention was drawn to a man in the street. In his thirties, fair-complexioned, neat, neutral-looking, he was not remarkable. Nor was he doing anything in particular. Perhaps that was why he was arresting. Except for the skateboarding kids from number twenty-one and barmy old Mr Fosse who conversed with his own woolly hat, people in her street never did nothing in particular. They walked at a fair clip to and from shops, buses, the Tube. They didn't loiter.

This man, however, strolled about, stopped, looked around, leaned on a low garden wall. Was he waiting for someone? He lifted his head and swung it slowly from left to right, panning the upstairs windows of all the houses. He glanced at his watch and walked off in a jerky uncoordinated way as if he were a perfect human replica. Heather was mesmerised. He was waiting for someone. It was the manner in which he threw a last, wistful look over his shoulder that told her he was waiting for, looking for, *her*.

The strange internal motor which had been quietly ticking over burst into life, accelerating like a dragster on a green light, powering her out of the flat in seconds. Heedless of bare feet and undress –

she wore only her red and black silk kimono – she hared towards the High Street, catching the man at the corner.

"You're... looking for someone?" she gasped. The man did not answer at once. His eyes took her in at leisure. A polite smile disturbed the symmetry of his smooth face. He took no notice of the odd looks passers-by were sneaking at Heather.

"News travels fast," he remarked at last. A red-hot streak, like a meteor, seared across Heather's mind, seeming to illustrate his words. "I've been looking for someone of your description. I've been asking around. An old woman in the market told me I might find her in this road."

"It's me," said Heather shyly. She was conscious now of the absurd figure she must be cutting.

"Clever of you to spot me." His words filled her with immense pride. She had passed the first test. Her task had been to find *him*, thus proving she was genuine.

"Won't you come to my flat for...?" She was going to say 'tea' or 'coffee', but stopped herself. It sounded so utterly banal. What would *he* want with tea or coffee? The very idea of exchanging small talk over tea instead of communing at once on the deepest level was nauseating.

The man smiled. He understood as, of course, he must. The notion of hot beverages was not ridiculous to him. The smile indicated that it was correct to preserve the outward appearance of conventional behaviour. His own appearance – the fashionable suit, the neatly-brushed beige hair – proclaimed it. Like spies they were to act as if nothing extraordinary was occurring.

"I have to be going, as a matter of fact," he said. "But I'm glad to have found you, Miss..?"

"Wright. Heather."

"OK Heather. I've an appointment in the area this evening. So how would it be if we got together? No reason we shouldn't mix business with pleasure, eh?"

It was exquisitely expressed. To describe their shared knowledge as mundane 'business' was delightfully ironic; to call their ecstatic encounter 'pleasure' was a masterly understatement, especially when their 'business' together was identical with 'pleasure', and vice versa. In fact, it was screamingly funny, the way he used conventional phrases to convey cosmic meanings. Taking her cue from the man's knowing smile Heather began to laugh. It was such a relief after the anguish and uncertainty of her last week or so, that she laughed until tears streamed down her face and her sides ached. The man's slight frown, the merest cloud shadow on the surface of a dead calm, bleached sea, restored her gravity.

"No reason," she replied. "No *reason* at all." She laughed again.

"Seven-thirty, then. I'll pick you up. You can tell me all about it."

"You'll collect me. I'll tell you about it," Heather repeated dutifully. The orders were crystal clear in her mind. She told him the number of the house and flat. He winked and, crossing the road, worked his limbs into an ordinary car.

It had been easy after all. If you didn't know better you'd think how incredibly lucky you were, coming across him like that. But luck didn't come into it. Whatever was necessary, was ordained. A few short hours from now instructions for salvation would be issued, orders given. At the very least they would work out together what was to be done, what was required to enter the luminous garden of the spirit where every flower was incarnate Beauty, every petal, Truth.

For the first week after Nanny Bryce's arrival at Eden, Maeve trailed everywhere behind her, agog at the sweeping changes that Nanny effortlessly effected in a domestic disorder Maeve had thought immutable. She gave instruction in dusting and general hygiene to the girl who came up from the village to clean; she organised the laundry; she arranged for a man to mend the guttering, and another the sash cords in windows which had never in living memory shut properly. Aromatic soaps, sent from Dublin shops, appeared in the bathroom to reproach, as sweetly and silently as Nanny herself, the dark age of intermittent washing.

Above all there was a new regime for meals, received with universal relief. Hitherto, Maeve's father had never been seen to sit down for a meal. He ate standing up like a horse (local opinion claimed that he also slept like one), hacking slices of boiled bacon or beef from the joint and shovelling them straight into his mouth. Her mother only nibbled biscuits at intervals throughout the day and night, sometimes with morsels of cheese which needed washing down. If it hadn't been for Mary the cook Maeve would have been forced to subsist on cress and nettles.

In England there was a war. Rationing had begun. Nanny Bryce couldn't get over the plenty that existed in Ireland. Her oblique references to the food situation across the water induced Maeve's parents to take meals more seriously. Out of politeness, if nothing else, Father took to sitting down for at least one meal every day; Mother took to eating something sensible in order to set a good example. At the same time she happily ceded the bother of arranging meals to Nanny, whose instructions to Mary were so pleasant, clear and direct that the very sight of her sent Mary's hands fluttering around her head and chest in the outline of a cross. All the same she was grateful for the order that was at last being imposed on the household, and she responded bravely to Nanny's notions of a balanced diet with meals whose quality startled even Father. It was apparent from the first that Nanny was more housekeeper than nanny, and, as Maeve soon learnt, more governess than housekeeper.

Maeve had difficulty adjusting to routine. A nine o'clock sharp start for lessons suggested to her some time during the morning. She saw no pressing reason to attend at all if there was something more rewarding taking place, such as the birth of a foal or the prospect of a trip over the bog with Patsy to cut turf. Nanny therefore added two minutes to a lesson for every minute that her pupil was late, until Maeve learnt to follow the dictates of the watch which she had been given. She also had to wear shoes and socks at all times. Any article of clothing dirtied, spoilt or lost had to be washed, mended or replaced out of her own meagre pocket money. She was an intelligent girl who quickly learnt that it was less painful to comply.

In any case she was not sorry to follow the routine. Her childhood freedom (or, as Nanny called it, indiscipline) had begun to pall. She welcomed regular hours and meals; she relished the opportunity to learn and work. She did not much care, it was true, for the hard end of education with its wall of numbers and diagrams, facts and figures; but she enjoyed geography, history and English composition which gave her a first chance to set down for an attentive audience the things she most valued about the world.

"Most imaginative, Maeve," Nanny would murmur, leafing through the scrawled pages. "Colourful. I don't know where you find such priceless yarns."

"They're not yarns, Nanny. They're *history*. They're the things that have happened all around here."

"You mustn't believe everything Mr Collins tells you, dear." Then, with a pencil as sharp as a cauterising needle, she would go through Maeve's narrative and punctuate its seamless flow with fine distinctions in the margin: yarn, superstition, old wives' tale, tall tale and so on. In extreme cases she would write 'Poppycock!' or 'I think this may be a fib!' Nearly all Maeve's history dissolved into a 'story'. Stories were admirable things in their place; they became 'stories' when you were asked in all seriousness to believe them.

Maeve could not explain to herself, let alone to Nanny, that it was a matter for yourself what you chose to believe, just as Patsy never unequivocally claimed to believe in the *Sídhe* from whom he was descended on his father's side, nor in the magical properties of raths, though he nevertheless gave them a wide berth at night. You believed and you didn't believe – that was the way of it. You were yourself free to provide variants, within strict unspoken rules, of the stories which attached as if by themselves to local objects, people and places. A 'story' might or might not be true; but all stories were 'true'.

Patsy, meanwhile, remained outside Nanny's jurisdiction, untroubled by inverted commas and all that they implied. He alone was unswept by Nanny's new broom. He was seen less about the house, preferring to hold to the stables, the grounds and the beyond. When their paths did cross the tolerant twinkle in Nanny's eye, which she reserved for the Irish, was met by something similar but friendly in Patsy's – hers just this side of irony, his the other.

In the early days, before Patsy began to tease Nanny (if it was teasing) with his baffling cry of 'One hundred and twenty-six acres!', Maeve sensed that Nanny was as near discomfiture in her encounters with Patsy as it was possible for her to be. What passed for conversation between them was enigmatic. They remarked on the weather, but Maeve couldn't help suspecting that something else was meant.

"Good morning, Miss Bryce," Patsy would say, with pronounced civility, "Isn't it a grand day?"

"It's raining, Mr Collins." Patsy would start and gaze about him in surprise.

"Sure, I wouldn't call that rain, Miss Bryce. Wait until winter now. Then you'll see rain."

Such exchanges made Maeve anxious. She was astonished at his daring to speak to Nanny in that tone. Occasionally he would go, as she thought, too far:

"Well now, I'm away to the pub, Miss Bryce. Will you be dropping in yourself, or will I bring you home a bottle of whiskey?" Maeve held her breath, waiting for the flare of Nanny's nostrils which signalled that she was about to come down on you like a dry-stone wall. The nostrils remained strangely inert.

"Thank you, Mr Collins, but I think not. As you well know, I hold no brief for strong drink." Was there, of all things, a touch of nervousness in her stiff reply? It could not be.

"Ah well, I'll bring you back a Guinness then. There's no harm in one of them."

"You're incorrigible, Mr Collins."

Patsy would wink at Maeve while Nanny avoided her questioning stare, almost as though Patsy had the power to impart a portion of his own ambiguity to clear-cut Miss Bryce. It was left to Maeve to ignore Patsy's wink and, lowering her eyes, she sensed some ancient tacit battle for the high ground, as much racial as personal, sweeping through the air above her head.

At the far end of the High Street was a triangular island in the centre of a confluence of three busy roads. It contained a war memorial and an angled bank with a flower bed whose different-coloured blooms were supposed to spell out a message. Maeve could have just lain down on that bank for a short rest, but it was surrounded by iron railings with no gate. She put down her basket and her two plastic bags and, leaning her elbows between the spikes of the railings, tried to make out what the flowers said. They were uneven – profuse in the yellows, sparse in the reds – so that imagination was needed to discern any words at all. She decided that they were 'We will remember them' – a reference to the dead Actonians of two world wars whose names were written on the plain memorial.

When she had rested her aching back for a while, she set off again in search of brass rings for the new curtains in what was now called Mwawa's room. She had been told about a suitable little shop beyond the usual limits of her shopping trips, right at the end of Acton where the High Street turned into the bare Ealing road. She found the shop. It had closed down. She crossed the street and found herself walking alongside a huge area of rubble, like a bomb site, where a sign advertised 'luxury maisonettes', no brick of which was yet in sight. Alone in the midst of this dereliction was a tall Victorian building which looked as though it had shrugged off its neighbours on either side and sent them crashing into tiny pieces. It might almost have been a Gothic revival church but for the sign which hung at the front: The Castle.

Maeve had never had the chance to examine the notorious pub before. She had passed it on the bus a number of times and noted that its front windows were permanently blacked out by curtains – indeed, it looked permanently closed. Local rumour alone told her that it was in fact permanently open. She peered at the door which was black with a brass knocker, like an ordinary front door. 'M.J. Ryan, prop.' was written above it; on it, in fancy lettering, was printed: *The Shebeen. Open Fridays and Saturdays from 9.00 p.m.* Rumour also told her that The Castle was a desperate, dangerous place, frequented entirely by Irish of the worst sort – gangsters who didn't care how much they drank or what it would lead to. IRA men could certainly be found in there, and Provos who dealt in guns and plastic explosives and who plotted bombing campaigns. The really illicit activities took place, it was said, in a kind of hall at the back, an inner sanctum or pub within a pub which, as Maeve now saw, was called *The Shebeen*. It was given over on the advertised nights to barbaric music, hard drinking and God knew what else – mad hoolies at any rate, which had ended more than once in police raids. Even from the vicarage she had seen the sky stroboscopically lit by the flashing lights from the convoy of police vehicles needed to quell *The Shebeen*'s army of violent subversives.

At that moment, the door flew open and a man reeled backwards through it, falling heavily at her feet. He was about thirty, still good-looking but – with bags under his eyes and a tendency to jowliness – not wearing well. One sleeve of his brown three-piece suit was torn away at the shoulder. The collar of his maroon shirt was open, lying outside his jacket and revealing a pale blue singlet beneath. Visible above his cheap slip-on shoes, purple socks clashed with his shirt. There was a gold chain around his neck and a ribbon of blood on his chin.

"Shite," he said. Then, loudly, "Fock you, McBride."

A second man appeared in the doorway, carrying a full pint glass of Guinness. Despite the heat he was wearing a heavy, intricately patterned cardigan with a turned-over collar. On his right wrist was a heavy gold identity bracelet; on his fingers, two massive rings above which the knuckles had been recently skinned. He lounged against the door post and raised a finger pedantically.

"No, no, Brady – fock *you*."

Maeve had been frozen with horror at the violent fall of the first man, but it was McBride who was the more frightening. His face was grey under the freckles and none too clean. His nose was snub and his eyes, tilted up, might have appeared retarded had they not burned with animal intelligence. He had the unmistakable look of a tinker, a look that was quaint in a tough little boy but, in a grown man, verged on the sinister.

"Come out here till we see what class of a man you are, McBride," shouted Brady, scrambling to his feet and raising clenched fists. The tinker considered this invitation for a second or two. Then he smiled, and threw the contents of his glass over Brady. One of his canine teeth, Maeve noticed, was missing. He turned to her and said softly:

"Did I splash you, Missus? I'm sorry if I did." He sauntered back into the pub. Brady, cursing and shaking himself, followed. Maeve did not wait to see the outcome. She was speechless with shock and anger. Really, these Irish men were impossible, brawling in public like that. They never learnt, never changed. A hundred yards farther down the road she had to stop because she was shaking so much. She breathed deeply and swallowed hard to prevent herself from bursting into tears.

TEN

Heather dressed with care. Remembering his own studiedly normal appearance, she chose a simple short blue dress with a deeper blue linen jacket to go over the top. She left her newly-washed hair loose for a change, to soften the outline of her face. She kept her make-up understated except for a bold gash of lipstick. Ready by six-thirty, she posted herself at the window.

The weather was warm and close. She forced herself to sit absolutely still. All the same, her skin prickled with tiny drops of perspiration. A number of possible speeches ran in parallel through her head, sometimes sliding sideways and garbling each other. She set herself to watch the clouds that floated like huge white barges high above the oppressive weather. Their motion soothed her. She decided to obey her instincts by blurting out everything she had experienced and thought and come to realise – in short, to submit entirely to his judgement. Then he would know how best to guide her towards... towards what? She couldn't remember for a second. Then it came to her: towards *enlightenment*. That beautiful word evoked an image of herself entering the immaculate white space of the Cube, where He had been expecting her for all eternity, like a true love. She could hardly wait for that moment, hardly wait for her new-found friend – colleague? Teacher? Guide? – to arrive and to start her on the quest.

"Let him find me worthy," she silently pleaded to the clouds. They were growing darker now, massing themselves around purple centres, presaging a storm. The stunted trees held themselves very upright in the electrical atmosphere; the grass phosphoresced. The important thing was to pay minute attention to everything he said and did, for he had already proved himself a master of subtlety. You had to be on your toes if you were to pick up the hints and clues he threw out so casually.

At a quarter past seven the doorbell rang. The grass quivered. The trees were rooted to the spot. Her hair crackled as she passed her hand over it. She ran to the front door and threw it wide open.

Murdo was standing on the doorstep. He walked briskly past her, straight down the narrow hallway to the sitting-room. Heather's brain froze like a waterfall overtaken by ice.

"You weren't at the last meeting."

She couldn't understand at first what he was saying. His voice was distorted by a dull echo from the bare walls. The empty room looked really very small with him in it. His leather clothes, wrinkled and shiny like a second skin, made her hot and itchy and bothered.

"I'm not coming again." Her own words frightened her. They sounded too defiant in the face of this man who, silhouetted against the window, resembled a Hell's Angel. She quickly switched on the light. His eyes were fixed on her, not in coldness or anger, but in the way a bird of prey simply *looks*. She was almost certain he was wearing mascara to heighten the effect. His face was drained of blood as if he had absorbed through prolonged contact some of Hermione's pallor. He looked like death. "I don't believe in the end of the world," she said quickly, before she lost her nerve. "At least, not in the way you believe in it. This world is dissolving into another more spiritual one. There won't be death and destruction, but a rebirth. The skyships are portents of a new dawning. They haven't come secretly, to move a few of us to another world – they come openly, for all to see, like Christ's promise to come again, trailing clouds of glory!"

Although she had spoken in a rush, she was not displeased with the result: she hadn't conveyed a fraction of the truth that was unfurling itself within her, but she had conveyed the gist of her differences with the Children of the Sky. A soppy name, now she came to think of it.

"Crap," said Murdo. "The planet's about to fall apart and you give me visions and baby Jesus. Mystical shit. Get a grip on yourself. The Guardians are not happy with you. If you come with me right now, they might make allowances."

"Please leave now. I'm expecting guests any minute."

"Sure you are." He pointed a finger at her head. "Hermione isn't going to like this. I don't like it. If you don't come with me now, you'll be sorrier than you've ever been. Once you've been marked out by the Guardians there's no escape. They know everything you do and think. If you're not for them you're against them... against us."

"You and Hermione... you're deluding yourselves. Leave me alone." He took a step towards her. It was not his change of expression which terrified her, but rather some awful withdrawal of expression. His face was blank; and, unable to bear looking at what might next possess it, she closed her eyes. Rain had begun to fall. She could hear its remote rustle turn to a roar, breaking the fever of the long evening. She prayed wordlessly to the Saviour in the Cube. The doorbell rang. Murdo's voice said:

"No-one can save you now."

When she opened her eyes, he had gone. Standing in the doorway was the man, her friend.

"Not a very sociable bloke. Who was he?"

"That was... excuse me." Heather walked stiffly into the bathroom and threw up. She knelt, trembling, in front of the lavatory for a while, clasping the cold white rim and studying the way her vomit swayed in the deep bowl: beautiful pale pinks, greens and browns, like sea anemones in a rock pool.

"That was Murdo," she said, returning to the sitting-room. "He's one of the Children of the Sky. They're in a bad muddle – but I expect you know that." The man's face admitted nothing. He pulled a notepad out of his suit and wrote in it. It was very professional, very reassuring. He was obviously compiling a dossier on Hermione and her crowd.

"Tell me your side of it."

There again, she only possessed one side of things. She was impressed at his objectivity, disgusted at her own sloppy subjectivity which assumed that she knew the whole when, of course, she knew only a tiny part. As quickly as possible she told him about Hermione and Murdo, Katy and Jeremy, Pete Kershaw and the military-looking man who loved his daughter.

"What do you think?" she said at the end.

"Tell me about their rituals. Sex, drugs. That sort of thing."

"There wasn't anything like that."

"Any kids involved?"

"No."

"Oh well. Not much to write home about, as cults go." He snapped the notebook shut as if the matter were settled. "It's your thing I want to hear about." Heather was aware of an enormous relief, like a cloak of chain mail slipping off her shoulders. The man's indifference to the Sky Children suddenly put them into perspective. They were unimportant. What had come over her, nearly being taken in by them? It was her encounter which interested him, hers which, as she had never doubted, had value.

"Am I allowed to ask your name?" she said timidly.

"Raphael." The pronunciation of the archangel's name caused a current of power to pass through her. "My friends," he added, "call me Raff." The self-effacing, almost comical abbreviation sang in her ears. She wanted to clap her hands and laugh aloud at his supreme modesty.

"May... may I call you 'Raff'?"

"We're friends, aren't we?" Heather was unable to reply. She was in his hands and, at long last, safe.

It was six p.m. The coast was clear. Alistair had gone off on some mysterious errand. Although it pained Maeve that they had recently become so estranged, it was not as pressing as the problem she now sat down, in her favourite armchair, deliberately to confront. She had got nowhere by beating her brains in an attempt to remember. It was time to try an approach that required considerable nerve, but there was no alternative. She had to get to the bottom of the haunting dream, or else – one way or another, she felt – she would lose her reason.

She closed her eyes and, breathing slowly and deeply, emptied her mind of everything except her memories of the dream. She retraced her steps through the labyrinthine servants' quarters of the house similar to Eden until she was again descending the stairs, first wooden, then stone, under the guidance of the Patsy-like figure. He unbolted the ancient wooden portal and – she gasped at the sudden access of helpless terror that swept over her on the threshold of that evenly-lit, circular room. She willed herself to stay calm – they were only a memory, they couldn't hurt her – as the 'children' came towards her. She couldn't look at them, could only feel her paralysed body being grasped and propelled towards the room's centre where she had glimpsed the outline of something like a dentist's chair with its back lowered to the horizontal position. Her legs were immobilised and she wasn't being carried – incredibly, it appeared that she was being floated, like a raft. There was a long moment of blackness during which she must have lost consciousness.

The next thing she knew, she was lying on the 'dentist's chair' with straps around her arms and legs, sick with fear. 'It's only a dream,' she reminded herself. 'You must find out what happened.' But she didn't believe for a minute that it was only a dream. With an enormous effort she was able to move her head a fraction, and her eyes. She saw that she was flanked, three on each side, by the 'children'. Except that they weren't. They were merely small, with disproportionately large hairless heads and – oh *God* – huge slanting pupilless eyes, completely black. Her body was taut with the screams she couldn't let out. She tried to repeat the Lord's Prayer in her mind, but the words were pushed aside by other words – words, it seemed, that they were putting there. She was saved from further horror – roused from her trance – by the sound of the doorbell.

Alistair scanned the row of terraced houses overlooked by the four towers of shabby high-rise flats set in their acres of wasteland. Number twenty-three was better kept than most, neatly painted in blue and white, with a bay window built out in front. He stood across the road from it, suffering a sudden attack of nerves. This annoyed him. After all, what could be more natural than to pay a call on her, albeit somewhat late in the day, in order to thank her for her concern? Common decency prescribed it. Caleb Duval, from whom he had obtained her address, saw nothing odd in it. But he hesitated all the same to approach the door. His stomach churned. His face tried to assume a look of both nonchalance and purpose in case the boys kicking a ball up the street should think he was loitering with intent. He had left Maeve sitting at the kitchen table, drinking tea. She had done nothing, as far as he could see, all day, except a spot of shopping. She didn't seem bothered that she had not bought the important rings for the Bishop's curtains. Her whole attitude bespoke apathy. How long was this going to go on? He was prepared to put up with a certain amount of irresponsibility and moodiness, but there were limits. She had been withdrawing from him for some time, and now the distance between them was too great for him to ask the questions that might bridge it. She would in any case probably respond vaguely, in monosyllables. Alistair felt sad and helpless and, yes, lonely. Maeve's condition – the word melancholic occurred to him

– deprived domestic life of a dimension. It was flat and cheerless, no longer the dependable refuge from whatever life outside threw at him.

If she didn't buck up soon, before the Bishop's visit, things could become extremely sticky. So sticky, in fact, that Alistair felt a flutter of panic. The idea that Maeve would be on less than top form for the crowning moment of his career was unthinkable; and so Alistair did not think it but, instead, crossed the road and rang the bell of number twenty-three.

He was conscious at once of his empty hands. Should be have brought something – flowers or chocolates, for example? But that was absurd. He wasn't a teenager on a first date. He was simply paying a helpful woman a courtesy call. No reason for his mouth to be so dry. He was seized by a premonition that, when the door opened, Hyacinth would be exactly as his vision had displayed her – the embodiment of some Madonna-like mystery. He heard the distant calling of children and brisk footsteps in the narrow passage. He prayed wordlessly for he knew not what. The door swung open and she was standing there.

The man on the doorstep was dressed in a black suit which, with its baggy trousers and wide lapels, seemed to belong to the nineteen fifties. His face was wan, his features bland, his washed-out hair stuck flat on his head by hair oil. When he left, Maeve would not remember anything definite about him except the way he walked – awkwardly, disjointedly, as if he were still learning how to work his limbs. Now, she was in any case too shaken by the awful memory, or reconstruction, of the events which her semi-trance experiment had induced. She heard herself say: "I'm afraid my husband's out at the moment. Can I give him a message or anything?"

"It's you I wanted a word with, Mrs Allingham." He spoke softly and carefully, not unlike a foreigner who was taking pains to speak colloquial English. "It's about your unusual sighting." Maeve realised at once that he had been sent by the Ministry to investigate her encounter with the cube. In the light of what had just transpired, his arrival was providential.

"Oh yes. Come in," she said with relief. "Thank you." He glanced, as if out of habit, up and down the street before entering. He had exactly the sort of bland, anonymous, cagey air that might be expected of a member of a sensitive Government department. He worked his legs as far as the sofa in the drawing-room and sat down. "Tea? Coffee? A drink, perhaps?"

"Whatever you're having. Thank you." He smiled confidentially. Maeve divined that he was on her side. She felt better already.

When she returned with two mugs of coffee, he was sitting as if frozen in the same position on the sofa. He had a notebook open on his knee.

"I'd be so glad to hear about it," he remarked. He looked into her eyes with such understanding, such encouragement that she felt sure he had heard many stories like hers – felt that he knew far more than he was able to reveal. Doubtless, when the interview was completed, he would let it be known, discreetly, that the existence of strange aircraft was nothing new. Maeve felt calm and greatly cheered.

He wrote down everything she said – the time of day, the clear sky, the early morning sun; the roses and the clock tower; the sudden appearance of the shining cube. Now and again he seemed about to comment but, changing his mind, only nodded and permitted himself a barely perceptible smile. She told him how the cube had abruptly come very close, how it was now inexplicably round or oval, filling her field of vision; how frightened she had been; how she had lost fifty minutes.

"Is that it?" he asked. Maeve hesitated.

"No. I can't explain, but I've been having these dreams. But they're not dreams. Memories, too. About what happened during the missing time." He leaned forward, raising his hand as if to touch her reassuringly and then withdrawing it. He took up his pen again instead. "I found myself in this round, brightly-lit room," Maeve continued. "I was paralyzed. The horrible creatures seized me. They were small, like children, with grey skins and hardly any noses or mouths, just slits; but their eyes were huge and black..." Even as she was speaking, recounting the nightmarish scene, a fresh piece of the jigsaw fell into place. "I remember something else, too," she said excitedly. "As they sort of floated me towards the centre of the room I could see a sort of round window, like a porthole, out of the corner of my eye. They didn't like it, didn't like me seeing. I could feel their agitation, a kind of wave passing through them, like the seething of insects. But they couldn't stop me catching a glimpse out of the window. Oh my God. I could see my garden and my neighbours', too – but from a height. We were about forty feet in the air, and then the garden suddenly grew tiny at a stunning speed. It made me dizzy. I think I may have blacked out." Maeve had to stop lest she begin to cry from the shock, the sheer weirdness of it. The man waited for her to regain control. He was neither embarrassed nor intrusive, but detached and sympathetic, like a competent doctor. At last he said:

"And did they do anything to you, these aliens?"

"Aliens? You don't suppose they really were, well, from... *out there*?" She gestured largely and vaguely at the universe. Aliens? Yes, she supposed they were. But *'aliens from outer space...'* She couldn't bring herself to credit that. And yet the man had said the word so calmly; and, then again, what else could they be? "Yes," she said. "They did something to me." She recalled again with dread the couch thing she was pinned to, like an operating table. She remembered how they clustered around, how one of them had a long instrument in his hand. "They did something... intimate." She remembered trying to cry out 'Jesus, please help me.' And then, 'Who *are* you?' And hadn't a voice suddenly intruded into her mind – she pushed it away now, as she had then. She couldn't go down that path. Madness lay at the end of it.

"What exactly?"

"I can't be sure. Or can I? It's coming back to me." Her tears began to fall freely. "You'll have to go now. I don't want to talk any more."

"If you could just give me some idea, Mrs Allingham," the man murmured. "It may be of great importance."

"Who are they? What do they want? You do believe what I'm telling you, don't you?"

"Certainly."

"The cube. It isn't a secret weapon or anything, is it? *Is* it?"

"Don't upset yourself. It's all over now. Did they... violate you in any way?"

"Yes. *Yes*. That's exactly what they did. I haven't been the same since it happened. They took something essential away from me. I'll never be the same again." Her hand flew involuntarily to the side of her head. "Oh God. My head. Please leave now. You can come back or I'll 'phone you, but you have to go now."

The man nodded slowly and moved in his jerky way to the front door. As soon as she heard it close, she flew to the mirror. She couldn't bear the idea of witnesses to what had resurfaced in her mind with terrible clarity. She scrabbled frantically at her hair, pulling it away to examine the skin underneath. It was as bad as she feared. There was a small oval scar on her scalp, about the size of a fingernail, just above her right ear. A cold shiver passed down her back. 'What,' she wondered, 'am I going to do now?'

The car swished through the deep puddles created by the recent rainstorm. Raff drove fast. His smooth hands were confident on the steering-wheel. Heather paid no attention to where they were going. He knew the way. It was more than enough to be off, at last, on the quest which ('Please let me be worthy') would end in truth's splendour. She was exquisitely happy.

Night was falling. The streetlights suddenly bloomed like marigolds. Their counterparts under the glassy road came on simultaneously like smears of ochre. Heather averted her eyes from this sulphurous underworld and fixed them instead on the dazzling grottoes of shop fronts which flashed past. In front of them human mannequins stood or loitered, apparently unaware of the wavering shades which hung beneath their feet like huge blurred bats. Even when she concentrated on the motion of the car as it skimmed along the diamond-strewn roof of that subterranean realm, she was drawn to look more deeply downwards to where a thousand eyes of white fire burned in the darkness. She gathered her mackintosh more closely around her, hating that dark inverted parody of the world the rain had opened windows on to. She heard her humming mind alter its continuous note, slipping off-key like a spinning-top starting to falter. She was so tired of it. She longed for that high white space, geometrically perfect, towards which, she was sure, Raff was taking her and where she could be at one with the One, in peace. A smudged eye, red as a Cyclops', big as a giant squid's, stared up at her from beneath the wet road. It had even arrested the car. When she looked up, she saw that it was only a traffic light. She did not look down after that, but kept her eyes on the wet windscreen which diffracted the lights of oncoming cars into pretty jewel-like streaks.

Raff's silence was tangible inside the car. He expelled it from his lips along with the blue smoke from his cigarette. It was a silence like no other. Pungent, pregnant with meaning, it pointed beyond itself like a pause in a drama or symphony. If she could only absorb it, she would unravel in a trice the mystery of things. It bred a veritable torrent of amorphous ideas which melted in the act of taking shape, flying out of her like phantoms and merging with the warm blue smoke which became richer and denser with significance by the minute.

When he spoke, the words unfurled like pennants on his blue breath. They were imbued, like everything he said, with an extraordinary subtle emphasis.

"*So. Why don't you tell me about your flying saucer?*" Heather inhaled this heady question and let out an involuntary explosion of laughter. The ironic use of the ridiculous term 'flying saucer' showed how conscious he was of the commonplace reaction to such phenomena as her Cube. He spoke like that deliberately, as part of her initiation: his irony and allusion were a method of illumination which embodied the very heightened awareness it evoked. You were forced to concentrate like crazy so as not to miss anything. You had to be as quick, as oblique as his remarks were. There wasn't even time to laugh.

While she was considering how best to reply, Raff parked the car and got out. Heather followed him through the damp night air. He turned sharply into a doorway – the sort you might walk right past if you didn't know – and entered a large, dimly lit room full of people. Two or three of them nodded at him unobtrusively; others studiously avoided acknowledging his presence.

"*What are you having?*" he asked, leading Heather to a table in the corner. Loud music blared out of a nearby speaker. She could think of no immediate response to this conundrum, so she sat down at the table. "What are you having," she repeated thoughtfully. He turned away and walked across the room. She had to clench her teeth to hold down her panic; but he only went as far as a plump moustached man behind a counter to whom he said a few words. Heather took a covert look at the other people present, chatting and drinking out of large glasses. They took no notice of her. She had inevitably to ask herself these questions: was she in a pub? Or did it simply look like a pub? How many of these people knew? Were they *all* members of Raff's fraternity or only some of them? And, if only some, *which*? The man behind the bar almost certainly, to judge by the understanding he had with Raff. But who else? Perhaps only those who had nodded at Raff when he first entered. She was prevented from exploring the possibilities further by Raff's return with two pint glasses filled with what looked exactly like lager. She began to drink without question.

She was unnerved when Raff took out his notebook. It seemed to her that she should have one. There was so much to take down, remember, assimilate.

"*OK. Fire away*," he said. It was time to tell her story, her 'side' of things. Obedient to his instructions she felt words begin to kindle inside her.

"You know more about it than I do. You know what it's like. You've seen it."

"*Others claim to have seen it*," he corrected her. Chastened, she let her head droop. Of course he had to be convinced of the authenticity of her experience. Her claim had to be substantiated – otherwise she was no more worthy than, say, the Children of the Sky.

"Where do I start?"

"*Begin at the beginning.*"

Her thoughts forked like lightning from the present moment back to the creation of the world. Where exactly could her story be said to begin? She looked at Raff miserably. Intuiting her dilemma he smiled thinly. "Just tell me about the morning of your sighting…" He sounded tired. Heather sensed the weight of his knowledge and responsibility, the burden of selflessness which tied him to ignorant and earth-bound creatures like herself. Her heart went out to him. She touched his arm hesitantly, tenderly.

"I know I'm holding things up. I'm sorry. I'll tell you all about it and then we can go wherever you say." His face brightened. He laid his hand over hers and a flood of heat passed into her as if a whole new circuit of nerves had been connected up.

"It was a Saturday," she began. "I dreamed that something earth-shattering was outside my window, and when I looked, it was true…" She recalled every detail – the weather, the time on the clock tower, the smooth texture of the silvery Cube, its flash of light that was more than light. She re-lived the way the world was illuminated for her and, for a split second, everything and everyone in the pub co-inhered, and were blessed, until they fell apart again into discrete entities. She described how, later, she had remembered – or had she dreamed it? – the concavity in the Cube's surface, through which she had glimpsed its sole occupant, the tall regal figure towards whom she was drawn like a moth to a still, jewel-like flame. Raff wrote it all down in his notebook.

"*Fascinating, love. Have another pint.*"

"It's all right to drink, then?" Retaining perhaps some trace of Murdo's warning against alcohol, Heather was in fact feeling a little strange after the first pint of lager.

"*It's essential, love.*"

While she was awaiting his return, two men came and stood near to her. They cradled beer tankards with one hand against their chests as they talked; their other hands were in their trouser pockets. The loud music prevented her from making out what they were saying, but there was something suspicious about them. Perhaps it was the way they had, apparently randomly, chosen to stand there or the way they glanced at her, looking away whenever she caught their eyes. She recalled Murdo's threats: no escape, no-one to save her. Was it possible that these men, his emissaries, had caught up with her already? Was she under surveillance? Then she heard the sound and there was no room left for doubt.

It would have been totally inaudible to someone less vigilant. Or it would have been passed off as part of the general cacophony. But, to Heather's sensitive ears, it was profoundly sinister: one of the men was clinking some coins in his pocket. She had taken no notice of such an innocent sound at first. Then the second man had rattled some keys in *his* pocket. Coins and keys conversed back and forth. Once she had detected these miniscule noises she could hear no other. They were as clear and insistent as the high-pitched crepitation of grasshoppers' legs. Beneath their ostensible chat the two men were communicating in an elaborate code. Heather could even discern a pattern – three chinks, for instance, were answered by a long rattle – but she couldn't crack the message. She dared neither move nor breathe.

As soon as Raphael came back, she opened her eyes wide and stiffly jerked her head in the direction of the two men.

"*Relax*," said Raff. At the same moment he squeezed her thigh under the table. A tremor of joy ran through her body. The hidden squeeze told her that he knew exactly what was going on, that she was to behave as naturally as possible. Immediately she set herself the task of relaxing, as he had bidden. The second pint of lager was easier than the first. She tackled it with a will. It was essential. Things were occurring at high speed now. The two men were joined by a third, but all three moved away when Raff put his arm around her shoulders.

"Time, gentlemen, please," the barman chanted. Heather thought of the face of the clock on the tower, its hands pointing to empty sky. The tower cracked. Huge lumps of masonry crashed soundlessly into the High Street, which opened like a jagged mouth. The sun began to turn red. "*Closing time,*" said Raff. "*Time to go.*"

ELEVEN

Heather followed Raphael up three flights of stairs. His hair sparkled from the fine spray of misty rain. No star had overlooked their short walk from the pub; no person had followed them. He had taken her arm when she swayed on the kerb, causing a car to hoot. He was unlocking a door. 'Now,' thought Heather, 'now he's going to unlock the secret. Now I'll comprehend the mystery.'

She looked around the small cluttered room, smelling of dust and sour milk. Raff removed her mack and hung it on the back of a chair.

"Is... is *He* coming?" she whispered. Raff silenced her by pushing his hand against her left breast, just above the heart which was pounding so hard that it ached. Talking was against the rules. She kept very still, watching Raff carefully, awaiting orders.

He led her into an adjacent room that smelt of unwashed clothes and switched on a dim light beside the bed. She peered around. There was, as yet, no-one else present. Raff's smooth face loomed close to hers. Strangely flat and lifeless, it was impressive as only an extremely realistic portrait can be, right down to such fine details as the large pores around the nose and the dewy cobweb which festooned the space between upper and lower teeth in the half-open mouth. Then the eyes in the painting moved, showing unexpected whites.

As he took off her dress his breath came in little puffs which burst like smoke-filled bubbles against her ears. Understanding the nature of the rite she had to undergo, Heather surrendered to the sensation of Raff's mouth on her flesh. Her body, however, remained oddly rigid, passively resisting its necessary mortification. She burned with shame when Raff had actually to manhandle her on to the bed.

"*Relax,*" he ordered in a low voice, jarring without breaking the rule of silence. But although she was sensible of the honour being accorded to her, still her body remained stubborn. It wasn't able to grasp the fact that she couldn't be deemed worthy until all of her, including the recalcitrant flesh, was raised up by the divine influx. Her jaw wobbled from the involuntary clenching of her teeth; her arms were stiff rods against her sides; her legs pressed tightly together. She was being squeezed out, shifted to the periphery of herself whence, floating slightly above her centre of gravity, she seemed to look down with disgust at her own stiff pale corpse.

"*Come on. Open up.*" The taboo against speaking shattered.

"Yes, I want to. But tell me," she begged, "who's behind it all? Who's above you?"

"*I told you, didn't I? The Evening Star.*" The name was like a neon strobe behind her eyes. That the Saviour should have taken it was staggering. Its meaning went on forever. It signified a beacon at the edge of darkness before nightfall; but it was also the *morning star*, heralding a new dawn. It stood astride the twilight between old and new worlds. Moreover it was Venus, goddess of the love that was returning from its long exile to shine – more softly and tenderly than the solar glare – on all mankind. Tears of happiness ran down Heather's cheeks and, as Raff pushed against her flesh, it meekly opened up.

"Yes?" Then, recognising Alistair, "Oh. It's you, vicar." Ignoring Alistair's speechlessness, Hyacinth showed him into a small sitting-room where she had obviously been working at a sewing machine. There were yards of cream silk-satin draped over the table. He could hear her admonishing her children in the kitchen. She re-appeared a minute later with a cup of tea which she placed at his elbow.

"If you do not mind, vicar," she said, settling herself behind the sewing-machine, "I will go on with this. I have to finish lining the skirt before I put the youngest to bed. As you can hear," she added, "the children are making their own tea."

"Yes. No. I mean, do please go on. Goodness, I had no intention of disturbing you. It's a pleasure to see people making their own clothes."

"Look at the material, vicar. It is a wedding dress. What would I be wanting with a thing like that?"

"Yes, so it is. I see." He watched her deft brown fingers working the material under the needle's staccato bursts of fire.

"Now, what is it I can do for you, vicar?"

"What? Oh, nothing really. I just came to say, well, thank you for helping me out the other Sunday. Made a clot of myself."

"The Holy Spirit is often unpredictable."

"What? Oh. Absolutely. But I rather think my keeling over can be attributed to more mundane causes, ha-ha. Anyway I hope it won't prejudice, so to speak, further co-operation between our respective churches." Hyacinth said nothing, but merely looked at him out of her deep-set intelligent eyes. He had to look away to avert a mild dizziness. "It's so important, isn't it," he went on, leaning forward earnestly, "to break down the barriers between communities. We mustn't let dogma, colour and so forth get in the way. We're all one family, after all."

"You sound like someone on the television."

"Do I?" said Alistair, flattered. "Well, you know, the 'telly' has a role to play. It can do so much good in bringing people together."

Hyacinth's fingers paused above the glossy material before setting the machine whirring with renewed force. Alistair was momentarily ravished by the juxtaposition of velvety hands and silk-satin, like coffee and cream. He longed to help this strong stoical woman; he felt the weight of her oppression, struggling on alone with no husband and three, or possibly four, children. Bad enough for those who weren't born into the double prison of female gender and black race.

"I don't want to seem presumptuous, Mrs, er... Hyacinth, but may I ask if you are being properly remunerated for this work you do? If not, I may be able to help. You may not be aware of it, but there are cases of, well, frankly, exploitation. Single women are notoriously vulnerable to unscrupulous employers. I mean –"

"Have no fear, vicar. I work for myself. I am well paid for dresses and similar. Especially such as these. People do not stint when it comes to wedding dresses."

"Ah. Good, good. I hope you're not offended by my asking. And as long as you're sure. It's just that –"

"I am not offended." Alistair sensed that he had committed a blunder. It was just that he wanted desperately to impress on Hyacinth his goodwill; wanted to show that they were on the same side. If only he could snatch her up and rush her to his colleagues and cry: 'Look! *This* is what we are fighting for. The problems aren't all in Africa or South America – they're right here, under our noses. Look at this woman. Talk to her. See how she isn't crushed by history and society, but tempered to the strength and value of a diamond!'

She wouldn't even have to speak; her very presence was eloquent. He could almost hear the respectful buzz of his fellow clergymen as he arrived at some august function with Hyacinth on his arm. The image conjured an idea of startling audacity. "Listen, Hyacinth. A rather important, er, African is coming to visit me soon. A bishop, actually. It would be wonderful if you met him. To exchange points of view and so forth. He'd be fascinated, I'm sure, to hear what, um, life is like here. I mean your sort of life..." In Alistair's imagination, the late-night discussions with Bishop Mwawa took on international import. There would be a few close colleagues present, perhaps the Dean, and above all Hyacinth, who was uniquely suited to presenting both the feminist and the Black viewpoint, but within a Christian context. "...I just know he would value, as we all would, your input – especially as he has little access to the West Indian perspective."

"I am not West Indian," Hyacinth interrupted mildly.

"Of course not – you're British. But I meant that he would value, as it were, an Anglo-Caribbean –"

"I am from Zimbabwe. Rhodesia," she added patiently.

"What? Yes, yes. Of course." Alistair was nonplussed by his own stupidity. Now that he looked at her he saw that of course her face was distinctively African.

"You are thinking of my husband, perhaps. He is from Barbados. I made a mistake similar to yours – I thought that our colour gave us more in common than our culture. But, I cannot deceive you, the man is actually a savage. A charming savage but, nevertheless, a bad influence on the children and a godless man. I had to pack him off, back to the West Indies."

"I see, I see."

"Perhaps you hope for too much when you hope that your Bishop and I will get along well together?"

"Oh, I think not. He could hardly be called 'godless', ha-ha."

"We might have some things in common. For example, it is true that neither of us can speak for the Third World. We were both brought up in Western cultures – I, in the mission school; he, at the University of London."

"Good Lord. How did you know that?"

"You are speaking of Bishop Mwawa? His visit is no secret. The newspapers are excited about your forthcoming conference. There is the promise of controversy and similar."

"Well, yes. As a matter of fact it is Bishop Mwawa. As to his staying in Acton, I can't say too much about it, you understand, because it has not yet been officially –"

"He takes refuge in Zimbabwe occasionally, when things are unpleasant in his own country. He is not a reticent man. He sides with the Shoshona people against the Matabele who are, to put it mildly, discriminated against."

"You're well-informed, I must say."

"I am a Matabele. Or, I should say, my family is. What is left of them." Sensing a hint of some issue which was not susceptible to analysis in terms of black and white (not to mention an opinion adverse to the Bishop), Alistair preferred to absorb only the tone of her words, lest their content lead him out of his depth. Their firm dignity re-evoked, faintly but unmistakably, her mysterious aureole with its swags of pink and gold. She assumed for him the extreme glamour of someone infinitely precious but outcast, like the goose-girl who is really a princess; like the rejected corner-stone on which the Kingdom would be built. If only he could harness for wider ends that power and presence out of which she spoke. What could he not achieve with her as an ally? Perhaps that was the meaning of his vision. Perhaps it was an injunction to help Hyacinth realise her potential for good. Indeed, he already felt that here was someone he could open his heart to.

"But what you say is exactly what I mean. We must address the wider issues, explore the possibilities of reconciling disparate cultures through a recognition of their common humanity..." Eagerly he began to sketch out his plans, all but abandoned until now, for the improvement of Acton. The battle against inequality had to begin with Christians, like themselves. Ideals would become reality. What began as exercises in community relations would end as love. His rhetoric carried him away; his voice quavered as he broached his own inchoate yearning for a peace which lay even beyond ideals.

"If you want me to join your church, vicar," Hyacinth interrupted, "I am afraid it is no use. I cannot deceive you, I am happy with my own."

"My dear..." He was astounded and flustered. "I mean, absolutely not. You misunderstand me. My concerns transcend churches. Don't think for a minute that I'd *presume* –"

"If you would excuse me now, vicar, I really have to put my youngest to bed."

"Of course. I've already taken up too much of your time. But please don't think... I mean, I only want to be of service. There's so much we might explore together…" He was still expostulating when, unaccountably, he found himself ushered firmly out of the front door and into the rainy street.

For herself, she could have run all night. A steady breeze at her back conspired to carry her along so that she hardly touched the pavement; the thin misty rain caressed her face, bringing refreshment as she sped through the gleaming streets. In the end her engines powered her at so high a pitch that her body threatened to break down. She slowed her feet and legs, and finally stopped, sitting down on a bench at the edge of a residential square.

It wasn't easy to remember how the facts of the matter had broken over her. Exhilarated by the dash through semi-darkness her mind was straining at the leash, thoughts egging her on in urgent whispers. She could get no purchase on them long enough to recall the exact sequence of events. However, the white-hot spot, like a brand, on the side of her face where the demonic entity had aimed its blow brought much of it back. It had been a narrow squeak: for a second she had believed that the Saviour had betrayed her most horribly; but now she discerned his handiwork even in this vileness. For what quest worth the name was free from snares and deceptions, false trails and ordeals? And, if not He, then who else had in the midst of her submission reminded her of that other Name for the morning and evening star? At the speed of light her high-powered logic had unravelled Raphael's skein of lies. As he lay slavering on top of her, probing her with his god-awful scaly thing, the Name had come to her: *Lucifer*. This was the other name for the morning and evening star. Satan was the moving force behind Raphael.

Heather glanced around her nervously. The entity was unlikely to have pursued her or, if it had, to have kept her flying feet in its sights; but there might be others, shadowing her. In this small hour, God only knew what was abroad. She sprang up and began to half-run up the street, away from the square where the street lights were spread too far apart. Away from the dark central garden whose shrubs dripped terror. Best to keep to the well-lit streets, even though they were exposed. As she jogged along the glistening pavement, Heather sent a desperate telepathic plea skywards for guidance. Nor did she forget to give thanks for the strength which had enabled her to overcome Raff.

She had dragged him off her body by his hair. He had given her a frightful slap. She had screamed and struggled like a wild animal, flinging him off, grabbing at her shoes and clothes, dashing out of the bedroom. With supernatural foresight she had slammed the door and rammed the back of a chair under the handle. All the same, her fear didn't allow her to stop and dress – she merely forced herself into shoes and mackintosh, stuffed her knickers into its pocket and ran down the endless stairs.

Gradually wind and rain had blown the reek of evil away. The event grew remote, a series of nightmarish flashes happening to someone else whom she had to lug along with her. A phrase floated into her head, something Julian had once quoted from some philosopher: 'The flight of the alone to the Alone.' It was apt.

A roaring sound made her look in sudden panic over her shoulder. She saw an enormous red beast, its face squashed in like a giant Pekinese, its forehead grotesquely high and emblazoned with words and a number: N137. The gust of wind it made as it raced past her caused her to swerve. It pulled up ahead, purring in anticipation. Heather recognised it as a double-decker bus, sent to collect her. It was lit up like a fairground and empty except for a man with a jet-black face and a fuzzy white halo of hair under a peaked hat. He seemed to be expecting her.

She sat as near to the open entrance at the back as she could. Slowly the wet grey conveyor belt beneath the bus began to grind backwards, carrying the lamp-posts and trees and railings out of sight.

"What you playing at, petal?" demanded the conductor. He had to shout above the clatter of the world as it was cranked past, picking up speed all the time; but his voice was not unkind. "Why you not properly dressed? You'll catch your death." Heather smiled at his mistake; she was perfectly safe for the time being. "Where you going?" Her smile broadened: if she knew *that*, obviously she wouldn't be here. It cost her a lot of effort to concentrate her mind on so meaningless a subject as the money he was asking her for. She preferred to watch his lips moving and the intriguing pinkness of his gums. She was surprised to find she had no money. Her pockets were empty except for a pair of knickers. The conductor shook his head. With relief she went back to observing the dark turning world roll scenery past her. You had to stay on this treadmill until your own bit turned up. But where was her bit? Had she missed it? She stood up shakily and edged towards the open doorway, ready to fling herself out on to the scudding surface of the Earth. A muffled bell made a 'plink' sound, signalling to the smoothly flowing belt to slow down. It ground to a halt. Buildings shuddered outside as they were brought up short. The bus ticked over like a bomb. She clambered off.

"Next time you take a bus, flower, bring some money with you!" the conductor called after her. It was sound advice. Heather nodded her head vigorously as she set off down a street that looked familiar to her.

In the interview with the man from the Ministry Maeve had remembered something so disturbing that she had to get rid of him immediately, had to be alone in order to cope with it. Outside, purple clouds smothered Acton. The sickly yellow light of the sun setting behind them made the colours in the garden look unnatural, the flowers feverish, the grass a neon green. The promised storm was by-passing the area. Distant flickers of lightning were visible but no accompanying thunder could be heard. Without warning rain came down in buckets and bounced off the lawn. Maeve drew the curtains, turned on all the lights downstairs and locked all the windows and doors.

Whereas before she had courted the memories of her encounter while sitting quietly in her armchair, it was now all she could do to keep them at bay. She moved restlessly from room to room, wishing Alistair would return, half-inclined to rush out and search for him, except that she was equally afraid of his seeing her in such a state. The rain sounded like handfuls of gravel flung against the window panes, and then it stopped as abruptly as it had begun. She went into the kitchen and splashed water on her face which was covered in a film of cold perspiration. She steeled herself to look again at the scar on her head. It could have been there for ages, the result of some childhood mishap. In fact, her unconscious knowledge of its presence might have caused the elaborate fantasy as to how she obtained it. But, somehow, this idea wouldn't wash. She recalled it all so vividly – the aliens around her with their thin bodies and grey skin, the rudimentary orifices in their faces, the huge up-tilted black eyes clamped to the contour of their heads. "Oh God, God," she moaned, splashing water more fiercely on her face and neck. She saw how one of them raised the long thin instrument at the end of his spidery arm; she felt the brief blinding shaft of pain in her head, the sensation of suction, of something giving inside her skull. 'They're scrambling my brain', she thought. 'No, they're stealing it.' Her extremity of fear might have communicated itself to her captors, not because of any expression on their blank faces, but because a collective shiver passed through them simultaneously, as it had before when from the porthole she had glimpsed the ground receding at a fantastic rate.

'Jesus, *Jesus*, please help me,' she had silently pleaded as the long instrument was inserted. She remembered the pressure of a voice, as if in reply, against the sensitive membrane of her mind. It was trying to thrust her defences aside. 'Telepathy' she thought wildly; and, as the words continued to push in on her, she abandoned herself to them in sudden exhaustion and fury.

'*Why me?*' she thought. The words formed:

'You are human.'

'What do you *want*?'

'Your world.' With these words she was released from her bonds and, raised upright, wafted across the room to the far wall where a panel slid back to reveal another window.

'Who the hell *are* you?'

'We are ourselves.'

'Why don't you answer me properly? Where do you come from?'

'We come from Pluto.'

With this answer Maeve knew that she was beyond help. There was no rhyme or reason to any of it. She suffered herself to be aligned with the window through which she looked sullenly out on to the surface of a barren planet – dark, rocky, ice-cold. Even as she watched, a horrendous explosion took place in the distance. There was no sound, only a vast shower of burning rocks. It occurred to her that she was not looking out of a window but at a screen on which film or TV images were being projected. She watched intently but there was nothing much more to be seen except the aerial view of hundreds upon hundreds of miles of devastated landscape. Little by little the unimaginable desolation entered her soul like iron, and she was unable even to weep.

Her next distinct memory was of standing, stunned, in her garden, gazing at the rose petals in the palm of her hand. Of her return she remembered nothing.

TWELVE

The drizzle had stopped. Dawn was breaking unobtrusively. A steady east wind, subject to sudden gusts, was being puffed out of the sun's pink cheeks as he toiled uphill towards the horizon. The canopy of raincloud was in tatters, allowing a few fading stars to peep through it in the west. Greenness was beginning to seep up into the expanse of grass that Heather now recognised as Turnham Green. She set off at a fast pace northwards. It was imperative to make home ground, a mile or two away, before the sun appeared in all his strength. The street lights were already extinguished; trees had ceased to merge into one another and were stepping forward out of the darkness to be counted; neat front gardens were throwing off their veils and showing themselves in their true colours. Sooner than she had expected the clock tower rose up behind the houses, its white face blushing pink under her fierce stare. The Tower! It had been right under her nose all along. It had been indicated from the very first moment, if she had just had wit enough to see it. She broke into a run, her damp mackintosh whipping her bare legs to greater effort.

It came as no surprise to her that the main doors of the Acton Assembly Rooms were open at that hour; nor that a blood-stained corpse was lying in the foyer. She prodded the body with her foot. It stirred. The man was not dead, but dead drunk. The stains on his white shirt were of red wine. From the main hall came the strains of 'You'll never walk alone', wailed by four voices in approximate unison. Heather jinked to the right, where she saw a staircase. Onward and upward – these were her watchwords. She emerged onto a gallery overlooking the hall. The singers were clearly visible, swaying over a sea of empty glasses, plates and wine bottles. A girl slept with her hand nestling in the smashed remains of a giant white cake. Confetti and coloured streamers festooned every surface like a fall of rainbows.

The door to the tower was locked. Heather burst open an adjacent fire exit and climbed some more stairs to the flat roof at the base of the clock tower. A fixed steel ladder ran up its west wall, to the right of the clock face, as far as the parapet at the top. She took a deep breath and began to climb.

She was seized by the momentous sensation of ascending beyond time. With every step she was more fully convinced of the rightness of her climb. She had been as mistaken in waiting for the advent of the Saviour as she had been in seeking colleagues on her quest. It was down to her alone, as it had always been, to rise up towards Him. If she could only climb high enough – especially here, at His chosen place of manifestation – she could at last meet Him face to face. 'The flight of the alone to the Alone': the beautiful haunting expression summed up her entire life. All her old preoccupations, activities or men had merely been an unconscious longing for this consummation.

On every ninth rung she took a rest. The thin soles of her shoes offered little protection to her painful feet from the sharp steel. Her left calf muscle suffered an agony of cramp. Her arms felt numb, empty of blood, from the effort of hauling herself up. Her hands were raw. But what was a little pain when you were within an ace of scaling the heights?

The higher she climbed the more violent the wind became, whipping around the corner of the tower, flagellating her face with damp hair, tugging at her flapping mac, threatening to pluck her off the ladder. It emitted a steady breathy moan which merged with her incessant mental engines. Together they broke into a strange singing sound, high and wild, advancing and receding: at one moment it was a distant sinister music of the spheres, at the next it swelled into a discordant gust of hallelujahs that made her want to shriek in reckless accompaniment. As she dragged herself up the ladder, past the enormous clock face, her whole body resonated like cut glass. It was being assumed into timelessness. Inches away to the right, around the corner, spears of orange light were glancing off the tower. She could feel it coming to life, humming with solar power. She laboured on in shadow, heartened by the knowledge that the sun would greet her from the east when she reached the summit. With every rung now she was becoming lighter, more sanctified, like a priestess or sacrificial victim on the Ziggurat of Ur.

At the end of her strength Heather hauled herself over the knee-high parapet and lay in the narrow walkway which ran around the central portion of the tower. This had a door, no doubt leading to the stairs whose lower door had been locked. She could climb no higher unless she somehow clambered onto the sloping tiles of this ultimate part of the tower, which continued to shield her from the full vehemence of the east wind. However, it seemed presumptuous to address the sunrise until she had recovered and composed herself. She stood up on shaky legs and looked back over the parapet she had just breached.

Half the kingdom spread out in a semicircle beneath her. You realised from such a vantage point how temporary civilisation was; for, unnoticed at street level, there was greenness everywhere, surrounding the houses, flowing into commons and parks, leaking through the cracks between buildings, encroaching on every road. Far away, beyond the unsightly island of Ealing, mist melted the green land and the pale blue sky into a continuous Elysian field. Closer to, a few tiny cars beetled along narrow channels. An even smaller creature, pathetic in its solitude, weaved through the back roads of Acton on a bicycle. It seemed so close yet so minute that you wanted to reach over and scoop it up like an ant. Heather saw with great clarity how its path would lead it inevitably to the edge of the old shopping precinct where another ant-like creature was busy with some rudimentary construction.

It happened as she knew it would: their lives intersected, they exchanged greetings. The worker in the market extended a feeler in Heather's direction. Two pinpoints of white appeared as their faces turned upwards. They had sensed her presence above them, controlling their destiny. The law of cause and effect was an illusion – once you were on high you perceived the simultaneity of things. You saw how lives ran on smooth ordained tracks which crossed each other, conjoining and separating. If you ascended high enough – as high, say, as the stars – you could see the whole of time, all of history, as a single instant. You could grasp with a single glance the world's millions of threads woven by an invisible hand into one fabric.

Heather stood on the parapet for a long time, holding this thought in her mind until the singing of the wind reminded her of her situation. It pulled at her coat, urging her to move around the tower. She offered it no resistance.

On the east side of the tower the wind buffeted her face. She closed her eyes and took off the encumbering coat. She heard it flap away like an enormous bird. She felt the air ignite in the sun's rays and dance around her in a frenzy of cold fire. Every time she breathed in there was less and less between her and the dance of fire and air; when she breathed out, more and more of her was blown away. She opened her eagle's eyes and stared steadfastly into the great copper disc which hung at eye level in the sky. The wind nudged her, catching her up and standing her on the low parapet. There was hardly anything of her left. In a second, any second now, she would be light enough, high enough – and then He would come out of the sun, encased in silver, to draw her away into eternity. Mesmerised by the single red eye, she silently addressed herself to the Alone. She would not take one step further towards Him unless He explicitly wished it.

The sun was very close, reddening her white skin. Something streaked like a meteor out of its heart and headed towards her. She closed her eyes again. It was not for her to gaze unbidden on His face. The tower trembled under a terrific gust of wind. Encased in her fiery nimbus, she sensed a great draught of air flowing up the wall and forming a solid moving slope. Heather swayed. Voices called out to her. She saw how she would be wafted up, ethereal as thistledown, on the calm stream of the wind to where He was waiting. She raised her arms and leant forward towards the sky. A powerful force seized her by the shoulders.

"Is there anybody waiting for you at your flat?" asked Alistair. "Anyone to look after you?" The girl made no reply, but continued to look out of the taxi's window. Her lips moved soundlessly as if repeating a prayer. Alistair was at a loss. 'What do I do?' he wondered.

He had been inclined to put the police off when they 'phoned. 'Surely a doctor... social worker would be more suitable?' he had suggested. 'She asked for you, sir,' the policeman had replied calmly, not to be put off. 'Personally.' There'd been no way out. He stared gloomily at the meter as it clocked up another fortune. He would have to pay for that as well. Really, it was too bad of the girl to have given his name. She was not a member of his congregation; he had only seen her once, barely remembered her. She was not flat broke, not a battered wife, not even (as far as he could tell) a single mother. What had possessed her to behave in this ludicrous, this exhibitionist fashion? It had been a 'cry for help' no doubt; but what help, really, did she need compared to so many?

Glaring across at the silent girl Alistair couldn't help but soften. Dishevelled was too mild a word to describe her tangled hair, her barked shins, the nasty bruise on the side of the face. She cut a forlorn figure. And yet, she carried herself with a composure he couldn't help but admire. When he had first seen her, he had thought for one incredible moment that the police had caught a species of extraterrestrial: wearing a silvery, one-piece space-suit it came flashing towards him down the corridor in a series of complicated leaps and pirouettes. It looked like nothing on Earth, unless a kind of sylph or hamadryad. The suit – very warm and made of a sort of reinforced paper – was in fact designed for victims of exposure or hypothermia.

A sergeant had explained the few facts of the matter: a woman who had a vegetable stall in the market had glanced up at the clock tower early that morning. Seeing someone suspicious climbing up the outside of it, she had alerted the police. With the station not two hundred yards away up the High Street, a rescue team had arrived in no time at all. It gained entry to the tower on the inside and, sprinting to the top, snatched the girl from imminent death as she swayed on the edge of the parapet. Outwardly she was in a bad way. Her nakedness was not the least of it. But inwardly she didn't appear suicidal. On the contrary, she seemed rather serene. She had suffered herself to be brought back to the station, dressed in the thermal garment, given hot tea. She gave her name and address in a clear voice and also, when asked to suggest someone who might claim her, those of Alistair. She would answer no questions concerning her escapade; but, since she had committed no offence worth mentioning, the sergeant took the view that she was best off in a hot bath as soon as possible. He had shrugged.

"What were you doing at the top of the tower?" Alistair asked her. She looked at him nervously and then said in a loud voice:

"I think I'll get out now." Alistair was about to hurl himself on to her lest she plunge to her death from the speeding taxi, when it abruptly drew up of its own accord in front of a house only two streets from his own. The girl – Heather – shot out of the door and began scrabbling in the earth of a small flower bed. She disinterred a small plastic bag containing front door keys – spares, presumably

– and let herself in to her flat.

Alistair could hear her splashing in the bath. He paced restlessly around the flat, trying to decide what should be done. That the girl's condition was more serious than he had initially surmised, was evidenced by the almost total lack of furniture in the principal room. If she wasn't mad already she'd soon go mad in these empty cheerless surroundings. She shouldn't be left alone. She might seem normal enough now, taking a bath on her own initiative and so forth, but there was no telling whether or not she'd take a razor to her wrists as soon as his back was turned. She had no friends or relations he could call on – 'I am alone in this world. We all are,' had been her portentous answer to his simple question. He would have liked to summon the professionals – doctors and so on. But would he be justified in doing so? The police had seen no reason to. Besides, how did you get hold of the social services on a weekend, other than by declaring a state of emergency? There was always the danger that he would be branded a scaremonger – an *uncharitable* scaremonger – and possibly a bit barmy to boot. He'd have to keep an eye on her himself.

Luckily there was Maeve. He thanked God for Maeve. She, if anyone, would know what to do. It was likely, even probable, that she would worm whatever the matter was out of young Heather in a jiffy. She excelled in that way. Heather would cheer up and, before he knew it, be off their hands. That was essential, of course, because preparations for the Bishop's visit were not as far advanced as they should be. Furthermore (Alistair felt even happier at this inspiration) the problem of Heather might be just what Maeve needed to take her out of herself, to jolt her out of this moping over delusions and memory lapses.

With the matter settled, Alistair fell to staring out of the window at the unkempt patch of garden, and to thinking (as he invariably did when not compelled to do otherwise) of Hyacinth. He would introduce her to the Dean. 'A colleague of mine from our Pentecostal brethren...' He savoured the look on the Dean's face.

Just then it occurred to him that he had not heard any splashing for a while. He hurried to the bathroom and knocked gingerly on the door. "Heather? Are you all right?" There was no reply. His blood ran cold. He tried the door. It was unlocked. He opened it, bracing himself against the sight of the pale body in the red water. But the bathroom was empty, and so was the rest of the flat. The girl had given him the slip.

What you have to do is watch the crowd – a hundred souls or more – moving around the cavernous stone hall. Quite soon it's possible to discern a pattern to the movement: they form lines in front of holes in the wall or else they interact with lit machines. No-one loiters. The logic of the pattern leads inexorably to a narrow gate presided over by a guardian in a glass booth. In order that the flood of humans may trickle through, each has to show the guardian a pass which he occasionally deigns to acknowledge with a slight nod. You've seen this operation before, long ago. It's coming back to you. There's another identical gateway, similarly manned, which allows passage in the opposite direction. This time, however, you have to hand over your pass in order to be released. The question presents itself: are those who are coming the same as those going? There is no discernible difference, no searing mark on their foreheads, for instance, to indicate that they have been down and re-ascended, transformed.

Heather had only the haziest recollection of the morning's events. She was too wholly absorbed in the present moment. She remembered clearly the later return to her flat, the planning of her campaign, the ritual purification needed to prepare herself for the ordeal that lay ahead. It would be appalling, she knew, but by the grace of the Saviour it would not perhaps last too long. After bathing, she put on a white shirt, red jacket, black trousers, flat shoes. Her feet hurt her, but it was a good sort of hurt, a reminder of the true path's necessary suffering. She put money in her pocket, almost laughing aloud at the absurd things humans lugged around with them. It only remained to give the evil one the slip. She waited breathlessly behind the bathroom door until she heard him moving about in the empty sitting room. Then she tip-toed down the corridor, eased open the front door and was away on the last leg of her quest.

You stand in line with the others, facing the wall. You watch how they push money through the hole and receive their passes in return. Your coin is moist from the sweat on your palm. When your time comes you perform the simple action, avoiding the eyes, if there are any, of the shadowy operator inside the wall. A yellow pass flips out in front of you. The first hurdle is triumphantly negotiated. You have been neither questioned nor rejected. It is easier to breathe. Although you can see no-one speaking at this initial stage of the journey, you can nevertheless hear the great hall re-echoing dully to the general sound of their passage. You look at no-one, nor they at you. For all the multitude present, this is a thing you undertake alone.

Her clothes felt tight and restrictive compared to the spacesuit the guardians had conferred on her when they retrieved her from the tower. They had been stern, under the impression that she had been about to harm herself; they had also been benign, feeding her and clothing her in the marvellous silvery suit which she now regretted leaving behind. It had taken her some time to work out, in silence, that although these guardians were agents of the Saviour, they were essentially ignorant of the larger scheme of things. Their purpose had been to bring home to her a single vital insight: *she was not ready to be raised up*.

It was a mistake to imagine that you could aspire through your own volition to the ranks of the twice-born. Only He who is on high can perform that miracle. It had been a wilful act of pride to climb the tower. However, the Saviour had been lenient. By placing her in the hands of his agents – guardians who were more or less automata – He had shown her the true path: *only by lowering herself could she rise*. This was the law, as beautiful and simple as the law of levers. Self-abasement led to self-exaltation. The way down was the way up. She had to take on the full weight of gravity, be ground down to dust, before her untrammelled spirit could soar into the empyrean aboard the holy Cube.

The guardians, fortunately, were willing to release her into the hands of someone they considered suitable. They didn't know you had to be alone. Cunningly she had given them the name and address of the churchman who, in due course, had arrived at the space station to take her back to her flat. She knew at once he was not to be trusted. Behind the mask of his smile and the bogus dog-collar she caught the unmistakable whiff of evil. It was another test, of course, which she had easily passed, for the evil ones are not always the most intelligent. Now, there's no turning back. You have to shuffle with others towards the narrow gateway, the threshold. It's no good regretting the daylight at the other end of the hall –

that's another world. There's light in here, of a sort – flat, yellowish, uniform. It casts no shadows. Here, you are your shadow, waiting to be processed, already released from the burden of identity. It's a strange feeling, enough to panic you, were it not for the crush of the others, especially as the gate is clogged and there's no alternative but to risk one of the steel passages, like traps, in which a bar magically swings open and shut to permit or prevent entry. You put your yellow pass into a slot, thus, and – yes! – the bar snaps back so that, if you're quick, you can nip through. You wait for the angry voice to ring out, but there's no sound except for the tramp of the feet of the crowd that carries you onwards.

Suddenly, the ground falls away before you in a smooth silvery stream. There's no time to go insane with fear – you have to take the plunge. You step into it. It holds, like a stiff metallic waterfall, carrying you down just as people parallel to you are being borne upwards by the same means. Their faces are blank, giving no clue as to what awaits below. Some of them seem familiar. They look like, of all people, the Children of the Sky. Perhaps there is no escape from them, as Murdo said. Perhaps they can get at you, even down here. A scream is not all that far away, and getting closer. You cling on for dear life to the moving rail at your side while the hard, stepped cascade slides down and – thank God – bears the blank-faced Children away. The danger fades; it is, dare you think it, almost exhilarating. Not as you'd imagined. It is not, for example, growing darker but, if anything, lighter; and, now, an eerie hollow music can be heard drifting up from the depths. As soon as the waterfall disappears underground, you jump on to the static floor. Ahead of you is a tunnel into which the music draws you. It consists of a mouth organ and a stringed instrument. Close to, it is less haunting – indeed, less melodious – than distance rendered it. The two youthful musicians are posted on one side of the tunnel, so you press yourself against the opposite wall to avoid having to hand over coins as one or two people are doing. They neither cease playing nor arrest you as you squeeze past. The strains of the music are gradually replaced by the single sound of drumming feet in the bare stone passage with the curved walls on which coloured hieroglyphs are scrawled. *Thatcher out, Kevin is a tosser, Shed Rules OK.* You strive to understand them. Who knows but that they are messages indispensable to the quest, written as aids by previous travellers on the same path? *Roz woz 'ere, Tracy loves Jason, Peace – or else, wogs go home, fuck.* The messages are indecipherable, belonging perhaps to some older civilisation, now lost.

Maeve sealed the envelope with a sense of finality. She propped it against the hall telephone where Alistair would be sure to find it, and then let herself out of the front door. The weather was dull. The early winds had dropped to a sluggish breeze. A grimy haze smeared the face of the sun. The piece of blue plastic in the fence flapped an indolent farewell. She never had removed it, but what did it matter now? She was worn out by the continual reliving of her abduction. She couldn't stop the images of the aliens and her painful operation from running through her head. They obsessed her. There were times when she thought that, if she did not somehow release them, her head would burst. The word 'psychosis' had come to mind. It had frightened her into action.

Her library books had been no help. Whenever she had been able to control her thoughts long enough to look at them, the accounts of UFOs and extraterrestrials had only fuelled her despair. None of the writers had been abducted. They simply quoted those who had. They calmly discussed nineteen-fifties reports of tall, blond extraterrestrials who delivered trite messages about world peace. They studied the 'evolution' of such benign 'Venusians' into the grotesque entities of recent sightings. These were frightening – animal-like and robotic. They came in a phantasmagoria of shapes and sizes, from huge, furry, clawed, headless creatures to small, silver-suited, four-fingered, faceless humanoids. No two encounters were the same. The books relentlessly documented a kind of mass insanity into which she had also been plunged. They said little or nothing of the havoc these sightings wrought in the lives of the hapless 'contactees'. All Maeve could think of – compulsively rubbing the tiny lump on her head – was that when *they* came again, they might come for good.

Last night's rain had fastened much of Acton's litter to the streets. Maeve paused to scrape a soggy carton off her shoe. The Tube station was in sight. She wanted to turn back and retrieve the letter she had left for Alistair. No matter how cheerful, even jokey, she had tried to make it sound, it would upset him beyond measure. The letter was a confession, a full account of the abduction.

She had no longer been able to shield him from the full extent of her madness. He would be forced to judge her as she had judged herself – as a case for treatment. She had not, however, mentioned her appointment with the psychotherapist in forty minutes' time. She could break it to him gently once her diagnosis had been confirmed. There wouldn't be any 'cure', of course, but at least she could not be accused of failing to seek one.

As long as the crowd is flowing smoothly forward, you can flow with it and ward off the fact that the roof of the tunnel is too close for comfort; that the air is warm and stale and used up; that retreat is impossible through the mass of bodies filling up the channel behind. It is only when, up ahead, a harsh chanting is heard, carried on a sudden sulphurous blast of wind, that the others falter, break step, either quickening their pace or pressing close to the walls. An excitation passes through them. Breath begins to come out in short bursts. The chant – half-sung, half bellowed – is deafening.

Around the corner there is turbulence at the confluence of three tunnels. A Bacchanalian rout of thirty or so young men is surging against the current, threatening panic and chaos. They wear uniforms of blue denim, striped scarves, heavy boots. Like some priestly caste they show no regard for the newer denizens of this underworld. They chant more loudly, clapping their hands above heads that are often half-animal. You hug the wall, craning your neck forward the better to watch their thrilling ritual procession. Two of them are kicking a shiny clattering object, identical to those from which others are drinking; another brushes you with his shoulder; a fourth leans against a wall and emits from his middle region a glittering stream of pure gold. The air bristles with danger; and yet you have the impression of a group mind, moving through the tunnel as a giant mole might move, ferociously but without personal will to harm. The ear-splitting cries sweep over you and recede into the distance.

So far, events have occurred with extreme rapidity, pulsing towards and away from you to the rhythm of your beating heart, your drumming brain. Now, things begin to slow. The crowd thins out as parts of it are filtered into side channels appropriate to their separate destinies. Your group is left to spill through a narrow opening and on to a long wide ledge, beyond which is a parallel trough with silver rails set into it. At both ends of the trough the shiny rails disappear into tunnels of the utmost blackness.

The sight of those gaping black mouths brings the first chill of foreboding. Now that there is no longer any movement among the crowd – not even a breath of wind to ease the congestion in the lungs – the surroundings themselves are compelled to move. Each time you catch sight of the tunnels' dark patches, they have crept a little closer. If you keep your eye on them they remain motionless; but it's not possible to watch them continuously because it reminds you that the time is coming when you'll have to broach that blackness – and this is not a thought to be easily endured. Also, the light is becoming more dim and the air more soupy and the other souls on the ledge more forlorn as they wait without hope for what can't be averted.

With vigorous arm movements you swim through the viscous atmosphere to the nearest traveller. His unnaturally blond hair is held in place by a curved strip of aluminium, on each end of which are balls of fuzzy material that clamp his ears to his head. A wire connects this headpiece to a compact box with something circulating inside it. Leaning nearer, you can hear a tinny whisper inside his head. Of course! The box contains a tape. It is recording the whispering thoughts which the head cannot contain. The blond hair nods in time to the thoughts; the lips move soundlessly. Now that you come to think of it, there are other thoughts at large in this strange place, a whispering conspiracy of thoughts, not all of them pleasant.

The twin mouths of the tunnels edge closer. The wall behind you slides forward, threatening to sweep you into the trough. The left-hand mouth is emitting a sound, a hollow exhalation; the rails begin to twitter. One of the faces in the crowd turns towards you. It is disguised but you see through it at once. It is the face of one of the Sky Children, surely, and it returns your look with hostility. The noise in the tunnel increases to a roar, signalling the imminence of some terrible presence, perhaps the Lord of this underworld. Your skin is cold and wet with sweat. All the faces turn; all are familiar yet strangely inhuman. They are dead faces, yet they move. The rails make a sound like a huge sheet of ice cracking. The dead people shuffle forward, closing in. It is quite clear what has happened: *an alien invasion has taken place*. The aliens have taken possession of people they have killed, people like the Sky Children who now have to kill you because you know their secret.

The Lord of the Underworld hurtles out of the blank tunnel mouth. He has come to transport you into eternal darkness where the aliens will perform their bloody operation. His head-splitting squeal drowns the sound of their slow footsteps. It is exactly the same as the scream which comes out of you – except that, in your case, there's no end to it.

Maeve was tired out by the twenty-minute walk to Acton Central. Her legs were like sacks of potatoes. The doctor's diagnosis of 'fluid retention' suggested that she was walking in the water-filled galoshes of her own swollen feet. The high airy ticket hall echoed dully with the indeterminate hubbub of a crowd. She was no longer afraid of seeing the psychologist. She just wished it was over. Feeling empty, merely resigned, it suited her to become a function of the transport system – there was a pleasure in its anonymity which enabled her, perhaps for the last time, to be taken for normal. She avoided the ticket machines which demanded actions and choices, and queued at the window instead. She looked with sadness at the ticket in her hand. As she turned towards the barrier, she regretted all the possibilities in the outside world which had been excluded by her acceptance of a single course of action.

She did not trust herself to negotiate the automatic barriers which snapped open like greyhound traps when the ticket was inserted in the slot. She wasn't nimble or interested enough. She joined the press of people who had likewise opted to pass through the narrow entrance next to the ticket inspector's box. She allowed herself to be funnelled through and carried by the crowd on to the slick new escalator. At the bottom, she was nearly mown down by a phalanx of drunken football fans – potential hooligans, if she was any judge – who burst out of the wrong tunnel, chanting and bawling and kicking empty lager cans in front of them. She stopped, dazed, as they flowed around her, their glazed eyes unseeing in their brutal heads.

Her fellow travellers regrouped and pressed on, not looking at each other, as if the hooligans had been a personal shame. As their coarse chanting receded, it was replaced by the sound of dreary guitar-playing and desultory harmonica. Maeve dimly recognised an old folk tune but declined to give money to its murderers. She hurried past them, eager now to be free of this place, despite whatever anguish awaited her at her journey's end. She paused at the convergence of three tunnels to ascertain which of them led to her platform. She found herself, depressingly, standing in a shallow pool of urine, some of which was still dripping down the graffiti-covered wall. *Shed rules OK*, the wall reminded her; and apparently it was so. Not, as Nanny would say, a particularly appetising prospect.

Passengers filled up the platform. There was not long to wait. The mouth of the tunnel gasped at the approach of the train. The rails twittered in anticipation. The crowd shuffled. A disturbance broke out further along the platform. Someone was in distress. Maeve wasn't surprised. Some wino or junkie or nutcase was always having a fit. She craned her neck discreetly and was able to make out the figure of a girl – a girl whom she recognised but couldn't for the moment place. Just her luck to know someone who was making a scene. With distaste she eased her way down the platform to where the girl had cleared a space among the stiff disconcerted travellers by walking rapidly round in tight circles.

The train roared like a dragon out of its tunnel. Its brakes squealed violently. The girl held out her arms feebly, but whether to ward it off or to embrace it, Maeve couldn't tell. She opened her mouth and screamed in unison with the train. The sheer terror in the sound as much as its volume rocked the crowd of passengers. Wearily, from the habit of duty, Maeve took the girl in her arms.

THIRTEEN

Alistair read the letter which Maeve had left him. He thought at first that it was a joke. When he saw that it wasn't, he wanted to cry. Aliens, eyes, operations, scars... It was simply insane. He would not think about it. He couldn't. Instead he mechanically opened the letter which had arrived by the second post:

Dear Mr Allingham,

Thank you for your letter. The Bishop and I look forward to staying in your home. In reply to your query, may I remind you that the Bishop's wife rarely accompanies him on official visits, and will not be with him on this occasion. She has been of great service to our cause over the years, but it is no secret, I think you will agree, that her efforts have been characterised more by enthusiasm than by effectiveness.

You need have no fears concerning accommodation. For a man such as Bishop Mwawa who has been, as you know, a 'guest' of the so-called Government, anything other than a bare cell may be deemed luxurious! However, since his incarceration, the Bishop's nights have frequently been troubled; and so it is necessary that our bedrooms adjoin. You will agree, I am sure, that his rest in these stressful times is of paramount importance. As to bathrooms, we would naturally each prefer our own (especially as the Bishop's hardships have left him with a certain fastidiousness about personal hygiene); but if this is not convenient, we can of course share one.

I am assuming that a room has been set aside, complete with telephone, fax machine, suitable desks/tables and so on, for the Bishop, myself and his chaplain to manage the business which necessarily pursues us around the world – an awful bore, but vital to the furtherance of the struggle, as I am sure you appreciate. (Please note our fax number at the head of the page. Let me have yours a.s.a.p. in order to facilitate communication.)

Since it is our intention to maintain a low profile on this visit, I am happy to say that we are able to keep the number of our security people down to three – the minimum, you will agree, to ensure the Bishop's peace of mind in these uncertain times. You need not concern yourself too much for their comfort, since all have a military background and may be presumed to be able to 'rough it'. At a pinch, for instance, two of them might share a room. Nor will they require any special diet, except that Enoch can eat no dairy products. Bwembwe is happy to subsist on his staple of mealies (maize). I will advise you of the Bishop's dietary requirements nearer the time.

Lastly, I have to say that there was considerable puzzlement here, not to say consternation, at the news that the wish of the nun from Chile, 'Mother Felicitas', to attend Christ in Action had been favourably received by your conference organisers. However admirable she may be in herself, her presence would be something of an affront to those who for years have carried on in conditions of emotional and physical suffering a struggle from which she has largely remained aloof. In addition, it is felt that she can only divert media attention away from the real issues and their upholders. We trust that you will lend your weight to whatever impulse there is within your country's Anglican communion to discourage this 'Felicitas' from making an appearance so untimely as to cause Bishop Mwawa, in spite of his deep loyalty and commitment, to reconsider the advisability of his own attendance.

Yours sincerely in Christ,
Barbara Mannheim (Mrs)

The letter induced just enough anxiety to enable Alistair to block out that other letter of Maeve's. He couldn't begin to think clearly how to resolve all the problems it raised. He hadn't imagined so many people. He was quite thrown. Could the 'chaplain' share a room with one of the 'security people' (were these bodyguards?). Was there time to install another bathroom and could he afford it? He would have to *improvise*: for a start he could make an arrangement with the local photocopying shop to use their fax machine. It might still be possible, providing Maeve co-operated (she'd have to sleep on the camp-bed in the attic, while he took the sofa downstairs). If she would just put her mind to the visit he was sure it could all be sorted out. There was nothing he could do about Mother Felicitas. He could almost hate her for being so thoughtless as to jeopardise the Bishop's visit. And yet, wasn't Mwawa taking her attendance rather too personally? Surely her presence was, in the final analysis, a good thing. No one would forget or overlook a conference to which she had lent her weight and reputation. The fact, too, that she was Roman Catholic would make the occasion really ecumenical for a change. Almost every sentence of the letter increased rather than diminished his unease. Having successfully forgotten all about Maeve's crazy claims, as if they were too far beyond the pale for his mind to absorb, he sighed with relief when he heard the front door being opened, and hurried to greet his wife.

"She must stay here," said Maeve. She was talking to Alistair in his study while Heather waited outside in the hallway.

"Absolutely not, Maeve. She must be taken to a doctor. Given proper treatment." Maeve's brief description of Heather's behaviour in the Tube had convinced Alistair that the girl's condition had deteriorated, if that were possible, from when he had last seen her.

"That's out of the question." Alistair looked into his wife's eyes. They were shining with a kind of triumph, a long way removed from their lacklustre heaviness of recent days; a long way from the eyes he loved of old. She was in a state of high excitement which frightened him. He hardly knew her. He held up the letter she had left him.

"Maeve, Maeve. What is all this? These terrible things you've been seeing... They're not true, Maeve. None of it is. It can't be. It's like some awful nightmare. It's..." He didn't trust himself to go on. It had been bad enough pursuing the crazed girl, running to the tower to see if she had climbed it again, wondering if he should call the police again, deciding to wait for Maeve, finding the vile letter. And now here was Maeve exultantly demanding that he perpetuate the insanity, bring it into his house.

"It's what happened to me, Alistair. I didn't want to tell you, but I had to, in the end. You must see that. Of course you think I'm going doolally – I did myself. But I'm not. You see, *Heather saw it as well.*"

As soon as Heather had said to her, 'You're from the Cube, aren't you? I knew the Saviour wouldn't desert me,' Maeve had been transformed with the force of a revelation. Her heart began to pump her sluggish blood through her clogged arteries at an exhilarating rate. Her head cleared; the clouds of oppression lifted. She wasn't doolally – this girl had seen it too! She had embraced Heather out of pure relief and joy, thanking Providence for having thrown the girl into her path.

"She's not at all well," said Alistair. "She was about to throw herself off the clock tower when the police intervened."

"Nonsense."

"It's not nonsense. She's in a dangerous state. I'm going to call the doctor. This sort of thing isn't in our province."

"I sometimes wonder what is in our province," Maeve retorted. "What can a doctor do? Sedate her? Tell her not to imagine things? Of course she's in a volatile state. If she has been through anything like my own experience, it's a wonder she's not barking. I suppose I need a doctor, too?"

"You know that's not what I meant. Heather might harm herself. You must see that. We're out of our depth here. We need professional help."

"Oh, Alistair. There *aren't* any professionals for what ails us." The fateful pronoun – 'us' – silenced them. Somehow they had become divided into opposite camps: Alistair versus Maeve and Heather, the sane and the reverse. They looked at each other, both aghast at how remote from each other they had grown, like two people shouting from different mountains. Maeve made a last plea.

"Help me, Alistair. Let her stay here until we can sort it all out. Please."

"We don't know how long that might take."

"What does it *matter*?"

"She can't stay here with Bishop Mwawa coming. Had you forgotten?"

"The Bishop doesn't need our help. Heather does."

"Believe me, Maeve – we can't help her. She needs treatment." He briefly consulted his address book and lifted the telephone receiver.

Heather marched into the room. "Maeve? Let's get started. The Saviour's waiting. What are the orders? Don't go near *him*" – she pointed at Alistair with a grimace – "He's an agent of Lucifer. You can smell it. But don't be afraid, Maeve, because perfect love casteth out fear."

"You see?" said Alistair to his wife. He began dialling.

"Come along, Heather," said Maeve.

Appalled at having driven Maeve away, Alistair did not finish calling the doctor. He stood for a while, breathing heavily, his hand clamped to the telephone. His impulse was to pursue his wife, but he knew that any further conversation at this stage would only make things worse. At last, in order to calm himself, he went out and rambled aimlessly down the High Street as far as the market.

"Is it yourself, Misther Allingham?" said Bernadette O'Rourke, exaggerating her brogue in order to amuse him.

"Top o' the afternoon," Alistair replied dutifully.

"What is it you're after? I've some grand broccoli." She regretted her words at once. The broccoli was all stalk; she had doubted whether it would go. She knew the vicar would not be able to resist any recommendation of hers. But, then again, it was probably good enough for the likes of him who, decent man though he was, was not one to notice what he was putting in his mouth.

"Well, since you recommend it, I'll have half a kilo, please. Also, I'll shortly be needing a supply of maize – corn on the cob – for a foreign visitor."

"Nothing easier. Just let me know a day in advance. Here y'are – a pound of broccoli. Annything else?"

"Two grapefruit and two peaches, I think. None of your fruit's South African, I hope?"

"Ah, not at all. And how's the poor girl that was up on the tower?"

"You know about her?"

"Wasn't it me who 'phoned the police? And I saw you taking her off down the street in a taxi."

"She's a bit poorly, I'm afraid."

"I knew it. I knew she was heading for trouble as soon as she came prancing along like a circus horse and started on about a thing that was up in the sky."

"Yes, I'm afraid she might be suffering from delusions."

"Ah God, she is not. Didn't I see the exact same thing myself? A great heavy thing, like a huge lump of steel sugar, and it just sitting there beyond the tower without the benefit of wings."

'Oh Jesus,' thought Alistair. 'Is there no end to this nightmare?' He said:

"You didn't by any chance see any... anybody inside it?"

"What? Like fallen angels, d'you mean? I did not." She handed him the fruit and took his money. "But I think God might go in for high strangeness just to keep us guessing. It was a class of thing you'd never get to the bottom of. It was more to be wondered at than enquired into." Mrs O'Rourke handed him his change. "And I know what you mean about the South African fruit. I don't like the idea of those black hands picking it myself."

"What are the orders?" asked Heather for the umpteenth time. Maeve looked into her white face. Blue veins showed their delicate tracery under the transparent skin. Dark rings, like bruises, circled her eyes in which the pupils were abnormally large.

"We rest," said Maeve. "Those are the orders."

"Rest. Right." But still she rattled to and fro between the walls of her all-but-empty sitting room like a caged animal, checking her step only to issue staccato bulletins.

"There's no time left. The world'll go smash. The Saviour's waiting. We've got to get up there. Got to become One. What's the plan, Maeve? What are the orders?"

While Maeve was in the kitchenette, scrambling eggs which she had had the presence of mind to bring from her own fridge, she kept one eye on her erratic charge. The strain was already telling.

"First of all we eat. To keep our strength up."

"Eat. *Strength*. Right," repeated Heather as if Maeve had uttered a great truth.

"Then we rest. Now tell me, Heather, where did you see the cube? Is the Saviour connected with it?"

"You can see it whenever you want. There! Up there by the clock tower!" Her eyes were unnaturally bright but unfocussed as she seemed to re-live her experience. "There's a flash! And another. His eye looks right into you. Everything is changed... everything's connected by golden threads. Beautiful. You don't need eyes to see – you see with your heart. *You know*. You saw it too."

"I didn't see it flash."

"Yes, yes. You saw it. The Saviour's invisible at first, but then you look harder and he's moving inside. He's in the Cube, and the Cube and he are One. And they light up the world."

Since Heather required it, Maeve ordered her to eat the scrambled eggs and listened attentively as the girl elaborated, between mouthfuls, on her experience of the cube and the Saviour. Although it was an experience in which, apart from the beginning, Maeve had not participated, she nevertheless felt attuned to it. Every disjointed sentence of Heather's produced a corresponding chime in her own mind. There was no doubt that she had missed out on a revelation, all the more stupendous for being virtually inexpressible to outsiders. Even as she struggled to piece together Heather's account, she was conscious of receiving something essential only at second-hand.

"It was different for me," she said sadly. "I can't tell you how much I regret not responding properly to it. Somehow I distorted it into a nightmare. I was snatched up, you see –"

"You weren't *looking* at it correctly," Heather interrupted. "Maybe you didn't see it at all. You probably imagined it, or else you saw an illusion. Do you suffer from hallucinations at all? If you'd seen the real thing you couldn't be in any doubt. The Cube grants the gift of vision. But you must know this really. After all, the Saviour sent you to me in that horrible underworld."

Maeve had also been struck by this coincidence. She rather wondered whether the fact of having admitted to a kind of madness in herself – enough to seek therapy – had opened a door on to Heather's world and enabled them to attract each other, as like attracts like. If only she had admitted it earlier – admitted, in effect, the full meaning of the cube instead of trying to explain it away. As it was, she had to agree with Heather (though not perhaps in the same way) that she had perverted some potential truth with muddle and meaninglessness and horror – that, in short, she had been deluded.

Heather talked on, fitfully, feverishly, long into the long summer evening. As the light faded on the air, Maeve was carried farther and farther away from understanding the content of the girl's incoherent story, yet nearer and nearer to grasping its vital, exalted mood. Drawing deeply on her store of patience, attention and goodwill, Maeve was imperceptibly drawn, as the shadows lengthened across the floor, into Heather's heightened and transformed reality.

At the same time, it was clear that Heather's discourse was suffering from her extreme fatigue. Thus, as soon as she had talked herself close to a standstill, Maeve put her to bed with a hot cup of Horlicks and instructions to sleep for a long time. She was calm now and drowsily grateful to Maeve, whom she saw as her benefactor. There was no sign at all, as Alistair had claimed, that she was in any way a danger to herself. Nevertheless, remembering how Heather had stretched out her arms to the roaring Tube train, Maeve left the bedroom door ajar and resolved to be vigilant. Then she settled herself as best she could among the variety of cushions on the sitting-room floor and tried to bring her hectic thoughts to heel.

Outside, the ragged little garden was in darkness. On its wall a fox was silhouetted, making its way to next door's dustbins. The last of the sky's delicate green light presaged a fine day tomorrow. As she caught sight of the evening star, Maeve understood with a kind of wonder that Heather's story – indeed her own, come to that – was as amazing as some ancient legend. It was as if their mundane lives had been shattered by the intrusion, in all its incandescent beauty and terror, of some myth – a myth that, one way or another, had on the instant seized them both.

In Heather's case it was obviously the high and noble myth of the redeeming Hero. Small wonder then if she seemed a little erratic, a bit unbalanced. Who wouldn't be under the circumstances? Those who had directly encountered sacred reality always appeared, like the prophets of old – like her old friend William Blake – a little mad to ordinary mortals. Perhaps she would also have been given a revelation if she had shown more of Heather's courage and humility, accepting the cube rather than fearing it. If Heather's revelation resembled delusion, it was because the world was deluded, not she; the world, not she, was mad.

Maeve's reflections were disturbed by a low whimpering sound from the bedroom. For a second she imagined that some wild animal had broken into the flat. She leapt to her feet and hurried next door. Heather was sitting up stiffly in bed. Her eyes swivelled in their sockets and she was breathing very fast. Her hands were held out in front of her; their fingers were splayed and rigid with what Maeve recognised as the first signs of hyperventilation. Worst of all, she was making a mewling sound of pure fear.

"What is it, Heather? There's no need to be afraid." The girl beckoned her over violently and put her mouth close to Maeve's ear.

"I think *they're here*," she hissed. "They come under cover of dark. They'll do terrible things to me. I know too much."

"Who's here?" asked Maeve, looking anxiously around. She switched on the bedside lamp. "You see? There's no one here."

"No." Heather quickly switched the light off again. "No light. It attracts them like moths. They're all around... outside... waiting."

"You're imagining things, dear," said Maeve uncertainly. "You're quite safe. You must get some sleep."

"Don't you know anything, Maeve? They come for you if you sleep. You have to be on your guard all the time."

"*Who* comes?" said Maeve, fearing from her own experience that she knew the answer already. She wasn't expecting Heather's reply:

"The Sky Children. Murdo especially. They're in the power of the Guardians. You won't believe this, but they're not human. They may look like us but they've been taken over. I saw them, down there, just before you came, when the tunnels were about to take you away into eternal darkness. *Listen*. Can you hear them?"

Maeve was alarmed. She strained her ears. She heard nothing at first, but the longer she listened the more it seemed that, behind the quietness, there might be the faint sound of a footfall outside on the street and the palpable silence of someone very near, holding their breath. She ran to the front door, checked the lock and put on the chain. Then she made sure that all the windows were secure, drawing the curtains quickly across without looking out, for fear of what might be pressed against the glass. All the time she could hear Heather's terrified sobbing.

Alistair had been profoundly shaken by Mrs O'Rourke's casual acceptance of the cube. Had everyone seen it except him? He wandered around the house, empty and unwelcoming without Maeve. He hoped she was all right. Perhaps he had been too hasty; perhaps she could help that loony girl. Alistair didn't know. With words like 'fallen angels' and 'high strangeness' ringing in his head, he wasn't sure of anything any more. But even worse was that he and Maeve had become so muddled that they were not on the same side any more. He should have paid more attention to her – and to her story, however wild. If he didn't do something drastic, he would lose her. But what?

He wandered restlessly out into the garden. The sun was setting behind rooftops; the sky was eggshell blue behind small ragged clouds. The flower-beds were looking unkempt; the grass needed mowing. He ought to do it now. There was so much to do before Mwawa's visit. But even as he reluctantly approached the shed at the end of the garden where the mower was kept, he noticed a large circular patch of discoloured grass which corresponded to the scorch mark he had seen on the morning of Maeve's... abduction, she had called it. For God's sake. The cube had changed shape, she said. Was she asking him to believe that he was looking at the mark left by the landing of an alien spaceship? Was she mad? No, Maeve wasn't mad. He had to cling to that. And she was asking him only to believe in the reality of her experience regardless of what its nature might be.

Alistair returned to his study, sat at his desk and took out pen and paper. He already knew what Maeve's aliens reminded him of. He was simply putting off the moment of writing the word down because then they would be out in the open, out of control. The word 'Christ' rose like a counterbalance in his mind. He was ashamed, in these absurd circumstances, to call on Jesus – it seemed too extreme – but he tried in any case to summon up His image. The vague robed Teacher, the defeated corpse on its cross, were less vivid than Maeve's creatures. His faith, it seemed, had grown too feeble to repel them. With a sense of slipping down into darkness, he wrote the word: *demons?*

He switched on his desk lamp. What was he suggesting – that demons existed, that Heather was possessed, that Maeve was about to be? Was there, in fact, any adequate explanation of demons? Psychiatry might deny or renounce them, but what did that amount to? Who were the experts? The real experts, he remembered, almost with a laugh, were upstairs in his attic. They had moved from house to house with him, most of them still in tea-chests, some hastily stowed away on remote shelves.

Alistair climbed the stairs to the attic where the books of his university days were stored. Out they all came – the Kabbalists and Gnostics, the angelologists and the Hermetic philosophers and, above all, his favourite Neoplatonists. As he leafed through the books, they called out a nostalgia, like sweet dread, for the carefree speculations of his student life. But they evoked, too, his brush with evil when he had woken, paralysed, at dead of night in his perverted room with that frightful Double twisting its preposterous head towards him.

The demons in his books were really the *daimones* of ancient Greece – daimons, like Eros, who mediated between men and gods. Socrates possessed or was possessed by one, like a kind of genius. They were strange beings, shape-shifters, who not only appeared as people but also as luminosities that moved with extreme speed and elusiveness. Napoleon's daimon, for instance, sometimes took the shape of a shining sphere he called his 'star', and sometimes visited him as a dwarf clothed in red who warned him.

So the daimons seemed to be both benign guides and frightening harbingers. Christianity had polarised them into angels and demons, but in reality they were always paradoxical: most extraordinarily, they were neither completely spiritual beings nor altogether material, but both, as if they had 'subtle bodies' such as the soul was said to possess.

Every book Alistair opened seemed to release small absconding shapes into the ill-lit attic whose air grew thick with their expanding presence. He became uneasy, seeming to see shadows move out of the corner of his eye. Jesus the Christ, the Anointed One, he reminded himself sternly, was the sole mediator between mankind and the true God. His Incarnation – the insertion of myth into history – stood once and for all as the means by which you were reconciled to God. Holding fast to that thought, he shut up the books and headed for bed. His anxiety had become, if anything, more not less acute after his foray into the past. He missed Maeve. It was madness to allow one's mind to run on mythical daimons. If one didn't cling to the eternal truth of Jesus as Saviour, who alone made relations with God possible, one would be drowned in a black tide of turbulent spirits.

Maeve held the distraught girl in her arms. In an effort to distract her, she said:

"Tell me about the 'sky children', Heather. Who are they?" The girl did not reply at once. She seemed to be trying to watch all four walls at once. "Are they by any chance small people, with big black eyes?" coaxed Maeve.

"Sssh. They're out there," said Heather. Then, in an urgent whisper, "Don't be *silly*, Maeve. I told you. They look like anybody. They're instruments of the Guardians, who are gradually taking them over. Hermione's already gone over. She told us so. Murdo's next. You think at first that Hermione's the leader because she channels their will down to Earth. But then you see that Murdo's behind it. He gives off cosmic energy, like poison gas. They're bringing the world to an end. They wanted me to help but I escaped. But there's no escape. Murdo was right..."

Maeve eased the girl into a lying position and stretched out beside her with both arms around her trembling shoulders. If only they could sink into blissful blessed sleep... But the night wore on, and, while Heather seemed calmer at times, even falling silent for long periods, Maeve could tell by the tension in her body that she was still awake. Just when Maeve decided that her fears were ill-founded, a shadow would pass in front of the streetlight whose dim beam seeped through the crack in the curtains. Then she would be gripped all over again by doubt and suspicion. But it was her own terror which prevented her from taking any decisive action: what if they – the black-eyed aliens – came back for her tonight? It was not beyond their power to walk through walls, to waft her up once again into that unspeakable laboratory, to inflict more pain, and worse, on her helpless paralysed flesh. Her scalp crawled at the thought, and she held Heather more closely, knowing how real fear could be, how useless to pretend that there existed any power on Earth that could banish it. Heather began to shake with sobs again.

Suddenly the streetlight went out. Its orange glow was superseded by the cold dawn. Heather caught her breath.

"I think he's outside the front door," she whispered, clutching at Maeve's arm.

"Who, dear?"

"Raphael. You think he's an angel but he's not – he's the worst of the lot. The last time they came he and Murdo pretended not to know each other, but all the time... I think he may come alone. I can't be sure. But he works for Lucifer. He told me. I thought he was taking me to the Saviour, but instead –" She broke off. Her sobs were dry now, simply causing her body to heave. Maeve wondered how long this fear could go on, and where it would lead. "He took me up to a poky little room," Heather went on. "There was a smell of sour milk. He took my clothes off, laid me down, tried to probe me..." Maeve's blood ran cold.

"In your head?" she asked urgently. "Did he probe your head?"

"No, no. Oh, it was horrible. But we mustn't think about him, must we. He knows you're thinking about him, he sees your thoughts, he homes in on you. Maeve, we have to get away from here. What are we waiting for? I only just escaped him. I've been blessed so far, but for how long? I've got away from them all. I got away from that man in the taxi who was dressed as a vicar."

"That was my husband, Heather. Alistair. He's a good man."

"No, no. He smiles and all the time he's plotting. I saw him down there with the others."

"Alistair? In the Tube?"

"Yes. Evil, *evil*."

Maeve remembered Alistair's set face, the way he picked up the telephone receiver. What 'doctor' was he going to call? Perhaps he had understood all along what had happened to both her and Heather. He was on their side, part of it all. They had *got to him first* and now, of course, he had to help suppress whatever Heather knew. She, his own wife, would be next. He would have her committed, too, in order to preserve the secret of the invading aliens.

For a moment Maeve trembled on the brink of an abyss. Then she sprang up and threw open the curtains. In a sudden rush she realised how close to insanity she had come. The street was empty and innocent under a pale sky. She breathed deeply, savouring this moment of great serenity. The night's madness fell away from her.

"There's nobody out there, Heather. Nobody threatening you. There never was. Look. It's a lovely day. Get up and dress while I make some coffee. It was all a bad dream, all in your –" She stopped herself. What was she saying? God only knew what was in Heather's mind. The girl was deluded. But she *had* seen the cube; and her revelation of Oneness, her quest for her Saviour – they were, surely, in some important sense, *true*. What had gone wrong?

Perhaps her myth, like all myths, was true but not literally so – just as the spiritual impulse to ascend to the Saviour was real but not to be confused with a literal ascent, such as climbing a mountain or clock tower. The cube and its promise of salvation had seized Heather so violently that she had been overpowered, usurped, compelled to act out what should have stayed a story. A story she could see the world through, giving it meaning, rather than a story that had become the world, too full of meaning. In this condition, revelation and delusion spoke to Heather in the same voice.

Alistair put on the blue brushed-cotton pyjamas Maeve had given him for his birthday and crept into the cold bed. There had been no point in waiting up any longer. Maeve was not coming home that night. He closed his eyes and tried to compose his mind for prayer. However, the harder he tried the less he was able to concentrate either on the words he repeated to himself, or on devotional images. They dissolved into Maeve's beastly little aliens, springing up behind his closed lids all the more vividly for having been only sketchily described by his wife. Of its own accord, his imagination fleshed out the vestigial features of their mask-like faces into horrible goblin visages. He squeezed his eyes as if to shut them out – only to find that they had changed into the ludicrous stereotyped devils of primitive Christianity: goat-footed satyrs with huge erect phalluses, slant-eyed succubi, horned demons.

As he tossed irritably under the strangling bed clothes, Alistair regretted opening those old books, like wounds. He was afraid of where his thoughts were leading him. He tried to reassure himself that the daimons no longer existed. He turned over on to his back and, with open aching eyes, stared at the intricate pattern the curtains cast on the ceiling by the streetlights outside. He saw there the cowled, incense-burning, exorcising armies of Christendom marching across medieval Europe, driving before them the pagan daimons. He saw the dryads creeping back into their trees, the trolls into their caves, the nixies into their streams. Satyrs and fauns slipped away into rocky places. He heard the knocking of kobolds peter out in the mountains and the hunting horns of Fairy fade beneath the hard ground. All the fabulous tribes of myth were exiled into the wilderness of superstition, fantasy and folklore. The trouble was, how could Christianity do away with them altogether when, as all the authorities agreed, the daimons were immortal?

As the dawn light began to make the curtains transparent, dissipating the patterns on the ceiling, Alistair fell at last into a fitful sleep, a prayer still-born on his lips – not that he would dream sweetly, but that he wouldn't dream at all.

FOURTEEN

St Joseph's psychiatric unit was a prefabricated hut at the far end of the hospital car park. Since Heather was passing through one of her new catatonic phases, staring blankly at the floor, Maeve was able to take her eyes off the girl for a moment and take in her surroundings. The waiting-room was painted in the kind of acidic green which had disappeared from the rest of civilisation nearly thirty years ago. The armchairs were upholstered in another such colour, a sickly orange which failed to impart the intended cheerfulness. The clothes of the mad people were also from a bygone era: the fat man with downy hair on his face wore beige flared trousers and a round-necked nylon cardigan. The clockwork woman wore a shapeless grey hat and a baggy dress with a faded zigzag pattern. Their two minders, both middle-aged women, wore predominantly brown clothes, perhaps out of an instinctive desire to camouflage themselves.

It was three o'clock in the afternoon. The day, mostly spent waiting, seemed to have gone on forever. Six hours before, Maeve had reluctantly telephoned Heather's doctor. The girl's mood swings had become so violent that Maeve had grown frightened. Heather seemed to have become trapped in a vicious spiral which led from aggression to fear to withdrawal, and back again, threatening to bear her beyond reach, into some nightmarish solipsism where she could only spin incoherently on her own axis.

In order to occupy the time between 'phoning and the appointment at ten-thirty, Maeve had taken Heather on the bus, hoping that some form of movement would calm her down. It had been a mistake. Heather demanded to see everyone's ticket. Some had complied, others had taken umbrage. "I'm not showing my bleeding ticket to a snotty kid," one belligerent old lady said. "You'll never finish the journey then," Heather predicted, with a superior smile. It was exactly this sort of scene, with the threat of worse to come, that Maeve could not abide. With her nerves already shredded by lack of sleep and the need for constant vigilance, she was close to the end of her tether. She had to issue sharp orders to Heather at increasingly frequent intervals simply to contain her worst excesses. She had closed her eyes, just for a moment, mindlessly repeating a prayer for deliverance. When she re-opened them Heather was leaning over the seat in front and clasping the hands of a surprised toddler whose mother had as yet noticed nothing. Tears were streaming out of the girl's tragic Pre-Raphaelite eyes as she gazed meaningfully into the child's face. Maeve quickly disentangled her fingers. "A couple of crazies," a rough-looking youth had remarked to his neighbour. Maeve was stung by the suggestion. She pulled out her compact and, looking at her reflection, confirmed the truth of the young man's words: a mad woman with dark circles around her eyes and hair straying all round her face in idiot wisps stared wildly back at her. "La-di-da," she practised under her breath. "Pooh-pooh." Under Heather's contagious sway she had slipped farther down than she thought.

It was perhaps no more than she deserved. She was, after all, betraying the girl with whom she had sworn to keep faith. She had established that Heather was on some sort of Quest; that she was caught up in some cosmic drama, living out a myth which, although crazy, was also profound. What right had Maeve to interfere with this sacred task? 'I'm protecting her from herself,' Maeve thought. But her words cut no ice. More likely, she had simply lost her nerve and taken it upon herself to prevent Heather from fulfilling the myth in which, with a life of its own, Maeve too was implicated. It wasn't madness to live out a myth because madness – Panic gods and Furies and Dionysian frenzies – was inherent in myth itself. No matter how painful, even fatal, the transformation was, Maeve wondered if she had the right to curtail its operation on, and within, Heather's soul. Might it not be as sacrilegious as ringing down the curtain on the madness of King Lear at the end of Act Three?

For a few seconds Maeve had dropped into a deep sleep and dreamed of a vast black sky in which something infinitesimally small was hurtling towards her at an astonishing speed. She jerked awake. Heather was looking at her curiously yet trustingly, putting her in mind of a dog destined to be put down at the vet's. She had not hidden from Heather that they were seeking medical help; and, indeed, her chief support in the enterprise, after all the heart-searching, lay in the fact that some part of the girl was collaborating with her. Some part of Heather was sick to death of the struggle, wished only to take 'orders' and to be done with the whole exhausting business. Both of them were pretending that the wearisome engagement with the medical world was part of the quest for ultimate enlightenment; and (since medicine too was not excluded from myth) who knew but that there wasn't a particle of truth in the pretence?

The clockwork woman was heading for the door. Her minder intervened by grasping one arm which was moving, as if mechanically, up and down in time to the stiff motion of her legs, and steered her towards the wall. When she could progress no further she did an about-face and walked jerkily as far as the opposite wall, where she repeated the compulsive sequence. Neither of the two minders acknowledged Maeve's presence. There was no exchange of sympathetic smiles, no complicity. They kept their heads down. Here, they came to beg for the magical pills that kept what was left of their loved ones from stepping off the edge of the world. The despair in their faces bore witness to the fact that love was not enough. No longer recognizing the person they had once known, they supported a simulacrum on which they in turn depended for justification of their own wrecked lives. Maeve sensed that this waiting-room was very far down, the last stop before you were swallowed by the abyss.

If this room was the last station of the Cross, the doctor's waiting-room that morning had been the first. Then she had had to explain to Heather over and over again that they were doing waiting. Heather would agree, sit quietly for a minute and then set off purposefully for the door. Every time she had to be restrained, returned to her seat, issued repeat orders. But then she would cower from other patients in whom she divined evil, or, worse still, address those whom she imagined to be friendly:

"You're so ugly," she said to one unfortunate woman. "No wonder you can't get a man to sleep with you." The woman's brimming eyes may have confirmed Heather's diagnosis. "What are you looking at?" she would ask another. "Just fuck off, will you?"

"She has been under a lot of stress," Maeve had begun by apologising. Every time another person emerged from Dr Purcell's surgery she prayed that they would be called next, before Heather's behaviour transcended the bounds of the possible. But, every time, the summons failed to come and the bounds became more stretched. Even Nanny Bryce would have been at a loss.

Maeve ceased to make excuses for Heather. She could scarcely be bothered to control her. She merely brazened out the reproachful stares of the other patients. It was, she discovered, quite different being the cause of a 'scene' rather than its recipient. Not as bad, in a way, once you were beyond embarrassment.

"Shut up and sit down, Heather," she said mildly, and stared defiantly around her.

Their turn had come at last, nearly two hours after the appointed time. Unfortunately the moment coincided with Heather's decision not to speak at all. Despite Dr Purcell's most reassuring manner she just sat there, with a spiritual expression on her face and her eyes full of tears. It was left to Maeve to tell him everything she had been able to piece together during the long night. She did not mention the cube.

"And how do you feel now, Heather?" the doctor persisted in asking. She seemed to deliberate, and then pointed a hieratic finger towards the ceiling. "If you won't speak to me, perhaps you could write down today's date. Will you do that for me?" Heather looked at Maeve and raised her eyes to heaven.

"She knows what day it is, doctor. She's not mentally retarded." Tiredness had made Maeve a bit short. Dr Purcell compressed his lips. "There is a procedure," he said.

"I see. Well, for God's sake stop playing the fool and write down the date, Heather." The girl wrote down the day's date, the month, the year, adding, after a pause, AD.

"Now, tell me, Heather," said the doctor earnestly, "do you hear any voices?" She nodded slowly and gravely. Dr Purcell leaned forward tensely, a glint in his eye. "Can you hear them now?" Another nod. "Where are they coming from Heather? This is very important. You must try to tell me."

There was a long pause. Then, with a slow artistic hand gesture, she pointed towards the door. There was a hush in the room. From beyond the door a woman's voice could be heard complaining: "I've never had to bloody wait this long before... "

"I see," said Dr Purcell. The remainder of the interview was brief and business-like. He told Maeve what she already knew

– that her charge was in a distressed state, with the danger of a psychosis developing.

"I'll look after her," Maeve assured him. "I'm certain that if she could just sleep it would be half the battle. She's worn out. You could give me some sleeping pills and I'll make sure she takes the right amount and so on."

But no. It was more serious than that, the doctor claimed. He overruled Maeve's pleading. He instructed her to take his letter at once, along with Heather, to the psychiatric out-patients' unit at St Joseph's.

"Take her at once," Heather repeated.

"I see you've decided to talk now."

"Not necessarily." And, to Maeve, "I think we're wasting time here."

A taxi had taken them to the hospital, a huge sprawling complex off a dual carriageway in the middle, it seemed, of nowhere. Much of it was built of dirty concrete and glass; some of it was tall Victorian blocks with barred windows. They had found the psychiatric unit. They had, inevitably, waited.

"Waiting," said the fat man suddenly and loudly, "it makes you fat. They're always saying I'm too fat, but it's waiting that does it. That and the pills. The red ones, not the green ones. It's not my fault I'm fat."

"You're not fat," said Heather unexpectedly. "You only think you are." Any further exchange was forestalled by the receptionist, who ushered the two women into the next room. The psychiatrist and the psychiatric social worker they met there had no trouble in deciding that Heather should be admitted to the hospital at once. Creighton Ward was telephoned, and Maeve given directions.

Maeve did not protest. Nor did she offer to look after Heather this time. Even she had to concede that it was more than a matter of sleeping pills. Sensing perhaps her air of gloom, Heather came over to her and, kneeling down, rested her head in the older woman's lap. All the fight had gone out of her. She began to cry softly.

"Someone very near here is going to be shut up and never let out," she said in a tiny muffled voice. Dizzy with tiredness and anxiety, Maeve thought for a moment that the girl was referring to her, rather than to her own remote self. She stroked Heather's tangled hair.

"No one's going to be shut up forever," she said. "We're both going to have a rest, that's all. I think it's what our Saviour wants."

Alistair was almost surprised to find himself ringing the doorbell of number twenty-three again. He knew perfectly well that it was sensible to avoid Hyacinth, at least until he was able to see her in proportion. But the thought of her filled him with such excitement that he simply had to see her – to feast his eyes on that wonderful skin, to hear her voice, to stand in that tangible aura of vitality and warmth. Their previous meeting had receded like a dream and blended in his mind with the angelic vision of her amidst the golden clouds. The recollection, acting like a counterweight to Maeve's ugly experience, made him feel less fraught.

Waiting for the door to open, he keenly anticipated the sympathy and practical wisdom she would bring to bear on his difficulties. Last night's diabolical images receded; sane daylight concerns pressed in on him again. He still had high hopes that she would consent to an informal meeting with Bishop Mwawa. How could he deny her the chance to voice her grievances to a religious leader of international influence? No longer would she have to remain silent about the subtle violation, on a daily basis, of basic human rights.

More immediately, Hyacinth could be relied on to advise him about Maeve's predicament, which had become his own. He was more than half-way to believing the whole frightful business. It haunted him, gnawed at him, destroying his concentration on the Bishop's visit. But if anyone was an expert on the supernatural, it was Hyacinth. Wasn't she at home with the 'Holy Ghost'? Didn't she interpret its messages? Maeve's chaotic experience was paltry by comparison. Hyacinth would let light and air in on the shadowy problem. Together they would reclaim Maeve and then all three would set about rehabilitating Acton. He hardly dared think it, but it was not impossible that his parish could become a model for the regeneration of inner city areas, even – why not? – the whole of London.

Hyacinth opened the door and smiled tightly. The sight of her was invigorating. Alistair's mood grew even more buoyant.

"I'm sorry I haven't called again before now," he said. "The fact is, I've been rather up to my neck in it." Hyacinth raised her eyebrows, but said nothing. He followed her into the sitting room. Disappointingly – for he had hoped to talk quietly with her over a cup of tea – she resumed her place behind the sewing machine and began to run some gauzy material through it. He sat down at a respectful distance.

"Still keeping busy, I see!" She nodded. "I was in the neighbourhood, so I thought I'd just pop in. I wanted to have a word about... about my wife." He had not meant to say that. He had planned to touch lightly on the subject at the end, when their intimacy was on a firmer footing. He was taken aback, too, by the crack in his voice on the word 'wife'. He had to take hold of himself. However, now that he had started, he might as well continue. Hyacinth's eyes seemed to glitter as she briefly looked across at him, but he couldn't meet them if he was to order his thoughts. "Maeve saw an extraordinary thing in the sky not long ago. A sort of shining cube. There's no easy explanation for it. I've come to believe that it was actually there. I'm sure now that she wasn't simply 'seeing things.'" The sewing-machine stuttered once or twice and then ran smoothly on. "I think I could cope – I think we both could – if the story ended there. Unfortunately it doesn't. Her strange sighting was followed by memories of an unpleasant kind. She talks of being... abducted by wicked little men with long black eyes..." Hearing himself speak like that made it difficult for Alistair to go on. "I don't expect you to believe me" – he gave an unconvincing laugh – "and I wouldn't mention it if I weren't worried sick." The sewing-machine stopped.

"I can very well believe you, Mr Allingham. Please don't say any more."

"But I must. I'm sure you'll be able to suggest –"

"No more. Please. The things you speak of are satanic things."

"That's putting it rather strongly, don't you think? I mean –" Hyacinth raised an adamant hand.

"Satanic. The kind of thing you wish to describe is to be expected in the last days – signs, portents and similar, as it is written in the Bible. As you should know, vicar."

"You don't seriously mean to say –"

"I am always serious. I do not know why you come here with your satanic tales. At first you come with your politics and your worldly ambitions and now this. My cheeks blush for you. A man of God has no business with temporal matters, let alone devilish things. He should be concerned with the eternal and the divine. You say: 'What about human rights?' I say we have no rights before God. We have only duties – the duty of each soul in the eyes of God. You say: 'Politics are a necessary thing.' I say that politics are a necessary evil. Jesus Christ was not political. He did not call us to a kingdom in this world but a Kingdom not of this world. There can be no happiness in this world and no goodness in society because, I cannot deceive you, those who build societies are in sin. There is only one hope of entering the Kingdom while we are still on Earth – and that is the hope Jesus gave to Nicodemus: we must be born again. Look at the children, running wild and sniffing drugs and similar. Who teaches them about sin? Where is the indoctrination?"

"Indoctrination? Surely not..." Alistair's protest was barely audible, so dumbstruck was he by Hyacinth's onslaught.

"Whoa, Mister Vicar. Of course indoctrination. How can we be reborn in the Holy Spirit without the doctrine of Christ? Why do you pretend you don't want indoctrination? You cannot rest until everyone believes in your philosophy of human rights and social justice and similar liberalities. I know you and your fanatical liberal friends. I know what you are up to. You want me to come and hob-nob with such friends. You want to say: 'Look here at this poor unfortunate black woman. We must convert her at once to the great truth of liberality.' But I say, what is this truth? It is a human, material truth. It is no truth at all beside Jesus Christ, who is the living truth."

"Of course," Alistair murmured, "it's not easy for white people to understand black experience."

"I don't care what colour you are. It is a matter not of colour, but of holiness. Look at your Bishop Mwawa. You think you know him? You do not know him. I know him. He also talks of human rights. But he was raised in the mission schools, like me, where they do not speak of such things. They speak of Jesus only. Where does he get his human rights from? I will tell you where – from London University and Durham Theological College. In such places he was indoctrinated and now he cannot remember Jesus. Now he hides in Zimbabwe and speaks out against my people. He takes tea with the President while Matabele are shot or burned. White people, you see, have no monopoly on racialist behaviour."

"I – I've never thought that Third World problems were simple, but –"

"But me no buts, Mister Third World. There are only two worlds – this one and the next; and Jesus is bringing this one to an end on His return. On the last day the bodies of the righteous shall be raised to glory. Do you believe this?"

"Well, er, naturally the Resurrection of the Body is an article of our Creed. But it is not, I suggest, a text to be taken too literally..."

"Doubting Thomas! You think it is harder for human beings to be resurrected in the flesh than for God to come down and make Himself man? It is not harder. It is easier. All things are possible through faith. And besides this, Jesus allowed his wounds to be touched so that there would be no doubt that his body was raised from the dead and no doubt that it would ascend with his spirit into Heaven."

In a state of shock and bewilderment, Alistair fell back on pedantry:

"Ah yes. But can we be sure, in the light of biblical exegesis, that these stories are, um, authentic? I would agree that there is most certainly a core of what I might term 'symbolic truth', but it has to be constantly re-evaluated if it is to remain relevant to our changing times."

"Goodbye, Mister Allingham," said Hyacinth, rising from behind her sewing-machine. "I will pray for you."

There was no gainsaying the finality of her words as she shepherded him out of the sitting room, along the narrow passage and out of the front door. "But... but..." Alistair stammered. The word was left hanging in the draught of air caused by the shutting of the door. He walked uncertainly into the street. He looked in vain for somewhere to sit, and finally slid down on to the pavement. He rested his burning forehead against the cool brick of a garden wall. His heart ached to be free of that eternal But which kept him out of Hyacinth's world. It was quite other than he had imagined it, quite different even – perhaps because it was hers – from that of the familiar fundamentalist Christian. With the intensity of nostalgia for childhood, he longed to link hands with Hyacinth and walk through that simple, self-contained, utterly pure landscape of Scripture. But...

FIFTEEN

It was as Maeve feared: Creighton Ward was in the older, dismal, Victorian part of the hospital, redolent of straitjackets and torture. As they crossed the car park towards it, the declining sun peeped through a gap in the tall buildings. Heather pulled on Maeve's sleeve.

"Wait! I see Him in the sun!" she exclaimed, gazing into the light with a far-away expression.

Maeve sighed. She was reminded of William Blake and his vision of the sun as a heavenly host. But he hadn't said the sun was a heavenly host; he had said it was what he saw. He hadn't lost the ability to see the everyday sun. His vision was like double vision, reading one version of the world in terms of another. To lose this sense of metaphor was to go mad. Heather had lost it and, with it, the battle for sanity. Looking into the heart of her sun she was blind to everything except the heavenly host.

As the sun was obliterated by the hospital block, tall and grim as a northern mill, Maeve pulled the reluctant Heather away.

"You know really, don't you, Heather, that you have to go through with this," she said, feeling like a murderer. "It's only a hospital. It's not the end of the world. You'll survive."

How bitterly she resented the cube and the pass it had brought her to. She hated its ambiguity and contradictions – the way it seemed to be both subjective and objective, delusion and revelation, there and not there. She loathed the way it couldn't be fathomed, as if that were precisely what it had come to demonstrate. Above all she hated the way it was dragging her in Heather's wake, down into the soul's inhuman depths.

"You're not alone," she said to Heather as they stood in front of the entrance. "I won't desert you. Now, chin up. We have to climb to the top. Are you ready?" Heather did not answer. She stood stock still for a second and then, suddenly, she put her head down and, dashing full tilt at the swing doors, threw them open and began to run up the echoing stone steps towards Creighton Ward.

"...Are you ready?"

Heather did not understand the words at once. She waited while they floated like bubbles towards her. As they melted into the transparent membrane which enveloped her, their meaning became apparent. Automatically she thought: 'Get set... *go*.' The idling engines of the Cube deep within her instantly accelerated to a pitch too high for hearing. As it began to lift off, her heaviness was dispelled.

She found herself being carried at high speed up the flights of stone steps. The higher she climbed, the more acutely she felt the Cube's angles expand outwards like a steel skeleton inside her skin. It was touch and go whether she would reach the summit before its superstructure, thrusting up into her skull, broke through the envelope and enfolded her so that she became no longer the container but the contained.

A second set of swing doors faced her on the top floor. She pushed through them just in time. The scream of the Cube dropped to a smooth purr as it became plastic, perfectly moulding itself to the inner contours of her form. Its sensors operated via the apertures of her eyes to compose an accurate picture of the space she was in. On the left, a glass-walled office; beyond it, some armchairs and a ping-pong table; on the right, a recess with more chairs and a television playing; at the far end, two rows of beds. It was clearly a kind of transit camp or embarkation point for which the hospital was a necessary front. The denizens who sat or slumped or walked about with stylised movements were strangely unaware of this. They were too dense; they lacked the lightning speed needed to compute the sensors' information. Heather was calm and supremely confident now that the final countdown had begun. She smiled warmly at a young woman who came out of the glass office. She wore a green jersey and trousers, and there was a green streak in her brown hair.

"I'm expected," said Heather.

"Mrs Allingham? Yes. The doctor rang. I'm Lizzie, the psychiatric nurse in charge of Creighton Ward. But where's Heather?" Heather's eyes filled with tears. "Oh dear," said Lizzie. "Been a bit of a handful, has she? Never mind. Ah, here we are..."

Maeve almost fell through the swing doors. She was gasping for breath after her pursuit. Lizzie was a little nonplussed; somehow she had been expecting someone younger.

"Hello, Heather. I'm Lizzie. How are you feeling?" Maeve felt a bit panicky. She looked anxiously around for a sign of someone in authority.

"Who's in charge here?" she asked, still out of breath.

"Well, I am at the moment," said Lizzie quietly. "But don't worry. The doctor will be along very soon to have a little chat with you."

"I mean, who else is in charge?" Maeve persisted; but Lizzie was distracted from answering by the sight of Heather, a stern expression on her face, pointing stiffly at an old woman in a dressing-gown who was making her way painfully along the ward, lifting each foot high above the ground. The surrounds of her eyes looked bruised, her complexion was yellow and her mouth sharply turned down like the mouth of a tragic mask.

"That's Mrs Rowley," explained Lizzie, puzzled by Heather's attitude. "She's just had a small operation and she's not feeling terribly well. But she'll be fine. Now, I expect you'd like to see around the ward. You come along too, dear," she said to Maeve.

"*I'm* Maeve Allingham," said Maeve firmly. "*She* is Heather Wright."

"Of course, dear." Lizzie crinkled her eyes understandingly. Then she paused while the past few minutes visibly rearranged themselves on her face. "Yes, *of course*. Come along, Heather," she said to Heather. And she said it in such a friendly yet competent way that Maeve felt like bursting into tears. A huge weight was lifted from her. At last someone else was in charge.

She was about to follow the two girls on the introductory tour of the ward when she was arrested by a tug at her sleeve. A small man, elderly, with a wrinkled puckish face, addressed her cheerfully in an Irish accent that, in spite of the circumstances, gave her a sharp stab of nostalgia.

"Are you visiting?"

"In a way, yes."

"I'd a visitor once."

"That's good."

"Good? 'Twas desperate. I had both me hands through the bathroom window." He lowered his voice, adding with pride, "That's what I do, d'you see? I put me hands through windows. There's no stopping me. Will you look at the state of them?" He drew back his cuffs to display hideously scarred wrists and hands. Maeve felt a little sick and faint. The ward was stuffy and possessed an odd cloying smell. "You'll have to excuse me," she began. But, as she spoke, a scream pierced the air.

The inmates reacted at once, as if galvanised. Some began to sway, some to jerk, and others to scurry to and fro in meaningless compromises between fight and flight. The small Irishman boxed himself twice on the ears. Maeve was dazed. In the light which slanted through the high barred windows and reflected off the blue walls, she had the impression that she was in an aquarium full of human sea anemones and crustaceans. Two inmates began to cry; a third screamed experimentally in imitation of the original.

Towards the far end of the ward Lizzie was struggling with Heather whose screams were not hysterical but methodical – a regular series of high-pitched notes like an animal's alarm signal. At her feet was the collapsed body of Mrs Rowley, her bruised eyes shut, her mask tragic in repose. Two white-jacketed men came through the doors and ran past her to join the fray. They were quick and efficient. Heather's flailing arms were pinioned, an injection was administered and she was frog-marched up a further flight of stairs at the end of the ward. Maeve lumbered heavily in her direction, her legs having apparently been filled with sacks of water. This was what happened when she let Heather out of her sight for more than five seconds. At the foot of the stairs the girl twisted her head around. The screams had ceased. Maeve glimpsed her white face, already ghostly and insubstantial, before she was pushed through the door at the top of the stairs. It closed behind her. The two attendants or male nurses returned to pick up Mrs Rowley. The tide of panic which had swept through the ward died down.

"What *happened*?" Maeve asked Lizzie.

"She hit Mrs Rowley. Don't worry – it could have been worse. Anyway, Heather will sleep now."

Heather recognised at once that the old woman had been possessed by the Spirit of Depression. The black-ringed eyes, the sagging mouth, the feeble eccentric steps announced an entity as far down in the natural order as it was possible to sink without ceasing to be human. She was forcibly struck by the idea that perhaps this walking corpse was not altogether beyond help. Perhaps it had been sent as a test to provide her with the final means of obtaining grace. If it could just be, for a second, resuscitated from its deathly trance by some Zen-like shock, then it might yet be saved.

Heather took aim with her finger at the slowly advancing creature. A sudden terror seized her: the entity was a sign, a warning of what it was possible to become if you were distracted from your high purpose. She set her teeth and focussed on the spot between the creature's eyes. It was coming up level with her now. She paused, waiting until her engines were revved to screaming point before engaging her will. It unleashed a line of force which carried her arm along it. She heard a sharp smack. The entity went down, with limbs splayed, as easily as a cardboard cut-out. Heather pinned it to the floor with a salvo of accurate screams which came out of her mouth in red jets of flame.

These she turned on the white-clad assailants who attacked her from behind. She struggled like a wild animal in their grip until, with a muffled roar like the tearing of cellophane, she managed to rip herself free. Calmly she watched her own carcase being thrown on to its back and held down by what appeared to be a pair of male humanoids. She almost laughed out loud at the way they were fooled by the continual heaving of the empty body beneath their hands. She watched, fascinated, as they inserted a long shiny needle into its arm. She could feel the sharp pain of the needle as her own. She began to waver like ectoplasm, and lose shape. She was being drawn back into the warm sheath of her body, becoming fluid, spurting into its bloodstream. She could feel it struggling and kicking around her, like a foetus, as she spread through its veins. Even as she was extruded into the hands, the feet, the crown of the head, she became aware that she was being man-handled, along with her body, up some stairs. She looked around for Maeve and sensed the head, like a heavy glove puppet, twisting around with her. After the split second of airy delirious freedom, the return to cumbersome flesh was exhausting. She sent out red waves of will-power to prevent her eyes from closing. Her legs were being tugged away by a numbing undertow of drowsiness. A great purple breaker swept over her, threatening to drown her in oblivion. She fought her way up to the surface and, hanging on for dear life, looked about her.

It was exactly as she had foreseen it: the brilliant white space was shaped like a perfect cube and, oh, like the Holy of Holies, perfectly empty. The endless welter of thoughts and images collapsed in upon themselves; their throb and roar died away into profound silence. She was alone at last and, high above the world, at rest. All yearning for meaning was fulfilled here, where the pure shining space was itself meaning, and she and the meaning were one. She lay down at the centre and sank into the plenitude that emptiness alone could bring. As her eyes closed, she seemed to hear a light footstep and to sense the majestic Presence bending over her, and whispering in her ear unspeakable words.

Maeve opened the front door of Heather's flat and walked along the dim passage to the sitting room. The silence was unnatural, intensified by her suspicion that her entry had interrupted somebody or something. She fancied she could hear the echo of pattering feet as if the rooms had been occupied by small creatures – slivers of Heather's sheared psyche, perhaps, which had been left behind to assume a life of their own. The temperature seemed several degrees lower than outside. Maeve shivered. The coffee cup on the table startled her until she recognised it as the one she had left there – good God – only that morning.

Although it was not yet dark she switched on the lights and nervously approached the closed door of the bedroom. She paused, unable to suppress a superstitious feeling that there was something inside the room, pressed up against the far side of the door as she was pressed to her side, listening…

"Buck up, Maeve," she scolded in her best Nanny-ish voice. Her apprehension, she knew, was caused by tiredness and by the memory of the previous night's terrors. But as she grasped the door handle she was immediately assailed by a mental picture of the grotesque aliens, clearer than at any time since she had first remembered the abduction.

Maeve recoiled from the door. What if they were in there? Her stomach convulsed. She tasted bile in her mouth. If she hesitated a moment longer she would flee, retching, from the flat. Bravely she threw the door open.

But of course they weren't there. She was no better than Heather, taking her experience of the aliens literally, imagining that she'd actually been abducted into a spacecraft. And yet her memory of it was so *real*. Maeve sank down on to the unmade bed and composed herself with an effort. What if, she thought, the physical and the literal were not at all the same thing? Perhaps it was just her own literal-mindedness that had made the experience seem so physical. After all, hadn't St Paul had the same problem when he was ecstatically caught up into the third heaven 'Whether in the body, I know not; or whether out of the body, I know not; God knoweth.'! That was just about bloody right: whether or not she had been snatched up into an alien craft, God only knew.

If she had learnt one thing from the past hours with Heather, it was the inappropriateness of looking for causes and explanations outside her experience itself. Both Heather's brand of insanity, and her own, belonged to another world whose laws could not be described in terms of this world. The key to her alien encounter – like Heather's quest – lay in its meaning. What, for example, was the significance of the aliens' eyes, their most outstanding feature? Maeve could see them now as they watched her – eyes without pupils like the dark glasses of torturers, concealing identity, giving nothing away; eyes as black and intransigent as those of the *Sídhe* were lustrous and flashing. If eyes – as poets and lovers testified – were windows of the soul, then the eyes of the aliens were paradoxical: on the one hand, they were unreflecting and opaque as if their owners had no soul; as if they were parodying Earth's own mad scientists and vivisectionists whose gaze, lusting after facts, was objective and emotionless. On the other, their eyes were emphasised, as if their owners were emblems of the soul. Was it possible therefore that the aliens somehow personified that remote part of her own soul which was both impersonal and non-human, like a god?

Maeve found a battered suitcase on top of Heather's wardrobe and began to root around for the things she would need: nightdress, a change of clothes, dressing-gown, towel, wash things, make-up, underwear. As she collected the items and packed them carefully in the case, she let her thoughts wander over the horrific operation the aliens had performed on her. If they really were a technologically superior race from another planet, they were surprisingly incompetent. She had been spared neither pain nor fear – unless these were essential ingredients of the operation, like some savage initiation. She recalled a fascinating television programme she had seen about just such rites. In Africa some young men were initiated into adulthood by elders wearing long demonic large-eyed masks, not unlike the flat faces of the aliens, who abducted them into the bush. The initiates were then painted to resemble ghosts, buried in symbolic graves, given scars and painfully circumcised, before being instructed in tribal lore. The initiation of tribal shamans was even more severe: marked out as having the shamanic vocation by a supernatural visitation, a dream or a sudden illness, they were dismembered while in a state of trance by supernatural beings and then rebuilt with new bones and eyes and brains. They flew into the sky or plunged into the underworld where they conversed with unearthly beings who conferred power on them by inserting celestial objects into parts of their bodies. Thereafter they could induce ecstasies at will. In Siberia shamans rode their drums into the heavens; or, climbing down through the smoke-holes into the dark yurts, they re-enacted the heroic descent into the underworld whence they recovered the souls of sick people otherwise doomed, soulless, to wither and die. Pain and fear were central to all these rites of passage, perhaps because they were necessary to induce the requisite sense of rebirth. Reality, it seemed, had to be driven into you, like nails, so that you could never again say 'I was only dreaming. I only imagined it...' Had the operation on her been an initiatory exercise of this kind? (She fingered the raised scar on her head: had something been *inserted* instead of removed?) But, if so, why had it been so unlike the thrilling Technicolor experiences of the shamans?

Maeve left the flat and began to trudge home in the failing light. The small suitcase weighed her down. She would bring it over to Heather in the morning. She thought of the girl, incarcerated like Rapunzel in that little padded room at the top of the building, and offered up a wordless but heartfelt prayer for her deliverance. She saw again the girl's white face turned in desperation towards her and suffered the sharp bite of remorse and guilt. Seizure, needles, pain, isolation, fear... wasn't medical 'treatment', too, a kind of initiation?

Maeve thought of Patsy and his stories of the *Sídhe*. The Good People. Everyone around Eden believed in them and many had seen them. They were, if not a fact, a fact of life. She too had believed in them unquestioningly until Nanny and her Englishness and her insistence on hard facts had made them seem insubstantial, dream-like, just 'stories'. Why had she gone along with this, siding with Nanny instead of Patsy, embracing that cold English literalism?

Her aliens had been clinical and cold. Their evenly-lit, cave-like space was as impersonal and sterile as their geometrical cube, a far cry from the rich and brilliant world into which the *Sídhe* abducted their victims. The aliens came as an advanced technological power because that was the only power modernity respected. But while the power was real, the technology was a mask, like the meaningless flashing panels on a science fiction film set. The operation was a parody of her own attitude, of her 'Englishness', probing her as she had rationally probed their truth into oblivion. Were the aliens simply mirroring the face she had turned towards them? Perhaps they were simply the old ones, like the *Sídhe*, who shape-changed, cutting their cloth to suit the times; whose real aim was to force her to recognise that there were powers she had forgotten about or denied.

But why had she denied them? Something had happened to make her forget, to lose her way. With a start she recalled the terrible day when she had, literally, lost her way in Five-Acre Field. She had never been so frightened before or since – until the day the aliens came. Had she done some violence to her imaginative life as a result of that fearful experience in the field – a violence which was now summoning up the aliens from deep inside herself to do her violence in return? But then again they had been quite explicit about where they'd come from: Pluto. It was *absurd.*

The vicarage was in darkness. Maeve averted her gaze from the malignant scrap of blue plastic, still adhering to the fence, and let herself in. She felt as though she had been travelling for days across a dark continent. She could have killed for a cup of tea in the warmth and safety of her own home. She wished only to be rid of the aliens who pushed up into her mind and evoked such disturbing speculations about initiations and shamans and, worse still, the precariousness of the world. But she was mortally afraid that if she did not find some way of making her peace with them, they would eventually come to possess her, as Heather in her way had been possessed.

She switched on the kitchen light and was startled to find Alistair sitting at the table with an empty mug in front of him. "What are you doing, sitting here in the dark?"

"Nothing. I had a coffee, I think." His voice was strained and flat. What had he got to be fed up about? He had been right all along – in a way – about Heather. Maeve put on the electric kettle. "Let me do that," said Alistair, "you look tired. Can I get you something to eat?"

"No. Thank you. I'm just dying for a cup of tea." The exchange sounded stilted, like an excerpt from some amateur dramatics. She added: "I had to take her to the mental hospital." She was going to say 'You were right', but didn't because he hadn't been. She waited for him to say he had told her so.

"I'm sorry," said Alistair simply. "I expect it was awful." He looked dazed, as if he had sustained some shock. Maeve wondered fleetingly what the matter was. It wasn't like Alistair to sit in the dark, brooding. But she was too tired to ask.

"I'll take this tea up to bed. I'm done in," she said.

"Yes. I'll be up in a while."

At the door, Maeve paused and turned. Wanting to break the constraint between them, she said:

"What does… Pluto mean to you?" He did not reply at once, as if his thoughts were elsewhere. Then, in a patient weary monotone, he said:

"Well, the Roman version of the Greek Hades, god of the underworld. And the underworld itself." Maeve's felt a prickle on her scalp. Why hadn't she thought of that? Pluto was not merely a planet, but a god. She heard Alistair add, with a surprising touch of bitterness: "Of course, no-one believes in an underworld nowadays. Except perhaps as the hell the Christians turned it into."

Maeve went to bed but, despite her exhaustion, she couldn't sleep. Alistair's words had made her a little dizzy. The world seemed upside down. What was above mirrored what was below. The aliens belonged to the underworld, yet they came from the sky. The more they were ignored or written off as hoaxes, fantasies or madness, the more they were forced to present themselves materially, as if they were 'spacemen', because that was the only language an unimaginative planet understood. If they weren't recognised for what they were, abductions and terror might be only the beginning.

Maeve's thoughts were interrupted by her husband who had quietly entered the room and begun to undress. She was touched by the stoop of his shoulders and his scrawny arms. It was sad the way he folded his shabby unsuitable clothes so carefully. He seemed old all of a sudden. As Alistair climbed into bed beside her, Maeve switched off the light and closed her eyes to shut out the aliens. But they were there in the darkness before her, pressing up close behind her eyelids. Their huge black eyes were fathomless. She held their gaze as long as she was able to bear it. Their faces gave way to the pictures she had been shown at the culmination of her abduction. On the screen she had mistaken for a window, she watched again the vast soundless explosion, the endless stretches of devastated planet. "What do you want?" she remembered saying or thinking. "*Your world*" the reply had come.

Perhaps the screen had been a window after all – a window from their world on to hers. The smashed planet was not their world. It was a warning, a prophecy. It was an image of what could happen to planet Earth if the aliens were not admitted.

"It comes from the Greek," said Alistair, his voice muffled by a pillow. "*Plouton*. Pluto. It means the Rich One."

SIXTEEN

Heather opened her eyes. Her bedside clock told her that she had been asleep for nearly nine hours, if indeed the heavy dreamless unconsciousness could be called sleep. She made an effort to rise, but someone had come in the night and sewn lead weights under her skin. And, when she tried to lift the tonnage of her head, the strain was almost too great. Her brain had been replaced by black icy slush which swayed when she moved, like thick bilge water. She had been warned to expect side effects, but there was nothing side about these effects. They constituted the whole of her, what was left after the wreck.

She had been out of hospital for two days. Inside, it had been three days before a panel of psychiatric people interviewed her. She had remembered not to go telling them everything. She had touched on the matter of the Cube, but deprecatingly, as if it were already in the past. Later, she saw the chief shrink alone. He was able to ascertain that her medication was having the desired effect, that the end of her 'manic episode' was already in sight. The official prognosis was optimistic: if she followed the treatment rigorously, she would probably be laughing about her aberration within a few months. Maeve had been allowed to collect her at the end of a week.

Heather heaved herself out of bed and stood up. Immediately she had to clutch her bedside table to prevent herself from falling. She suffered from permanent vertigo, a sensation of being always on the brink of toppling forward on to her face. She pulled on her dressing-gown and teetered like a neurotic old woman to the kitchen. Her arms, bent at the elbow, were held feebly out in front of her; her feet were numb slabs of meat she could only move in small dragging steps. Her joints – her very flesh – ached as if she had been beaten with blunt instruments in some secret police cell. She looked out of the window. There was nothing to detain her. The garden was grey and two-dimensional, as if she were missing an eye. The world was uniformly dull, drained of all meaning. The only thing she was not yet used to was the quietness. She was suspended in a single enormous silence, like the silence after a car crash. It was as if her interior engines had overheated, gone critical, and smashed themselves to pieces. The feverish din and clatter had ceased. Now, even quite ordinary sounds appeared muffled, as though buried by snow.

She was grateful. The pandemonium in the ward had been enough to drive her mad. All day patients had bickered and shouted above the blare of the television; all night they cried out or wandered around. Heather had requested to be re-interned in the White Room, where everything rested in perfect equilibrium and tranquillity. Her request was refused. She had to learn to adapt and, luckily, she was just mad enough to be able to. With the help of her drugs she slept for long periods; she watched television; she painted her toenails and hit a Ping-Pong ball idly about. It worried her that she couldn't read. Her eyes could not decipher the little grey marks on the white pages. She wondered if she had suffered some permanent brain damage. She accused Lizzie of administering electric shocks to her head while she slept. She had Maeve's visits to look forward to, of course; but, having too much to say and too little command over language, she said nothing. When the ward became unbearable, she stationed herself at one of the high barred windows and stared fixedly at the scrap metal yard on the other side of the dual carriageway. She liked to watch the huge machine with the steel piston-like ramming device as it crunched whole cars into neat cubes. When, two days before she left, Lizzie hit her with the serious tranquillizers, she knew what the cars felt like.

Slowly and deliberately she filled her kettle from the tap, placed it on the cooker and lit the gas. Then she wrapped herself in a rug and sat on the floor while the water boiled. The cold was probably the worst thing of all. It was not a coldness she could describe, unless it was that of a drowned person brought up from the ocean bed. Unrelated to outside temperature or weather, it was the climate she carried around her. Whereas in the halcyon days of mania her volcanic heart had flung scintillating images up into her head, her cardiac engines were now barely able to force the freezing slush through her arteries. Her mind was locked in ice, her organs petrified, her intestines coiled like ammonites in their lead casing of flesh. No amount of vests and jerseys made any difference. Although she was mortally afraid of the Cube as the occasion of her insanity, she also craved the laser flash of its warmth to thaw her impacted heart and fire her into life again. Nor could she resist probing her mind, like a sore tooth, for traces of it.

At once she saw herself standing alone in the centre of a gleaming arctic waste, under a vast canopy of frosty stars and a huge snowball of moon from which something silvery detached itself and hurtled soundlessly towards her. An electrical shock of exhilaration and terror ran through her. She immediately blocked the image and grasped the bottle of pills in her pocket, like a talisman. Little more than a week ago, she reflected, she might have marched off into that trackless polar region, never to return. Now she was back in the real prosaic world where such regions were images of her state of mind and no longer states of mind she was in.

She shook two pills out of the brown bottle. She loathed what they were doing to her and at the same time she was terrified of losing them. She carried them around with her, like a life-line. They were the fragile barricade between her and her marching army of madness. She made the tea and swallowed the pills down. She did not consider that the deep depression they induced was so much a cure as a punishment, whose justice she accepted. Her crime had been to deny the depths and now they had engulfed her, all at once and to the utmost extremity.

Dear Alistair,
Yes, your lack of personal fax facilities is unfortunate, but I am sure you will be able to remedy this before our arrival. (Don't forget to check that you have the correct telephone socket.)

I can tell you now that we shall be flying into Heathrow from Zurich on either the Monday or Tuesday of Conference week, having spent a day or two in Switzerland where the Bishop has some Party business to complete. Naturally I will telephone to confirm our exact time of arrival, and trust that cars will be awaiting us. I imagine, incidentally, that transport for the duration of our stay has been arranged. Your Church authorities will no doubt defray any expenses. Perhaps you would inform them that the Bishop prefers the reliability of German cars? It may be that Mercedes or BMW will make new models available, free of charge, in the light of the publicity which the Bishop's visits inevitably attract.

I am reminded that we have not yet touched on the matter of the Bishop's diet. Alas, the frailty of his disposition after many years of hardship forbids any foodstuffs which contain additives. However, he likes to eat simply – a little seafood (scallops, scampi, salmon, sole etc.), green vegetables (no root crops, including potatoes) and, as staples, brown rice, freshly-made pasta, rye bread. While essentially vegetarian, the Bishop can also eat (on doctor's advice) some lean meat, such as chicken and fillet steak. His drinks are orange juice (freshly squeezed), tea (Formosa oolong), mineral water, claret, Burgundy, Armagnac. (Nor do we begrudge, bless him, the occasional single malt before dinner!)

Lastly, his Lordship will be pleased to meet at your request (time permitting, of course) one or two local Church activists. If you would be kind enough to submit their names and qualifications to me in advance, I will be able to give you my thoughts on the matter. For example, it would be desirable if he were to meet them against the background of some sort of demonstration for which the media should have at least three days' notice. We have found that the late afternoon is an auspicious time for such events to attract television coverage and fill slots in the early evening news broadcasts.

Yours sincerely in Christ,
Barbara Mannheim

P.S. Re *the Felicitas issue: sources in South America have assured us that she intends to monitor the Conference rather than play an active part in it. The Bishop is prepared to accept her presence on these terms; but we would all agree, I presume, that it would be desirable if she came out and spoke in his support. I have written to your Dean and Bishop, urging them to bring what pressure they can to bear on the disturbing reticence of this nun, and I naturally urge you to do the same, should you have an opportunity.*

The letter threw Alistair into a fit of anxiety. He could not begin to concentrate on the more important difficulties it raised. Instead he wondered wildly if he should rush out and buy a machine for squeezing oranges. At last he was driven to ringing the Dean to ask about money for a car. Cars. The Dean was out. His secretary felt confident that there was little likelihood of any money being made available to him. Next, he phoned several car hire firms until he found one, in Knightsbridge, which supplied German cars. He wondered which parishioner he could ask to act as chauffeur. No one came to mind.

He slumped back in his chair. There was so much to think of, to do. Surely Maeve should be helping him. She had needed a respite after her trauma – he understood that – but nearly a week had passed and she was still spending the bulk of the day in bed. Her only excursions had been to visit Heather at the hospital. He had offered to take his turn but was rejected. Apparently Heather had, well, mixed feelings about him. Still, he had shown willing. Was it too much to ask that his wife should lend a hand in the arrangements for Mwawa's stay? There wasn't any hostility on her part towards him; she was simply not co-operating. Her mind was elsewhere. And without her reassuring presence and her powers of organisation, Alistair was all at sea. Apart from anything else, the house was a pigsty. He had tried at odd moments to clean up essential areas but, really, he couldn't be expected to do everything. There were times – and this was one of them – when he wanted to bellow at Maeve to snap out of it.

Alistair stared at the plumber's estimate for installing a second bathroom. It was too high. More to the point, it was too late. He had kept putting off the moment when he would have to take serious action, and now the moment had passed. He lapsed into one of those bouts of listlessness to which, ever since Hyacinth's attack, he had been increasingly susceptible. What did he care about the bathroom? Perhaps the Bishop was less fussy than the Mannheim woman implied. His thoughts switched, unbidden, to the accusations Hyacinth had levelled at him.

He had refused to dismiss out of hand her fundamentalist beliefs, if only because the chief feature of the very liberalism she had attacked was tolerance. He couldn't subscribe to Satan and Armageddon and all the rest, but neither could he scorn them as Hyacinth had scorned his beliefs. This was admittedly something to do with Hyacinth herself. She had authority. Her dark eyes blazed with a visionary fire to which he was unaccustomed. He had the uneasy feeling that she bore a stronger resemblance to St Paul than he ever would.

In addition, her onslaught had come at a moment when his system of beliefs had been unusually vulnerable. He had visited Hyacinth in part to shore up his Christianity against the daimons who were undermining it – only to find that ever since she had spoken to him as a disembodied oracular head set among golden clouds, she was unwittingly on their side. It was not impossible that she was right;

that his liberalism (or 'liberality' as she would say) which prided itself on being free from assumptions, was in fact blind to the daimon (or god?) who underwrote it. Jesus had not been a noted liberal. Was he guilty, without knowing it, of serving Christ falsely or of serving another god altogether – guilty, in short, of idolatry?

He heard Maeve's slippers on the stairs, slapping against her feet in that irritating sloppy way. To think that she used to be up and dressed and ready to go at dawn...

"Maeve, do you know what time it is?" he asked, intercepting her on the way to the kitchen.

"Nearly eleven, I should imagine, dear." Her eyes focussed on him briefly. "You look a bit hot under the collar. Is anything the matter?" Alistair wanted to shout: 'Yes, yes, *yes*. Get up, get dressed, get *cracking*,' but instead he smiled miserably and said:

"I've had another despatch from that Mannheim woman."

"Oh dear."

"She and the Bishop seem a bit exercised over Mother Felicitas. I don't quite know how to respond."

"Saints make people uneasy, dear. Say nothing. They'll manage."

"I suppose so." He shrugged helplessly. "The Bishop has to eat a lot of seafood."

"We'll stock up on fish fingers."

"This isn't a joke, Maeve. They'll be here on Monday. I don't know what I'm going to do with them. For a start the house is a mess."

"It won't take long to clean it."

"Yes, but who's going to clean it? I can't do everything."

"It's simple. I've got the number of a cleaning agency. I'll ask them to send a cleaner round the day before."

"More expense, Maeve."

"Oh, I'll pay, Alistair. I've got a few pounds saved."

"That isn't the point."

"I'd rather do it that way. Leave it to me. And don't get into a state." Alistair pushed the previous day's paper towards her.

"Something here that might interest you," he said gloomily, pointing to a small article on an inside page.

Maeve took the paper and her tea back to bed. She felt vaguely sorry for Alistair but his problems failed to engage her full attention. She didn't even have to worry any more about Heather, whom she had taken home from the hospital two days before. After all that had occurred to bind them together, she was shocked by Heather's coldness, as if she were a different person. She had tried to re-establish personal contact with the new dull slow-moving Heather. She had grown over-solicitous until Heather had insisted on being left alone. She had explained, in a remote monotone, that she could not cope with the weight and responsibility of relationship. She preferred, for the time being, to deal with officials: the psychiatrist she would visit once a week, the social worker who would monitor her daily, the staff at the Day Care Centre who would provide therapy. With these she wouldn't have to be grateful or cheerful; she wouldn't be required to have emotions. Maeve understood. Recognising how she had come to depend on Heather as a means of avoiding her own problem, she resigned herself to letting go. With a sigh, she looked at the item Alistair had indicated in the paper.

The TASS agency reported that a UFO had landed in a public park in Voronezh, somewhere in Russia. Many people saw it, and also some aliens who had three eyes and silvery overalls. Children had drawn pictures; one of them, reproduced, was of a large 'alien' resembling a yeti. A policeman admitted to seeing less distinct giant forms. Another witness was quoted as saying: 'I saw them, and have no doubt they exist. But when I remember them now it seems like a fairy tale.' Maeve sighed again. Still, the item reminded her that her abduction, whether or not it was some kind of initiation, or some form of retribution for a failure of imagination, was not exclusive to her or to Heather. People were seeing some very funny things all over the world. She didn't need to take her experience altogether personally. Yet, at the same time, there must be something about her or something in her life which made her especially susceptible to such traumas; some precedent she had overlooked or forgotten, just as she had once nearly forgotten the abduction itself. In her heart, she knew it was time to disinter the memory of what had happened to her in Five-Acre Field. Even now, from the safety of her warm bed, she had to nerve herself to retrace her steps.

The two women stopped dead in front of each other. Neither could immediately place the other but they were both reluctant to pass by.

"Heather, isn't it?"

"Yes."

"I'm Katy. Do you remember? From the... the house in Chiswick."

"Yes. I remember." Heather recognised her now. Katy had looked different out of her former context, especially as she had cut her mass of glossy hair and was dressed, well, almost sloppily for her. Her face gradually came into sharper focus, like a face emerging out of a dream. It seemed years ago since they had last met. It seemed extraordinary that Katy should be in Acton, and not altogether desirable, since she brought back memories Heather would have preferred to forget.

"What are you doing here?"

"Oh, picking up bits and pieces. Inks, mostly. I'm into silk-screen printing these days," Katy replied.

"I never knew what you did before."

"It doesn't matter now. What are you doing?"

"I'm on my way to the Day Care Centre."

"That sounds like an out-patients' department for loonies!"

"That's what it is."

"You look after loonies?"

"No. I am a loony."

"Oh God, Heather. I'm sorry. You don't look like a loony."

"That's because of the drugs."

"Are you OK? I mean, are you getting better?"

"They think I'll recover."

"I wasn't far off madness myself, what with Murdo and all that."

"Murdo. Yes, I remember him." Heather felt a small surge of dizziness and nausea.

"I don't see him any more. Actually, I'm with Jeremy now."

"The Lord."

"That's right."

"How did you... escape from Murdo?"

"It wasn't easy. Although he had no feelings for me – he said our 'destinies weren't intertwined' – he wanted to keep me. Power, I suppose. And I hung on, hoping he'd have a change of heart. But it got worse. He kept hitting me. I don't know why I stuck it. There didn't seem any choice at the time. You may find it hard to believe, but he had a way of making you dependent on him. A way of taking away all your will. I don't know what would have happened if Jeremy hadn't pulled me out of it."

"How?" asked Heather, interested to note that she was still capable of curiosity, however feeble.

"Of *course.* I forgot you weren't there in the last days. You were denounced as a heretic! I remember thinking how brave you were. And you were right, too. Looking back, it was frightful. Murdo more or less ran the whole show. Hermione couldn't seem to channel any more. I saw Murdo giving her pills. To 'help' her. But she just sat around in a kind of daze, claiming that it was all part of taking on 'Guardian consciousness'. Then she would have sudden outbursts of rage or tears, slating everyone for backsliding or feeling sorry for herself because no one understood the burdens she was carrying. She'd issue statements, too – really wild stuff, impossible to swallow – which Murdo had to 'interpret' because he was a Guardian as well by this time. She leant on him more and more and, towards the end, she said nothing without his approval. Some people managed to leave; most were sort of mesmerised by it all, too far in to back out. We all policed each other and ourselves for the slightest sign of faithlessness or impure thoughts. It was a nightmare of paranoia. Thank God, Murdo gave me one black eye too many and Jeremy drew the line."

"I can't imagine Jeremy standing up to Murdo."

"Nor could anyone, I think. He went very red in the face one day and ordered Murdo out of the house. In front of everyone, too. Murdo just laughed so Jeremy punched him. They started fighting. Murdo looked different in the middle of an undignified tussle. It seemed to wake everyone up a bit. They ended up in the hall where there were all those animal heads on the wall. Do you remember? Jeremy's grandfather shot them. Well, Jeremy had some kind of deer's head down and gave Murdo a good pronging with its horns. He actually drew blood. It was rather magnificent." Katy laughed.

"Was that the end of the Sky Children?"

"Oh, no. There's a few left. Murdo's taken them down to Glastonbury. The Guardians have nominated it as the place where they'll land their ships. Quite soon, I think. It's funny, but I always suspected that Murdo only really believed it up to a point. I thought he was just on some ego trip. But he does believe it. He's the maddest of the lot. Hermione had a nervous breakdown or something. She pushed off to stay with her sister in Hastings. Her real name, by the way, is Vera."

"Why are the Guardians landing now?"

"Because the world is ending any minute, of course. The Sky Children – what's left of them – will be lifted to safety. Oh, I'm sorry, Heather. Don't look like that. It's nothing to worry about. I shouldn't really joke about it – after all, I believed in it all once."

"Me too."

"But none of it's true. I'm not upsetting you, am I?"

"No."

"I mean, was it the Sky Children business that drove you...?"

"No. I was already barmy."

"You must come over to the house some time. It's changed a lot. Jeremy and I would be pleased to see you."

"Thanks. Perhaps when I'm more myself."

"Of course. Give me your 'phone number." She wrote it down. "Good. 'Bye for now."

"Katy... Before you go... don't you believe in your... your sighting any more?"

"The UFO? Of course I do. I know what I saw. But I can't, you know, waste the rest of my life agonising over it. I'd advise you to forget yours, too. Get yourself a nice bloke. Works wonders."

It had happened a few months after Nanny's arrival at Eden, not long after Maeve's ninth birthday. She had been sent by father to Phelan's farm to ask Michael Phelan would he come over to Eden the following day and give his opinion on a horse's strained tendon. For a small girl, but with long legs, the trip across five meadows could be completed in fifty minutes there and back. Maeve set out after tea, delivered the message, refused the Phelans' usual kind offer of another tea, and began the return journey at a trot because time was getting on and it would be dark before too long.

It was a chilly blowy evening, and Maeve was glad of her new red coat. The sky was a strange dark blue, richly pigmented like lapis lazuli. Compact clouds flew low overhead; the sun dimmed and dazzled in quick succession. Shadows skated over the long rippling grass of the meadows. Maeve felt that she was very high up, or perhaps far out at sea among green waves.

She climbed the gate into Five-Acre Field, which was the third of the five meadows, and began to walk diagonally towards the stile in the far corner, from which she would see the chimneys of Eden. Gate and stile were the only entrances to the field which was otherwise sealed by ditches and dense impenetrable hedgerows. The only landmark was an old blackthorn near the centre. It was about thirteen feet high, and Maeve – who had made this journey dozens of times – habitually averted her gaze from it because the wind had swept its branches up and to the left, so that it looked like a scarecrow with its spiky hair standing on end. That day, she noticed, its lengthening thorny shadow was unpleasantly precise on the long grass at its foot.

When she reached the spot where the stile should have been, it wasn't there. She was surprised. Although she had been day-dreaming a little, she could normally rely on her feet to carry her surely along the well-worn route. She must have cut too sharply across the field, she decided; and so she followed the hedge to her right, confident of stumbling at any moment upon the stile. She didn't. The thick undergrowth presented a tall black wall. It was obvious that she had gone the wrong way. Irritably, half running, she retraced her steps and followed the hedgerow to the left. Flashes of light from the dying sun forced their way through the foliage.

When she had gone much further than her calculations warranted – and there was still no sign of the exit – she concluded that, odd as it might seem, she had not gone far enough to the right the first time. She tried again, following the hedge around the field for what seemed a long time. There was still no sign of the stile she had crossed less than an hour ago.

Maeve stopped for a breather. It was impossible. The stile had to be there. She had been too anxious perhaps, in too much of a hurry; she had somehow missed it in the fading light, overshadowed as it was by the tall hedge. Once again she retraced her steps, scrutinising every inch of the barrier to make absolutely sure of not missing any opening. As the minutes passed she became aware that she was no longer very hot but, in spite of her new coat, suffering from a peculiar creeping kind of cold. The wind had dropped; the silence and darkness grew, and still no stile presented itself. She stifled the instinct to begin running in mad circles and forced herself to move more and more slowly so that she would miss nothing.

At last she stopped and turned around. She was absurdly far from where the stile should have been. At least, she thought she was – each side of the field looked very much alike in the dusk. But one thing was clear: someone had somehow removed the stile. There was no choice but to go back to the gate. She was so eager now to be out of the field and back in the safety of Phelan's farm that she did not hesitate to head for the thorn tree by which she could easily orient herself. It had almost merged with the darkness by now, its shock of branches bristling, like Struwwelpeter.

It was a simple matter to discern the direction of the gate. Maeve broke into a run. She could even make out the faint path in the grass her feet had made earlier. When she got there, the gate had gone. No longer trusting her eyes, she ran to and fro, beating at the tall hedgerow with her hands, stumbling into the ditch, wiping away her tears lest she miss the longed-for break in the barrier. She ran back a little way, the better to see any gap; but by then she knew that the gate, too, had been spirited away. She turned round and round again, her breath impeded by sobs, searching for a chink of light. Nothing. She was trapped. Yet still she continued to run, hopelessly, at random, around the perimeter. Her sobs sounded so loud in all that stillness that they frightened her into stifling them.

Suddenly she stopped. Surely there was someone on the other side of the hedge? She peered through the tangled darkness until her eyes ached. Weren't there two small shapes on the other side? Yes, she could hear them talking in low voices. She couldn't make out what they were saying. The words sounded foreign. Perhaps they were conversing in Irish.

"Help," she shouted. "Help me." The two figures seemed to ignore her, only continuing their murmured talk. "Help, *help*, it's me, Maeve, *help*, I'm trapped..." But even as she yelled, the two shapes appeared to move away into the night. It occurred to her that they couldn't hear her. She was inaudible, invisible, non-existent. Perhaps she was dead and damned – doomed to circle the field for eternity. Her mind seemed to retreat far down inside herself. There was one further thing she might try. She took off her red coat and, turning it inside out, put it on again. It was a charm Patsy had taught her as protection against the Good People.

It was of no avail. In her fear and desperation she found herself, in some obscure way, blaming Patsy for all this. His stories of the *Sidhe* had brought it on her. He had tempted fate and now she was suffering the consequences. Half fairy that he was, it was all right for *him*. He was safe while others were left at the mercy of the unspeakable creatures.

Maeve recalled very little after this, except backing away from the suffocating hedge and calling on Jesus, sweet Jesus, to help her. She remembered hearing the sound of Nanny's voice shouting her name.

Miss Bryce found Maeve curled up quiet and white beneath the blackthorn. She did not respond to her name at first. She was stiff when Miss Bryce picked her up. Only when they were over the stile and within sight of the house lights did she whisper: "I thought I was going to stay there forever."

After her ordeal Maeve was given cocoa and tucked up in bed with a hot water bottle which failed to remedy completely the lingering shivers in her body. Patsy looked in on her. He had hurried to Phelan's farm by road and returned on foot across the fields, looking for her.

"Are you all right, pet?" he asked in a low anxious voice. Maeve pretended to be asleep. She could hear Nanny and Patsy talking outside her door.

"What happened, Patsy?" Maeve stiffened with amazement, not only because Nanny had used Patsy's Christian name – something she had never heard before – but also because of the unprecedented fear in her voice.

"Ah, leave it alone, girl" – *girl* – "There's nothing to worry about."

"But how could she get lost? Did she have a fit or something?"

"Not at all." There was a pause as Patsy, perhaps reluctant to speak, lit a cigarette. Nanny's fear was contagious, causing Maeve to press her hand against her heart as if to suppress its loud beating. "She was only after being led astray."

"Astray? What are you saying? This is no time for one of your stories. Speak plainly, please." Maeve might have been reassured by Nanny's words, had their tone been more controlled. But she sounded shaken, her voice – uniquely – tremulous.

"Well, now. They say the Good People will put the glamour on a bit of ground – the stray sod, they call it – so that we're led astray when we tread on it." Maeve waited for Nanny's peal of laughter, the cry of 'Priceless, Mr Collins!'; but it was Patsy who laughed, softly. "I'd say you wouldn't have to fret. I never heard now of an English man or woman going astray."

The soft laugh terrified Maeve. It seemed to her inhuman, pitiless, like fairy laughter. She couldn't bear to hear her appalling experience treated so matter-of-factly. She would have blocked her ears, but did not, for fear of missing Nanny's snort of derision, her clipped exclamation – 'Poppycock!' – to break the spell.

It never came. Instead there was a silence stretching between them. A silence in which Maeve sensed the tension between Patsy's knowledge and Nanny's incomprehension. Almost tangibly, the balance of power seemed to shift from one world to another, from Nanny to Patsy, from English common sense to Irish unreason.

Maeve buried her head under the bedclothes. She had an intuition of the danger that Nanny Bryce's silence portended. She vowed to be a good pupil from now on, to give up her wild ways and compel all Nanny's attention, holding them both fast to the curriculum. She would cling to Jesus who had brought her out of that terrible field, merciful Jesus whom she now thanked in heartfelt prayer. Above all, she would learn Englishness and its immunity to the stray sod.

"Hi! I'm Roddy," said Roddy, clasping his hands together and cocking his neatly cropped head to one side. "It's Heather, right? I've been looking forward to meeting you. Hey, don't look so surprised."

"Sorry. It's just that I thought you probably see enough nutters," said Heather vaguely. She looked around the small room which was painted yellow and had bright pictures, like those on a calendar, pinned to the notice-boards. She wondered if she had wandered by mistake into a children's play group. She was startled by the speed at which Roddy moved from behind his desk. He laid a warm hand on her arm.

"You," he said, looking straight into her eyes, "are not a nutter, OK?"

"Sorry," said Heather humbly.

"And hey. Don't be sorry. You've nothing to be sorry about." He smiled, showing a row of even white teeth. He looked fit and supple. His complexion was smooth and lightly tanned. His spotless jeans had a crease down the centre. A discreet silver earring added a roguish touch.

"You're not related to Jane Hughes-Goodall, by any chance?"

"You know Jane? Amazing!"

"She used to be my therapist. Before... all this."

"Yeah? Well, Jane and I were in the same encounter group, when one still went to encounter groups." He laughed. "Still, welcome to the Day Care Centre. It ain't much but we like to call it home!"

"Thank you, Roddy."

"Don't thank me! Listen, I'm here for *you.* If you have any problems – anything at all – talk to me. Any time. Talk! OK? Now I know you're on tranks right at the moment. They can be heavy, I know. But we're going to have you off them in no time and feeling good about yourself. Right?"

"I hope so."

"Good. You see? You've made a start! The important thing right now – the reason you're here – is to stop you curling up into a little ball and retreating into your shell. I don't pretend it's not going to be tough, but you've got to keep in touch with people. You've got to hang on in there. OK? We don't want you isolated from the community. That's what we're all about here. We're a kind of family, learning to care for and support each other. But I have to say, Heather, that in the end it's down to you. You have to do it on your own. You only get out what you put in! How do you feel about that?"

"I'll do my best."

"Great. I know it's difficult to be really positive right now, but you're doing fine. We'll just take it one day at a time. Your social worker has been sharing one or two thoughts with me. We both agree that you should come off the tranks as soon as possible, even though they're levelling you out at the moment – stopping you from, like, flying off in all directions. That's been the problem, yeah?"

"Hmm."

"OK. So somehow we've got to get you earthed! That means a lot of physical stuff. Lots of activity. Especially things like cooking. Gardening. How do you feel about those things?"

"I like cooking and gardening." Heather pictured herself baking and hoeing, up to the elbow in dough and soil, growing large breasts and wide hips. Yes, she would try hard. The days of fire and air were over. From now on she would devote herself to the dumpy comfortable goddesses of hearth and earth.

Roddy continued to explain and exhort. But the momentary warmth his buoyancy had imparted was slipping away. She felt tired. The black glacier of depression closed her in. She wanted to crawl into a corner, away from other people. She tried to move her face in response to Roddy's earnest words but she could barely keep her eyes open. She felt centuries older than he, as if in her mania she had burnt up several lifetimes. She was not so much levelled as razed, a scorched husk with no resistance to the encroaching ice age.

"Once you're earthed," Roddy was saying, "you can begin to grow again... begin to, like, integrate yourself into a whole person. I'm told you used to do a lot of dancing, yeah? Well, you'll be able to show the others a thing or two!"

He ushered her next door, into a large communal room where his subsequent remarks were drowned in a blast of disco music. He mimed an introduction to a girl in a blinding pink and turquoise track suit whose name she didn't catch. She was steered into the centre of the floor and encouraged by vehement gestures to dance. Strongly reminded of her kindergarten days, she obediently shuffled from one leg to the other and, keeping her arms extended in front of her, worked them minimally in time to the head-splitting beat. In other circumstances she might have found it funny that she, who could once pirouette across a stage on her points or fly effortlessly through the air, was now reduced to a kind of palsied St Vitus' dance; as it was, she merely wanted to die.

There were about a dozen other unfortunates moving around the floor with varying degrees of gracelessness. They were mostly younger or older than Heather. The younger ones, especially two black boys, danced with speed and agility but had somehow mislaid their sense of tempo. The puzzled, glazed looks on their faces suggested either that they recognised this, or that they were moving to the rhythm of some private beat. The older people, mostly women, swayed and jerked without any reference to the music which, Heather couldn't help thinking, wasn't at all suitable for them. Perhaps they were, like her, too doped to care; perhaps they had learnt, as she hadn't yet, to keep in motion, no matter how mechanically, in order to escape the attentions of the track-suited girl. For Heather had only rested a second when her hands were seized and pumped up and down by the girl who gyrated in front of her and tossed her head about. Heather knew that, if she were ever to free herself, she had to react; so she swung her own leaden head, feeling the black icy slush shift painfully from side to side. The girl looked delighted and, with mock clapping movements, pranced away.

After this, Heather kept her head down and confined her activity to walking warily around the perimeter of the room like a prisoner in an exercise yard.

SEVENTEEN

Remembering the terror in Five-Acre field had stirred Maeve more than she cared to admit. She had been especially struck by the similarity between the missing time after her cube sighting and the events after treading on the 'stray sod' – the one was like a temporal equivalent of the other. Her memory had been blocked off; her life had gone astray for fifty minutes. But what tormented her and filled her with despair was the dark suspicion that perhaps, one way or another, she had stepped again on the stray sod; that years ago she had lost her way – wasted her life – without even noticing. She was no longer confident that Jesus had protected her all this time. Where had He been when she was pinned to the aliens' chair? What if He was as ineffective as reversing one's coat?

Maeve remembered how fiercely she had thrown herself into the books which Nanny had brought over from England: real books she could read rather than leaf through, like mother; or, like father, merely consult. She studied Latin and French, pored over maps and graphs and geometrical figures. Above all, she learnt proper history with dates she could memorise, and reasons for things – causes, such as economics and foreign policies. She relished the routine and regular hours; she loved the way Nanny took a subject, like the Hundred Years' War or Latin subjunctives, and clearly dissected it, laying out its entrails for analysis. It was such a relief to be calmly inducted into a world as clearly defined as Nanny's well-cut clothes, as precise as her neatly-pinned golden hair.

Miss Bryce never criticised the Irish, but her attitude towards them remained, on the surface at any rate, consistent: she disapproved. Maeve remembered, for instance, how, outside Slattery's bar on a visit to town, Nanny had been jostled by arguing men in a way that recalled her own encounter with the hateful Brady and McBride outside The Castle. Even then she had said nothing, only giving her gorgeous head a little shake so that the piled hair trembled. For a moment, too, the amused tolerant twinkle went out of her eye. Burning with shame, as if she had been responsible, Maeve was all for remonstrating with the men; but Nanny drew her away, murmuring between pursed lips: "Come along, dear. Never make a scene."

"They're simply impossible, aren't they?" Maeve whispered, dimly aware even as she spoke that 'they' extended beyond the knot of intoxicated men to embrace the Irish race. Nanny did not disagree. And so, little by little, without an explicit word, Maeve came to see the Irish from what she imagined to be Nanny's point of view. They were shiftless and irresponsible – like unruly children, really, and good for nothing but a lot of fantastic gab.

In retrospect then, it was not surprising that Maeve became estranged from Patsy. They were still friendly, of course; and, to begin with, she was eager to pass on the new truths Nanny taught her, in order to illuminate poor Patsy's muddy twilight world. If he ever grew tired of hearing the words 'Nanny says...' he never showed it. On the contrary, he was inclined to shake his head in wonder at the things Nanny was alleged to have come up with. At the same time he remained infuriatingly calm in the face of revelation, and immune to instruction.

"Nanny says that Maeve's Grave can't possibly be an entrance to the land of Fairy. It's not even her grave, because she never existed. She's a myth, Patsy. The grave's probably just the burial place of some old petty chieftain."

Patsy took a lively interest in such theories, as he did in all stories, but Maeve was never able to wring from him any concessions.

"I never heard of any bones being found in one of them things," he would say, but in a non-committal way. "Treasure maybe, but not bones."

Unfortunately, she was not prepared to argue the toss too closely about Maeve's Grave. It was both a subject and a place she now avoided. She ceased to treat it with a proprietorial air and, it just so happened, never found herself within its vicinity. Besides, there were plenty of other matters to excite her. She recalled rushing to Patsy with the news of Darwin's theory of evolution.

"Nanny says you can't be descended from the *Sídhe*, Patsy. I'm sorry but it's all poppycock. Darwin found out that we're all descended from monkeys."

Patsy opened his eyes very wide:

"Monkeys, is it? Jaysus. All the same, I could never tell from looking at the pair of yez."

"Be serious, Patsy."

But Patsy declined to be serious. He continued to manifest that passive resistance of the Irish to any authority but their own. And so he receded, by day, into the stable-block which Maeve no longer visited, or into the wilderness beyond Eden's walls. By night he returned to his Irish life, which had always been mysterious to Maeve. If she saw him at all it was in the half-light. Rising sometimes at dawn she watched from her window as he moved like a spectre across the field, forming himself out of the waist-high mist, weaving and hopping as he spread one cow-pat after another with his boot, the better to fertilise the pasture. Or, at dusk, she would look up from her French irregular verbs and glimpse him sniffing the air in the distance by Maeve's Grave, a fishing rod like a lance at his side, some bloody trophy hanging at his belt.

Just before her departure for the English boarding-school, her homework was further disturbed by the sight of another figure silhouetted against the fairy mound. Miss Bryce had formed the habit of taking the air at about that time too. Maeve could see her elegant shape in front of Patsy, who stood very straight-backed. It seemed impertinent that they should have any contact with each other without her as intermediary, almost as if she were superfluous. What were they talking about? About her? What secrets were they sharing? Maeve was too proud to ask. She was lacerated by an obscure, violent sense of betrayal. As the summer evenings lengthened, the pair lingered, before Nanny glided back over the lawn and Patsy melted, straight as a wand, into the darkness.

The sound of voices dragged Heather out of her heavy doze. It was the television. She had fallen asleep in front of it. Idly she watched some women in bright summer clothes laughing together. One of them was giving away videos to a lucky member of the public. They seemed to be happy and positive and, oh, warm. In the perpetual summer of the TV studio, they had no trouble feeling good about themselves, while she lay on the sofa like a stone.

Suddenly she realised with horror that it was past four o'clock. She had missed taking her lunchtime pills. It was nearly time for the next ones. She leapt up and stumbled over to the sink where the brown bottle was kept when she was not carrying it around with her. Should she take a double dose to make up for the lapse? If she did, she would never do the gardening she had vowed to begin that day. It wasn't possible to do anything when you were tranked up.

But, just now, she had leapt to her feet. Had it been from pure fear – or had the omission of the pills made a difference? Yes, there was a difference: the task of gardening, prescribed by her therapy, no longer seemed insurmountable. Was it possible that she had taken enough pills, that she was ready to manage without them? Her pulse beat faster at the idea. She felt as if tiny spurts of hot blood were breaking out of her impacted heart and injecting an iota of warmth into her arteries. Her hand trembled with her own daring: she would leave the pills right there, in full view, where she could get at them if anything went wrong. She would go outside and work as hard as she could in the garden. Honest toil would prevent any wayward thoughts from entering her head. At the same time it would return the life to her numb body, exhausted but grounded in itself, earthed.

Heather changed into a T-shirt and baggy shorts and went out into the garden. It was warmer outside than in. The sun was white behind a thin uniform layer of cloud. Swathed in her leaden sheets of depression, she looked with despair at her dreary washed-out surroundings. The grass seemed bleached; colourless flowers hung limply on long weedy stalks; flinty stones poked like bones through the crusty soil. She hauled her garden fork and spade to the far end of the plot and surveyed the flowerbed beneath the wall. She would build a pond. The earth which she dug out could be piled up to form the base of a rock garden. It was not a particularly inspiring plan, but it was as good as any.

She began to dig painfully and clumsily. Her progress was impeded at almost every stroke of the spade by stones, old bricks, roots. She had to go down on her knees and hack at them with a trowel or scrabble them out by hand. It was murder, but so much the better – she wasn't there to enjoy herself but to work, to force earth, as it were, into the fabric of her body.

Sweat ran down her face as she worked grimly on. Her head felt warmer, more malleable. Inside, her brain expanded and rose like dough, fermenting thoughts. She could not suppress doubts about the aims of her therapy. It was a fine thing to be positive and hopeful, to feel good about yourself and, finally, to grow by a kind of psychic photosynthesis into a higher, more integrated personality. But wasn't it just such a hedonistic philosophy which had encouraged her madness in the first place? All that meditation and striving after higher consciousness, all Jane's cushion-bashing to release blocked feelings – wasn't this a way of pressing spiritual life into the service of an overweening ego? Didn't it lead to crazed quests for ultimate unities and 'saviours'? There were things in the depths, as she knew to her cost, which should not be dragged into daylight at all. They had to be faced where they lived – in the dark, at the bottom of the world, like the dreadful underground inhabited by aliens and zombies and the Lord of the Dead himself. It was dangerous to be always feeling good about yourself. It might make you feel good, for instance, to slit someone's throat.

This thought made her intensely nervous. Maybe it had been a mistake to leave off taking the pills. She dropped the spade and hurried back to the flat. Superstitiously she touched the brown bottle beside the sink. A couple of pills now would put an end to her thoughts and crush the pathological images which could spring up at any time in their wake. On the other hand, this hadn't happened yet. Her thoughts had no life of their own; they were under control. She drank some water and splashed her face under the tap. She was grateful to the pills. They had saved her from dissipating her soul in the universe. They had, to say the least, brought her down. But, the trouble was, they had also brought her out – out of the region in which her madness had been running its course. The tranquillisers rode rough-shod over the rules of her mania which decreed that she be tempted by false saviours, like the Sky Children, or that she struggle with demons, like Raff. They ignored her insanity's internal logic which, for example, counterbalanced her ascent of the clock tower with her descent into the Tube. She realised that the reason why she had freaked out in the Underground was that she had carried down with her attitudes and preconceptions which were only appropriate to the world above. She had tried to armour herself against the descent, against the latent depression of which her phobia about the Tube had been a sign. Thus, when it came, it came violently and all at once, bodied forth in delusions and paranoia and the long scream from which, without Maeve's providential arrival, she might never have escaped.

The secret, thought Heather, was to complete what she had never finished: to get *farther down*. This was the hidden meaning of 'earthing' which no amount of pills could counterfeit. She returned to her digging with renewed determination. Already she felt lighter, her head clearer. The sun dropped; the garden filled with long shadows; the dry stalks of shrubs and plants rattled in a sudden insistent wind. Bent on widening her pit, Heather noticed none of these things.

She had intended the pond to be a circle but it had turned out more rectangular. It continually mocked her by narrowing itself at the bottom. And, when she tried to remedy this, its walls kept caving in. It grew difficult to see what she was about in the failing light. Blindly she tossed spadeful after spadeful of earth on to the rampart which – the rock garden forgotten – grew high all around her. Whenever she was forced to dig with her hands, the soil had a different feel. It was colder, moister, darker; it smelled musty, and immeasurably old. It occurred to her that no one had ever dug this far down before. She was breaking new ground. So deep was her absorption in the task, that she did not at first register the sound.

It was familiar to her, distant but coming closer. She vaguely assumed it was something large and clanking, like a traction engine, on the High Street. She stopped digging in order to listen. The sound was rhythmic and metallic, like soldiers clashing swords against shields, and it was coming from the hole. Heather scrambled out in a panic. She must fill in the pit at once and prevent the sound from breaking out. But she had no sooner heaved the first spadeful of earth into the bottom when the noise changed to a higher pitch. It was not in the hole at all; it was in the breeze, all around her, growing stronger with every gust. She clamped her hands to her ears but the sound was, if anything, louder still. It was as much inside her as out. She didn't know which way to turn. She knew it now for what it was. Jumping back down into the hole, Heather began to dig furiously, as if by sheer speed she could outstrip the barbarous army of her old madness, marching towards her.

Maeve felt strange. Strange but, on the whole, better. The gnawing hopeless sense of having lost her way was still present, but muted. The bruising edges of the world had been smoothed. Alistair was out, so she was free to wander about the house, enjoying the unwonted sensation of lightness in her legs and the warm glow which emanated from familiar objects. In the drawing-room she poured more sherry into her glass.

"Just one more," she said aloud, "for the joy that's in it." But that was Patsy's ritual remark, and her involuntary echo of it first saddened her and then evoked that curious, indeterminate, angry feeling of betrayal. If only she could remember what had happened in her last days at Eden to excite such turbulent emotions. There had been, she thought, some sort of row – bitter enough to make her glad she was leaving, serious enough to make her disinclined to return, even for the holidays, which she spent with friends or with her cousins in Gloucestershire.

She had gone back, of course, in her first term for mother's funeral. She was surprised that Nanny was still there, although she had left soon afterwards. She had written Maeve a letter or two which had been left unanswered. In fact, now she thought of it, Maeve clearly recalled holding the envelopes in a hand which trembled with anger; and, since she had no memory of their contents, it was quite possible that she had, for some reason, never opened them. The vague feeling that Nanny had somehow let the side down could doubtless be traced to the vagaries of a difficult thirteen-year-old who wished to detach herself from her old Nanny and make her own way into adulthood.

The last time she returned was for father's funeral, three years later. Patsy was there, having travelled over from his hundred and twenty-six acres in Galway to oversee father's last days. She remembered nothing about him, no conversation even, except an irritating personal remark to the effect that she had lost her Irish accent. He had also mentioned, as a compliment, the way her hair was up – a fashion she had adopted because her friends' parents agreed that it made her look older, mature for her age, sensible. It suited a girl with a reputation for being independent and strong-minded, with her feet firmly on the ground. Such qualities made her ideal for school-teaching; and, since she was known in the parish to be devout without being pious, ideal as the helpmeet of an idealistic young curate.

As she raised the glass to her lips, Maeve tried to assume the look which Patsy had reserved for the activity, both serious and joyous, of drinking. If you treated it with respect, your body was lightened, your eyesight enhanced, your mind pleased. She drained the glass and reached for the bottle. It was empty.

"Jaysus," she admonished. "This is no time to go letting a woman down." She glimpsed herself in the mirror above the mantelpiece and stepped up to inspect herself more closely. "*Jaysus*. You look like Nanny Bryce! A fat old caricature of Nanny." She began to take the pins out of her grey hair. "Look out now, Nanny. You're being dismantled." She removed the pins clumsily so that her hair suddenly cascaded around her shoulders. The sight made her catch her breath. For a second she saw, not her own hair, but the falling of Nanny's golden tresses – where had she seen that? – and it upset her more than she could say. The spectacle of her own hair depressed her. A grotesque parody of Nanny's, it looked ludicrous on an elderly woman.

"You miserable old baggage," said Maeve to her reflection. She felt a kind of scornful pity for herself. She felt lonely. She wondered whom she could call up and talk to on the telephone. There wasn't really anyone, *except…*

She had forgotten all about the young man from the Ministry of Defence who had called on her in what she thought of as the early days. She had come a long way since then. Perhaps he was still floundering around, investigating spaceships and foreign secret weapons. The least she could do was put him straight.

The switchboard reminded Maeve that it was Saturday and therefore that there were very few people in the MOD. Luckily, the duty officer was the same air vice-marshal's aide to whom she had originally spoken. He remembered Maeve very well. He even sounded less irritable than the first time. Unfortunately he couldn't give her the name and address of the young man who had visited, firstly because it was not the ministry's policy to reveal private details of employees; and, secondly, because no one from the ministry had visited her. Yes, he was quite sure about this – he had handled her... case himself. Her name was even on a file marked 'No further action.' He hoped she was feeling better. He rang off.

Maeve received this news with consternation. Who had the man been then? He had been, come to think of it, a creepy sort of chap. That smooth face, that jerky way of walking... Was it possible that he was somehow in league with the aliens? A sort of by-product or side-effect? He had not said much, she remembered. He had let her do the talking, let her say too much perhaps. He hadn't drunk his tea.

However, Maeve did not dwell on the creepy man. The sherry had put her more in the mood for action than thought. Drastic action. She fetched the kitchen scissors and, after a short but intense struggle, cut off her hair. The result wasn't quite as she had pictured it: the hair, bobbed to just below the ears, stuck out in thick wedges. There was less resemblance now to Nanny than to the bag lady in the Co-op.

"Well, la-di-*da*," said Maeve. She giggled. The haircut made her look mad, yes; but, more importantly, it made her look younger. What had she been playing at all these years to have gone about with all that poundage pinned on top of her head? The release from the weight of it made her feel quite light-headed. The important question to be addressed now was: where could she get another drink? And what class of drink should she get? Vodka perhaps. She had heard that this left you not stinking of alcohol, and that was good because you didn't want your husband to know you'd been boozing. On the other hand, there were times (as Patsy used to say) when a brace of whiskies was your only man. This was the sort of time he must have had in mind.

While Maeve was taking her first sip of sherry, Raphael Screeton – Raff to his mates – was sitting in a fifth floor office of a popular Sunday newspaper. He stared, frowning, at the screen of his word-processor. The story had been in the memory bank long enough. The time had come to bring it out and polish it up. His old editor at the *Evening Star* had rejected it out of hand; but this was typical of a man who would sack an investigative journalist, on the slenderest grounds, for unethical conduct. Luckily, the new editor had a lot more nous: he wanted the story splashed over the centre spread. It was just the job for the summer dog-days – the 'silly season' – when hard news was short.

Raff re-worked his first draft. Too long and involved, the editor had called it; keep it simple. It pained him to remove whole bits of an investigation he'd taken trouble over, but that was writing for you. With a sigh he pressed the 'delete' key. The subsidiary personnel disappeared, beginning with the batty old Irish woman who kept the fruit and veg stall. Raff had found her simply by asking around the market. She had given him the lead on the second character to be cut from the story – that little prick-teaser Heather Wright. Definitely a few bricks short of a load, that one. He still had some of the clothes she left behind at his flat, silly bitch.

The real story was the Allingham woman. It had been by the merest chance that he had dropped in on Acton police station and discovered her report. Her 'sighting' had made him look around for other 'witnesses'. He wondered briefly if there was anything in it. After all, if there were three people... No, it was impossible. They were three hysterical women. They probably got it off each other. What gave the story its edge, of course, was the big Christian conference thing. She was the wife, it turned out, of a vicar who was involved.

Raff paused. Should he ring up the Reverend for a quote? Better not. He might reveal that his wife had a long history of mental illness, and that would dilute the story. Instead, he began his re-write. His fingers flew over the keys. The trick was not to think too much but to get the main thrust of the story straight, and then bash it out in one go. In that way the facts were less likely to interfere with the felicities of the house style his paper favoured.

A gust of warm wind struck Maeve in the face as she stepped outside. To her surprise, it was dark. She had assumed that it was about eight o'clock, but the clock on the floodlit tower told her it was getting on for eleven. And where was Alistair? Still down at the Dean's, no doubt, liaising and co-ordinating and checking schedules. He should be here with me, she thought, walking in the wind warmed by a thousand take-aways.

Still trapped in the fence, the piece of blue plastic fluttered like an eyelid. She flicked a V-sign at it and set off down Marlborough Gardens, marvelling at the sensation of air breezing through her shorn hair. Half way down the High Street she found a shop still open, but it sold no alcohol. She pressed on to the nearest pub, but last orders had already been taken. The barman became quite offensive when she asked if she could buy a bottle of Irish whiskey to take away. She knocked on the doors of two off-licenses and another pub, but in vain.

She found herself at the end of the High Street, facing the barren stretch of road which ran to Ealing. No joy there. The pavements were empty except for an old drunk who was talking and gesticulating violently to himself. A car swished past, blowing a batch of dirty papers against her legs. Across the street, standing alone amidst the rubble of waste ground, Maeve saw the tall Gothic outline of The Castle.

She crossed over and inspected it. There was no chink of light in its windows. It looked not just closed but deserted. But hadn't she heard that it was often open when other pubs had closed? If she could just breach its walls, surely the tinkers and terrorists wouldn't garrotte her for requesting a bottle of whiskey? She could be in and out before they twigged that she wasn't one of them. She looked around her. There was no one in sight. She would just try the door on which, in white lettering, *The Shebeen* was advertised. It was probably locked.

Resigning herself to going home and to bed with something beastly like cocoa, she pushed half-heartedly at the door. It opened.

Alistair struggled through the front door, staggering slightly under the weight of the fax machine. It was the only one he had been able to hire at short notice, a heavy antiquated model very different from the briefcase-sized version he'd envisaged. He laid it gently on his desk, which had been cleared in readiness for Bishop Mwawa, and began to set it up. He managed to cut his finger attaching the plug. He felt like weeping. He shouted for Maeve and, receiving no reply, went in search of her. She was not in the house. The only sign of her was the puzzling empty bottle of sherry in the drawing-room. Had there been guests? It seemed not, since there was only one glass in evidence. But Maeve rarely, if ever, drank. What was going on? Was she going off the rails again? It was too awful to contemplate.

He sat down heavily in an armchair and pressed his knuckles against his closed eyes. He felt like giving up. He was too tired to fend off the searing doubts and questions which had only been kept at bay by continuous activity. Chief among them were the intolerable daimons which, now that they had gained a foothold in his imagination, plagued him at every turn. They were like an insidious whispering campaign conducted inside his head. He even dreamed about them, in the form of provocative nymphs and snaky melusines and black gory-locked Furies. Old Freud would've had a field day. Alastair didn't hold much of a brief for

Freud; but something he'd said had stuck, something to the effect that whatever is repressed returns in another guise. Of course, the immortal daimons could not be done away with – every culture, all folklore was full of them. They could only be repressed, and then only temporarily, by the blunt instruments of Christianity and the bare knuckles of rationalism. They would always return, trickily, by the back door, in one form or another. So where were they now? Judging by his own mental condition, it was obvious. Driven out of the world, they had hidden where they were least likely to be looked for, nearer to humans than humans were to themselves – in the unconscious mind, where they bided their time, waiting to erupt whenever guards were dropped. They'd come back to him, Alistair realised with a shock, as Hyacinth's image: the black ambiguous visage contradicting the gold rococo clouds – partly her, partly not-her; part human, part divine; both sexy and sublime. The more the daimons were denied, it seemed, the more they gathered power until perhaps, at some extreme limit of suppression, they were driven to become substantial, autonomous; and, bursting forth like madness, to resume their ancient high position, hanging like swords over the heads of men.

Alastair smiled wryly to himself: he was becoming a bit of a pagan. Oddly, the thought caused him no anguish. If Christianity couldn't banish the daimons, the reverse was also true. His belief in one God remained intact. It was just that he'd have to learn – had already learnt – to temper it with a belief in the existence of other godlings, even other gods, just as the old philosophers had taken for granted.

EIGHTEEN

A row of dim lights above the bar of The Castle caused the bottles to gleam in their optics but left the rest of the pub in semi-darkness. It was smarter than Maeve had imagined. A thick carpet lay underfoot; tall-backed benches, like pews, lined the walls; black-painted tables and chairs were grouped here and there. Past the bar, the L-shaped room narrowed towards the back. Strips of wooden panelling affixed to curved walls suggested the hold of a ship.

Four men were drinking at the bar. Maeve had not noticed them at first because they sat so still and silent. She now saw that they were looking at her. As she walked towards them, they returned to their drinks. A fifth man, standing behind the bar, stopped polishing a glass and held it up to the light. He stared at it for a long time, scrutinizing it for imperfections. He was a large, corpulent fellow of about thirty. His face was plump and very smooth. His hair was expensively cut.

"Didn't I tell you, Declan," he said, picking up and examining another glass, "to lock that door?" One of the men slipped off his bar stool and went over to the door. With the bravery born of more than half a bottle of sherry Maeve said:

"Good evening. A whiskey, please."

"We're closed," said the barman. "Show the lady out, Declan." Maeve quickly sat at the table nearest to her.

"I'll wait until you're open then," she replied, adding with drunken inspiration, "if you don't mind, Mr Ryan." It was written outside: M.J. Ryan, prop. Who else would the man be? The expression on the barman's face did not change, but there was a perceptible intensification of its studied blandness. The use of his name seemed to have put matters on a slightly different footing. He lifted his chin in the direction of Declan, who opened the door, looked to left and right, and then shut it again. Maeve gripped the arm of her chair a little harder as she heard the lock click.

"You've a long wait," said Ryan neutrally, "we don't open till eleven tomorrow morning."

Maeve could think of nothing to say in reply, so she sat back in her chair. The men looked at her, speaking to each other out of the sides of their mouths. She couldn't make out what they were saying because their voices were too low and their accents were too strong. Or was it because they were speaking Irish? At least two of them were, she decided. One of them was now talking to Mr Ryan while the others listened and nodded. She began to feel a deeper unease. There seemed to be a kind of vibration under her feet as if someone were playing the radio too loudly in a room below. It was stuffy, too, in the pub. She undid the top button of her dress but she still could not breathe comfortably.

Suddenly one of the men was standing in front of her, holding a glass. No more than a boy, really, with a narrow head and the pale undernourished but cunning look of a Dublin gurrier.

"Yes?" Her voice was cold from apprehension.

"You'll have a drink while you're waiting?"

"Well, yes. Thank you." The impression of cunning was dissipated by a smile of great sweetness.

"The consensus of opinion was that an Irish would be more to your taste than a Scotch."

"Quite right."

"I had him put a drop of water in it for you."

"Very nice."

"Not too much, I hope." Maeve took a sip of the whiskey and then a mouthful. It brought tears to the backs of her eyes.

"Just right. What's your name?"

"Kevin."

"I'm Maeve Allingham."

"Ah. Well, I'm off down below so. Goodbye now." He walked purposefully through the dark narrow part of the bar and disappeared behind a red curtain which Maeve had mistaken for a wall-hanging. After a few seconds, a weird sound was heard and then abruptly cut off. Even though she had only heard the sound momentarily, it seemed to chop the air into segments. It was, unmistakably, a double jig being played on the uilleann pipes. Maeve was already on her feet, heading towards the curtain which, of course, was the doorway to *The Shebeen. Open Fridays and Saturdays from 9.00 p.m.* The bulk of the landlord smoothly intercepted her.

"You can't go down there."

"Why not?" He thought for a moment, impassively.

"You're not a member."

"Can I become one, please?"

"I'd advise against it."

"Why's that?"

"You could see things down there would alarm you. It's not a place" – he hesitated – "for a lady."

"You mean an English lady?" His small eyes seemed to soften for a moment, but he did not contradict her. "I was born in Mayo," Maeve added, feeling foolish. Ryan shrugged.

"I'd advise against it. But I'll not stop you."

"How much is it?" She fumbled in her purse.

"Ah, go on." He waved a hand towards the red curtain. "Annyway, I'll be shutting up shop in a minute or two."

"Thank you very much, Mr Ryan."

The whiskey was taking effect. Maeve walked unsteadily to the curtain and pulled it aside. She was not certain now that she wanted to go through with this. What did she hope to gain by entering *The Shebeen*? There would only be drunkenness and mayhem, and worse. Ryan was right – it was no place for an English lady. He had been too courteous to put it more strongly. He had not liked to mention the possibility of knee-capping.

She was in a short corridor lit by a single naked bulb. At the end was a steep flight of stone steps leading down to a heavy door. It had a sheet of metal fixed to it, like the door of a strong-room. Once she was in, there'd be no escape. She felt helpless and vulnerable. She began to tip-toe down the stairway like a little girl playing Grandmother's Footsteps. She thought of how Nanny Bryce would take a very dim view of this behaviour. She could see Nanny's lips compress and her perfect head give a little shake of exasperation. She was simply being wilful and childish, just as when she had cut off her hair. Yet, all the same, her feet carried her to the bottom.

She could hear a rumble of voices behind the sound-proofed door; and, behind the voices, music. The faster, it seemed, the sadder. Pierced by the sound, she leant against the door. The fiddles were underpinned by the thrilling intricate tattoo of a bodhrán. The rattle of the baton on goatskin sent the whiskey racing to her head. She put her hand on the door-knob. She tried to picture Patsy, smiling encouragement. Instead, out of the blue, she saw the look he had given her, once, towards the end. A devastating look she had never seen on his face before. It had been no less chilling in its way than the blank black stare of the aliens. What had she done to deserve such a look? What had happened that they should have parted without a kind word? She could neither remember what she most needed to, nor forget what she most wanted to. She wanted to bang her head on the door and weep. Instead, she turned the knob and pushed it open.

It was pitch dark now, but with the help of a torch lodged at an angle on the lip of the hole, Heather was able to keep working. She dug frantically, mindlessly. If she ceased for an instant, she felt, she would be overrun by the clashing ranks of crazy images, crushed to a pulp by the drumming engines. She was crying now with fear and exhaustion. Her breath came in dry desperate sobs. With every chop of the spade she told herself that she was nearly far enough down. Just one more and one more – and she would be finally earthed.

As she battled against a seam of clay at the bottom of her trench, a single persistent notion, like the advance guard of the mad army, came into her head. The more she tried to fight it off, the more clearly defined it became: the whole process of digging was absurd. If she were ever to be 'earthed', the operation should take place, surely, in the mental realm, where her airy inflated mania had originally occurred. It was crazy to believe, as her therapy required, that she was a plant. It was as mad to act out 'earthing' as it had been to climb the tower in search of a saviour 'on high'.

Heather threw down her spade and heaved herself on trembling arms out of the hole. She shone the torch into its depths. For a long moment she forgot the darkness and the exhaustion and even the frightful clamour of imminent madness. She saw only the profound and terrible meaning of her gaping hole: it was the ancient mouth of the earth which, out of the silence, spoke to her. It told her that, beneath the green surface of the world from which growing hopeful things put out shoots towards the light, there was a deeper level, as cold and inhuman as the Cube, where she would find a cure. Only there, in the earth's indifferent mineral embrace, could she find release. Only the grave was far enough down.

It was nearly midnight by the clock on the floodlit tower. Heather went back indoors and counted out the tranquillisers on the kitchen table. That had been the problem – one or two at a time could never take her deep enough. But, taken all together, there was hope. She had a few sleeping pills, too, which would help. They might not be needed. She was already worn out.

She poured a jug of water from the tap and set it in front of the pills. The clatter and rumble of her madness was very close now, and very loud. The martial clash of steel on steel brought the blood to her cheeks. Her body vibrated to the throb of its heavy machinery. She laughed. She had not felt so alive since the White Room at the hospital. She was not afraid to face her insanity now. It could have no dominion over her because the spectral dead were also found among its ranks, marching forever across the endless wind-swept steppe beyond the grave. With a thin smile she lifted the first pill to her mouth.

The music stopped as soon as Maeve opened the door of *The Shebeen*. The band had finished their set and was trooping off the low wooden dais which served as a stage. As they left the lighted area they disappeared into the dark throng of the audience. More or less pinned to the door by the crowd, Maeve peered through the gloom around her. Cigarette smoke and alcohol fumes made her eyes water. *The Shebeen* was larger than she had expected. Its ceiling was low, but what it lacked in height it made up for in extent, stretching away into the distance where some more lights, dimmer than those of the stage, could just be discerned. The heat generated by the press of bodies was fierce. The atmosphere of raw excitement seemed to embody itself suddenly in random surges of shadowy people. Maeve was appalled by the possibility of violence, but also relieved that she was unlikely to be singled out for special attention. She had no sooner thought this than she felt an urgent pluck at her sleeve. She froze. It had begun.

"Hello! Mrs Allingham!" A voice rang out in the amazed and delighted tones of one who has found a long-lost friend.

"Kevin!" Absurdly, she shook hands with the pale boy whom she had seen not ten minutes before.

"Will we have a drink?"

"Yes!"

"Follow me." Kevin ploughed into the wall of people which miraculously opened in front of him. Maeve followed as best she could, feeling clumsy and conspicuous among the preponderance of young people. Twice she was rudely, almost brutally, jostled; but, looking round in alarm, she saw only excitable youths, as prey to the capricious tide of people as she was. She passed a number of tables invisible from the door. They were surrounded by groups of drinking boys and girls. She shied away from one at which a shaven-headed man was pouring beer on to the head of another amidst hoots and jeers. Kevin shouted over his shoulder:

"Swiss! They've no manners at all!" Maeve put a hand on his shoulder to steady herself among the slippery patches of spilt beer on the stone floor. Gradually they progressed to where the noise was less and the people older. There were lights, too, from the bar, masked by large men standing three deep against it. In the far left corner of the huge cellar-like room, Maeve noticed a door behind a curtain of plastic strips. It made her alive once again to the dangers of this place. God only knew what was being hatched behind that door. What was Kevin leading her into? She glanced back at the packed space behind her. She could no longer see the entrance – which was also the exit – through the seething crowd. Occasionally a face, catching the stage lights, flashed white in the blackness. The eyes looked glassy, the expression blurred by drink. It frightened her.

When a small gap appeared at the bar through the departure of a customer with a tray of full glasses, Kevin was able to nip in and catch the eye of the barman. Maeve, red in the face, squeezed in beside him.

"I'll pay for these," she said, holding her handbag tightly in front of her.

"OK so. What'll you have? Will you try a drop of porter?"

"Guinness? Yes, why not." Maeve had never tasted the stuff, but that seemed irrelevant when everything else was also unprecedented. A man standing next to her, with shaggy hair and an alarming beer belly, laid a restraining hand on her arm. He glanced furtively around him and then, bending his head close to hers, spoke quietly out of the side of his mouth. She couldn't make out what he was saying. Was it some kind of warning or advice? Was he friend or foe? She strained to catch his words. The man repeated them:

"You're better off in this place with Murphy's. It's a smoother drink altogether."

"It's a decent enough pint," conceded Kevin who had no difficulty hearing him.

"Oh, I see," said Maeve. "Well, Murphy's then."

"Fair play to you," said the man. He had the broad red face more appropriate to a farmer than to the criminal class. Maeve was heartened.

"You've to pay now," said Kevin patiently, "and your man will bring the drink when it's ready." This didn't sound right at all. She stubbornly held on to her purse. She would pay up when she was served, and not before. A new band struck up on the stage, distracting her. It was a folk band. Acoustic guitars and raucous singing replaced traditional instruments. Suddenly she noticed that Kevin was paying the barman. She went hot and then cold with shame. She thrust her purse towards him but he only smiled and shook his head. She saw now that the hiatus between paying for, and receiving, the drinks was caused by the need to nurse the Murphy's: the barman was coaxing it out of the tap and gently creaming off superfluous froth with a wooden spatula. When at last it had been caressed to perfection, the barman placed the two pints in front of them. Kevin raised his glass to her. Maeve bit into the white head, slightly warmer than the cool black fluid beneath. It looked like diesel but tasted smooth and bitter. She drank deeply. The porter swept through her like a blood transfusion. The crown of her head seemed to lift an inch or so into the air.

"Fair enough," she called out to Kevin. He smiled.

"God in velvet trousers!"

Despite the heavy grating rhythm of the ballad the band was playing, Maeve felt a flush of pure well-being steal over her. It was short-lived. The sound of breaking glass instantly plunged her into deep dread.

A man lay full length on the floor. Others regarded him morosely. The tallest of them, a snub-nosed fellow with pale red hair and a tinker's face looked unpleasantly familiar to Maeve. He spoke softly, meditatively, yet his voice could be heard through the strumming music.

"Get that man up and make him drink his pint. There'll be no wastage this night." Two heavy rings sparkled in the bar lights as he raised his glass slowly to his mouth. He caught Maeve looking at him. "Don't I know you?" he said. Maeve pursed her lips and gave her head a little shake. Kevin shifted uneasily. The man seemed about to speak again when another voice, behind Maeve, intervened:

"I know you, McBride." She recognised the speaker. The flash of gold at his neck and wrist recalled the last time she had seen him – knocked flat outside The Castle by the menacing McBride, who now sighed and said:

"And I know *you*, Brady."

"Why don't you pick on someone your own size, McBride?" Brady indicated the fallen man who was being helped to his feet. Four or five of his cronies bunched close together and nodded in agreement. McBride smiled, revealing a missing canine.

"I never laid a finger on him, did I, Missus?" All eyes turned on Maeve. She tried to pray, but the singing of the band prevented her: their lyrics described the iniquities of the British and the bravery of the rebels who fought them.

"I... I didn't see..." she began.

"He fell down by himself," interrupted Kevin. "I saw him."

"That's right," said McBride softly. "That's exactly right, Brady. Your friend here is as legless as the Morrigu." At this, a shock passed through the assembled men. Maeve could see sinews tightening beneath their shirts. Brady pointed a finger at McBride's head.

"The Morrigu was queen of the White City till you had hold of her, McBride."

"So you say, Brady." The two men looked hard at each other. Maeve could see surreptitious hands reaching over to the bar and grasping empty bottles. The younger people were joining in the chorus of the rebel song. McBride's lips were moving as he lightly brushed imaginary dust from his rings, but his words were lost in the deafening singing. Brady took a step forward, undoing the middle button of his jacket. Maeve willed her legs to move but, as in some nightmare, they were rooted to the spot. Several more men had imperceptibly joined one group or the other now – both of them bunched and tense on either side of Maeve. In the second before they seemed certain to fly at each other's throats, Maeve found herself being propelled from behind by Kevin.

"Go on. Quick. Head for the door." Maeve hastily pushed through the singing, stamping throng towards the coloured plastic curtain in the corner.

"What's the matter between those two?" she called out to Kevin. "Who's the Morrigu?"

"Jaysus, it's only an old dog," he shouted back, swaying his body to avoid spilling the two full pints he held in his hand. "A greyhound. Brady had great success with it at the White City track. But when he sold it to McBride, sure it never did another thing. That was two years ago. They've been fighting ever since." They were on the fringe of the crowd now, standing in space near the door. "We'll nip in here where it's quieter," said Kevin casually. "And listen. Don't mind the words of the songs now."

Maeve was grateful for his tact. She was beginning to trust Kevin – but not to the extent of entering the notorious back room. However, she had no choice: a mass of heaving bodies in the bar area was sending ripples through the packed room. People were flying towards her. She was barged in the solar plexus by a small black-haired girl. Kevin dropped one of his pints. He opened the door and pushed Maeve, gasping for breath, through it.

At one o'clock in the morning the telephone rang. Alistair tripped over the hall rug in his rush to answer it. He had been beside himself all evening, wondering where Maeve was and whether he should call the police. Also, knowing that the Bishop and his entourage would be arriving the day after tomorrow – no, tomorrow – made him unable to eat or sleep or do anything except write panic-stricken lists of tasks to be completed, each list longer than the last. He was at his wits' end.

"*Maeve?* Where –"

"Allingham." It was the clipped voice of the Dean.

"Yes." Alistair nearly added 'sir'.

"Have you read the Sunday papers?"

"What? Of course not. It's one o'clock in the morning. They don't come until –"

"I've got first editions here. Can you come over? I don't want to read this over the 'phone."

"*What?* Come over? At this hour?"

"It's imperative that you read the article I have here."

"Well... Look, whatever it is, you could fax it, I suppose."

"Right. Give me a minute to go across to the office. And ring me as soon as you've read the article." The Dean sounded even more than usually tight-lipped. He suddenly exploded. "Good God, Allingham, can't you keep your wife under... Never mind. Call me." The line went dead.

Alistair connected up the fax machine in his study and sat next to it, waiting miserably for whatever fresh disaster was in store. The machine buzzed and began to extrude a copy of a newspaper page. His eye fell on the headline before the transmission was completed:

VICAR'S WIFE IN ALIEN BONKING HORROR

He read the first paragraph. It was enough. He rang the Dean.

"Well?" said the terse voice.

"I don't know what to say," said Alistair.

"You'd better think of something. The credibility of the Conference is at stake. You'll be knee-deep in journalists any minute now. We can't stop Mwawa from finding out about this. We can only hope that Mother Felicitas doesn't read newspapers. You'll have to issue a statement to the press as soon as possible. It's vital that you distance yourself absolutely from this lunatic business. Is that clear? Let me know the minute you've done it. Goodnight."

Alistair continued to sit numbly by the 'phone, staring at the newspaper article. *Pinko vicar's Missus, Mavis Allingham, 62*, it began, *claims to have been molested by saucy spacemen in broad daylight. "I was terrified," said the prim-and-proper wife of campaigning lefty, the Rev. Al Allingham, leading light of tomorrow's international church conference...* There was more about 'Christ in Action' which Alistair could not bring himself to read. Both Mwawa and Felicitas were mentioned. It was a nightmare. *The incident occurred on a sunny June morning while Mave, dressed only in a flimsy nightie, was picking roses in her garden at 14, Marlborough Gardens, Acton. "They came out of the blue in a flying saucer shaped like a box," wept a shocked Mave, pillar of her local church. But the randy extraterrestrials certainly weren't square. Slipping out of their slinky silver spacesuits, they tied the mortified Mave to a divan and probed her with their intergalactic appendages. "I was VIOLATED," confessed the terror-stricken housewife. Little green men from Mars? "I don't know where they came from," sobbed Mave, "but whatever they stuck into me wasn't green and it certainly wasn't little."* Alistair felt sick. He skipped the rest of the article, his eye catching only the final sentence: *Page*

3 stunna Kiki Katkin, current Miss UK Wet T-shirt, commented sadly last night: "They sound like the kind of fellas you just don't see around any more."

Alistair stood up, swaying, as the scaffold of all his hopes collapsed beneath him.

NINETEEN

The door was heavier than it looked, and lined with cork. As Kevin closed it behind her, cutting off her retreat, the rebel songs outside were instantly muted to a whisper. Breathing hard, Maeve gazed wildly around her. The back room of *The Shebeen* was as she feared – small, dim and filled with smoke as much from the unexpected coal fire as from cigarettes. She could barely make out the far end of the room where there was an unused pool table and a public telephone fixed to the wall. Otherwise, there were four tables. The nearest was unoccupied; the other three were surrounded by shadowy figures. No one spoke, as if some secret parley had been interrupted. Maeve concentrated on trying to breathe in the stifling airless atmosphere.

"Who's that?" an old man called out sharply from the second table. Maeve dabbed at her smarting eyes with her sleeve. The man's face was deeply lined and tanned like leather, his nose severely hooked. He stared stonily ahead of him as he spoke.

"It's only Kevin, Grandpa," said the girl sitting next to him. The blankness of her expression masked a natural prettiness.

"Kevin!" exclaimed the old man. "You've no business here. I know you. You've come in here, the way you can disturb Teresa. Will you not leave the girl alone?"

"Sssh, Grandpa. He has Mrs Allingham with him."

"Who?"

"You don't know her, Grandpa. She's the vicar's wife."

"Vicar, is it? Ah well." He sounded resigned. Kevin stepped forward. "Hallo, Mr O'Sullivan," he said formally; and, shyly, "Hi Teresa."

"Hallo, Kevin." Teresa's smile allowed the prettiness to break through. Maeve listened anxiously to these exchanges. She did not know what to make of them or of the speakers. The overall picture was blurred. Wiping her eyes made no difference. And yet, when she focused on something, it leapt out with startling clarity, as though she had tunnel vision. She couldn't decide whether the fog was in the room or in her own head, or both. A huge bear-like man at the same table lumbered to his feet. His leather jerkin and drooping moustache vaguely suggested a war-time member of the Resistance.

"I am Tomas," he said to Maeve, smiting his barrel chest. "I am Polish. These –" he swept an arm over the group – "are Irish people. Fine people. We drink Irish whiskey. It is very good for me. Do you wish to drink also? I am singing now."

"You're welcome here," added the old man. Maeve was installed on a chair between Teresa and a plump woman with very pink cheeks who giggled when she was introduced as Mary Donaghue. Two middle-aged men, bald, with neat paunches beneath their waistcoats, completed the party. Kevin preferred to stand behind Teresa, leaning against the mantelpiece on which there was a row of empty glasses and three small silver trophies. On the wall behind these were some old framed photographs depicting teams of men holding hurling sticks.

Meanwhile, true to his word, Tomas had launched into a lugubrious song about his mother country. Generous measures of golden whiskey were poured. Maeve gulped at hers, hoping to clear her head. By screwing up her eyes, she could see that another of the tables was surrounded by five men quietly playing cards. The third table was occupied by three silent women, all knitting. When the Pole had ended his song on a long vibrato note, the only sound in the polite silence was the clicking of their needles. Then there was a smattering of applause and, from Mr O'Sullivan, a non-committal tapping of his glass on the table. The Pole beamed with pleasure. "My friends," he began, spreading his arms wide. He did not finish. Instead, he slumped down in his chair and let his large head fall on to his chest. His eyes closed.

"As you see, we're all doing our little party-pieces," explained Teresa. "You missed mine. I sang *Sé Fath mo Bhuartha*," she added, more for Kevin's benefit, Maeve suspected, than for hers.

"I'd like to have heard that," Kevin remarked, leaning towards the girl. "Watch the Dooleys now," she advised Maeve. "That's Con and that's Mick." The Dooley brothers, hearing their names, caught Maeve's eye and nodded guardedly. They resembled bank managers, with their suits and ties and bald heads.

"How do you know my name?" Maeve asked Teresa.

"Ah, you're well known," she replied vaguely. "You're in and out of the chemist's. I work there."

"Oh. Yes. I recognise you –"

"Look. They're starting." However, the Dooleys did not seem to be starting. They seemed to be looking at each other, dead-pan, with perhaps a faint suggestion of surprise at having come across each other in this unlikely place. Teresa laughed. "God, they're a scream, those two. They never speak at all. Not even to each other. Isn't it great?"

The Dooleys simultaneously reached inside their jackets. Mick produced a long fat tin whistle and looked at it with a perceptible increase in his expression of surprise. Con pulled out a tiny whistle and stared at it with gloomy resignation. They looked at each other with immobile faces. Maeve couldn't help laughing. The brothers then returned the whistles to their inside pockets and produced two more, identical ones, somewhere between the sizes of the first two. "Hooray," said Mary Donaghue, immediately clapping her hand over her mouth. As if this had been some kind of signal, the Dooleys began to play.

They opened in unison with a brace of hornpipes, virtuoso pieces with intricate trills. It was difficult to believe that simple metal tubes could make such an unearthly sound, disembodied like the singing of spirits – detached even from the Dooleys who were as still as stones except for the delicate fluttering of their fingers. Effortlessly the duet glided into a solo with Mick performing a slow air. The high lonesome notes evoked a picture of Patsy, treading his rain-swept acres. Staring into the glowing fire, Maeve seemed to see him turn and fix her with that terrible neutral look. The eerie tune paused and flowed on. 'If I hold my breath,' she thought, 'I'll remember everything.' Mick's sad grace notes wafted a wave of pain across the room. Distant images returned to her: Nanny's golden hair cascading around her; Patsy, straight-backed, walking away; herself shouting, gleeful, ugly. As the whistlers launched into a set of tripping reels, she let out her breath. The sadness inside the music's gaiety desolated her.

The pates of the Dooleys shone pink with the applause. The bottle of whiskey was passed around. The needles of the knitters, silent during the whistles, clicked more vigorously. The card-players nodded over their hands.

"Give us a story, Grandpa," Teresa urged; and, to Maeve, "He's a great man for stories. The strangest things you ever heard."

"I will not," said the old man, maintaining his stiff, dignified attitude, staring straight ahead.

"Ah go on, Mr O'Sullivan," coaxed Kevin.

"Yes, come on, my friend," boomed Tomas, surfacing briefly from his stupor. The Dooleys tapped encouragement with their glasses.

"I'll tell no stories this night," said the old man sternly. "I'd rather hear from Mrs Allingham. Will you favour us with something?" He turned his head for the first time towards her. With a shock, she realised he was blind.

"Me? Oh no, I couldn't." As soon as she spoke, she regretted her words. It was not, she knew, the performance that mattered; it was the taking part.

"You could, of course," prompted Teresa.

"Anny ould thing," added Kevin

"Yes. Well, I could tell you something I've just remembered. It's not really a story. It's something that happened to me. A thing you might understand better than I."

"Hooray," said the Pole, clapping his hand to his moustache. Mary Donaghue giggled. His head fell forward again. Mr O'Sullivan struck an attentive attitude, and the others followed suit.

"The story has a beginning but no end," began Maeve.

"Very good," said Kevin.

"Not yet, at any rate. I was brought up in a big house in Mayo. In a corner of the grounds was a mound known as Maeve's Grave. I knew, of course, that Maeve was queen of the *Sídhe* and that the mound could not truly be her grave because she is immortal. But it was a fairy spot, held in high esteem by Patsy Collins, a man who worked for my father. I used to play there as a small child, feeling connected with the place because Maeve is my own name. But one day I thought I heard music, and afterwards I didn't play there any more. It made me shiver to think of it, as if it were my own grave." Mr O'Sullivan nodded slowly. Encouraged by the sympathetic attention she was receiving, Maeve lost her self-consciousness and warmed to the story. Taking a drink of whiskey, she continued:

"I went to Maeve's Grave for the last time a day or two before I left Ireland for school in England. It was late September. A cold wind had been blowing all day from the North, directly into my face. The mound was all overgrown, invisible to those who wouldn't know it was there. I brought with me a scythe and a spade. It took all morning to cut a wide swathe through the bracken and brambles. In the afternoon, I began to dig."

"Was drink taken?" enquired Kevin, with the air of one who wants to set the scene correctly.

"Would you ever shut up, Kevin?" said Teresa.

"No," said Maeve. "I wasn't yet fourteen. I barely tasted whiskey before today." The Dooleys exchanged incredulous looks.

"Very good. Go on," said Kevin.

"I dug deeper and deeper. I didn't want to, but there was a kind of frenzy on me: my clothes stuck to my back, my eyes were stinging with sweat but I was cold with fear of what I might unearth. I kept seeing things" – Maeve broke off, remembering the mineral glint in the blackness she took for fairy treasure, the white twisted flints she took for bones. Deeper still, she thought at any moment to hear the stamp of dancing feet and the blood-freezing stutter of pipes. But all she heard was the whine of her own breath, the cold wind, the rooks mourning in the high beeches.

"After a while, the fear and frenzy passed. I was calm and controlled. I threw down the spade and sat like a princess at the top of the wide scar I'd opened in the heart of the mound. The sun was setting. There were pink clouds, like candy floss, and long shadows lying on the meadows. I waited for Patsy to come, as he always did at that hour. I was triumphant." Her voice quavered. She stared for a moment into the dying fire. Her audience shifted in their chairs but didn't speak. The knitting women clicked away. "It was my Nanny – Miss Bryce – who arrived first. A person brought over to make an English girl of me. A fine, lovely woman with gold hair piled up like mine... like mine used to be. I knew she would applaud my victory over Irish superstition and ignorance. I beg your pardon, but that's how I felt. I can see her now, looking up at me where I squatted on top of the mound with a grin on my face. I can see her breaking into a little nervous run as she came up to the beautiful black trench I'd dug. I called out to her. I said: 'If Patsy wants proof, here it is!' I never saw a stupid look on that woman's face until then. 'Proof?' she said. 'Proof of what?' Her hands fluttered up to her cheeks. Then she pitched forward and sank to her knees in the fresh earth."

For a moment Maeve was speechless as she saw once more how Nanny, as if with an access of grief, had picked distractedly at her piled hair; how, with a sudden shock, the tresses fell like the petals on a spent rose. Gold hair flowed over her shoulders and down her back. "I couldn't believe what I was seeing – Nanny rocking to and fro and moaning: 'Oh what have you done? Oh what will Patsy say?' But Patsy said nothing at first. He came round the back of the mound and quietly helped Nanny to her feet. I wasn't as confident as I had been, but I put a brave face on it. I wasn't going to let the pair of them break me. I called down to him: 'You see? There's no treasure, no fairies! Nothing. It's just a heap of useless earth!' Maeve's voice cracked now as it had then. An enormous pain drifted like smoke around her head. "Patsy didn't reply. I yelled again, hysterical: '*See*? There's nothing.' He gave me a look then such as I'd never thought to see. It wasn't hostile or angry. It was the brief glance you'd give to a perfect stranger. I heard him say, almost casually, to Nanny: 'The Good People have taken a soul for less than what she's done,' and then, as they both walked away, he said something I didn't catch. I was raging. 'What did you say?' I shrieked at him. 'Nanny, what did he say?' She called over her shoulder. 'You'll probably get away with it, being English.' Bitter words, like a blow. 'Go to hell,' I said; but really it was I who..." Tears ploughed down her face. She had left for England two days later – never, except in fact, to return. "I'm sorry. I must be a bit drunk."

"We're all of us the better for drink," Teresa reassured her. Mary Donaghue surprised herself as much as anybody by patting Maeve's arm and saying:

"Don't fret yourself over that ould mound now. I know many who wouldn't think twice about digging them up in the hope of gold."

"You don't understand," said Maeve sadly. "I hardly spoke another word to Patsy again. I saw him at father's funeral, but that's all. He disappeared to his land on the Galway border. He always promised me when I was little that I could see it one day. All hundred and twenty-six acres of it."

"I'd say he had a lot more than that now," remarked Kevin. Maeve wondered if she had misheard him.

"You *know* him?"

"Patsy Collins? On the Galway-Mayo border? God, everyone knows him."

"He invented a portable sheep dip," added Mr O'Sullivan. "Some say his wife invented it. Made him a fortune. Smart man."

"But I didn't imagine he'd still be alive. He must be eighty odd," said Maeve excitedly.

"He's not so old."

"How is he?"

"Why don't you ask him yourself?"

"I could. I suppose *I could.* I could write to him."

"Telephone him," said Mick Dooley, his words taking on great authority by virtue of their rarity. Everyone was surprised into silence.

"I couldn't possibly," said Maeve at last.

"You could," called out one of the knitting women whom Maeve had thought was out of earshot.

"Ah do," said Teresa.

"Has anybody any change?" asked Kevin. All except Maeve pulled coins from pockets and bags and pooled them on the table. Kevin scooped them up and headed for the 'phone. "I'll get on to Directory Enquiries. It won't take a minute."

"You're not going to 'phone him *now*..?" Her heart was hammering against her ribs.

"I may as well."

"Isn't it great gas?" added Teresa. The palms of Maeve's hands were slick with sweat. The huge obscure pain seemed to have settled inside her head. She shook it, trying to think clearly. It was impossible that this was happening. Yet she could hear Kevin joking with someone on the 'phone, ringing off, redialling. The room was unbearably stuffy; she, unbearably hot. Kevin called out to her.

"Mrs Allingham! It's ringing for you."

As she raised the first pill to her mouth, Heather had paused to listen. Now that there was no longer any need to shut out the raucous inner engines, she could afford to take the risk of admitting the sound and its accompanying host of images. And it seemed as though she could hear, beneath the clattering battalions of noise, a deeper bass note, as regular as a heartbeat. And again, above the dissonance, like the sighing of high winds, she could hear a rudimentary harmony. Involuntarily she began to tap her foot in time to the bass and to whistle through her teeth in tune with the airy top notes.

Curiously, the awful tumult – the sound of the mind's wheels turning against themselves – did not increase. Her recognition of something akin to music within the grinding, whining machinery appeared to keep it at bay. The more she tapped and whistled and swayed, the easier it was to discern the musical components.

Heather rose from her chair and improvised a few dance steps. The music – half-heard, half-imagined – was lost for a second in the background clamour, only to re-emerge more distinctly as if it had drawn some of the discord into its own order. She laughed incredulously and began to move her feet and work her aching arms more methodically, until she had created a repetitive dance pattern. At first her sluggish body resisted the music like a clogged sieve, slowing it down; but then, as the music imparted new energy to her straining limbs, it flowed more freely, speeding up, until she was no longer leading it but following. The repetitive rhythm became relentless. She was forced to dance faster and faster to keep up. The pounding beat bore down on her; the high harmonies swelled like remote wailing choirs. If she were to stop moving for a second she would be drowned before she could reach her pills and cram them into her mouth.

Panic-stricken at the thought, she lost her footing, stumbled and, in a flash, waves of sound were breaking over her. She flung herself about the room, gyrating and jumping in her attempts to recapture the pattern of the dance. She lost all control, banging against the walls and flailing her arms as if to beat off the mad surge of music. Miraculously her feet knew what to do. Even as her gasps for breath were turning to screams, they responded with a last exhausted charge, executing the steps which kept her head above the waves. She found herself whirling at the heart of a wild vortex in which, for one long mindless moment, she was both the music and the dance. Then she was through the far side, perfectly balanced on white crests of ecstasy, flying down steep foaming slopes towards terra firma.

Gradually the music retreated into the distance, sinking down deeper inside her, until it was no more than a single faint beat. Heather dragged herself into the next room and collapsed on the bed. Through her dazed senses she was aware of a new sound, strange and lovely. It was the sound of birds singing in the pre-dawn. She fell into a deep sleep.

Maeve listened to the peremptory ringing of the telephone in far-off Galway. She imagined the grey farmhouse as Patsy had described it, overlooking the Atlantic; and, behind it, the dark-green, mountainous sweep of the famous land.

"Yes?" said a woman's voice. Maeve was not prepared for this.

"Can I speak to Patsy Collins?" she said faintly.

"Do you know what time it is?"

"I'm afraid I don't," whispered Maeve.

"Oh well, hold the line." She held the line, with the huge silence of all Galway filling her ear. Her throat was constricted; her heart beating fit to break.

"Hello there."

"Patsy? It's me, Maeve."

"Maeve?" said the voice, older but still profoundly familiar. "Well, well. Aren't you the girl!" He sounded as though he had been speaking to her only the day before. "Where are you, Maeve?"

"I'm in a pub in London."

"Are you now. How's the crack?"

"It's fine, Patsy. Fierce!" He laughed. He might have been in the room with her. "I'm drinking whiskey with some friends," she said foolishly.

"Ah God, are you a ruined woman, Maeve? Fair enough. Are you coming to see us?"

"I'd like to, Patsy."

"That'd be mighty. Hurry up and come over then. I was expecting you for the wedding. Caroline wrote to you. Twice. Did you not get the letters?"

"Was that Caroline I spoke to, Patsy? Is she your wife?"

"Do you not know your own Nanny? And wasn't I after telling you she'd fall for the acreage?"

"I didn't realise, Patsy... no, that's not true. I suppose I really knew all along. I never read the letters. I'm sorry."

"It doesn't matter, pet. As long as you're well."

"I'm well, Patsy."

"Wait now till I tell you about the sheep dip she dreamed up. Jaysus, it's a powerful contraption..." Maeve listened, smiling. The pain lifted and dispersed in the smoky room. The money ran out and Patsy's voice was cut off in mid-flow. Slowly she returned to her seat.

"Would you ever bring us another bottle, Kevin?" she asked, handing him a twenty-pound note. Kevin disappeared through the door, letting in a gust of music. The traditional players had returned and were galloping away on some fast Kerry slides.

"While you were on the 'phone," said Teresa, "we were discussing your fairy fort – it's a lovely name, Maeve's Grave – and I was saying that I believe there used to be, you know, fairies and that in Ireland, but they're long gone now."

"They're fallen angels," broke in Mary Donaghue, her cheeks reddening. "A priest told me."

"There's no harm in them," opined Con Dooley, made talkative, perhaps, by his brother's earlier dramatic suggestion.

"There is and there isn't," said Mr O'Sullivan with the air of one settling a dispute. "As for their going, Teresa – my grandfather was saying the same thing a hundred years ago, according to my father. Sure they're always going – but they're never altogether gone. I could tell you stories now..."

Kevin returned triumphant and replenished the glasses. Maeve was toasted by all present, except Tomas who was snoring gently, his head on the table.

"Tell us the story, Grandpa," begged Teresa. "But not in Irish or I won't understand a word." The old man nodded, his sightless eyes already surveying the events he would describe. Maeve listened in a kind of trance, every word penetrating her, like truth.

"I had an uncle lost a wife to *them*." Mr O'Sullivan paused meaningly. "She was out stacking the turf he'd cut, up by an old rath – that's to say a fairy fort" he added for Maeve's benefit, "when she heard music in the air and the clatter of horses; and, seeing no one about, she knew it was no *right* thing she heard, and she ran back home and told my Uncle John. He only laughed. But that night, when he was blowing on the fire the way he might get a bit of a spark to light his last pipe, he heard music coming from the next room where his wife was asleep. He was up then like a rabbit and, putting his eye to the keyhole, saw nothing for the bright lights dancing around inside. He knew then that the Good People were there in the house. Sure enough, when he burst into the room his wife was gone and only her likeness left behind in the bed. And that same night Michael Casey, coming home from a spree, passed her on the road and she wearing only a nightdress. And there was a queer tall man with her, says Michael, with long hard legs, who had her by the sleeve."

"I thought they were small people," said Mary, immediately covering her mouth with both hands.

"They are and they aren't," said Mr O'Sullivan severely. "Some say that there's something in your eyes makes them seem bigger or smaller. Annyway, two weeks later the wife comes to John where he's working in the fields. Pitiful to look at she is, and thin, because, you know, to eat their food is to stay amongst them forever. And she says to him will he go up to the rath three nights from that night, the way he might save her. How will I do that? says he. You'll see a troop of horses going into the rath, says she, and I'll be on the last horse. And if you throw a handful of nails over my head, says she, you will save me surely. For iron has the power to charm *them*, that's well-known. So my uncle John, who was afraid of no man, goes up beyond to the fairy fort on the night appointed by his wife. Sure enough, along comes a troop of tall riders, laughing the way they do, with fine clothes of green and gold, and shining eyes you'd be alarmed to look at. And on the last horse to go into the rath was his wife with a forlorn face on her. John was so amazed now, and so afraid, that he couldn't lift a hand to throw the nails. And that was the last he saw of her."

"God save us all!" said Teresa.

Maeve drifted towards wakefulness. Her bed seemed to be damp and she felt chilly, but nothing worth the effort of getting up. *The Shebeen*'s music was running through her head – a continuous thread of reels, jigs, slides and polkas on which were strung, like beads on a rosary, isolated memories of the remainder of the night. There was Kevin's face, luminous and looming close to hers, saying something that made her weep with laughter. There was a wonderful lady dancing to the tunes of a lone fiddler. People had cheered even before she began. Six times dance champion of all Connaught, someone had said. She wore a dazzling red evening gown and flashing jewellery, and she danced in the Irish fashion: her hands pressed to the sides of her perfectly still body while her feet darted to and fro with exquisite precision. Her sudden stallion-like kicks high into the air brought gasps from the audience. She had smiled at Maeve, and waved, like an old friend. For a moment Maeve had fancied that it was Heather; but the lady's face was much older, perhaps timeless, reminding Maeve of an icon she had once seen of the gorgeously caparisoned Shiva, dancing the world into being and back into non-being.

Behind her, like a caricature of her graceful dance, a pair of men clumsily circled the fiddler. Laced in each other's arms, their foreheads were pressed together, their bleary faces fixed in drunken concentration – Brady and McBride! It was as though Maeve knew everyone down there – as though she knew everyone in the world! She even (it came to her now with a shock) knew the female dancer. It was, of all people, Mrs O'Rourke of fruit and vegetable fame. Perhaps everyone had a secret other life which was invisible by daylight.

The last thing she remembered was her surprise and pleasure at the blueness of the sky and the crystalline sharpness of the early morning air. There had been an inviting grassy bank and a luscious bed of flowers – a special place, kept inviolate for her by iron railings. Tired, light-headed, not altogether steady on her pins, Maeve decided that, before going home, she would just rest for a minute, just close her eyes for a second. She had swayed through a narrow gate in the railings and laid her grateful head among the scented blooms.

"Mrs Allingham!" A voice broke into her dreamy reminiscence. "Wake up, hah! You are in the papers!"

Maeve sat up and looked around her, blinking in the sunlight. A black-suited man was leaning on the railing, brandishing a newspaper. Behind his thick spectacles his eyes seemed to be popping out of his head.

"Ah, Pastor Duval," she said, shading her eyes. "Good, er, morning."

"I am on my way to church, Mrs Allingham, but, but…" Caleb Duval sounded agitated. "But now I find you sleeping rough!" Maeve studied the flower-bed in the small memorial garden not far from the Pentecostal church. Her head had crushed the last word of the sentence, spelt out in flowers: 'We will remember them.'

"Yes. It is odd, isn't it?" She was soaked with dew; her neck was stiff. Her head, though aching, was unusually clear.

"You had better come out of there, Mrs Allingham, before you get, hah, arrested for trespassing on municipal property."

"I expect you're right, Caleb. I seem to remember a gate around here somewhere."

"No gate, Maeve. You will have to climb over these railings. Quickly. I will give you a hand." He looked to left and right, as if expecting imminent arrest. He was right, too, about the gate. She must have imagined it. Considering the trouble it took, even with Caleb's help, to clamber over the railings, she wondered how she had managed it earlier that morning. Perhaps Irish whiskey possessed magical transformative properties. Several church-goers paused on the far side of the street to watch her ignominious egress from the municipal property. Once she was safely over, Caleb took a nervous step back.

"What does it all mean, Maeve?" he asked with concern. "Look at you. Look at your hair. What is this sleeping rough and this strange tale of hanky-panky with spacemen…?" He shoved his newspaper towards her and pointed at the unsavoury article. Maeve scanned it. 'Oh God,' she thought. 'Poor Alistair.'

"It's all a mistake, Caleb. Thanks so much for your help. Now do go along – I don't want to make you late for church."

TWENTY

As the Dean had predicted, a crowd of reporters and photographers was gathered outside the front gate, baying for a statement. Every so often one of them would sally up the short path and press the doorbell. They knew Alistair was inside. They had seen his drawn anxious face at the drawing-room window. He scarcely dared to go into the rooms with windows in case he found reporters pressed against them. He was forced to stay in the hall, where he dithered to and fro, steeling himself to issue the statement that would make them go away. If only his mind weren't so confused by lack of sleep, if only his head didn't ache – if only he weren't so *thrown* – he could easily come up with the swift, decisive dismissal which would save the situation. He could make light of the newspaper story, countering ridicule with a little joke about the well-known extravagances of the tabloid press. He couldn't procrastinate much longer – the Dean would be on to him any minute, demanding an account of what he had said. Besides, Mwawa was flying in from Switzerland that evening. Someone was certain to have faxed the news to him by now. If Alistair did not scotch the story, or somehow laugh it off, straightaway, it would simply be the end of everything.

But still he hesitated. He wanted desperately to talk to Maeve first, to be reassured by her. Her absence was profoundly worrying. Shouldn't he call the hospital or the police, or something? Was that over-reacting? No, surely it wasn't, not when his wife was missing. He would say something to the press now – anything really, just to stall them, just to gain a breathing-space – and then he'd start 'phoning. He took a deep breath, composed his face and opened the door.

He was confronted by a small elderly woman, her hand frozen in the act of ringing the bell. Alistair stared, uncomprehending, at her wrinkled face, her grey headscarf, her long maroon coat.

"Good morning," she said, with an unmistakable Irish accent. "I was sent to see Mrs Allingham."

"What? Oh. Yes." He remembered that Maeve had said she would hire a cleaner from an agency, to help organise the house for the

Bishop's visit. "You'd better come in. My wife's not here just now. I expect she'll be back shortly. Quickly..." He ushered her inside and shut the door as the press, emboldened by the sight of someone breaching the walls, surged up the path. There was a long blast on the doorbell and the sound of voices calling his name.

"Sorry about this," said Alistair. "I wish I could stop them ringing."

"Why don't you fix the bell with a bit of paper?" The woman tore a sheet off the notepad by the telephone, folded it, and handed it to Alistair. He reached up to the bell above the door and inserted the wedge between it and the clapper. Silence.

"Good thinking," said Alistair. "It's all rather trying, this... my wife... well, anyway, you'll want to press on." He led her into the kitchen where the floor stuck to the soles of shoes and the table was piled with dirty plates and cutlery, opened packets, used cups. "We may as well start in here." He peered vaguely into the cupboard under the sink. "All the cleaning stuff is kept in here, I think."

"I'll find everything," said the woman briskly, taking off her coat. "Sure, you go and put your feet up. I'll have a word with Mrs Allingham when she comes in." Alistair was alarmed to see how thin the woman was. He hoped to God he wasn't in the business of exploiting the labour of little frail old ladies. However, she seemed confident enough, and was already stacking things at a good clip. Despite her suggestion that he should rest, he was about to wade in with assistance when he heard the rattle of a key in the front door.

"No," Maeve's voice was saying, "no, I've nothing to say." Alistair ran into the hall. Irrationally, absurdly, he felt as if things would be all right. Maeve would see to it, somehow. Relief gave way to dismay. His wife was a sight. He hardly recognised the damp bedraggled person with the deathly pale face. And her *hair*... He swallowed the sudden lump in his throat. Her hair was a cropped thatch, sticking out at odd angles. She looked like a tramp.

"Maeve... what's happened to you?"

"You've seen the papers then?" she asked, ignoring his question.

"Yes, yes. But... but where have you *been*, Maeve?" Incredibly, she laughed.

"Not now, dear. It's a long story. I absolutely must have a hot bath. I'm done in. But first of all –" She broke off and pointed towards the kitchen where clattering sounds could be heard. She raised her eyebrows.

"The cleaning agency sent a woman," explained Alistair.

"Good. Now listen, Alistair. This is important. You have to go outside and talk to those reporters. I'd do it myself but I'm afraid it would only make matters worse. You must pooh-pooh the whole story –"

"You sound like the Dean," said Alistair, bemused by the sudden return of his wife's old incisive self.

"You're not listening, Alistair. You must denounce me as temporarily off my rocker. They must be made to feel sorry for you, stuck with a crazed old baggage for a wife. Put yourself in the clear. I will not have this business messing up your big chance. It's nothing to do with you, after all. Do you understand? With luck, it'll all just peter out and Mwawa won't take any notice." Alistair lightly brushed her pink indignant cheeks with his fingertips. "Do you understand?" she repeated more gently.

"Yes, dear. Thank you. Now go and have your bath."

As she mounted the stairs, Alistair was surprised to hear her humming a jaunty sort of tune under her breath. He retired to his study, lay back on his divan like a tubercular poet and tried to compose the simple, strong press statement. He would have to hurry because he was due to take matins in less than two hours' time. The thought of having to conduct a service appalled him. He could already see his parishioners whispering behind their hands, even talking loudly in church – perhaps openly walking out as he took to the pulpit. How could he hope to disassociate himself from Maeve's aberration? He would always be the vicar whose wife had been ravished by diminutive aliens. He would never be entirely free of the stigma. He imagined the Powers That Be in Westminster shaking their heads, jowls wobbling as they turned away at his approach. His ears burned as if they were already discussing him, pronouncing their *anathema sit*. His legs writhed against the divan cushions. He had always been ready to endure martyrdom. Those who had been jailed or tortured for the Cause in barbarous countries were, well, almost to be envied. But this imminent, inglorious ridicule was a new refinement of such persecution. He would be shunned by his own party, cut off from the centres of decision-making, doomed to spend his declining years on the fringes. He would be merely tolerated, like a village idiot, by his superiors; his parishioners would be replaced by cranks, flat-earthers and ninnies who believed that God was an astronaut.

Alistair closed his eyes. If only he could sleep for a minute or two – just long enough to clear his head for the task in hand. He never had been able to think well under pressure. Perhaps it would be best all round if he threw in the towel and gave up a ministry he wasn't fit for. Hyacinth had been right: he was too *worldly*. He had allowed ideology to usurp his religion. He had bent the eternal verities to suit his own notions of what was important. His obedience to Jesus had atrophied, leaving him vulnerable to the host of pagan daimons. He longed to pray, but no longer knew how, nor to which god.

There was a light tap at the door.

"Sorry," said the cleaning woman. "Did I wake you?"

"No, no. Just resting my eyes. Do you want to have a go at this room?"

"Well, it could do with a duster running over it. But it can wait."

"I'll tidy up a bit."

"Not at all. You're all right where you are. You look tired."

"I didn't sleep last night." Alistair lay back and closed his eyes once more. The small domestic sounds of tidying and dusting were soothing rather than disturbing. He relaxed slightly. It might be possible now to think of the right words to ward off the reporters.

"The thing in the sky. You didn't see it yourself, then?" The woman's question, quietly spoken in her soft brogue, cut across his thoughts. His heart sank. So they had begun already, the curiosity and faint mockery.

"No, I didn't see it. But," he added defiantly, "it wasn't at all how it appeared in the paper."

"I guessed that." There was no trace of scepticism in her voice. "As a matter of fact, I've seen a similar class of thing myself."

"Really?"

"It was in the mountains, sitting – landed, you might say – on a bit of flat ground. Shaped like a cigar it was, and two little lads standing beside it. Big heads they had, bald as eggs, and long black eyes they pointed at me, the way I couldn't move of my own free will. They tried to draw me towards them, into the cigar thing, but I fought them off with a prayer."

"What sort of a prayer?" asked Alistair, interested.

"Something the women used to say when I was a girl. It doesn't fit into English altogether, but it could be put like this:

Seven paters seven times,
Send Mary by her Son,
Send Bridget by her mantle,
Send God by his Strength,
Between us and the fairy host,
Between us and the demons of the air."

Unexpectedly moved by the simple piety of her recitation, Alistair said: "Maeve would like that. Your... 'lads' sound very like hers."

"I thought as much. Would you know what they were?"

"Not really – although lately I've been having ideas."

"They've troubled my mind more than once. I always hoped that if I were to see anyone, it might be, you know, Our Lady or that class of a vision. But not those lads. A thing like that can test your faith."

"Yes."

"For a while I thought I must be a great sinner to run into them. I thought they must be *divils*. But, you know, I wonder now whether setting my face against them didn't help to make them so. Sure, when all's said and done, they did me no harm, bar putting the heart across me."

"That's an interesting theory." Alistair could hear her rubbing vigorously at the rings left by coffee cups on his desk.

"Ah, you don't mean that. But maybe we don't understand them because they're partly in us and partly in the world – but they're God's creatures for all that, and a part of His mystery. They're not human, but then neither is God – and neither are we half the time." The sound of rubbing ceased. Alistair waited, taken aback by her speculations. "Then again," she mused, "they might be divils." They both laughed at the same time. Alistair could hardly believe that he had done so, under the circumstances.

The thin little woman slipped discreetly out of the room, leaving Alistair to construct his statement. Instead, he dozed off – waking twenty minutes later, surprised and refreshed. There was still more than an hour before matins, time enough to talk to the press. He found that the words he would use had been neatly laid out, like fresh linen, while he slept.

Maeve sank down into her hot bath. Whether because of her hangover or, more likely, because she was still not altogether sober, she felt slightly shaky, her head not unpleasantly detached from her body. Inside it muted Irish music hummed under its own steam. When, inevitably, images of the aliens bubbled up before her mind's eye, she was able to look at them curiously and without fear. Grouped as always in their evenly-lit circular space, they looked more like a huddle than a menacing phalanx. She could almost feel sorry for them. Perhaps they were a sort of poor relation of that tall fair race whose fixed abodes – ancient earthworks and rocky outcrops – had once been venerated on Earth. Perhaps it was their sad fate to roam the lonely air in volatile make-believe craft, parodies of the technological objects which now commanded the attention of men. Might it not be possible to coax them back to Earth? Perhaps if they were acknowledged, without fear, they could be persuaded to change their shape and, with it, some part of their nature. They would always be weird and even dangerous – that was the hallmark of the interaction between one world and the other, between the earthly and the eldritch. Distance must be maintained. But was it too much to imagine that they longed to abandon their colourless sterile capsules and return to their old pastimes of dancing and feasting? Maybe they even yearned for human contact – men to enlist in their battles and games; women to marry rather than rape.

Maeve rose from her bath, dried herself, dressed in clean clothes. She pictured Nanny married to Patsy and living on the legendary one hundred and twenty-six acres. She tried to picture his marvellous ancestors, the tall riders of the *Sídhe*. Surely, deep down, in the depths of the soul, there was something otherworldly, something of the *Sídhe* about everybody. Brushing her hair in the mirror, she thought: 'One way or another, we're all changelings.'

Dreamily, Maeve went downstairs. The sound of the vacuum-cleaner drew her to the dining-room. Through the open door she saw an elderly woman at work. She made Maeve feel uneasy. There was something not right about her. For instance, she was small – too small for comfort, somehow. Her face was too lined. Her clothes were old-fashioned but, perversely, had an unworn look about them. Just then she threw a bird-like glance, sharply intelligent, in Maeve's direction.

"Mrs Allingham, is it?" she said, switching off the machine. "I'm glad. Do you feel up to a bit of a chat?" Maeve realised what was bothering her most of all: she had completely forgotten to request a cleaner from the agency.

"Who are you?"

"Ah well, I was coming to that," said the woman. "I meant to tell your husband but he was a bit preoccupied, the poor soul."

Matins had been uncomfortable but – such was the power of the press – better attended than usual. If the members of the congregation had felt any urge to utter cries of protest or catcalls of derision, they had suppressed it. Mercifully the reporters had dispersed. Alistair quickly ascertained that the cleaning woman had also left and that Maeve was asleep upstairs. It was an opportune moment to 'phone the Dean, a thing he should have done as soon as he had issued his statement.

"You heaped scorn on the whole story?" the Dean asked abruptly.

"I deplored the deliberate distortion of Maeve's account for the purpose of sensationalism," Alistair answered carefully. The Dean sighed with exasperation.

"Did you or did you not disassociate yourself completely from this wild tale?"

"No, I didn't. Rather the opposite, I'm afraid. I told them I believed that Maeve underwent a traumatic experience at the hands of what appeared to be alien entities. I emphasised that these entities were not necessarily from outer space, as the newspaper seemed to take for granted; nor were they a product of my wife's mind. I stressed her sanity. I went on to say that the origins of the so-called aliens were mysterious. I mentioned that the world might well be rather different from how we commonly imagine it. In conclusion, I repeated that I believed my wife and fully supported her." There was a brief silence.

"I commend your loyalty to Maeve," said the Dean dryly, "but good God, Allingham, are you telling me you believe she was sexually assaulted by little green men?"

"Little grey men, actually. And sex didn't enter into it."

"All the more reason to dismiss the tabloid version of Maeve's story. No matter what you believe, couldn't you at least have done that?" Alistair considered. The newspaper story had contained a core of truth, however distorted. In some sense it recognised the supernatural. That was why tabloid journalism was so popular. There might be millions of people, like the humble cleaning lady, who were troubled by daimonic experiences. *Someone* ought to champion them in the face of official, orthodox scorn.

"It seems that I couldn't," he said apologetically.

"You'll be made to look very foolish, Allingham. I hope you made it clear that you were not speaking as a representative of the church?"

"No. Sorry. I forgot."

"I see. It gets worse, doesn't it. As if I hadn't enough on my plate, with taking over the arrangements for the Bishop's arrival tomorrow."

"Tomorrow?"

"He's been delayed. Some last-minute hitch." The Dean sounded momentarily perturbed. "Anyway, it no longer concerns you, Allingham. Your copy-book is blotted. No doubt this business will be pursued at the next diocesan meeting. Meanwhile, I don't want to see you within a mile of the Conference."

"Of course not. And I'm sorry."

"It's a pity, Alistair. A great pity. You might have... Oh well, never mind." He rang off.

"Goodbye." Alistair replaced the receiver. He thought: 'what shall I do?' But there was nothing – only the empty week stretching away in front of him. Only the sensation of loss, as if someone close to him had died.

Then Maeve appeared. She came down the stairs two at a time. She looked rested and well and, with her short hair brushed back and curling, younger.

"Alistair! Snap out of it. I'll finish the hoovering and make up the beds. You go and chop vegetables. Chop everything. I'll knock up a lovely casserole. Don't look so tragic. I still have a few marbles left. We've got all afternoon, we'll manage, I promise."

"He's not coming."

"What? *Why*..? Not because... because of *me*?" He shrugged. "You didn't go telling them..? You didn't back me up?" He nodded. "Oh Alistair. And the Dean? What did he say?" Alistair drew his finger across his throat. Unexpectedly, she put her arms around him. It wasn't the sort of thing she often did. "You set your heart on this," she said, her voice muffled by the shoulder of his jacket. "It's my fault."

"No," replied Alistair, returning her embrace. "It happened, that's all."

The ring of the telephone startled Heather. She moved stiffly to answer it. Her muscles ached, but not unpleasantly. After her orgy of dancing, she had slept deeply for eleven hours.

"Heather. It's Katy. How are you?"

"Much better, thanks. Fine, in fact."

"Are you up to hearing some gossip about the Sky Children? I don't want to, you know, *stir you up*, but I couldn't resist 'phoning."

"I'm glad you did. Go on. Tell me."

"I've had a call from Pete Kershaw. The ex-policeman, abductee, remember? He says Murdo's been arrested."

"*Really?* What for?"

"Apparently there was what Pete called an affray in Glastonbury High Street. The 'children' were confused – angry – when the end of the world failed to arrive and the Guardians' spaceships didn't turn up either. They'd been living rough for a week and fasting and some of them, Pete thinks, were a bit mad. One or two turned against Murdo. He lost his rag and lashed out at them. By the way, he calls himself the Lord Omega now, claims to be a Guardian himself, of course. Anyway, blood was spilt, but no serious injuries. Then a policeman took him away. Pete says that they were all sort of stunned that Murdo would allow it... that the sky didn't fall in. He says they all sort of woke up, as if from a bad dream. Pete's not so much concerned about the money Murdo extorted from them all as the corruption of his 'handmaidens' – he had these impressionable young girls attached to him. He had them convinced he was a sort of god, and took advantage of them. Pete's very bitter. He can't believe he let it happen. He's not even sure about his abduction any more. Anyway, he and some others are collecting evidence against Murdo, who's going to be charged with something or other. It's weird, isn't it?"

"Very weird. Hard to take it all in."

"What about a drink and some supper tomorrow? Do you feel like it? Are you still on the tranquillisers?"

"No. I've been doing a lot of dancing instead. It seems to be working. The mania has receded, at any rate. I've been tip-toeing about all day in case I wake it up. It's funny really."

"Do be careful, Heather."

"Don't worry, I will. I've got the tranks handy. But a dose of normality would be just the job. I'd love to see you tomorrow."

"Good. I'll pick you up at about seven. Jeremy's brother is staying. You'll like him. They can cook while we're in the pub..."

Heather sat out in the garden. The sun was sinking peacefully. The London dust was settling through the warm air. The sky glowed. Tomorrow looked like being equally fine. She would look for a temping job. Something ordinary in a lively office. She would fill in the ugly hole at the end of the garden.

A bright light twinkled low on the darkening horizon. The evening star. Or was it moving? An aeroplane, probably. Heather went inside. She danced quickly for a minute. Then she drew the curtains, switched on the lights and made herself comfortable in front of the television.

It was Sunday evening. With time now on her hands, Maeve had decided to do something about the patch of front garden. She knelt down on the dry earth and began to uproot the weeds. She had not seen much of Alistair. He had clearly wanted to be left on his own. She had heard with concern the way he moved restlessly about his study. She had watched him from the window, mooching around the garden, staring distractedly at portions of the lawn. They had taken tea together, quietly, even affectionately; but both were enclosed by separate moods. She had wanted to speak – to relate her unusual news – but his silence seemed to forbid it. Besides, she had drawn enough attention to herself for the time being.

As she tugged at a recalcitrant knot of couch grass, her eye was caught by the flutter of blue plastic trapped in the fence. She recalled how, not so long ago, it had seemed the epitome of all the litter which threatened to obliterate the Earth. Involuntarily she thought of the awful vision the aliens had presented to her through the window or on the screen: the soundless explosion, the desolate surface of the planet. It had been a warning of world-destruction. But not, it occurred to her, the destruction of this world. It was an image, as they had intimated, of their own world's extinction. Pluto, they had called it. Both lord and land of the Dead. Pluto, 'the Rich One', whose riches were not of this world but of the underworld, our dark unconscious life which, in its depths, revealed a treasure-house of strange beings, marvellous images and myths. The aliens were warning against the denial of the imaginative world. To lose the sense of a heavenly host was to extinguish the sun. The blue plastic alone reminded her that there might well be an end to the literal world; but there could be no literal end to the world because its fate was tied to that otherworld without end.

Maeve reached over to the fence and tried to work the fragment of plastic free. Goodness knew how it had become so tightly wedged between the slats. She ceased to pull at the plastic and, instead, wiped the dust and grime from its surface. It was rather a lovely colour, when you came to look at it. On the whole, it deserved to stay.

It was Monday morning, the day of 'Christ in Action'. Alistair was in the kitchen, preparing a breakfast tray for Maeve who was still asleep. He had woken early after a restless night. As he waited for the kettle to boil he listened to the news on the radio: Hungary had opened its borders to East German refugees. Gorbachev and the Soviet Union were not intervening. It was too good to be true. A few short weeks ago Alistair would have been electrified by this event – surely the most reliable sign that Gorbachev really did mean what he'd been saying; that the great Soviet block of ice was thawing and the trickle into Hungary would soon become, the Communist dykes broken, an uncontrollable torrent. But he couldn't get worked up about it, couldn't really concentrate. Instead he found himself wondering whether Bishop Mwawa had arrived yet and where the Dean had arranged for him to stay. In his own well-appointed house, perhaps; or at the palace. He looked at the clock on the cooker. In two hours' time everyone would be taking their seats for the Archbishop's opening address. His own seat, flatteringly near the front, and only a few feet from Bishop Mwawa's, would remain empty. He leaned his forehead briefly against the cool door of the fridge.

The telephone rang. Alistair reluctantly picked up the receiver. He had learnt to be apprehensive of 'phone calls.

"Hello? Alistair?" It was the Dean's voice. It sounded urgent. Alistair went cold with foreboding. Surely he hadn't said anything to fan the flames of controversy. Or had he? Had the newspapers printed something to make matters worse? It was hardly possible.

Gently he replaced the receiver. He'd had enough of the Dean for the moment.

A knocking at the door made him jump. The bell, he remembered, was still wedged into silence. He peeped through the drawing-room curtains and groaned aloud. The reporters were back. He racked his brains to recall exactly what he had said the day before. It must have been spectacular. Nothing came to mind. The words that had come to him during his short sleep had seemed so right. He decided he ought to rise above the whole thing, ignore the lot of them.

Five minutes later he had scrambled over two garden fences and run half-crouching along a back alley, to arrive undetected at the newsagent's. The serene and taciturn Mr Khan was, uniquely, agitated.

"Mr Allingham! You are here! It's in all the papers!" He thrust one of the heavyweights at Alistair whose eyesight, abnormally heightened by the crisis, immediately caught the words 'Nelson Mandela', 'P.W. Botha' and, finally, 'Bishop Mwawa' at the foot of the front page. He raced through the article. Mr Khan had recovered himself. His voice was neutral, but tinged with amusement:

"Gentlemen of the press have been here, Mr Allingham, asking questions about you and your wife. 'What newspaper are you taking? What are we discussing on a daily basis?' I have, of course, said nothing at all, Mr Allingham. But I'm thinking you are in a pretty pickle, appearing daily in the newspapers under debatable circumstances..." Alistair laughed. He could hardly take it in. Mandela had actually met in secret with the South African prime minister. They were actually negotiating to end apartheid. First the Communist Bloc crumbling, and now this. But the really momentous news from Alistair's point of view, ashamed as he was to admit it, was also there, in black and white: Bishop Mwawa was not coming after all. He had flown home from Switzerland. He and his 'advisor', Mrs Mannheim, had been summoned by their Party to answer questions about the use of funds raised in Europe. Swiss bank accounts were mentioned; so were expensive cars and houses in Harare and Lausanne; a Parisian couturier had made unfortunate disclosures. And this at a time when everyone associated with Mandela had to be whiter than white. Mwawa was about to be cast into outer darkness. He'd be even less welcome at any conference than Alistair was now.

"Why are you laughing, sir? Why are you reading this newspaper and not looking." He snatched the paper out of Alistair's hands, unfolded it, and stabbed a finger at the top half of the front page.

A large photograph showed two women standing hand in hand outside an ordinary house, not unlike his own. They looked rather sweet, like children about to cross a busy road. The woman on the right, smiling shyly, resembled Maeve. In fact, it was Maeve. The other one, smiling more broadly, her free hand pointing to the sky, was the little cleaning lady. Under the photograph a caption read: 'Mother Felicitas and Maeve Allingham outside Acton vicarage yesterday.' Under the caption was a headline: 'Saint backs "alien" woman.' Alistair thought: 'I made her clean the house.'

"You find this also funny ha-ha, Mr Allingham?"

"No. Well, yes. I don't know."

"This holy woman has been visiting you?"

"Yes."

"A great honour, I think."

"Yes."

"Sir?"

"Yes?"

"I was mentioning one or two things to the press. For example, I told them that we have spoken together about cricket. You are not offended?"

"Not at all, Mr Khan. I'm delighted."

"The Dean 'phoned," said Maeve. "You'll never guess, but –"

"The Bishop's not coming," supplied Alistair.

"Oh. You know. Well, listen. The Dean wants you –"

"You forgot to mention this." He held up the photograph.

"Ah. Sorry. Good God, it's on the front page. I didn't imagine that. I didn't think it would be in the papers at all. It was more of a, well... a lark. Yesterday didn't seem a good time to tell you."

"I made her clean the house, Maeve."

"I know. Isn't it a scream! She just heard about me and wanted to compare notes. Anyway, listen, the Dean was very civil... asked how I was, how you were, and so on... tried to get a bit of gossip about her, of course. I was polite, unhelpful and so on. But he... they want you to contribute to the debate at the Conference, on the last day – isn't he shameless? – and you will, won't you?"

"Oh, I don't know. It's a bit late now. And besides... all that political jockeying and nonsense..."

"Oh, go on."

"You think I should?"

"You've got things to say."

"Have I? I used to have... It doesn't have to be political, I suppose..." He struck an attitude. "What about 'Demons of the air: the daimonic nature of reality'?"

"You've been thinking, haven't you?"

"In a modest way. Thanks to you and your..."

"The Dean and his pals won't like that title one bit."

"I know. But, Maeve, I feel suddenly... *subversive* again. Like in the old days before everyone became one sort of radical or another."

"She'll be on your side. Or perhaps not. She's not predictable."

"She didn't just wipe the kitchen floor. She scrubbed it."

"She thought it was great gas."

"You Irish... I sometimes think you're from another planet."

"Yes," said Maeve. "I suppose we are, rather."

THE END

STRANGE ATTRACTOR PRESS 2017